THE VENTIFACT COLOSSUS

DORIAN HART

THE VENTIFACT COLOSSUS

© 2015 **Dorian Hart**

Cover art by **Gareth Hinds**
http://www.garethhinds.com

This is a work of fiction. Any similarity between the characters and situations within its pages and places or persons, living or dead, is unintentional and coincidental.

Comments and inquiries should be addressed to
Dorian Hart
27 John Street
Reading, MA 01867

or sent via e-mail to
Dorian.hart@comcast.net

ISBN-13: 978-0692609521 (Jester Hat Books - paperback)
ISBN-10: 0692609520

For Cris, Frank, Jodi, Kate, Kevin, Kristi, Lonnie, Peggy and Rob

I could ask for no finer Company

CHAPTER ONE

Despite the woolen hood that masked his face, a few drops of wind-blown rain found Dranko's cheeks and wiggled their way through his latticework of scars. The largest and deepest scar—earned eight years ago when he was caught applying glue from the church bindery to the inside of the head chaplain's hat—tended to divert rainwater into the corner of his mouth. Every minute or two he wiped his cheek with a damp sleeve.

He lurked in an alley's shadow and watched the citizens of Tal Hae hurry along the street. A chilly breeze whipped stinging needles of water sideways into their faces, which made it the perfect day for Dranko to ply his trade; people were inattentive to their surroundings in a rainstorm. They would be casting their eyes downward to avoid puddles, while their minds would be on dry rooms and warm fires.

His patience was rewarded in the hour before noon when a likely looking mark walked past his alley. A fancy merchant was trying to keep the rain from his fancy clothes with a fancy umbrella, while the wind played havoc with its fabric. A bodyguard walked ahead of him, head tilted down to keep water from his eyes. The bottom of a coin purse peeked from beneath the hem of the merchant's silk tunic.

Dranko smiled. *They never learn.*

After drying his face one more time, he slipped out of the alley and started the tail. At first he ignored his target and instead scanned the foot traffic for the two blocks ahead and the block behind. He took stock of everyone in his field of view. A doddering old woman lurched around pools of rainwater; a pair of waifs chased a weaving path between rain barrels and dripping vendor carts; a despondent young man with a basket of bread took shelter beneath an awning. Dranko didn't need to locate the city guardsmen, as he knew their routes and positions by heart after years of experience. He'd long since memorized every side street and narrow lane that might be useful during a hasty exit.

Satisfied he had plotted a safe approach, Dranko strode forward, drawing a small knife but keeping it concealed beneath his cloak. He caught up with his prey. The knife flashed. The coin pouch dropped into his off hand. The merchant kept walking, oblivious.

There was always a chance of such thefts being spotted by a meddling third party, so Dranko turned calmly down a small side street, then darted into an even narrower alleyway before scaling the back wall of a dilapidated chandlery. Once on the rooftops he scooted from building to building in a low crouch until he was several blocks from the scene of his crime. Only then did he sit with his back to a crumbling chimney and examine his gains.

It wasn't much. Given the tailoring of the merchant's clothes and the muscles of his bodyguard Dranko had expected better, but turned inside out the money pouch produced only one silver talon and six copper chits. Still, it would pay a week's rent and keep him fed for a couple of days, and "fed" was not a condition he took for granted. He returned the coins to their purse, stuffed the purse deep into his pack, and splashed along the puddled rooftops towards his home.

Four blocks from his abode on Fishwife Row, on a gently tilted roof atop a row of weather-beaten tenements, Dranko stopped, lay flat, and cocked an ear. Over the din of the rain came an unusual cry from the street below. Had he been spotted by the Tal Hae constabulary? Had someone been tracking him since his bit of larceny? It was always a danger in his line of work. But he heard the cry again, and this time there was no mistake: it was one of pain. He peered down from the roof. An old beggar crawled into a narrow alley, its cramped width littered with damp, smelly refuse. The poor man slumped against the wall and clutched his ankle. Dranko squinted; there was a pool of blood forming beneath the beggar's leg, mixing with the runoff from the building wall. His filthy rags were soaked through.

"Gods damn it." Dranko pulled his head back and out of sight. He'd wait, is what he'd do. He'd wait, and someone else would come along and give the man aid.

Three minutes later there came another pained shout, and the sounds of sobbing cut through the hammering of the rain. Once more Dranko poked his nose over the edge of the roof. The beggar attempted to stand but collapsed and lay still.

I'm wet, thought Dranko. *I'm cold. I'm tired. I just want to get home and drink something besides rainwater.*

Thunder pealed in the pipe-smoke sky.

Damn the Gods. You especially, Delioch.

Dranko unslung his pack and pulled out a rumpled cream-colored robe with faded gold trim. It was too small for him; now in his mid-twenties, he'd grown broad-shouldered and pot-bellied since the church elders had given it to him. It was a struggle to get the wet fabric sorted out, but he managed to pull the robe over his street clothes. From a small pocket inside the pack, he fished out a cheap pendant on a silver chain and forced it over his hood. Both robe and pendant featured the stylized open-fingered pattern that indicated Delioch, God of the Healing Hand.

Properly attired, Dranko carefully descended the wall and approached the beggar. The old man's ankle was broken, a compound fracture, bone poking through the skin and blood leaking out.

"What happened?" Dranko's voice was low, gruff, almost guttural.

The beggar looked up, squinting into the rain. When he saw Dranko's face, he shrank away, cowering against the wall. Dranko sighed—he knew the beggar had ignored his robe, his necklace, and probably even his alarming network of scars. Others, including some in the church, had looked at him in the same way many times over the years. What the beggar noticed were the tusks. Two thick teeth like small boar tusks protruded from Dranko's lower jaw, marking him as goblin-touched.

"I'm not gonna stand here in the rain all day," Dranko growled. "You want me to heal that ankle, or would you rather bleed to death in a pile of garbage?"

Water plastered the vagrant's straggly hair to his face. "I was begging for coins," he croaked. "All I wanted was a chit or two for a meal, but he pushed me aside. I fell, and my leg…"

Dranko leant down and examined the break. Gods, it was an ugly one. For all his expertise at healing—the one skill for which he had shown aptitude during his time at the church, if one discounted scaling walls and picking locks—he wasn't sure he could fix this. He didn't have any of his salves in his pack, only a small roll of bandages along with a few dirty rags. In the best case this poor fellow would live out his days enduring a painful limp.

But maybe…

Some of the more senior priests at the church could channel the divine restorative power of Delioch, but Dranko and his church had parted ways years ago, long before he had mastered any sort of proficiency in the art of divinely inspired healing. Faith, piety, and devotion—these were the things that determined the strength of healing one channeled through Delioch. That's what Mokad had always told him, especially during his scarring sessions. But despite Mokad's sharp-edged ministrations, or perhaps because of them, Dranko's devotion had never been a thing worthy of mention. Though Dranko had tried channeling several times, he had never been successful.

He took a deep breath.

"This is going to hurt." Dranko offered the man a leather strip from his pack. "A lot. So bite on this and not your tongue."

None too gently he put the strip in the beggar's mouth, and before the old man could protest, he twisted and pulled on the broken leg. His patient screamed through clenched teeth.

"It beats being dead." Dranko prodded the wound with his fingers, felt the bone beneath the bloody shreds of flesh. "Now hold still and scream quieter. I've got to get this right or you'll live out your life a cripple." He nudged everything back into place as best he could.

Delioch, please let this work.

With one hand clutching his pendant and the other gripping the old man's ankle, Dranko shut his eyes and entreated his God. "Lord, I pray for healing, that this man be made sound and whole."

Nothing happened. He spoke the words again, louder. "Lord, I pray for healing, that this man be made sound and whole!" The beggar spat out his bit and screamed in agony. Dranko had rolled the divine dice and lost.

"Lord! Please! I pray for…"

A chill ran through his body, like he had swallowed a bucket of ice water. The beggar stopped screaming. Dranko's hand grew bright, and a thrilling warmth flowed down his arm into the man's wound. For all of Dranko's transgressions, and surely Delioch knew them just as well as Mokad, the God of Healing found him a worthy vessel.

Bones knitted, veins reattached, skin closed. It was more than his own body could endure. Dranko passed out a second later, falling limp beside the beggar in the rain.

* * *

Sometime later Dranko awoke in a fit of coughing, a rivulet of rainwater seeping into his open mouth. The slick wet cobblestones pressed cold against his scarred cheek as he lay on his side, still in the tiny street where he had cured the beggar.

I did it. I channeled.

His body felt drained of its defining energy, as though he had gone a week without food or sleep. He tried to recall the feeling of Delioch's divinity rushing through him but couldn't muster up the memory. What he had was a surety that he had served as a conduit for a power infinitely greater than himself. Also, a splitting headache.

There was no sign of the beggar. Dranko set his back to the alley wall and surged to his feet, an unwise maneuver that brought dancing lights to his eyes. He leaned heavily against the wall and willed himself to stay conscious. When his senses returned in full, he cast about for his pack, but there was no point. Someone had lifted it while he napped. His hand dropped to his belt; at least his knife was still there. But his newly acquired coin purse was gone, along with an old apple and some expensive burglar's tools he'd kept in the bottom of the pack.

Dranko's first instinct was to rant and rail against the heavens. He had offered up a piece of his soul to heal a stranger, and this was his thanks? To be robbed? A curse upon his god came to his lips, but he left it unspoken. Yes, he had taken Delioch's name in vain on dozens of occasions before now, for all the indignities of his life, but this time he lacked the animus. He had channeled! Forget all of the scorn heaped upon him at the church; Delioch had worked His perfect grace through Dranko's scarred body.

Now he was feverish and weak. A channeler was not merely a conduit for Delioch's might; some of his own essential vitality was given irrevocably to the supplicant. A bit of his soul was gone forever. Doubt and fear crept into his heart.

I'm not doing anything better with my soul these days. Maybe that's why Delioch let me put it to good use.

He glanced up at the wall of the building, and the thought of climbing it made his head spin. But he was in his priestly raiment, soaked though his robes might be, and seeing as no one had come along to arrest him while he was unconscious, there was no reason not to walk the rest of the way home.

Dranko lived on the third and highest floor of a rotting tenement that leaned precariously over Fishwife Row. He rented a squalid room from a coarse woman named Berthel, who in four years had shown a complete lack of interest in repairing the holes in the roof or purchasing any charms to keep away the bugs. The climb up two flights of stairs left him winded and faint, and he barely had the wherewithal to strip off his drenched robes and change into dry clothes before collapsing into a rickety chair.

He had set out a collection of pots and buckets to catch the drips on days like this. One of them nearby was misplaced, and a puddle was forming on the warped wooden floorboards. Dranko stretched out a foot and nudged the bucket beneath the drip. When the sound changed to the plunk of water into water, he closed his eyes. All he wanted now was to have a few minutes of relaxa—

"Drank-ooooooooooo!"

The sound of his name carried over that of a fist pounding on his door.

"Go away," he groaned. "We're closed."

"Dranko, open up. Rent's due."

"That's why I want you to go away."

The door opened. Berthel was large, loud, lazy, and never waited to be invited in. She stepped carefully over the drip-catchers while pretending not to notice them.

"And how are we today, beautiful?" she asked.

"Poor."

Berthel laughed. "Then being a bit poorer won't matter much, will it? How about that rent?"

Dranko rubbed his temples. "I had it, but I got rolled on the way back here. Someone took my pack, and my pack had your coins in it."

"You? Someone robbed *you*?" Berthel gave him a look of pure skepticism.

"Yeah. Me. So how about I pay you next week with an extra silver thrown in to reward your patience?"

Berthel crossed her arms and said nothing.

"Hey, look, when have I ever gone more than two weeks without paying rent?"

"Last month."

"Er, okay, fine, but when have I ever gone more than *four* weeks without—"

"Yes, yes," said Berthel. "One week from today, with *two* extra silvers, and I won't kick you to the curb."

Dranko sat up a bit. "Thanks. Though maybe I should hold off paying you until you've done something about this drafty strainer I live in." He looked pointedly at his collection of containers.

"Right." Berthel laughed again. "You got somewhere else to go?"

Dranko paused. He imagined the sanctuary of the Church of Delioch, God of the Healing Hand, where those who needed succor were given harbor and comfort. Six years he had spent beneath that roof, wearing out his welcome day by day and year by year until, drained of patience, they had turned him out. His one friend there, a girl a couple of years his junior named Praska, had tried to warn him, but he hadn't listened.

"No," he said. "I guess I don't. Now if you don't mind, your perfume is obscuring the aroma of my chamber pot. Also I have to figure out where my next meal is coming from, and after that your rent. One week, I'll have your money."

"I know you will," said Berthel. "And…are you okay? I mean, whoever took your money, did they hurt you much? You look like crap, even more than usual."

Dranko grimaced. "I'll be okay. Thanks, Berthel."

His landlady turned and picked her way between the buckets to the door. "Oh, almost forgot. Some kid came by today and left this for you. Said it was important." She produced a small envelope and tossed it to Dranko, who caught it deftly before it could land in a puddle. "I didn't know you could read," she added, then gave one last braying laugh before departing.

Dranko turned over the letter in his pruned fingers. Its beautiful wax seal and fine calligraphy were an absurd opulence in his grungy apartment.

"What in the twelve Hells is this?"

He ripped open the envelope and slid out a thick beige card.

You will appear at the tower of the Archmage Abernathy in the city of Tal Hae at sundown on the first day of spring in the year 828.

Dranko peered with suspicion at this unlikely invitation, its words glowing with faint enchantment. He flipped it over, saw that nothing was written on the back, then ran his fingers along the heavy parchment. From his time working in the church's bindery he knew that this sort of paper was rare and pricey. (Among his dozens of scars from Mokad was a long one on his elbow, testament to a moment of carelessness wherein he had knocked over a pot of ink and ruined a sheaf of vellum.) The expense of the paper made the obvious conclusion—that this was some odd prank—harder to countenance, though it was still more likely than him being summoned by the elusive archmage of Tal Hae.

His life not having much overlap with wizarding circles, assuming there even were such things, Dranko knew only the usual street gossip about the archmagi. Powerful, mysterious, and never seen outside of their stone towers, the archmagi were said to be working on some grand project on the orders of King Crunard himself. Typical citizens had heard only faint rumors of them, rumors they probably disbelieved.

Other possibilities: the letter was a ploy to lure him either into a trap, or out of his house so someone could rob the place. The first of those was more likely. Unless someone desperately needed buckets of rainwater or a stiff straw mattress with a few fleas in it, his apartment was not much of a target for premeditated burglary. But a trap, that he could believe. Careful though he was, his cutpurse hobby had occasional repercussions. Someone may have tracked him home after one of his outings, and now was planning revenge.

The letter…there was certainly some sort of glamour making the words glow. Had he inadvertently robbed a wizard on one of his extralegal excursions? Or maybe, maybe, the invitation was on the level. This was already a momentous day, the day he had channeled Delioch's healing energies, years after being cast out of the church. Was the letter related? Had Abernathy used his wizardry to sense the power he had so briefly touched? Who knew? He didn't have much time to think about it—the first day of spring was tomorrow—but the possibility made it worth the risk.

* * *

Dranko Blackhope arrived at Abernathy's tower the following afternoon and noticed for the first time that it had no doors. Though he had ranged far and wide through Tal Hae over the years in search of prospects, targets, and cheap liquor, Dranko had never visited the wizard's tower in the city's northwest corner, in an old park that offered few opportunities for his ignoble trade. He had seen the upper portion of the smooth stone cylinder from afar but had no clear picture in his head of what the place looked like at ground level. Now that he stood before it, he found that its bottommost section was no different than the rest of it—seamless stone, unsullied by carving or graffiti or anything else. The tower was a tall featureless post thirty feet across and nearly a hundred feet high, rising from the grass like an ancient menhir. Indeed there was no reason to think it was hollow, save for the fact that a mighty wizard was purported to live inside of it.

There were no windows either, and Dranko didn't give himself good odds of being able to scale the smooth tower wall to check out the roof. His mind flashed to his friend Praska, a fellow novice in the church and a co-conspirator in many of his childhood pranks. She'd try to climb the tower, no question; she could climb almost anything. Gods, what would she say if she could see him now, answering an invitation from an archmage? Whatever happened next, this might occasion his first trip back to the church since his exile, just to tell her all about it.

After a quick scout-around that revealed no immediate ambush, Dranko walked a slow, careful perimeter of the tower, running his hands over the stone in case there was a door masked by illusion. That seemed like the kind of thing a wizard might do—test Dranko's reasoning and resolve to see if he was truly worthy of whatever it was he'd been summoned for. But, no, there was nothing. The sun had already dropped behind Tal Hae's western wall, and sunset was imminent.

He cupped his hands to his mouth. "Hello? Abernathy? I'm here. You going to let me in, or what?"

A bird chirped and the sound of a dog barking came from several blocks away, but Abernathy, if he was really inside this pillar of rock, did not respond.

"Great," Dranko muttered. "I should have guessed this was some kind of idiot joke. Maybe someone from the church who still—"

With no noise, lights, or warning of any kind, Dranko found himself somewhere else. He blinked his eyes. Gone were the park and the tower and the fish smell of Tal Hae, and in their place was something more like a parlor, or a library. (Not that he had much experience with parlors and libraries; the church of Delioch had both, but with his reputation for troublemaking Dranko had seldom been allowed to visit them.) This place had a cozy, comfortable, happily disorganized feel despite being quite a large room. Bookshelves lined the stone walls, and many of the scrolls and books lay on their sides or had spilled onto the floor. A half dozen small tables were heaped with more books and leaves of parchment, as well as inkpots, quills, pots of wax, and an assortment of small curios. Among them were valuable figurines and objects d'art, small and easily palmed.

But while the objects and furnishings of this scholar's lounge were interesting, Dranko quickly focused his attention on the people who stood nearby. Five others, three men and two women, were looking around in confusion or wonderment, and Dranko guessed that they had not been expecting to get magicked directly into Abernathy's tower, or to find themselves part of a larger group. They stood in different parts of the library, none too close to any of the others. It seemed that each of the six of them was waiting for someone else to speak, so Dranko broke the silence. "I don't suppose one of you is Abernathy?"

Everyone looked expectantly at everyone else.

"Did all of you get one of these?" asked a sandy-haired kid, holding up a card that matched Dranko's. "I'm Ernest Roundhill, by the way. My friends call me Ernie. Nice to meet you." He was an honest-faced young fellow with a sword at his belt. Dranko pegged him at eighteen years old.

"I'm Aravia Telmir," said a girl on his left. She looked out at the others from beneath the brim of a large and ridiculous conical hat, purple, adorned with little stars and moons. Did she think she was going to impress a powerful wizard by playing dress-up? The hat shaded her face enough that he couldn't know her age, though from her voice he guessed late teens or early twenties.

On the other side of Ernie was an elderly woman holding a cleaver dripping with blood. She was in her sixties, and dressed like Dranko imagined someone's mom would dress: long peasant skirt, dingy blouse, tattered scarf, bonnet around her gray hair. Laugh lines dominated her face.

"My name is Ysabel," said the old woman. "You young people can call me Mrs. Horn." She held up her cleaver and graced the room with a friendly smile. "Try anything, and you'll be my next victim." When Ernie took a quick step away from her, she laughed. "No, no, don't get the wrong idea, young man. I was butchering a deer a moment ago. Never thought that invitation was really from a wizard."

Dranko grinned at her. "Noted." Her return smile went straight to his eyes, not his tusks. He liked her.

"Tor. Tor Bladebearer." Tor was a tall, muscular, and well-dressed youth who carried himself with a grace and confidence Dranko didn't see much of in the poorer parts of town. A nobleman's son, maybe? There was a sheathed sword strapped to the boy's back, and the kid could doubtless do some serious damage with it, but his face was guileless and full of wonder. Dranko would have bet a gold crescent that "Tor" was a pseudonym.

Closest to Tor was a grim, dour-faced man, probably in his mid-forties, and like the two youths he carried a sword. His right hand was on its grip, though he had not yet drawn it, and his eyes were wary, flicking around between Dranko and the others. Of his fellow guests in the library, this guy was the only one sizing *him* up in the same way he was doing to them. Competent and humorless; probably a soldier or mercenary.

"I'm Grey Wolf."

Dranko tried not to laugh, but a poorly-stifled snort came out. "Your name is Grey Wolf?"

"No," said Grey Wolf. "But it's what I prefer to be called. Is that a problem?"

"Hey, no, that's great. Whatever makes you happy. I'm Dranko Blackhope."

Grey Wolf scowled and narrowed his eyes.

Ernest squirmed uncomfortably at the exchange. "So, anyone know why we were…magicked here by an archmage?"

"Teleported," said Aravia. "The correct term is 'teleported.'"

Dranko updated his impression of the girl. Maybe she was a wizard herself? The hat was still outlandish.

"Teleported," Ernie repeated. But no one answered the question, and an awkward silence lasted almost half a minute.

Dranko hated silence as a rule. "Maybe this is a test. Maybe we're supposed to find Abernathy somewhere in his tower, and the first person to catch him wins a sack of gold."

Ernie laughed and Grey Wolf rolled his eyes, but Dranko was only half-kidding. He walked to the door and tried the handle. It was locked. He shook it, turned it both ways, and even put his shoulder into the door in case it was merely stuck, but they appeared to be trapped in the library. Maybe there was a hidden exit somewhere, but it would take hours to search properly through all the clutter. He glared at the door. If only he had his tools…

Grey Wolf sighed and sat down in one of the room's wooden chairs.

The boy who had called himself Tor Bladebearer (a name no less silly than Grey Wolf) picked up a little onyx dog from the table nearest him and examined it idly. "All of the archmagi work for the king, right? I'll bet King Crunard asked Abernathy to assemble a team for some kind of secret mission. He must have picked me because of my swordsmanship. What about the rest of you?"

"I am a wizard," said Aravia proudly. "I have been studying under the master Serpicore for over two years and have learned several significant spells."

That answered that, then. A young wizardess, full of herself.

"Really?" exclaimed Ernie. "That's amazing! What kind of spells do you know?"

Aravia smiled, straightened, and spoke in a crisp and practiced manner. "I've learned *heatless light, minor arcanokinesis, minor lockbreaker…*"

"Lockbreaker?" Dranko interrupted. "Now we're getting somewhere!" He gestured to the door. "How about lock-breaking us out of here so we can find Abernathy and let him know we're waiting for him."

"Do you really think Abernathy would have locked us in here if he wanted us to break out?"

All eyes turned to the far side of the library, where a woman stood mostly hidden in a shadow. She was almost a ghost, with cheesecloth-white skin and hair so pale it must have been bleached or dyed. But the odd thing was, she was wearing black Ellish robes, and everyone knew that all Ellish sisters had dark hair. Maybe she was part of a weird secret sect within the Ellish temple? Who knew? But like the rest of her sisters she didn't like the light; though she stood in the darkest corner of the room, both of her hands were shielding her eyes from the library's lamps.

She also had a weapon on her belt, a stout club with a spiky flanged head. Dranko frowned. Had he missed a follow-up message that warned the wizard's guests to come armed? Was there going to be some kind of arena battle staged for Abernathy's amusement? The general feeling among the citizens of Charagan was that the mighty wizards in their towers were of a benevolent sort—wouldn't they have taken over by now if they weren't?—but no one knew for certain. Perhaps Abernathy was a cruel, ruthless sorcerer who enjoyed making strangers fight one another for sport. Dranko hoped not; the tenets of his faith would put him at a severe disadvantage.

"Maybe," he said. The closer he looked, the more freakish he found her appearance. It was possible that Ell had put a curse on her, but he didn't know much about the Ellish religion. Ell was the Goddess of Night. Her clergy were all women, who never went outside during the day.

"What's your name?" he asked her.

"Morningstar of Ell."

"Well, Morningstar of Ell, maybe Abernathy is testing our initiative, and *wants* us to figure a way out. Aravia, what do you say about that lock?"

An eager expression came over Aravia's face and she moved toward the door, but before she had crossed half the distance the door swung inward without needing her arcane persuasion. In walked an elderly man, in his seventies at least, with a long hooked nose, wrinkled face, and startling blue eyes. An untended white beard sprouted from his chin. He was dressed in a plain white robe and had white slippers on his feet.

Dranko repressed a snort. The wizard was certainly dressing the part.

The old man stopped inside the doorway and sighed with relief. "Ah. Good." His voice was aged and crackly. Wizardy. "All here then?" He counted them with a wrinkled finger, but frowned when he was finished. "Are there any more of you? Did anyone leave the room?"

"No, sir," said Ernie. "It's just the seven of us."

"There are supposed to be eight," said the old man.

"You must be Abernathy," said Dranko. "Nice place you have here."

"I must be, and I do. Now, tell me your names, please."

One by one the guests introduced themselves to the wizard. When Grey Wolf gave his nom de lupine, Abernathy shook his head. "No, I mean your real name, Mr. Wolf."

Grey Wolf stared at the wizard for a moment. "Ivellios Forrester."

"And you, 'Tor Bladebearer,'" said Abernathy. "That's not your real name either, is it?"

"N…no," stammered Tor. "But I'd rather not say it in front of strangers. Uh, no offense."

Abernathy scratched his face through his beard. "Very well. Are your initials 'K.B.'?"

"No."

"How about 'D.F.'"

"Yes."

"Fine."

Dranko held his breath, but Abernathy didn't come back to challenge him. Was it because he had chosen the name "Dranko" at such a young age?

Abernathy looked around the room one more time, then stooped to glance under the nearest table. "Do any of you know a man named Kibilhathur Bimson?"

The question was met by blank stares and shaking heads.

"Well, it was an old spell, and my tower is built to prevent…oh, never mind. You seven will have to do."

"Do what, exactly?" Dranko asked. At the same moment Morningstar said, "Why have you brought us here?"

Dranko expected the old man to launch into some grandiose speech, but instead the wizard merely brought his fingertips to his lips. Several seconds passed during which Abernathy did nothing but pass his gaze around his guests.

"The world is in some danger," Abernathy said at last. "It has been for some time. Recently that danger has grown more immediate, to a degree such that I felt I needed a team of…agents would be the correct term, I think. For—"

"I knew it!" Tor interrupted gleefully, only seeming to realize afterward that he had interrupted one of the (supposedly) most powerful men in the world.

Abernathy smiled indulgently at Tor and continued. "…For reasons I don't have time to explain, we archmagi don't leave our towers and don't have an adequate sense of what goes on outside of them. You will be my eyes, ears, and hands out in Charagan."

"For how long?" asked Grey Wolf. "I have a job to get back to, you know."

Dranko wondered the same thing himself, but he bristled at the guy's self-important impatience. He forced out a smile, showing his tusks.

"What are you, a bouncer, Mr. Wolf? Or can I call you 'Grey?'"

Grey Wolf glared at him silently.

Abernathy fixed his penetrating blue eyes on each of his guests in turn. When they were turned to Dranko, he squirmed in spite of himself. Could wizards read minds?

"I don't know for how long, exactly," Abernathy admitted. "Maybe a long time. And perhaps this will become a permanent arrangement."

"No thank you, then," said Morningstar. "I appreciate the offer, but I should not stay away from my duties at the temple for very long."

The wizard sighed and walked to the nearest wall. With a wave of his hand a window appeared in the stone; he gazed out of it upon the rooftops of Tal Hae.

"I could compel you," he said wearily. "Some of the others felt I should."

"Others? Others who?" Tor's voice was clear and deep, but his inflections were boyish.

"The other archmagi," said Abernathy. "Some disapprove of me summoning you at all, and the others feel that I should simply coerce you with threats. For instance, I could say something like, 'Serve me in our kingdom's hour of need, or I will turn you all into toads!' But I am disinclined to that sort of bullying."

Grey Wolf looked meaningfully toward the door. "So we can say no?"

"You may," said Abernathy. "But I will put one condition upon you, in return for my forbearance regarding transforming you into amphibians. And that is, I would like each of you, in good faith, to allow me to try convincing you *without* threat of force, or blackmail, or any kind of improper strong-arming. I'll visit you each tonight at the Greenhouse. If you promise to hear me out, and should I not sway you to service of the Kingdom of Charagan, you will be free to return to your lives."

"That sounds more than fair, Mr. Abernathy," said Mrs. Horn, every bit as polite as Grey Wolf was insolent. "But if you don't mind my asking, why did you summon *us* to be your...agents? If the world is in danger, shouldn't you have picked great warriors or other powerful wizards?"

Ernie Roundhill's eyes went wide. "Am I here because of the statue of me in Murgy's basement? Do you need us to hold up the sky?"

Abernathy's expression became hard to read. "I don't know who Murgy is, or about any statues, although I'm sure that's an interesting tale. And the sky is not falling, except in the most metaphorical of senses. No, you were chosen by a very unusual spell I cast three days ago. The spell was designed to select several people who will be instrumental in helping protect Charagan from the evils that beset it. It chose you. But why you specifically? I don't know."

The old wizard didn't have much experience in lying to people, that was certain.

"What kinds of missions are you going to send us on?" asked Tor. He looked like a puppy eager for a walk.

"Scouting, initially," said Abernathy. "After that, it will depend on what you learn."

Tor's shoulders slumped a bit. "Will there be fighting? Battles against the forces of evil? Monsters?"

Dranko snorted. "Monsters? Forces of evil? Are you serious?"

But Abernathy wasn't laughing. "That is entirely possible," said the old wizard. "My boy, whatever your life was like before today, it is likely that should you accept my offer, you will be afforded opportunities for adventure and glory that few in a generation are given."

Tor grinned like a six-year-old offered an entire apple pie, but Ysabel—Mrs. Horn—clicked her tongue. "Abernathy, don't you think I'm a trifle old for adventures and glory? And I'm just a farmer. Unless you intend adventurous sewing, or a glorious feeding of the chickens, I can't see that I'll be much good."

Abernathy gave the old woman an apologetic look.

Ernie's voice had a noticeable wobble. "So it's, uh, dangerous, then?"

"Very likely," said Abernathy. "I won't lie to you. Though some among the archmagi feel you should be left in the dark until you earn our trust, I think it is important for you to know what we're dealing with."

From somewhere distant in the tower, a single chime sounded. Abernathy tugged his beard and looked nervously at the door to the library, at which point the conjured window, deprived of the wizard's attention, shrank to a point and vanished.

"I will briefly summarize, as I shouldn't be away from my work any longer than necessary. It would be a bitter irony if I let things get out of hand because I took too much time talking with you."

He took a deep breath before continuing.

"There is a very powerful and dangerous man—no, not even a man, a monster, a being of a sort we do not know how to kill. He is currently locked away, but we believe he is figuring out how to escape. If he succeeds and comes to Spira, he may decide to conquer the world or destroy it, but it would be best it not come to that. I and the other archmagi have spent many, many years maintaining the locks on his door. Your first assignment will be to go to where that door is and inspect it. It's all much more complicated than that, and I'll explain in detail when I have more time, but for…"

He was interrupted by a low grinding roar, a nearly subsonic groaning, as if giant hands had grasped the tower and now were trying to bend and twist its stones. Dranko was overcome by a sourceless vertigo and lurched involuntarily. Holy Hells! Aravia stumbled and fell to the floor, though nothing was actually moving. Abernathy braced himself against a table, his eyes wide.

"Is it the monster?" cried Ernie.

Then it stopped. A burly red-faced man in workman's clothes, with a bulbous nose and a bristling black beard, had appeared in the center of the library. He was in the very act of bringing a hammer down upon a chisel. When his swing did not meet with any resistance, the man overbalanced, stumbled, and dropped his tools.

He looked around as he bent to pick up his instruments. "Well, damn. So that fancy card weren't no joke then."

Dranko let out his breath; it was only the missing invitee.

Abernathy held up his hand and, eyes closed, turned a slow circle in place, muttering syllables beneath his breath that Dranko couldn't quite make out. When the wizard opened his eyes again, he was obviously relieved.

"The tower's wards appear to be uncompromised," he said. "Good. I'm surprised something like that didn't happen when the rest of you arrived." He walked to the newcomer. "Please tell me you are Kibilhathur Bimson."

"Be glad to, seein' as it's true," said the man. "And you must be the Archmage Abernathy, and this here's your tower?"

"Welcome to the team!" said Dranko. "Abernathy here was telling us about our new careers as prison door inspectors."

Abernathy gave Dranko an aggrieved look. "Kibilhathur, as I was telling your new companions, it's not quite so simple."

The man with the chisel scratched his beard. "My new what?"

Dranko cleared his throat. "Do we get paid to be your lackeys? 'Cause I have some back rent to pay."

"Hmm," said Abernathy. "I confess that I have an unusual relationship with money. I can't simply produce it from the aether. Creating permanent solid objects is extremely difficult even for the most skilled wizard, and the spells for it are typically limited to wood, stone, and poor-quality iron. Conjuring up gold or gemstones would be quite out of the question."

"Yeah," said Dranko. "Okay. But what about money you get the old-fashioned way? Does anyone *pay* you to be a wizard?"

"I used to have a decent amount saved by, but that was a long time ago. What I had left, I've recently spent on things for you. I've purchased you a house, a converted bakery called the Greenhouse on the Street of Bakers. As for working expenses, I think that in the course of your employment, should you choose to accept it, you may find valuables that you will be welcome to sell or keep."

"Great," said Dranko. "What about up-front money?"

"Oh, well." Abernathy looked around the library, made a few halting steps in several different directions, and finally strode to a tall bookshelf where he took down a jade owl figurine. It was six inches tall and had small rubies for eyes. He handed it to Dranko. "How about this? Are there still jewelers in Tal Hae who will give you coins for it?"

Dranko's eyes nearly bulged from his head. Having done a bit of fencing in his day—and not the kind where you poked holes in people—he had a decent sense of the value of things, and even if the gems in the eyes were fake, he could imagine fetching ten gold crescents for this little owl. More, if the rubies were authentic.

He composed himself. "That'll do for a start."

The chime sounded again from somewhere deep in the tower's heart. Abernathy flinched at the noise. "I have to go," he said hurriedly. "Our enemy is ever battering at the door. As soon as I'm able, I'll visit you at the Greenhouse. Good luck!"

Before Dranko could even open his mouth to ask one of the dozens of questions he still had, the bearded wizard wiggled his fingers and the library disappeared.

CHAPTER TWO

Morningstar of Ell was thankful that the sun had set, but she was annoyed at everything else. She stood in a cluster with the others, looking upon the exterior of Abernathy's tower and the scrubby park that surrounded it. The goblinoid man, Dranko, stood closest, reeking of cigar smoke and stale alcohol. She took a step away from him, as did Ernie and Grey Wolf.

Her head still spun from the whirlwind of the last hour. She had been aboard a ship from Port Kymer to Tal Hae, safely ensconced in its hold to avoid the sunlight. The invitation, so vaguely worded, had made her think it was her responsibility to reach the wizard's home, though it had arrived too late for that to be possible. Morningstar had decided to come anyway, risking the wrath of her church elders and the additional scorn of her sisters by traveling abroad after sunrise.

She had wanted to tell Abernathy that his arrangement was impossible unless the entire group was willing to travel after nightfall wherever they went, but there hadn't been time for that. As for the old wizard's tale of a powerful enemy trapped in a cell, she needed more time to reflect.

The tall boy with the sword on his back, Tor, was looking every which way, eyes wide, a smile on his face. "I've never been this far from home before!"

"Young man, where are you from?" asked Mrs. Horn.

"Forquelle." As soon as the words left his mouth, the boy looked mortified, as if he'd given up some terrible secret.

"We should go to the Greenhouse, right?" said Ernie.

While Morningstar was irked at the wizard's presumption, the Greenhouse *was* her best option at the moment. She had never been to Tal Hae, and Abernathy was offering her free lodgings. (She briefly considered the local temple—supposedly one of the largest in the kingdom—but she wasn't emotionally prepared for the questions that introduction would raise. Or, worse, for the possibility that her reputation had preceded her.)

Grey Wolf gestured to the tower. "I'm giving him one day to make his case. After that I'm on the first ship back to Hae Charagan. I'll be in enough trouble as it is for abandoning a job."

"You're from the capital?" asked Tor. "I've never been there. What's it like? Is it true that there's a garden of walking topiaries? And that—"

Morningstar interrupted him. "Are any of you from *this* city and know where the Greenhouse is?"

Dranko answered, "Yeah. I've lived most of my life here. I can get us to the Street of Bakers. Follow me."

He set off, and Morningstar trailed along with the rest. The walk took them half an hour, from the corner of the city where Abernathy had his residence, through a grocer's district, then skirting a series of small plazas before turning down a wide street loud with the clanging hammers of smiths. Though the sun was now an hour below the western wall, Tal Hae was full of a thriving city's industrious cacophony. Stores with brightly painted façades were open late, criers hawked their wares, children and dogs played in streets and yards by lamplight, the occasional beggar shook a rattling cup of copper chits at passersby, and the air lay heavy with the smells of fish and salt from the harbor. It was a larger, busier place than Port Kymer, which made sense. Tal Hae was the capital of Harkran and one of the largest cities in the kingdom.

A pair of scampering urchins stopped a game of tag to stare at her, then turned to whisper and giggle to one another. Once this would have stung, but her years at the temple in Port Kymer had built up around her an armor of calm equanimity. Having withstood the relentless cold suspicion of her sisters for so long, she was no longer troubled by the snickers of children. Her refuge, an inner calm and measured observation of the world, served her well as she floated through the strange streets of Tal Hae, following in a crowd of mismatched strangers. Her life could hardly have taken a more unexpected turn, summoned by a great wizard to help prevent calamity, but there was no use panicking. And besides, even if Abernathy somehow convinced her to stay as part of his team, she could not accompany them during daylight. His choice of her—or his spell's choice—must have been in error.

The Street of Bakers was quieter than most, two blocks removed from the nearest plaza and the busier nighttime thoroughfares. Where most streets saw shops and houses huddled shoulder-to-shoulder, the half-dozen bakeries kept their distance from one another, separated by lawns and fences. To Morningstar they looked like nobles' houses.

"Here we are." Dranko gestured grandly at a small manor house painted a uniform forest green. "The wizard's flophouse."

A large wooden sign hung from a post set in the front yard. "The Greenhouse," it announced, and the words were imposed over a painted baguette. A smaller sign had been tacked beneath the large one, warning "closed for repairs." There were large bay windows—made with actual plates of glass—set in the street-facing wall of the house, covered with translucent curtains that only revealed the lamps lit within.

"I hope the Greenhouse has food," said Mrs. Horn. "I feel Abernathy owes us dinner for a start, especially since mine is going to rot on my butcher's block."

"I'm starving!" Tor said, sounding like he just wanted to be agreeable. Morningstar didn't think the lad would take much convincing to stay on as Abernathy's servant.

They approached the large, thick door of the house, a slab of lacquered oak inscribed with unfamiliar letters. Grey Wolf tried the knob. It didn't turn.

"It's locked," he grumbled. "Abernathy didn't give any of you a key when I wasn't looking, did he?"

Aravia stepped up and rubbed her hands together. "I can take care of this."

Except for the appearance of Abernathy's window (and, technically, the summoning and dismissal of the group), Morningstar had never seen wizard magic up close. It wasn't expressly forbidden at the temple, but divine magic was a different thing altogether. Was she about to witness Aravia's *minor lockbreaker*?

"Wait," said Ernie. "I thought I saw someone in there, behind the curtains."

"Maybe our great wizard forgot to tell some baker we was movin' in," said Kibilhathur. "Old geezer seemed like the sort what could overlook that sort a' thing."

"How about we knock, like the civilized people I'm sure we are." Mrs. Horn winked. "We're not vandals yet, are we?" She rapped her knuckles on the door.

A few seconds later there came the sound of a bolt being drawn back. The door opened, revealing a tall gentleman in a spotless butler's uniform. His face was gaunt, his hair graying at the temples, and his bearing exemplary.

"May I have your names, sirs and madams?" His voice was precise and cultured, if a bit gravelly.

Dranko stepped into the light spilling from inside the Greenhouse. "Dranko Blackhope," he said affably. "Who are you, and why are you in our house?"

"You may call me Eddings," said the butler. "Master Blackhope, I am pleased to welcome you to your new home. I will allow your friends to enter once they have named themselves."

Sighing at this pointless rigmarole, Morningstar made her introduction next. The rest followed her lead and were allowed to cross the threshold.

The modest foyer was cheerfully decorated with potted plants and paintings of fruit. Two opposing staircases with carved wooden railings spiraled to the upper story of the house, while a wide archway opened into a spacious living room complete with couches, a fireplace, low tables, and empty bookshelves lining one wall.

On the left-hand wall of the living room was a black-painted door, the only thing in sight that would have looked at home in her Ellish Temple. But she had not eaten in hours, and a second door opened onto a dining room already set out with goblets of wine and plates of roasted chicken, the smell wafting out to greet her and setting her mouth to watering.

"You may leave your weapons in the foyer," said Eddings. "Dinner awaits your pleasure in the dining room."

"Does this count?" Mrs. Horn produced her cleaver from the waistband of her skirt.

Eddings was unfazed. "If you would prefer, I can clean that off in the kitchen."

"That's very nice of you."

The interior of the house was much too bright; lanterns on the walls filled every room with a peculiarly even glow. It could hardly have been more starkly contrasted with the austere, unlit halls of her temple. Morningstar unbelted her weapon and set it against a wall inside the door, shielded her eyes with one hand to ward away the glare, and joined the others in the dining room. In addition to the chicken and wine there was a huge bowl of yellowbeans, cooked to an almost unnatural perfection.

A chandelier hung directly above the center of the round dining room table, with magic lights in place of candles. Morningstar kept her hood drawn close and her eyes squinted. She didn't speak much as she ate, preferring for the moment to observe and listen to the others.

Dranko was unrestrained in his assault on both the food and the alcohol; he ate like someone for whom lavish meals were a luxury, and drank like a man for whom wine was a regular habit. Tor had laid his napkin carefully on his lap and held his wine glass with a practiced hand, but though his table manners were exquisite, the rate and quantity of his intake were alarming. Young Ernest seemed embarrassed at having a butler hovering nearby, and stole worried glances at Eddings between each mouthful.

"Mr. Eddings," he asked, "have you been a butler for a long time?"

"Yes, Master Roundhill."

"Oh, you can call me Ernie."

"As you wish."

Ernie reddened and looked back at his plate.

Dranko belched. "So, Eddings, how did you get this job working at the Greenhouse? Seems pretty cushy."

"Master Blackhope, I was hired some months ago by our mutual employer, Master Abernathy. Though the circumstances of this arrangement are most unusual, the compensation is more than adequate. Also our employer suggested that I might find your company most entertaining."

"Really? He said that about us?"

"He did, Master Blackhope."

Dranko smoothed his shirt and sat up a bit straighter; he obviously enjoyed being addressed as "Master Blackhope" by a servant.

"Abernathy didn't say he had hired us a butler," said Morningstar. "He said very little, all things considered. Did you also do the cooking?"

"No, Lady Morningstar."

"Just Morningstar will be fine. Do we have a cook as well? Because this is quite delicious."

"No, I regret to say that we do not. Your food has come from Mr. Abernathy's extraordinary Icebox, a magical compartment that creates food or drink upon request."

"That seems like cheating," said Ernie.

"Can you have it make us apple pies for dessert?" asked Tor.

"I cannot," said Eddings. "While miraculous in its magical workings, the

Icebox can only produce three separate items of food or drink each day. I have already used up its daily allotment by asking it for roast chicken, yellowbeans, and wine."

"Tomorrow you should ask it for a watermelon made out of pure diamond," said Dranko. "Or if that's pushing it, a pie filled with silver pieces."

Such a clever one, that Dranko. How did he make his living? She doubted it was something entirely on the level.

Eddings didn't crack a smile. "I'm afraid the Icebox does not work that way, Master Blackhope. It only produces real, edible food."

Morningstar's hood slipped slightly and the light stung her eyes; she winced and pulled the fabric closer. Kibilhathur looked at her with concern. "You okay, miss?"

"I'm not used to lights this bright," she answered curtly. "I'll manage. I won't be here very long, I think."

"Why not? You don't want to help Abernathy keep his critter locked up?"

That was the kind of passive-aggressive sort-of-accusation her sisters tended to make, but there was no nastiness in Kibilhathur's voice, just curiosity.

"My desire to help is immaterial," she said. "My sisterhood will not tolerate a priestess abroad during the day, and I doubt Abernathy will be content to limit us to nighttime excursions."

"Oh. Suppose that makes sense." The bearded fellow gave her a sheepish glance, as though remorseful he had taken up her time, then returned to his meal.

Grey Wolf looked across the table at her. "Morningstar. Isn't that an unusual name for a priestess of Ell?"

Yes, yes it was, and she had resented it from the moment it had been given to her. In the halls of the Goddess of Night all names were supposedly born in the eye of Ell, but her fellow priestesses regarded hers as an effrontery. Between her name, pallid skin, and white hair, she had earned the nickname (whispered behind her back, but loudly enough for her to hear) the White Anathema. Her sisters felt that her name and appearance were punishments for some sins of her family, or childhood, or even deeds she had not yet done.

"It's the name I was given," she said simply. "I have learned to accept it."

Tor dropped his fork to his empty plate. "This is fantastic!" He spread his arms to indicate the room and everyone in it. "Hired by a wizard to help him keep the kingdom safe, with our own headquarters and a butler and magical food-making box. I wonder when we'll get our first mission."

Grey Wolf gave Morningstar an apologetic glance, then rolled his eyes. "Kid, how old are you?"

Tor lowered his arms and turned a bit red. "Sixteen."

"Sixteen," repeated Grey Wolf. "This must all seem like a dream come true for you, but I have a decent job and a life to get back to. Abernathy can say what he likes to me, but I can't imagine what will convince me to start over at my age."

"My life needed changing anyhow," said Tor sullenly. "This one will be better, I'm sure."

That was curious. Tor was obviously well-fed, carried an expensive sword, and had upper-class table manners. But the boy's dissatisfaction wasn't her business, and like Grey Wolf she'd soon be taking her leave of this ad-hoc band.

"I thought Mr. Abernathy was very nice," said Ernie. "Remember what he said about the toads!"

"Are you sixteen too?" asked Grey Wolf.

"I'm seventeen."

"Pikon preserve me," grumbled Grey Wolf. "Half of this group are children."

"Some of us might count you among them," said the elderly Mrs. Horn, flashing a mischievous smile.

"Abernathy's spell chose us for a reason," said Aravia. "I'm sure we each bring something to the group, so let's talk about our skills. I personally am—"

"Yeah, a wizard, we know," Dranko interrupted. "If you don't mind me asking, do you have to wear a stupid-looking hat to be a wizard? Abernathy wasn't wearing one."

Aravia blanched and swept the hat from her head. "I forgot I was wearing it," she mumbled. But she recovered impressively, lifting her chin and meeting Dranko's eyes. "I am the student of Master Serpicore, a formidable practitioner of the arcane arts. He has always insisted that I wear a hat in his home. It improves one's casting focus."

"He's pulling your leg," said Dranko. "That, or he has a weird thing for hats."

Aravia ignored this and gave the table a superior smile that reminded Morningstar of some of her less congenial sisters. Holding her fork in her right hand, she twirled the fingers of her left while mumbling strange words under breath. After ten seconds of this the tined end of the fork blossomed into cool yellow light, much like the enchanted candles in the chandelier. Morningstar flinched instinctively.

"Fantastic!" Tor exclaimed.

"I can do that too," said Dranko. "All I need is a torch, a tinderbox, and the time to run home to get them."

All of this banter was becoming tiresome, Dranko's in particular. He was the sort of person who needed to hear himself talk and turn everything into a joke. But who knew what kind of insecurities a goblin-touched man would build up over time? She could almost empathize with him, were he not so unapologetically crude.

"Your home?" asked Tor. "Do you live in a cave? With goblins? What's it like to have tusks?"

Morningstar winced, and everyone else stared at the boy, who gulped and seemed to immediately regret asking. But Dranko laughed.

"Makes it easier to eat babies," he said. "First I scare 'em, like this." He opened his mouth wide and let his gray tongue loll out. "Then, when they start crying, I eat 'em. They taste better that way."

Tor let out a relieved breath.

"But let's get this out in the open," said Dranko. "All baby-eating jokes aside, I look a little like a goblin because somewhere generations back in my family a goblin got involved. But I am not a goblin, I've never seen a goblin, and aside from my lovely face I have absolutely nothing in common with them. Now, anyone else have inappropriate questions for me? Anyone want to know about my sex life? Because I could tell you—"

Morningstar cut him off, appalled. "No, thank you, please. In fact, maybe it would be best if you stopped talking altogether."

Into the awkward silence that followed, Kibilhathur said quietly, "I'm a stonecutter."

Morningstar wondered what had prompted that, until she remembered Aravia's attempt to learn everyone's profession.

Dranko flashed a grin. "Hey, that's great. I'm sure we'll need one of those at some point!"

Kibilhathur either ignored or didn't notice Dranko's sarcasm. "Always had a knack with stone. I can make it do what I want, in some small ways. It don't feel like magic. Just feels natural-like. Almost like I'm part a' the rock, and it's part a' me. Know what I mean?"

Morningstar didn't have the slightest sense of what he meant and guessed that no one else did either, but Mrs. Horn answered warmly, "That sounds extraordinary, Mr. Bimson. You'll have to show us some time."

"There's no need for 'Mr. Bimson.' Folks just call me Kibi."

"So what do you bring to the table, Dranko," asked Grey Wolf, "besides a glib tongue?"

"My tongue is more than just glib," said Dranko with an exaggerated leer. Morningstar felt sickened. She had been living exclusively among women for many years, and her experience with men was extremely limited, but Dranko was a match for the most exaggeratedly lewd caricatures she had heard.

Dranko smirked at her. "Here's my serious answer. I have street smarts. I can procure things quickly in an emergency. I know where I can get the most gold for Abernathy's little bird friend here." He held up the jade owl. "Also I am a man of the cloth, or at least I was. I'm an expert at first aid, and I can channel Delioch's healing might."

Morningstar's eyebrows went up. "You? You're a priest of Delioch? That would explain the scars, but you don't strike me as the pious type."

"The church elders felt the same way, which is why I'm sort of on leave at the moment. But if you don't believe me, I can put my hands on you and prove it."

Ernie made a choking noise and blushed. "Dranko, don't be such a…such a pig!"

Dranko laughed it off. "I'm harmless. Just trying to add some levity to our new situation." He poured himself another glass of wine. "So, Ernie, what do *you* do? What great talent do you bring to our merry band?"

Ernie sat up straight. "I…well, I'm a pretty good cook. My parents are bakers. And though I wouldn't describe myself as having any 'great talent,' I have been training as a swordsman since I was a boy."

"So," said Grey Wolf, "about six months then?"

"Four years," mumbled Ernie.

Morningstar herself had extensive combat training, serving in the order of Shields at the temple. Hers was the martial wing of her sisterhood, who would protect the people from dangers that dwelt in darkness. Though she was slight and not possessed of great strength, she was quick, practiced, and able to spar for hours.

Of course, in this time of peace in the Kingdom of Charagan, sparring was most of what the Shields of Ell did. She frowned. Abernathy's spell must have picked them for their fighting skill, which meant he expected there'd be battle. Was it possible that his locked-up monster was already free, and they'd wind up fighting against it? But, no, Abernathy had admitted they didn't know how to kill it, and if the archmagi with their great powers of wizardry were helpless, there was no way this little band of summonees would have any hope.

"You fighting types should have a tournament tomorrow to see who's best," said Dranko. "Mrs. Horn, you've got your butchering cleaver. Care to test your mettle?"

"Oh, that wouldn't be fair," said Mrs. Horn. "None of you would hurt an old woman, so I'd simply chop off all of your heads, and then where would we be?" She shook her head. "No, no, I'm too old for that sort of thing. I'm a farmer, not a warrior-maid. When we hold a cow-milking contest, count me in."

"Fine," said Dranko. "You can sit this one out. Hey, Eddings, does the Greenhouse have a backyard? My friends here could use it for combat practice."

"Indeed it does, Master Blackhope," said the butler. "The back lot is quite large. Master Abernathy said you might find it useful to have a large outdoor space at your disposal. It is also enchanted so that anyone looking over the fence will see only an empty lawn."

"Huh," said Dranko. "What sort of things did Abernathy imagine we'd need to do in secret out there?"

"I couldn't say, Master Blackhope. But perhaps you could count sword practice among those activities."

Dranko turned to Morningstar. "So I saw you had a weapon like the rest. Any good with it? What do you call that thing, anyway?"

Morningstar had first seen the picture in an old book of arms in the Chroniclers' library. She had only been a Shield for a month, but when she saw the drawing, she knew in her bones that one day she would swing such a weapon in the service of Ell.

"It's called a morning-star mace," she told him.

"They named a weapon after you?"

Morningstar blew through her lips. "Are you really as stupid as you pretend to be?"

"I'm probably stupider," said Dranko agreeably. "But can you swing that thing?"

"Yes. So take care not to stand too close to me."

She was surprised at how confrontational she was being, but something about Dranko stirred up a long-dormant anger inside of her. He was a like a toddler who liked to poke his elders to get attention.

"It can't be a coincidence," said Tor. His grin had returned, his faux pas already behind him. He had the attention span of a mayfly. "It can't be chance that Abernathy's spell picked a group with lots of fighting skill, plus a wizard, and a channeler, and a…um…" He looked apologetically at Kibi and Mrs. Horn. "A stonecutter and a farmer. The missions he's going to send us on must be very dangerous!"

Grey Wolf gave a bitter laugh. "Have you ever killed anyone?"

"No. Not yet," said Tor defensively. "But I could, if I had to."

"You can't know that," said Grey Wolf. "Not until the time comes. And you shouldn't look forward to it."

"What about you?" Dranko asked Grey Wolf. "Ever killed someone? I'm guessing you're no stranger to the blade."

Grey Wolf nodded. "Not often, but yes. I've spent the last fifteen years as a sword for hire. It pays the bills. Well, *paid* the bills, until we were kidnapped. Abernathy swiped me right in the middle of a job, which is not going to do my reputation any favors."

After the meal Eddings gave Abernathy's makeshift team a tour of the Greenhouse. The kitchen was large but not yet stocked; its only remarkable feature was the Icebox, a silver metal crate four feet on a side that sat on a large table. As they walked back toward the staircases, Eddings waved at the black door and mentioned a spacious basement, currently empty.

He stopped before leading them upstairs. "Before I go further, I will give you each one of these." The butler produced a large key ring and started detaching keys from it. His voice became even more formal than usual. "These open the Greenhouse doors. Each of you gets one. Without a house key, the only way you, or anyone else, can enter is by a verbal invitation from someone already *in* the house. Abernathy made it clear that crafting spare keys would be a great bother to him, so I implore you not to lose them."

Morningstar hesitated before taking a key she was sure she wouldn't need, but decided not to make a fuss.

"Morningstar," said Eddings, "I have noticed the light seems to bother you. I suggest you shield your eyes." Once she had done so, he said, "Stairwell lights on please," and a number of small heatless torches sprang to magical life along the walls.

"I will now show you the most important room in the Greenhouse."

In the upstairs hall Eddings stopped halfway between two of the bedroom doors, where a large oil painting of Abernathy's tower hung on the wall. "Please watch," he said. He grabbed the sides of the painting and spun the whole thing upside down. Once it was fully inverted, a tiny doorway appeared near the base of the tower's exterior. Eddings flicked the doorway with a finger. A whole section of the wall swung silently inward on invisible hinges.

Beyond the concealed door was a small room, large enough for all of them to squeeze inside, but not much larger. In its center was a table, and on that table, resting upon a squat metal tripod, was a large glass globe.

"Abernathy," Eddings said to the globe, "we need to speak with you."

The glass ball filled with a swirling gray fog that soon cleared. A face appeared, though it did not belong to Abernathy. It was the dull red visage of a metal bust, its cheeks composed of gem-like facets, its eyes two silver marbles, its head a tiered dome.

Its mouth, a thin black line of dark iron, didn't move as it spoke. "Greetings! Abernathy is indisposed at the moment, but I would be pleased to convey your message to him."

"Handsome fellow," said Dranko.

"I would be pleased to convey a message to Abernathy," repeated the metal head.

"What's your name?" Dranko asked.

"Abernathy refers to me as 'Mister Golem.'"

"Well, Mister Golem," said Dranko with a grin, "tell the boss we appreciate him hiring us a butler. Eddings is great!"

"I will convey your message to Abernathy at his earliest convenience. Is there anything else with which I can assist?"

"Do you have anything of substance to say to us?" Morningstar asked the creature. "Abernathy said he would try persuading us to sign on with him. Have you any idea when that's going to happen?"

"No," said the golem.

When several seconds passed with no one speaking further, Mister Golem's face vanished, and the polished glass sphere returned to transparency.

"That was amazing!" cried Tor.

"That was underwhelming," said Grey Wolf.

"And creepy," added Ernie. "You'd think Abernathy would make it so Mister

Golem's mouth moved when it talked."

* * *

Morningstar was still awake an hour after midnight, which was not unusual. Sisters of Ell typically woke in the midafternoon and retired at sunrise, so for her this was the middle of her "day." On an ordinary night she'd be sparring with her Shield trainer, Clariel, in the hour before two-bells services.

At least they each had their own bedroom—a luxury she hadn't expected, especially one well furnished with a wardrobe, desk, and enchanted tub that filled with hot or cold water on command. Morningstar sat on the edge of her featherbed in the comforting darkness, head bowed. Would she bother describing this experience to her sisters when she returned home? Most of them wouldn't care, and the rest would merely add it to the tally of her peculiarities. Would they even believe that she'd been in the tower of one of the most powerful wizards in the kingdom?

Someone knocked on her door.

"Morningstar? It's Abernathy. May I come in?"

She stared at the door. Hadn't the old wizard said he couldn't leave his tower? Goddess, was Dranko playing a drunken prank? He had been far into his cups when he had staggered upstairs an hour earlier.

Morningstar sighed, stood, and opened the door. Abernathy was in the hall, still in his long white robe, slightly bent and leaning on a tall staff. His body was outlined in a flickering blue corona.

"Come in…" She wracked her brain for the proper honorific. Sir? Your wizardliness? He shuffled into her room and sat in the chair at the desk.

"I'm not really here," he explained. "I'm projecting myself. I can do that into the Greenhouse."

She nodded blankly.

"I've visited all the others. I'm here, as promised, to try convincing you to stay on and defend our kingdom."

Morningstar squinted; the wizard's blue aura hurt her eyes. "It's not that I don't wish to see Charagan defended. But it's hopelessly impractical that I be part of your team. Ellish priestesses are forbidden from the outdoors while the sun is up. However worthy your cause, I cannot betray my faith. Are you proposing that we eight perform all of our tasks for you at night?"

"No, I think that would be infeasible." The deep blue glow about him cast eerie shadows over his features, and outlined every hair of his abundant eyebrows. "But I have already taken the liberty of contacting the upper echelons of the Ellish hierarchy, in case some accommodation can be made."

Morningstar tried not to read anything sinister into the word "accommodation." Abernathy hadn't promised not to turn anyone *else* into toads.

"I trust you issued no threats?"

"Certainly not. I merely inquired if there might be some compromise that would allow you to remain in my employ."

"The Ellish religion is not amenable to compromise," she told him.

"You are not very popular in your temple, Morningstar."

It was not a question.

"So you have been talking with the sisters of Port Kymer?"

"No. I'm simply good at reading…certain people. I'm not wrong, am I?"

"No. You're not wrong, and I'm not popular."

"It must be tiring, going through life without the acceptance of one's peers."

Morningstar reached for her inner calm, an island in choppy seas. Was this meant to make her angry? "I've learned to live with it. I serve Ell with all of my being, and that is enough."

It was true that Morningstar had no close friends, and could count her friendly acquaintances using only her thumbs. Her sisters judged her harshly while at the same time treading lightly around her, as if they feared what her purpose would be, placed in their midst by Ell. She made her sisters distinctly uncomfortable, and this they reflected back at her in defense.

"I don't pretend to know the will of the Gods for certain," said Abernathy, "but I suspect that Ell would consider service defending all the Kingdom of Charagan to be within your general remit."

Possible, but irrelevant.

"What do you think of the others?" asked the wizard.

That was an oddly abrupt change of subject, but she could humor him. They were decent people. Ernie and Tor, the kids, were friendly if naïve. Aravia was a little full of herself and her wizardry, but not so much as to be annoying. Kibi, the soft-spoken one, was hard to get a read on, but she didn't sense any malice there. Mrs. Horn was quiet but had a wry sense of humor. And Grey Wolf, though rough around the edges, had a rugged, world-weary competence she could appreciate. It didn't hurt that he was also quite easy on the eyes.

But Dranko…ugh. He was rough around the edges, rough in the middle, and rough everywhere in between. He was a rude and wholly unpleasant con artist who was obviously lying about being a Deliochan acolyte. His only redeeming feature was an ugliness so profound that it was liable to make *him* the freak of their group, a role she was all too happy to forgo.

"I like most of them well enough," she said. "Except for Dranko. I don't see why your summoning spell included a boorish drunken felon."

"He's also a Deliochan channeler," Abernathy pointed out.

"He wasn't lying about that?" Morningstar tried to picture Dranko as a pious healer but couldn't summon up imagery that absurd.

"I don't think so, no. I ask about your fellow summonees because they represent something you've not had in your adult life, not truly. They will accept you, Morningstar of Ell. They could be your friends and allies, your confidants, even your family if you allow it. They don't care about your skin, your hair, your name. You might find that quite liberating."

Morningstar was good at reading people, but Abernathy—or this shimmering projection of him—was a puzzle. He seemed sincere, but she sensed that he was uncomfortable with his words, like he was reading from a script and hoping its author had his facts straight.

But for all that, he was right. Somewhere buried beneath her protective layers of emotional detachment was a desire for acceptance. No, that was too strong. Better to call it a curiosity about what acceptance would be like.

"I'm sorry, Abernathy," she said quietly. "I'm sure the kingdom is full of people both able and willing to help you, but I'm not one of them."

Abernathy gave her a long penetrating look, his eyes shaded nearly purple by his nimbus. She looked back at him, unabashed. What a strange life this old wizard must lead, stranger than hers, and no less lonely. How long had he lived alone in his tower, keeping his monster at bay?

He quickly turned his head, as if he had heard something unexpected from the next room. "Do as you must," he said sadly, "but I must return to my work at once."

He vanished, a blue flame instantly snuffed.

So that was settled then. Tomorrow she'd ask Eddings to book her passage back to Port Kymer on a ship departing after sunset. In a few days she'd be back at the temple. As intriguing as this business with Abernathy was, life would return to its normalcy, its isolation.

Sometime after three o'clock Morningstar drifted to sleep.

She stands upon a platform atop a narrow spire of rock. The platform is swaying in time to a series of massive booming thunderclaps, as though a giant is striking the base of the spire with a hammer. The tower is going to fall, and if she were real, if she were truly standing there, she would plummet to her death.

A man is standing at one edge of the platform, a man plated in red mail. He ignores her—she is not truly there, in this dream—and looks south over a hazy ocean. In one hand he holds a shimmering black sword, and in the other is a polished gem-studded horn. His face is cruel and triumphant, a combination Morningstar finds troubling. He seems unconcerned with the spire's oscillations.

"This seems like a great deal of trouble to go through, Forkbeard," he says to the air. "And my master is not entirely convinced any of this is necessary. He thinks his victory is already inevitable."

Another thunderbolt rocks the tower.

"But it's quite the spectacle, either way," he murmurs. "Even more so if you're wrong about how this will end."

"I think you'll be surprised about how this ends," says another voice. It's Tor, who has appeared on the far side of the platform. Tor charges at the man in red armor, crashing into him and sending both hurtling off the edge.

Morningstar sat bolt upright in her bed, drenched in sweat, her heart thudding heavily in her chest. Late morning light spilling in the window immediately blinded her; she threw an arm across her eyes and staggered to draw the curtains. It took almost five minutes for her vision to return.

A Seer-dream! Certain sisters were Dreamseers, trained to interpret dreams and provide guidance based upon those interpretations. All Ellish priestesses understood that some dreams were prophetic though usually in small or ambiguous ways.

Dreamseers were also, on rare occasions, granted prophetic dreams of their own, called Seer-dreams. They had been described to her as unusually vivid, and unlike most dreams which burned off like morning mist, Seer-dreams were as easily remembered afterward as any waking experience. Not for a second did she doubt that was what this was. She could still hear the sound of the thunderous booms, as clearly as if she had been there.

Would she tell the others? Morningstar was unused to sharing…anything, really. Opinions, revelations, spiritual experiences, even mundane pleasantries had been too often turned back on her by her Ellish sisters. For something as intensely personal as a Seer-dream, all of her instincts warned her to keep it to herself.

But then there was the boy. She didn't see him strike the ground, but the implication was clear enough. Should she warn young Tor about what she saw? Seer-dreams could be anything from obscure metaphors to near-literal foretellings. She ought to tell him, though he'd probably forget all about it before lunch.

Downstairs Dranko and Tor were sitting together at the living room table. Dranko was pulling on a cigar, the smoke of which was so thick and heavy that it curled downward to form a spreading cloud by the floor. Tor was methodically stacking coins. Mrs. Horn was curled up on a couch nearby, sewing up a hole in a sock that wasn't hers. The old woman looked up at her.

"Are you feeling well, dear?" Mrs. Horn glanced at the window and shook her head. "This won't do at all. Boys, we need to remember that Morningstar isn't used to sunlight." She carefully set down her needle and thread, crossed the room, and drew the curtains across the bay windows. "There's still plenty of light for you two to enjoy your coins."

Morningstar nodded gratefully to Mrs. Horn. "Thank you."

The old woman smiled as she sat back down. "We all need to look out for one another, now that we've been thrown together."

Dranko gestured proudly at the table. "*I'm* looking out for us."

There was quite a lot of money there—the pile included at least twelve crescents, plus a handful of silver talons and copper chits. Dranko took a long draw from his cigar and blew out a downward-streaming slug of dark smoke. "You know that owl Abernathy gave us? Turns out those ruby eyes were the real deal. Figured there was no point in waiting to turn that birdie into some seed capital. Now you can buy yourself a blindfold."

"I'm not staying," she told him. "Abernathy tried his best to convince me, but it's not going to work."

"Shame," said Dranko. "What about you, Grey Wolf?"

Morningstar turned to see Grey Wolf on her heels. He wrinkled his nose. "I have a favor to ask. How about no cigars in the…wait. Is that gold?"

"Dranko sold Abernathy's owl this morning." Tor flipped a gold crescent to

Grey Wolf, who caught it deftly.

"Right," said Grey Wolf. "And Dranko, I'm sure you wouldn't have held anything back for yourself. Yes?"

"I could argue that I deserve a small fee for my service," said Dranko. Grey Wolf took a step forward, but Dranko held up his hands. "I *could* argue that, but I won't. I promise you, every last chit is on the table."

"I'm counting it so we can divvy it up fairly," said Tor.

Dranko gave Grey Wolf a toothy smile. "So, Mr. Wolf, will you be staying on as part of Abernathy's team?"

Grey Wolf looked thoughtfully at the coin. "For a little while, at least. Abernathy told me that a…personal goal of mine may be easier to achieve if I join this merry band. So I agreed to give him a couple of weeks, see if there's any progress."

"Going to share?" asked Dranko.

"No."

Morningstar did not fault Grey Wolf for not being the sharing type. And on the subject of sharing, should she tell Tor about her Seer-dream now, or wait until they were in private?

Eddings came in from the dining room. "Ah, Lady Morningstar. A letter arrived for you, not more than an hour ago." From his jacket pocket he pulled a slim black envelope.

A letter from the temple? A swift rejection of Abernathy's query, she assumed. She tore open the envelope and read.

Sister Morningstar,

We have learned of your changed circumstances, and your recent employment by the Archmage Abernathy of Tal Hae. Though I do not personally condone it, the High Priestess Rhiavonne in Kallor has allowed you special dispensation to walk abroad in daylight and to suspend any other church traditions that may conflict with your duties in the service of the archmage, so long as they do not violate specific temple laws. This dispensation shall be in effect until you and the Archmage Abernathy together agree that your service to him has finished; until then, the High Priestess prefers that you remain based in Tal Hae and follow the archmage's instructions.

Morningstar, I know this will be a difficult transition for you, but we all must do as Ell demands, and the High Priestess Rhiavonne speaks with Her voice on this matter. We will miss you at the temple.

May the Goddess guide you,

Sister Fithawn

The blood pounded in Morningstar's ears. Her skin prickled. Her eyes swept over the letter, two times, three times.

...walk abroad in daylight...

...suspend any other church traditions...

...High Priestess Rhiavonne speaks with Her voice...

"No," she whispered. "They wouldn't..."

"Wouldn't do what, dear?" asked Mrs. Horn. Morningstar raised her head; the others were looking at her expectantly.

"I...they..."

How could she explain it? Though her sisters didn't like her, or were scared of her, the Ellish temple was her identity, her lifeblood, her foundation. *We will miss you at the temple*, Fithawn had written. But what had been left unwritten was *...because you will not be welcomed back*. How could she be, if she walked beneath the sun?

This was going to confirm every suspicion that had ever been leveled at her, that she was not truly a sister, that she had no place in the black halls of Ell, that she had been a mistake. For those who had wanted to see the White Anathema expelled, Abernathy's summons had provided the perfect excuse.

Worst of all, there would be no appeal to authority. The High Priestess Rhiavonne was the mortal leader of the Ellish religion in Charagan, and for sisters her decrees carried as much weight as the laws of the kingdom itself.

A roiling anger filled her. Her armor of composure shattered under a blow like none she'd ever faced.

She couldn't keep her voice from trembling. "I need to speak to Abernathy. Alone."

Morningstar stormed from the dining room and rushed to the secret chamber with the crystal ball. "Abernathy!" she demanded. "I need to speak with you."

The glass ball filled with mist, and after a minute Mister Golem's face appeared. The thing's emotionless visage enraged her. "Not you," she snapped. "I want to talk with Abernathy."

"Is this an emergency severe enough to require his immediate attention?"

"Yes. I want his *immediate* attention."

"One moment, please."

Mister Golem's face vanished into the fog of the crystal ball. Soon Abernathy's aged face looked out at her. His stringy white hair was plastered to his cheeks with sweat, and his torso heaved with heavy breath, as though he had sprinted up several flights of stairs to answer her call.

"Morningstar," he panted. "What has happened? Quickly, please."

Morningstar held up the letter. "What is this? What have you done?"

Abernathy's face grew larger in the crystal ball. "Is that a letter?"

"It's from my temple! It allows me to go out during the day running your errands."

"Er…oh. That was faster than I had expected. I'm pleased to hear it!"

Morningstar nearly hurled the crystal ball against the wall. "Pleased to…Abernathy, you've effectively had me thrown out of the temple! Kidnapping me was one thing, but this…this is…you've ruined my life!"

Abernathy's wrinkled face grew grave. "You were thrown out of your temple? That was not my intent, dear girl. I only requested that you be given more latitude in your work for me, so that your obligations would not clash with those of your religion." He glanced over his shoulder, then back at her. "Now, I don't mean to belittle your anger, but is there some disaster or problem such that you truly need my immediate help? Because I need to return to my work right away."

"No." She spat the word, her fury blunted though hardly diminished. "Go back to what you were doing. Keep your prison door closed."

She walked haltingly down the stairs and wished there were someone else nearby deserving of her rage. Tor looked up from his coins, and without thinking she said, "Tor, I had a dream about you last night. A Seer-dream."

Tor immediately reddened.

"Hey, I had a dream too!" said Dranko. "But not everyone in it was fully clothed, so you might not want to hear about it."

Goddess, but the goblin was relentlessly vile.

"What's a Seer-dream?" asked Tor.

"A dream that is prophecy." This was good to talk about. It was something *else* to talk about. She willed herself into a semblance of calm.

"Dreams are prophetic?" Dranko showed a tusky grin. "Then I know one fellow who's gettin' lucky sometime soon, if you know what I mean."

Morningstar ignored him, and looked Tor in the eyes. "There are sisters of Ell who are Dreamseers. They are tasked to interpret the dreams of others, but sometimes they have their own dreams that mark the future."

"And you're one?" asked Tor.

"No," said Morningstar. "I'm not a Dreamseer, or wasn't until today. But last night I dreamt the future, and you were in it."

"Neat!" said Tor. "What happened? What's my future?"

"Do you mind if the others hear?" She could at least offer him the choice of privacy.

"No, I don't mind! Tell me!"

And Morningstar did, including every detail she remembered, which was all of them.

No one spoke when she was finished; they were all looking at Tor. Defying all expectation, he smiled hugely.

"That's great! I'll bet the guy in the armor will be up to no good, and our job will be to stop him, and I'll push him off the edge and kill him before he does his evil deeds. Maybe he's even the monster Abernathy has locked away!"

Did Tor not understand? "But in my dream, you die too,"

"Did you see me hit the ground?"

"No, but—"

"That must have been on purpose! I bet I land on something soft, or I grab onto a flagpole or something. Thanks, Morningstar! It sounds like Abernathy was exactly right. Adventure, glory, excitement, we're going to have it all!"

Morningstar sighed. "Tor, you should take this more seriously. Not just my dreams, but all of it. Didn't you hear Abernathy? I think we won't be going on picnics in the park."

"We?" asked Dranko. "So Abernathy convinced you to tag along? What about you staying inside all day?"

The Goddess knew that she didn't owe Dranko, of all people, any explanation, but now the others were looking at her. Aravia, Ernie, and Kibi had even come in from the dining room. She was suddenly too weary to deflect or dissemble.

"The letter from my temple. It gives me permission to travel outside before dark."

"Uh, isn't that good?" asked Dranko.

"You don't understand."

"True. So why don't you explain it to us."

There was mockery in his voice, she was sure of it. She flailed about for her island, her rock of equanimity, a swimmer caught in an unexpected undertow. Was Dranko any worse than the cruelest of her sisters? No. He was just a revolting street thug trying to get a rise out of her.

Anger was filling her. "One of the defining traditions of our church is that we do not allow the sun's rays to touch us. It reminds us of how we are different and of the role we play in society. I am a Shield of Ell. My path was that of protector, against the dangers that come in the dark, against the creatures that prey on the sleeping. But now all of that is gone."

The tide surged. The rock was slipping from her fingers.

"All of that is gone," she repeated. "I was always one step away from being pushed out." She grabbed the end of one white lock of hair and shook it at Dranko. "I was already an outsider! The Goddess gave me a sunlit name! Morningstar? She might as well have named me Pariah! And this!" She held up her arms, pale as moonlit snow. "I was born an outcast, and now Abernathy has made it stick. A sister who walks in the sun is no sister at all, and every single one of my peers is nodding to themselves right now and saying it was all for the best. Morningstar was never meant to be one of us. And now she's not. I'm not. Now I'm one of you instead."

Dranko took a deep breath.

Don't speak to me, goblin.

But he did. "Do you have so little faith in Ell that you don't think She has a plan for you? You don't think She gave you your hair and your skin and your name for a reason? Ell wouldn't torture one of Her own children, even if she had a tendency to whine. Have a little faith."

She was swept out to sea on a swell of rage. She took two steps forward and slapped Dranko hard on the side of his face. He took a step back from the blow but turned again to face her. Goddess, but he grew uglier every time she looked at him. All those scars on his goblin face, his stringy hair, his wire-coarse stubble...his was a filthy countenance to match his filthy soul.

She turned and stalked to her room.

CHAPTER THREE

T hat was nice," said Grey Wolf acidly. "You're a real diplomat."

"And you're an overbearing arse with a stupid name." Dranko felt he could really use a drink. "I think I'll go for a walk and enjoy some fresh air."

"Take your cigar," said Grey Wolf. "That way we can enjoy some too."

Dranko didn't bother closing the door behind him, and prowled the streets in a snarling funk. He had a half a mind to rob someone, but his heart wasn't in it. A few times over the years he'd barely escaped following botched petty thefts attempted without a clear mind and full concentration. "Never pick a pocket if either of you is drunk," he once told Berthel. "One of you will be swaying too much."

He had lied to Grey Wolf. He *had* kept a handful of coins for himself, though it was much less than the typical take for a professional fence. After an hour of wandering, he bought himself a mug of beer and a bowl of hearty stew at a dockside tavern. Sitting at a corner table and nursing his drink, he thought about Abernathy's visit to his room the previous night.

Dranko hadn't taken much convincing to sign on. The Greenhouse was a palace, the bed was vermin-free, a magic box made magic food, and he had a patron who could turn his enemies into frogs in a pinch. But Abernathy's pitch had gone beyond that. The old wizard must be able to see right down into his private dreams. He had zeroed in on the thing in life Dranko desired most. Which reminded him, it had been a while since he had thrown his last bottle.

With the extra cash, Dranko had another ale or three and drank away the afternoon, belching defiance at anyone who approached. Sometime after sunset he lurched to his feet, leered at the barmaid, and stumbled out the door. Rain began to drip from a quilt of low gray clouds as Dranko sulked his uneven way through the busy nighttime streets of Tal Hae. He tried and failed to banish the image of Morningstar's face from his mind.

You're so Gods-damned good at poking people. You've been doing it for so long, I think you're addicted to it. That's what you do. You pick at scabs, you get under peoples' skins. And then they get rid of you. Praska always told you to tone it down, and you always ignored her warnings.

Dranko stopped. He had arrived at his tenement on Fishwife Row. Quietly as he could, he crept up the creaky stairs to his little apartment, hoping Berthel would leave him alone for once. Inside he went first to a sealed jar full of paper scraps and pulled one out, then groped behind his beat-up dresser until his fingers closed upon a half-drained bottle of cheap wine.

By the time he emerged back on the street, it was entirely drained. Drunken and angry—at the world, at Morningstar, at himself, at Abernathy—he made his way up a scrubby hill to a familiar cliff-top path above the sea. To his left was the harbor, with lanterns winking at him from dozens of ships as they bobbed and creaked. He turned right. Half a mile later he had rounded a wide headland and now stood above the Middle Sea, where the currents swept around the coast and out into the wide blue. The sea wasn't blue now—it was a moonlit black—and Dranko gazed out over the murmuring water, listening to the slow song of its chop.

He fished the paper scrap from his pocket. Three words were scrawled upon it: *Dranko was here.* He uncorked the bottle, stuffed the note inside, and replaced the cork.

From the earliest days of his memory, Dranko had wanted to be famous. His grandmother told him stories of Cencerra the Bold, a mighty warrior maid who slew dragons by the dozen, and while the dragon parts scared him, he loved how at the end of the tales Cencerra's name was shouted by throngs of grateful peasants, or the king proclaimed her a Dame of the Realm and showered her with gifts. He dreamt of someday doing great deeds, such that crowds would cheer and statues would be raised. What deeds those would be, he was never quite sure. That was less important. But in the little circle of his aggrieved childhood, his own name had been known and despised, and that filled him with shame and a burning dream of redemption. One day his name wouldn't be spoken with a curse and a glob of spit. One day he'd make a difference, and Mokad would regret every scar he had carved into Dranko's flesh, and his grandfather would stop blaming him for all the ills of his family.

He hurled the bottle—not the first and not the last—as hard and far as he could, out into the sea. The waves swallowed it up.

I'm going to be famous, Praska. Abernathy said I would be.

The thought of his old friend, and the wine in his blood, filled him with a maudlin nostalgia. Instead of returning to the Greenhouse, he detoured into the so-called Pious Quarter where most of the churches, temples, and shrines to the Travelers were set in a ring around a sprawling public park. He hadn't shown his face at the Church of Delioch in several years. How old would Praska be now? Twenty? Twenty-one?

The grounds of the church were surrounded by a high fence of iron bars, and the main gate was closed, though two Healing Brothers stood guard. He thought he recognized one—Nolman, wasn't it? Not a bad sort, if he recalled rightly. Dranko straightened his shirt, hoped the wine on his breath wouldn't travel too far, and approached the gate.

"Greetings, brothers!" he announced. "Long time no visit. Is Praska still here?"

One of the guards squinted. "Who's asking?"

"Dranko?" said the other, the one he recognized. "Is that you, Blackhope?"

"S'me!" said Dranko, wincing at his own slurred speech. "Nolman, isn't it? I never forget a fa-name. Name. Or a face. Either one."

"You're Dranko Blackhope?" asked the first man. "I've heard…" He stopped and smirked at his mate. "Your reputation is remarkable."

"Praska is not available," said Nolman. "She is serving out a punishment in the Closet."

"The Closet?" Dranko shuddered. Isolated confinement had been a controversial disciplinary measure back when he was a novice. The scarbearers claimed it was effective, but High Priest Tomnic had nearly always overruled any suggestion of its infliction. "What did she do?"

"That is not your concern," said the second man.

"Never mind," said Dranko. "When she gets out, tell her Dranko came by to see her, okay? I live in the Greenhouse on the Street of Bakers now. Praska can stop by any visit. Any time for a visit."

"Go home and sober up," said Nolman. "I'll give your message to Praska when she's released."

Dranko bowed so low he nearly toppled, wind-milled his arms to keep his balance, and staggered into the night.

CHAPTER FOUR

The first thing Ernie Roundhill did the next morning was sit at his desk and write a letter because he really ought to.

Dear Mom and Dad,

I'm writing you from my new house in Tal Hae. I never even got to the city on foot since Abernathy, the wizard, did some magic to pop us right inside his tower. Aravia had a word for it, but I can't remember it right now. Oh, and it's "us," since there's eight of us, not just me. Abernathy wanted a whole team to help him. The others all seem very nice, though one of them is part goblin and involved in a mysterious gem-trading business. His name's Dranko, and he's also a Delioch channeler.

There's also a young man like myself, Tor, he's a swordsman, there's a tough older gentleman who calls himself Grey Wolf who I think was a bodyguard. The others are Aravia, she's a wizard, though not near as powerful as Abernathy, another woman named Morningstar who's Ellish, and a stone-worker with a funny accent named Kibi. Oh, and Mrs. Horn, who's kind of like the grandmum of the group. I think she must be older than Mrs. Appleford. They're all such nice, interesting people, but also I think more complicated than the folks in White Ferry. It's hard to explain.

Abernathy has given us a house to live in, and we even have our own butler named Eddings. It feels weird to have someone serving me. Our house is called the Greenhouse, and it's on the Street of Bakers here in Tal Hae. Isn't that great? Our house even used to be a bakery, and I've already become the house cook, even though we also have a magic box that makes food.

Abernathy said we have to help keep the kingdom safe, and that it may take a long time. But I bet I can convince him to let me come back and visit. I'll keep writing to you to let you know how everything is going.

Love, your son,

Ernest Carabend

Ernie folded up his letter and stared at it thoughtfully. He didn't want to worry his mother unduly, and he had gone back and forth in his mind about whether to include any references to Abernathy's world-threatening monster. His parents had hammered the importance of honesty into him like a blacksmith pounds a blade, but he could stomach small lies of omission to spare his dear mother distress.

Now he faced another difficulty: how did one send a letter to a small village a hundred miles away? He found Eddings downstairs, scrubbing the kitchen floor.

"Eddings, could you arrange to have this letter sent to my parents? They're in the town of White Ferry, at the Roundhill Bakery."

"Of course, Master Roundhill."

"Oh, good. Thanks, Eddings."

"It is my pleasure, sir."

Having a butler sure was handy. He didn't deserve a butler, of course. If anything, *he* should be the servant.

He started to ask Eddings if there was anything *he* needed, but was interrupted by a truly horrific noise, like a songbird being tortured. After ten seconds it hadn't stopped. Aravia and Grey Wolf were already in the dining room, and they looked every bit as alarmed as Ernie felt. Only Eddings remained undisturbed.

"That is Abernathy summoning you to the globe room." The butler gestured toward the stairs. "Announce your arrival and the summoning noise should cease."

On the second floor the others had staggered into the hall. Dranko, his face haggard, had his hands clapped to his ears and was moaning, "Make it stop, make it stop!"

Grey Wolf flipped the painting, flicked the tower, and shouted over the din, "We're here! What is it?"

The ear-splitting warble cut off, thank the Gods. They crowded into the small room while the mist inside the globe coalesced into Abernathy's wrinkled face. There was sweat beaded on the wizard's spotted cheeks and his hair was mussed.

"I'm sending you off on your first assignment."

A thrill of excitement and fear flowed through Ernie. Mostly fear, he'd have admitted if anyone had asked.

"Did your monster get out?" he asked. He felt his face flush with embarrassment for having wondered that out loud. Could he sound more pathetic?

"No, no," said Abernathy. "But the aspect of our enemy's assault on the door has…shifted recently, and we need all the information we can get. I've already told you the nature of this task, yes? To inspect the door behind which my monster, as you say, is trapped. You will find it unusual, but what I need to know should be simple enough for you to learn."

"Where is it?" asked Aravia. "And will you have time to send over some of your spellbooks before we go? You promised me, remember? It's why I agreed to join your endeavor. Also, my cat is still at Master Serpicore's house. Can you arrange to have my Pewter brought here?"

Abernathy sighed. "The door is near the town of Verdshane," he said. And as for your…"

A deep chime sounded from within the glass ball, and Abernathy flinched at the noise. When he spoke again, his words came rapidly. "Very quickly now, go to Verdshane, cross-country will be fastest, leave within the hour if you can, there are some ruins north of the town, and one building looks like there's no way into it, close your eyes and walk through the door with the bear head, inside there's a magical blue field—don't touch it—but in that field is a person, floating, and I want you to measure, as precisely as you can from as close as you can get, the distance between that person's left heel and the floor beneath him, after that, return at once and tell me that distance." He finally took a shallow breath. "Don't talk to anyone about anything you see near Verdshane. Good luck!"

The chime rang again, more loudly this time, and Ernie remembered the sound from their first night in Abernathy's tower. The old wizard's worry-stricken face vanished from the crystal ball.

Back in the living room, Grey Wolf took charge. "You heard the boss. Leave within the hour. Let's get packing, and get this over with as quickly as possible."

Grey Wolf was obviously used to giving orders and being obeyed, and that suited Ernie just fine. Someone needed to lead, and it certainly wasn't going to be him!

"Where's Verdshane?" he asked the room. His voice trembled, for which he silently cursed himself. None of the others even seemed nervous. How could that be? And did any of them understand that stuff about a bear head and a blue field and a floating person?

"It's in the Greatwood, to the north," said Aravia. "Master Serpicore has a map of the kingdom on the wall of his library. Naturally I memorized it in its entirety. The Greatwood is only about a week's journey from here, I imagine. Dranko, Tal Hae is your home. Have you never been there?"

"I'm more of a city boy," said Dranko. "Forests give me hives."

Yesterday afternoon, suspecting that Abernathy would soon be sending his team far afield, Eddings had taken the majority of Dranko's windfall and purchased all kinds of traveling supplies. Ernie took it upon himself to carry the cooking gear, which nearly overbalanced him when combined with his spare clothing, travel tent, bedroll, and provisions. He looked at himself in the mirror that hung in the foyer, at the water skin hung on the hip opposite from his sword Pyknite. He felt almost glamorous, a true outdoorsman, and he showed a brave face to the others, as if this were something he regularly did for fun back in White Ferry. Kibi was looking back and forth between Morningstar and the sunlit open doorway. The Ellish priestess, Ernie reminded himself, was about to take her first steps into daylight.

Everyone had accepted Abernathy's offer, even the elderly Mrs. Horn. Tor's beaming face balanced the scowls from Morningstar and Grey Wolf. Kibi had packed the most—Morningstar's tent, his own gear, and even a heavy mining pick—but moved about as though entirely untroubled by the extra weight.

"Ain't got no weapon," he explained. "Figured if there's fightin', I oughta have something with a sharp point I'm used to swingin'."

Ernie made a point of checking on Mrs. Horn before they left.

"Ma'am, will you be okay? Walking for a week, I mean?"

The old woman laughed. "Ernest, I've been running the farm solo for almost five years, ever since I lost my husband. I daresay I walk more miles in a day than you do."

"Oh! I'm sorry about your husband," said Ernie. "How did he die?"

Mrs. Horn became serious. "I didn't say he died. I lost him. Or, rather, he lost himself. Dear old William was a fisherman, and one afternoon his boat didn't come back. I prefer to think of him as washed up on an island somewhere, building a new ship as fast as he's able, and that one day soon he'll be sailing home again. It helps me stay positive."

"Say," said Ernie. "Maybe in return for helping Abernathy, he'll help you find your husband."

Mrs. Horn smiled at him, wrinkles forming an oval around her face. "When I first read Abernathy's magical card, a thought like that did cross my mind."

* * *

They marched out of the Greenhouse and a pack mule was waiting for them, cropping the grass on the front lawn. "I did not have enough coin to buy you horses," said Eddings, "but purchasing you a beast of burden seemed prudent. It can live in the back yard." It was a sad-faced but sturdy animal that accepted much of the group's paraphernalia without complaint. Dranko announced that he was naming her E.R—short for Emergency Rations.

They headed off down the Street of Bakers, then wound their way through Tal Hac's unimaginable crowds and out the city's wide north gate. Once into the countryside, they followed a northwesterly course along hedge rows and sheep tracks. The air had the cool bite of early spring, but Ernie was soon sweating and huffing from the fast pace Grey Wolf had set. Hours later, as the sunlight was starting to fail, his feet were blistered and one of his calves was cramping, but he only needed to glance at Morningstar to banish any tendency to self-pity. Poor Morningstar! She had her black robe pulled down as far over her face as it could go, and her hands were pulled into her sleeves so not an inch of her skin was exposed. Ernie asked her from time to time if there was anything he could do for her, but she merely shook her head. They had stopped several extra times when she had gasped requests in cracked whispers, but she uttered not one word of genuine complaint.

Aravia claimed in her know-it-all way that there was a small road that went more directly toward Verdshane. Grey Wolf decided they should detour slightly and march up a small steep hill to see if they could spot it before it became too dark. It turned out to be a tough climb. Morningstar had to stop half way up to catch her breath, and Kibi always seemed to be falling behind. Ernie's heart was thumping and his legs ached by the time they reached the top, but from the high vantage it was easy to spot the thin ribbon of the road curling into the northern haze.

"See?" said Aravia. "I knew it was there."

Grey Wolf paced around the flat top of the hill. "We've made good enough progress for one day, and this is a good place to camp for the night."

Ernie sat down gratefully and propped his back against a boulder. Who knew that hiking all day would be so tiring? He allowed himself a few minutes to recover, then broke out the cooking supplies and started on supper. At least cooking was something he was good at.

* * *

Mrs. Horn sat down beside him as he ate. "Ernest, these are excellent carrots."

"Oh, well, they're from Abernathy's food box. I just cooked them."

She smiled at him the way his grandmother used to before she passed away. "When someone gives you a compliment, it's yours. Don't turn around and hand it to someone else."

Ernie felt himself blushing. His trainer back in White Ferry, Old Bowlegs, used to say similar things. Ernie still remembered what the old man had said to him the day he left White Ferry. "You're the best student I've got, and I don't mean your skill with a pig-sticker, though that's good enough for a start. I mean what's in here." Old Bowlegs had thumped Ernest on the chest. "You won't misuse your gifts, Pyknite included. Copper to kettles, that's why your great wizard picked *you* to visit him. You are destined for great things, Ernest Roundhill."

Pyknite was Old Bowlegs' sword, the famous blade he had used twenty years earlier to singlehandedly slay the seven goblins that had raided White Ferry. It had been unthinkable that Ernie should accept it, but Bowlegs had insisted.

Mrs. Horn wiped her mouth with her sleeve. "So, young man, tell me about your statue. Do I remember correctly you saying there was a statue of you in your hometown?"

He had almost forgotten about that! "Yes, but it's not because of anything I did. It's so odd. Murgy Thorn owns a tavern, the Rusty Mug, next door to my parents' bakery, and he's having his wine cellar expanded. The pick-men working for him uncovered the top of a stone head while they were digging. They cleared out the earth around the head and neck, and guess what? It was me! At least, it looks exactly like me, but it's been buried down there for hundreds of years, and

I'm only seventeen."

"Amazing," said Mrs. Horn. "How do you think it got there?"

"I have no idea. No one had any idea. But that was the day after Abernathy's card arrived, so everyone was convinced it was connected somehow."

Ernie's invitation to Abernathy's tower had already been the talk of White Ferry. His father, Hob Roundhill, had made sure the whole town knew about the glowing letter. Every farmer, every merchant, every craftsman had a theory about what Abernathy of Tal Hae wanted with Ernest Carabend Roundhill, and Ernie had been obliged to listen to them all over drinks at the Rusty Mug.

"Bet the old wizzy needs an apprentice!" grizzled old Bannick Greengrass had opined, before slapping Ernie on the back—a habit which Ernie had learned to endure with a smile.

"Or a bodyguard more like," added the carpenter Marb Mudcat. "Old Bowlegs always says you're goin' places, Ernie. Now we know where!"

"Tell you what I think," Lefty Appleford had said. Lefty was the oldest man in the village, but he still tended his riverside orchard every day. He had leaned over the table and managed to be loud and conspiratorial at once. "Abernathy is raising an army for King Crunard, and wants you to be part of it, Ernest!"

The only reason anyone in town even knew what an archmage *was*, was that Sally Cooper told them. Sally Cooper lived two hundred yards away on the far side of town. She was known for reading lots of books (and was considered an odd duck for it), and she said that "archmage" was a fancy word for "a damned powerful wizard." Every big city had one, she claimed. They lived in enormous stone towers, hundreds of feet high, and no one ever went in or out of them.

"They keep the sky from falling," Sally Cooper had told him, dropping in on the Roundhills after the news of Abernathy's letter had shot through White Ferry like brushfire. "The wizards, I mean, not the towers. I'll bet they need someone strong to help hold it up."

Ernie told all of this to Mrs. Horn, who nodded and said, "It would be an unlikely thing if they *weren't* connected, don't you think?"

"I suppose. I can't think of any *other* reason for Abernathy to choose me. I'm still not much of a swordsman." Ernie felt embarrassed to have talked about himself at such length. "How are you holding up? That was a long day of walking."

"Oh, fine, fine," said Mrs. Horn. "I'll feel it in my calves tomorrow to be sure, but it's nice being out in the open country. William and I used to go for long rambles like this. Our farm was in a valley, and we had to go over the hills when we traveled to Minok."

Mrs. Horn was the kind of woman Ernie's mom would call a "tough old bird." It made him feel safe to have her as part of their band, in the way that his parents made him feel protected back home in White Ferry.

"Why do you think Abernathy chose you to be part of our group?"

"Ernest, my parents both died when I was young—younger than you by a couple of years. I inherited the farm and was running it myself when I was fourteen. William didn't come along until I was in my twenties, and he was never much of a farmer even afterward. He preferred his fishing boat, his pride and joy."

The campfire caught a far-away gleam in her eye.

"I'm a survivor," she continued. "I can mend a fence or build one up from nothing. I can kill just about any animal you can name, skin it, gut it, and cook it. And I know where to put my knee if a young man gets fresh with me."

Ernie blushed, and Mrs. Horn laughed. "I don't understand magic," she admitted. "But I recognize the burden of responsibility on someone's shoulders when I see it. Abernathy is bearing a heavy load, and he's put a great deal of faith in us. I daresay each of us has a good reason for being here, and before long we'll have a good idea what that is."

"I don't know that I'm ready to be a hero," said Ernie, and that was, if anything, a terrific understatement.

Mrs. Horn smiled encouragingly. "I don't think anyone's ready for that."

CHAPTER FIVE

ccording to Aravia, the Greatwood stretched a hundred fifty miles east to west, filling nearly the entire western half of Harkran. Their little band reached the forest's southern border just before noon on their third day of hiking, and Morningstar, in near-desperation, dashed the final ten yards to the tree cover. Reaching the shade was like breaking the surface of the ocean just before drowning. She threw back her hood and gingerly touched her raw, blotchy cheeks. Her nose stung when she wiped the sweat from it, and her head ached.

These past couple of days had been hellish. Though the temperature had remained moderate, there had been no cloud cover, and the road was dry and exposed, with trees growing only infrequently beside it. The walking itself had been tiring, too, as the long march worked muscles that were never strongly tested during her sparring sessions at the temple. But while that would be overcome with time and miles, her feelings about daylight were not so optimistic.

Now, finally, blessedly, the road ran beneath the canopy of the red pines and mighty elm trees of the Greatwood, its thick green ceiling filtering away the harshest rays of the sun.

She shook her damp hair away from her cheeks. "Thank Ell."

"How are you holding up?" asked Ernie. She smiled at him; the young man had asked that at least a dozen times over the past forty-eight hours. This time, as with every time, his brow was furrowed and his voice filled with genuine concern.

"Fine, Ernest, but thank you for asking," she said. "Now that we're under cover, I think I'll be more comfortable."

"Maybe Dranko could heal your sunburn," Ernie suggested. "Him being a channeler and all."

Dranko looked up. "Channeling is serious business. Maybe Dranko should save his energy for something more debilitating, like if someone rips a cuticle, or stubs their toe."

"Dranko, have some sympathy! Morningstar hasn't had to—"

"It's okay, Ernie," said Morningstar. The last thing she wanted right now was to cause a row or (worse) get Dranko riled up enough to start his mouth going. His company was much easier to endure when he was quiet, and since they set out from Tal Hae, he had hardly said a word.

Mrs. Horn was rooting around in the underbrush beside the road, and soon she pulled up a bunch of purple-flowered weeds. She pressed them into Morningstar's hands. "Buckthorn. Mash this up and rub it on your sunburns. I always find it helps after a day in the fields."

Morningstar blinked. She hadn't realized that Mrs. Horn had been paying attention to her. "Thank you," she managed. "Are you an herbalist?"

"I'm a farmer, so yes." Mrs. Horn smiled her crinkly smile. "Hang in there, young lady. There's nothing so terrible that a body won't adjust to it in time. Human beings are designed to endure hardships."

Grey Wolf cleared his throat. "We'll stop for lunch the next time the road widens out."

Dranko made another one of his sour faces at Grey Wolf's command, and that made Morningstar smile. Grey Wolf was a natural leader—confident and decisive. She saw how Ernie and Tor in particular looked up to him.

"Morningstar, if you—"

Grey Wolf abruptly stopped talking and clutched his stomach. His face contorted. "I think I'm going to be sick."

He walked a few paces off and doubled over, but nothing came up. Morningstar took a few steps toward him. "Do you need water?"

"I don't know." Grey Wolf groaned. "It feels like...mff...like someone is reaching into my guts and grabbing my stomach. Not nausea or...or like any pain I've felt before, but...Gods, it's awful."

"Ernie!" called Dranko. "Did you poison Grey Wolf's breakfast?"

"No!" The baker's son looked scandalized at the suggestion.

Grey Wolf stood up, color returning to his face. "Huh. It's over. Yeah, I must've eaten something off this morning. Ernie, check the supplies, make sure nothing's moldy or rotten." He immediately set off again at his brisk pace.

Grey Wolf's intestinal troubles aside, this was the nicest day of travel by a wide margin, and it helped drain some of the agitation from Morningstar's mind. She had been trying, without success, to convince herself that the letter from the temple was not as damning as she had originally decided. There was nothing explicitly mentioned about excommunication, or even an extended leave of absence. But it was all too easy to read between the lines.

Morningstar had always taken pride in her even-keeled nature, and her fury at the church's "dispensation" now embarrassed her after the fact. In the comforting shade of the trees, she made a conscious decision to regain control of the situation. If they wanted her out, they would have to make it overt. Let them wear their bias in plain sight if they felt they must reject her. In the meantime she would treat her new designation with all the stoic grace she could muster and deal with Abernathy's assignments as professionally as possible.

When the sun had set beyond the trees, the eight made camp by the side of the road and lit a fire. The spring evenings were cold, and though Morningstar had to sit with her back to the flames lest they blind her, she appreciated the warmth.

Tor rummaged through his pack. "I didn't bring enough extra food."

The boy was always hungry, even after Ernie's generous meals.

"That's why they're called 'rations,'" said Dranko. "You're supposed to ration them out."

"We should reach a village called Walnord the day after tomorrow," said Aravia. "We can get you some more food there, I imagine."

After that they munched on their provisions in relative silence, as the forest outside the circle of their firelight grew darker. Nighttime was home to Morningstar; she breathed out the troubles of the past few days and inhaled the cool comfort of the evening. Aravia sat next to her and scrawled in a small notebook when she was done eating. Morningstar asked the young wizardess what she was writing.

"Oh!" said Aravia. "I write down my ideas for improving the spells I know. Abernathy promised me access to his spellbooks in return for joining his team, but in the meantime there's no reason I should not continue the refinements and efficiencies I was working on under Master Serpicore." She spoke with an affected eloquence, as though every sentence was an opportunity to demonstrate the quality of her education.

"Did you understand what Abernathy was talking about when he gave us our marching orders?"

"I believe so," said Aravia.

"Good," said Tor, who had moved to join them. "I've already forgotten what he said. Something about a body in a field in a building? How can a field be in a building? Unless it's a *really* big building…"

Aravia graced Tor with a condescending smile—not that the boy noticed. "He said a magical field. You know the circle of light around a lit candle? Think of that as a 'field' of light. Now substitute 'magic' for 'light.' There must be a source of magic near Verdshane that's emanating a magical field."

"With a person in it!" said Tor. "I wonder if it's a live person or a dead one."

"Almost certainly alive," said Aravia. "As a wizard, Abernathy chooses his words with care. He would have said 'body' instead of 'person' if they were dead. I noticed some other interesting tidbits among his speeches to us so far. For instance, recall that he said in regards to his monster, 'If he succeeds and comes to Spira.' From that I deduce that the monster's prison is extra-dimensional, not of this world. I could imagine that the interior of Abernathy's magical field is not part of the world either, and even that the person suspended in it is the monster itself."

Morningstar couldn't help but be impressed, even though she knew that was part of the point. "Aravia, how old are you?"

"Nineteen. I'll be twenty next month."

It was curious that Abernathy's spell had picked three teenagers and an old woman, given their enlistment was so important. But then she realized something that must be related. "None of you are married, are you?" she said, sounding it more like a statement than a question.

Dranko grinned. "Morningstar, that was the worst proposal I've ever heard."

Morningstar cringed.

"I'm married," said Mrs. Horn quietly.

"Yes, I'm sorry," said Morningstar. "Do you have any children, Mrs. Horn?"

"No, William and I never had any children."

"I meant no offense. We don't know why Abernathy picked us specifically, but I'd wager his magic worked to choose people not tied down to their old lives by family obligation."

"But it stole you away from your temple," said Ernie. "That's almost as bad, isn't it?"

"I don't know," Morningstar admitted. Though her mother was a priestess, Sisters of Ell swore to place all family ties beneath their devotion to the temple. Marriage was outside the realm of her everyday consideration.

Grey Wolf idly picked up a piece of bark and flicked it into the fire. "It makes sense. Some of us are a bit skeptical about this whole arrangement. Can you imagine how we'd feel if Abernathy was asking us to give up wives and husbands? Children?"

"I'm sure he'd have let them move into the Greenhouse with us," said Ernie.

"I'm not," said Grey Wolf. "Abernathy never even brought the subject up."

Morningstar sighed and unfurled her bedroll. "Strange as this is to say," she told the others, "good night. I'm going to sleep."

* * *

Morningstar is observing a turtle. She stands above it, watching it plod forward, step by unhurried step.

Someone has built a tiny model of a city, a model of astounding detail. Houses, inns, shops, streets…every feature has been lovingly crafted by some supernaturally talented artisan. But the model sits on the ground directly in the path of the turtle. It is inevitable that its stumpy soft-clawed feet will smash the model unless something is done.

Eddings appears, also watching the turtle, and his eyes shine as though a lantern has been lit inside his skull.

"Are you going to watch?" he asks.

Morningstar cannot answer. As far as she knows, it is impossible for her to speak inside a Seer-dream. It is odd, though, that Eddings is talking to her.

"Maybe you should stop it," says Eddings. "And maybe you shouldn't. There are reasons, either way. But here is my opinion."

The butler produces a letter opener, and with shocking violence jams it straight into the left nostril of the turtle, nearly to its entire length. The turtle stops, twitches, and falls dead upon its underbelly, its corpse smashing the city before erupting into flames.

CHAPTER SIX

Ysabel Horn looked back at Kibi. The bearded gentleman was the slowest walker of the group, and so tended to wind up by himself, quietly trudging along the road with his eyes downcast. In four days, Ysabel didn't think he'd had a single walking companion. Maybe it was time to draw him out.

She slowed to let him catch up, and squinted up through the canopy at some cotton-ball clouds. "Nice day for a stroll."

"Can't disagree," said Kibi.

"William and I always enjoyed walks around the farm on days like this. Though he used to joke that there was something wrong with me, that I preferred the smell of manure to the tang of salt."

Kibi gave a slight smile but said nothing in reply. And his reluctance to engage in conversation, while stronger than everyone else's, was not entirely atypical of the group. If their little band wasn't willing to talk to one another, they'd have a tough time working together for Abernathy. Maybe Kibi would be willing to chat about something more substantial.

"How are you feeling about all of this? About all of this wizard nonsense, I mean."

"Ain't nonsense, don't think," said Kibi. "Abernathy needs some folk, and we're it."

Ysabel could have believed he was talking about how much he liked Ernie's porridge at breakfast, he was that matter-of-fact.

"But we're kind of the oddballs of the group, don't you think? Tor was right.

Neither of us is a warrior or wizard or an agent of the divine."

"Can't disagree with that, neither," said Kibi with a shrug.

"But Abernathy convinced you to go along. Would I be prying too much to ask what he said to you?"

Kibi didn't answer right away, and when he did the words came slowly.

"The old wizard told me...told me..." He scratched his beard. "Listen, this ain't gonna sound sensible, but he told me that the earth said I oughta help."

On the surface of it, yes, that sounded like nonsense, but over her long life Ysabel had learned that few things made sense right on their surface. She studied Kibi's face. His lips twitched and he licked his lips, as though he wanted to say more but didn't know how to continue. She gave him an encouraging smile. "And you believed him?"

Kibi looked at her and smiled back. "Yeah," he said eventually. "I guess I did."

Sometimes getting someone to come out of their shell was like pulling up stubborn weeds from the field, but they had to come up in the end. "And that was enough to convince you?"

"Yup."

"Do you believe the earth can speak?"

Kibi answered with silence, but again the movements of his face betrayed something like reluctant anticipation.

"Does it speak to you?"

Kibi stopped walking and let out a breath. His smile vanished. Had she pushed too hard? "Ysabel, you're a good-hearted person, anyone can see, and I know you mean well. But I ain't quite ready to talk about everythin' just yet. This whole arrangement is confusin', and we ain't known each other for a week."

"That's all right," she told him. "But if you ever think it would ease your heart to talk things out, I'm always here to listen. Truth is, I'm not sure what *else* there is for me to do. I'm twice the age of the rest of you, except Grey Wolf, and even he's twenty years my junior. Someone needs to keep you youngsters on the straight path. I don't know why Abernathy put me in such an outlandish venture as this, and Pikon only knows what I'll do if things get dangerous, but that's as good a reason as I can think of."

"Guess that makes sense," said Kibi. "And I'll do my best to protect you."

"Thank you, Kibi."

* * *

Ysabel Horn's parents had both died when the blood cough found their farm, going on fifty years ago now. It was a quick and ruthless thing; her mother had lasted four days, her father six. Ysabel's parents had always given their prayers to Pikon, God of the Harvest, but at fourteen, bereft of her family, she had harsh words for her god. The Pikonish priest had visited her several times in the weeks after, but he never had a good answer as to why her parents had been taken from her so quickly.

"Was it one of the Travelers?" she had asked him. "Is one of them a god of disease?"

"No, child," the priest had said.

"Then it was Pikon," she had accused.

"The Gods need not explain themselves," the priest had said. "And all men and women die, at different times, for different reasons. Your parents, they were good people, but it was their time to go. Pikon gives us no guarantees in this life. He expects you to make the most of your years and give back to the earth, and not make war upon your neighbors. Beyond that, life is our own to live."

The priest had patted her on the shoulder. He was a good man with a goodly store of platitudes. "Be strong, Ysabel. Be strong."

And she had been. At fourteen she took over the family farm, first with the help of some folk from nearby farms, but soon enough on her own. Her family's acreage was nothing to boast about, but it had cows to milk and eggs to collect, two small fields to plant and harvest, and endless repairs to make on an ancient weather-beaten barn. By eighteen Ysabel Newfield was as tough and brown as an oak tree.

At twenty, she met William Horn. William was a fisherman's son who plied his trade off the gray coast of Minok, a young man of modest means and sunny disposition. He was returning from visiting some inland cousins when his horse pulled up lame, and her farmhouse was the first one he came to. He knocked on her door, seeking a place to spend the night.

He had stayed for a week and a day, returned four more times before the month was out, and they were soon after married. He moved into her farmhouse, but spent half his time away in Minok; the sea was in his blood, and he could no more give it up than Mrs. Horn would have abandoned her farm. But it worked. They were both independent souls, and their love was not lessened when a few miles of fields and ocean lay between them. Always he would come back, bringing her gifts from the city, helping the farmhands that his fishing income allowed them to hire, and warming her bed through every chilly night.

The only shadow over their marriage was the absence of children. They both wanted them, but it was not Pikon's will. She and William were into their forties before they became resigned to it, and after that things were better. The farmer and the fisherman, they knew how to survive life's rough weather.

That remained true until five years ago, when a storm surged up from the south and William didn't come home from a simple overnight excursion. She waited, patiently, knowing he had washed up somewhere along the coast and would soon make his way home. When a week had gone past, she knew he must be adrift, riding a piece of wayward flotsam, waiting for rescue. After a month, she realized he had fallen upon an unmarked and uninhabited island, unable to return to her. Yes, they had talked about the dangers of a fisherman's trade, but her heart wasn't ready to let go.

And so she waited, patiently, for five years. Though there was no logic in it, she still repeated her wish like a mantra. William was lost, but not gone, and one day he'd sail home to her.

Then Abernathy's letter had arrived. Ysabel didn't know anything about magic or wizards, but it reignited a spark of true hope in her. Abernathy could help her find William, or at least his magic could confirm her husband was truly dead. And when he had come to her room two nights before they departed, she had put it to him directly. He wanted her help with his monster? She wanted his with William.

The old wizard had smiled at her. "I don't have a great deal of spare time these days," he had told her. "But I will do what I can to help you and William reunite. Understand, though, that if I find him, and he is alive, I would still like you to stay a part of the group."

And that had been fine with Ysabel. Knowing, that was the thing.

* * *

The next morning she woke early to collect more buckthorn for Morningstar, the poor dear. The only other person up and about was Grey Wolf, prowling the forest beside the road.

He tilted his head. "'Morning, ma'am."

"You're old enough to call me Ysabel," she said. "Are you looking for something?"

"I'm looking for trouble," he said, and she knew that he hadn't meant it to come out like that. It made her grin. "I mean, I'm keeping an eye out for anything that might cause *us* trouble," he clarified.

She gestured to where the others slept. "It's good that they have you. They're so young, aren't they?"

"Yeah, and that worries me," said Grey Wolf. "Morningstar, Tor, and Ernie, they may have fought against sparring partners and hay bales, but that's no substitute for the real thing."

"Whereas you are well versed in 'the real thing.' So teach them. We're all here for a reason. Could that be yours?"

"Maybe."

"You didn't sound like someone keen on joining up when we were all in Abernathy's library," she said. "What did Abernathy say to you?"

"Not your business," he said gruffly. Then he looked down at the ground, sheepish at having been brusque. "It's personal, I mean."

"Is it the same personal not-my-business that makes you call yourself Grey Wolf instead of Ivellios? I quite like the name Ivellios."

"Yes," said Grey Wolf. "Abernathy told me that in the course of running his errands, I stand a decent chance of learning something related to…to my personal business."

"I see. So that's what's important to you. To learn something."

"Yes."

"And you don't think sharing with our young friends, who mostly look up to you, could have an effect on that? Ernie alone would bend himself backward to help you out, and he hardly knows you yet."

Grey Wolf smiled at her. "Are you certain you're not a priest? You talk like one."

"Heavens, no," she said. "I'm just a farmer, whisked away by a mighty wizard like the rest of you."

Grey Wolf peered westward down the Greatwood Road. "Ysabel, I'll think about what you've said. I promise. I don't trust people as a rule, but I'll think about it."

That was the best she was going to get, so she returned to the buckthorn.

CHAPTER SEVEN

E rnie peered over the sidewall of the wide stone bridge. The rapids churned up the ruddy soil, giving the water a reddish cast.

"That river is called the Redwater," said Aravia. "It parallels the Greatwood Road all the way from Tal Killip to Minok on the western coast, probably two hundred miles."

Ernie stared at her. Over her shoulder he saw the little village of Walnord, nestled where the sparse track they had been following met up with the broader and better-maintained Greatwood Road. "You really have memorized the entire map of the kingdom?"

Aravia smirked. "I have. One of the most important faculties a wizard must develop is her memory, and I've worked very hard on my recall. I can remember the details of most things I've looked at."

Ernie smiled back, but she reminded him, more than any of his companions, of how absurdly unworthy he was. She was unfathomably smart, just as Tor and Grey Wolf were (he was certain) such natural warriors. And Dranko had his healing (or so he claimed), and Morningstar her dreams, and Mrs. Horn was so wise and insightful, while Kibi...well, Ernie wasn't sure, but probably something impressive.

And what did he himself have?

He could cook.

He shook his head and kept to himself as his companions debated whether they should stop in Walnord for the day or get another four hours of travel under their boots and camp on the road. Grey Wolf pointed out that Walnord had a clean-looking inn, and they would all benefit from a night's sleep in real beds. Morningstar felt the same, but Aravia had reminded them of Abernathy's need for haste, and Tor had immediately agreed with her. Dranko added that lodging for eight would eat into their remaining funds. In the end they stopped only long enough to purchase more food, before putting Walnord at their backs and continuing westward until nightfall.

As they made camp that night in a grassy clearing, Tor let out a long sigh. "I was hoping for more adventure," he complained. "This is just…walking and camping."

"Just be happy we haven't been beset by bandits or bears," said Grey Wolf. "I think because there are eight of us, we're unlikely to be troubled."

Ernie hoped it would stay that way. Abernathy hadn't needed to sell him on the idea of helping protect the kingdom from danger, but Ernie was terrified when he thought about the particulars. The evening in Abernathy's tower had been blurred in his memory by confusion and excitement, but he remembered clearly what the wizard had said to Tor: "…afforded opportunities for adventure and glory that few in a generation are given." Adventure and glory sounded great in the abstract, but his knees knocked when he thought about facing down monsters or highwaymen or mountain lions or whatever else they might encounter. He never admitted his cowardice to Old Bowlegs—he couldn't stand the thought of letting his old master down—but a coward he was, and the whole "Golden Boy of White Ferry" thing was a sham, a bubble he hadn't the heart to burst.

Well, he could stand in the back with Mrs. Horn, behind Tor and Grey Wolf. They were skilled and brave, you could just tell.

* * *

Two days later, as the shadows of trees lengthened in the woods around them, the group shuffled into the tiny village of Verdshane, six days after setting out from Tal Hae.

Calling it a village was generous; it made White Ferry look like a thriving metropolis. All of five buildings clustered in a scared-looking huddle around the road, with another half-dozen set back among the trees. There were no people in sight.

"Is that an inn?" Tor pointed to the largest of the buildings, the only one with a second story. A battered signboard named it the Shadow Chaser.

"Only one way to find out," said Dranko.

Ernie followed Dranko across the road. A strange and unpleasant odor grew stronger as they neared the building.

"Something in there smells pretty rank," said Dranko. He opened the door, and a dreadful stink rolled out of it. Ernie grabbed the front of his shirt and lifted it over his mouth and nose, even as he looked in. At first glance the inside of the Shadow Chaser reminded him of the Rusty Mug back in White Ferry. There were tables set with mugs and plates, plenty of chairs, and a long bar at the back.

Except its half-dozen patrons were as dead as stones. All but one were sprawled on the floor; the remaining body was draped stomach-down over a table. Flies busied themselves about the corpses. Many of the chairs were overturned. Plates and silverware, some whole and some shattered, were strewn about the wood-plank floor.

Dranko murmured under his breath, "May Delioch have mercy on their souls."

Ernie's blood ran cold. It hadn't occurred to him that adventure and glory would include dead people! Around him the others were crowding to look in. Aravia gasped; Kibi coughed. The smell was indescribably foul.

Ernie felt bile rise in his throat. "What…what happened?"

"Looks like the stew didn't agree with them," said Dranko.

Tor pushed his way to the front, shouldering past Ernie and taking two steps into the commons. "There could still be someone alive in there!"

"Kid," said Grey Wolf, "That's not a great idea."

Tor stopped and looked around, then drew his sword.

"Do you see something?" asked Ernie.

"No," said Tor. "But I thought I heard a—"

Something buzzed toward them from the back of the commons, like a hard-thrown rock. Tor slashed at it with his sword but was much too slow, and the thing bounced hard off his shoulder. But instead of falling to the ground, it rebounded back and hovered in the air. It was a muffin-sized oval of fur-covered muscle, with one enormous eye, a pair of insect wings sprouting from its middle, six tiny insect-legs, and an open mouth full of sharp little teeth.

"Pikon's pancakes!" Ernie exclaimed. He tried to fight down a wave of fear as he fumbled for Pyknite and stepped into the building. A huge smile spread over Tor's face, and the hulking boy took another slash at the strange creature. It dipped and dodged like a hummingbird, then dove toward Tor's neck, latching on with its teeth. Tor shouted in pain, dropped his weapon, and grabbed the thing with both hands, sinking his fingers into its fleshy fist-sized body. Blood stained the boy's face, but was it from Tor or the creature he was squeezing? Ernie felt faint. Oh Gods, what if he *did* faint?

By the time the others had dashed inside to see what the commotion was about, Tor had dislodged the strange one-eyed monster and pinned it on the ground beneath his boot. His face and neck were smeared with blood.

Kibi stepped up and drew the mining pick from his belt. The little monster squirmed beneath Tor's foot, but before it could wriggle free Kibi slowly pushed the sharp end of the pick into the thing's body. It stopped squirming.

"That...that didn't seem so dangerous," Ernie stammered. Brave face! "I wonder how it managed to kill all these people."

Like a pod of little furry meteors, another half-dozen of the things burst from an open door behind the bar and streaked toward him, filling the air with the drone of their wings. Ernie shrieked and chopped the air wildly with Pyknite, but the things were too quick; one thumped into Dranko's chest, and a second landed on Grey Wolf's head. Morningstar was the only one to land a hit on one of the monsters; she swung her mace and a furry ball wound up impaled on its spikes. Mrs. Horn gave a little shriek and dropped to a crouch behind a chair.

It was all of his nightmares come to life. He wanted to run out the door, away from the corpses and monsters, but the thought of abandoning his friends was as unthinkable as discovering his courage. While he was frozen with indecision, a flying abomination landed on his sword arm and bit right through his shirt. Ernie yelped in pain, staggered to the nearest table as the thing chewed on him, and flailed his arm down as hard as he could. Plates fountained upward, but the tenacious little biter was still attached. Twice more he thumped the monster onto the table, harder each time as panic gripped him, until it finally let go, buzzing drunkenly back into the air. Ernie held out his sword in front of him, his body shaking with terror and adrenaline. The furry thing bobbed up and down, its buzzing erratic now, probably because Ernie had damaged its wings. Ernie set himself to take a swing, took a deep breath...and Tor's sword came down from the side and split the monster in half.

"Take that!" Tor cried. He winked at Ernie, but Ernie was far too flustered by the blood and chaos to acknowledge the gesture. Behind Tor, Mrs. Horn was still hiding, hunkered behind a chair—and one of the monsters was climbing up her shoulder toward her neck. As Ernie opened his mouth to shout a warning, another flying monster slammed into the side of his head with enough force to spin him around. He turned, dazed from the impact, and while the creature had caromed away, it was already returning. He chopped frantically with Pyknite, forgetting every lesson Old Bowlegs had ever taught him, and to his great surprise he cut right through an edge of the creature's body, severing one wing in the process. It dropped and scooted in pathetic little circles on the ground, trailing blood.

When Ernie looked up from the mortally wounded thing, he found that yet another was flying straight at his face. There was no time to duck or bring his sword to bear. His mind wasted his final thought wondering if it would eat his nose.

Mom always told me I had the cutest nose.

He was spared having to find out. Aravia shouted something he couldn't quite make out, and the monster changed course in midair as if it had been knocked sideways by an invisible frying pan. It tumbled head over wings and splatted against the wall, bursting into a cloud of blood and brown fur.

Slowly Ernie's muscles unfroze, terror reluctantly releasing its grip. He turned to see how the others were faring, and at first things seemed good. All of the monsters had been killed, or at least none were still flying about and posing a threat. There were now two stuck on the spikes of Morningstar's weapon, and the remaining critters had been chopped, crushed, or impaled.

But Grey Wolf was kneeling down beside Mrs. Horn, and his hands were on the old woman's throat. Grey Wolf had gone mad and was throttling her! But no—blood was fountaining out between Grey Wolf's fingers. Mrs. Horn's face was almost as pale as Morningstar's.

"She's bleeding to death!" shouted Grey Wolf. "Damn thing bit right through a vein in her neck."

"How did we miss it?" asked Morningstar, just as loudly.

But he hadn't! He had seen it, but that one banged into his head, and in the rush of panic and excitement…oh Gods…

Dranko hurried forward, pushed Grey Wolf aside, and put both hands on Mrs. Horn's neck, heedless of the blood gushing forth. "Lord Delioch, I pray for healing, that this woman be made sound and whole."

Nothing happened. Bright blood continued to jet from Mrs. Horn's neck in sickening spurts, and the woman's eyes were wide and confused.

"Gods damn it, Dranko!" shouted Grey Wolf. "Are you a channeler or aren't you? What are you waiting for?"

"I can do this," Dranko growled. "Shut up and let me concentrate!"

Dranko had medical supplies in his pack. Shouldn't he be using those instead? Ernie thought about speaking up but feared distracting Dranko from his prayer. Grey Wolf loomed over Dranko and Mrs. Horn, angry, muttering, which couldn't be helping Dranko's focus. But Dranko ignored him and continued to pray, whispering entreaties to Delioch, his hands now as red as if he'd dipped them in paint. Ernie held his breath. The blood coming from Mrs. Horn's wound was slowing down, but he didn't know if that was a bad sign or good. Mrs. Horn closed her eyes, her face the color of birch bark.

"Dranko!" Grey Wolf shouted again. "She's going to die!"

"Delioch, please!" Dranko whispered. His face was nearly as pale as Mrs. Horn's. "I pray for…" His face contorted and he slumped to the side, shaking hands falling away from Mrs. Horn's neck. Blood continued to pump out, more and more slowly.

Ernie knew he should do something but seeing Mrs. Horn bleeding on the floor left him stunned. His head swam. This was all wrong.

"Worthless," snarled Grey Wolf, as he rolled Dranko onto his stomach. He tore open Dranko's pack and pulled out bandages.

"Morningstar, hold these against Ysabel's neck. We can't let her lose any more blood."

Morningstar did as she was told, taking the cloths and pressing them to the poor woman's throat. Grey Wolf tossed items from Dranko's pack until he came up with a handful of small pots.

"Dranko, I don't know which of these to use!" he barked. "Does one of them stop bleeding?"

But Dranko was barely conscious. His mouth moved slowly, and nothing intelligible came out.

"Dranko!" Grey Wolf was frantic, shouting directly into Dranko's ear. "She's dying! Do something, you miserable bastard! It's the only reason you're here!"

Ernie knelt and took Mrs. Horn's hand; it was cold and brittle. Her eyes fluttered open.

"Ernest," she whispered.

"I'm here, Mrs. Horn. I'm sorry I didn't warn you in time." His tongue felt as thick as a rope.

She smiled, and her face filled with laugh lines, but her eyes were unfocused, staring at something far away. "Abernathy kept his promise."

"What promise?"

"Ernest," she whispered. "Stay positive."

And then she was gone.

CHAPTER EIGHT

T he world contracted.

Dranko's mind was a distant thing, seeing his surroundings from far off. His chest was cold, as though his heart in one frantic surge had pumped out all of his blood and left him hollow. He had wanted so badly to channel, so Gods-damned badly. (Did he, though? Now that he knew the cost?) It didn't matter. Just the attempt had left him dulled, enervated. It had all been for nothing. Mrs. Horn was dead.

Above him Grey Wolf was in a rage. "What in all the Hells is wrong with you? You were lying this whole time about being a channeler, weren't you? Are you even a healer? She needed you! Ysabel needed you, and..."

There was more, but Dranko hardly heard it. The sound of Grey Wolf's anger came to him distantly, as though he sat at the bottom of a cold dark well hearing noises from the surface. He closed his eyes and wished he would pass out, but that relief was denied him. Now Kibi was speaking.

"I promised I'd protect her." His voice caught in his throat. "Just a few days ago. But when them things started flyin' around, I lost my head. I didn't..."

"It's not your fault, Kibi." That was Morningstar. "We all should have been watching out for her."

Dranko opened his eyes again. He was lying on his side, looking into the pallid face of Mrs. Horn, his hair matted to the floor with her drying blood. Ernie was sitting beside her, massaging her hand as though he could knead life back into her if only he tried hard enough. His chest heaved with sobs while tears streamed down his cheeks, mixing with snot and blood from the battle.

"It's my fault." Tor sounded so young. Dranko flicked his eyes upward to look at him. The boy had a vacant stare. "I shouldn't have rushed in like that. I'm sorry. I'm sorry…"

"No." Grey Wolf's voice was a blade of anger cutting through the shock and sadness. "If it's anyone's fault, it's *his*." He pointed down at Dranko. "Have you ever actually channeled? Have you?"

Dranko tried to answer; his mouth opened and his lips moved, but nothing came out, not even a breath. *Yes*, he mouthed. Then there was a sharp pain in his ribs; Grey Wolf had kicked him in the side. The pain jolted him back into focus.

"You are *useless!*" Grey Wolf shouted. "Worse than useless. Ysabel was worth a hundred of you!"

He made to kick Dranko again, but Kibi grabbed him around the torso and pulled him back a step. "Grey Wolf, you ain't makin' anything better right now."

"Yes," Dranko croaked. Everyone around him became quiet. His words came slowly, but they came. "The…day before Abernathy summoned us, I…healed an injured beggar in the street. Delioch's power shot through me, and I healed his…broken leg. I thought I could just…do it again. But it was hard…hard…"

A surge of fury welled up inside him, coursing through the hollow spaces in his body. Was he angry at himself? At his god? It hardly mattered; both of them were failures. He had called upon Delioch at the moment of his most desperate need, and the God of Healing had abandoned him. Even if Dranko was an unfit vessel, was it fair for a god to punish Mrs. Horn for His son's inadequacy? It was a doubled cruelty—first to deny Mrs. Horn her life, and then to place the responsibility on his mortal shoulders, leaving him to the unavoidable judgment of his companions.

"You failed," said Grey Wolf flatly. "Ysabel needed you, and you failed."

Dranko stared into Mrs. Horn's glassy eyes. Grey Wolf was right. Sadness and anger and resentment warred in him. He pushed himself to a sitting position.

"It was because you were yelling!" he shouted hoarsely. "I couldn't concentrate! With the beggar I could focus, but with you swearing in my ear, I—"

"Don't you blame this on me!" snapped Grey Wolf. "If you thought there was a chance you couldn't channel, you shouldn't have wasted time with it. You've told us you're a healer. You had a bag full of remedies. You should have practiced your Gods-damned medicine. You should have—"

"Stop it! *Stop it! Stop it stop it stop it!*" Ernie was shrieking and shaking. "Why are you fighting? Who cares whose fault it is? She's dead. Mrs. Horn is dead. She was so nice, and now she…she…" He burst into fresh tears.

Dranko's eyes fell to the pool of blood beneath Mrs. Horn. "It wouldn't have worked. That thing's teeth cut her jugular. As a *healer,* I can tell you that's a death sentence without divine intervention."

And where was divine intervention? Delioch, this is your fault. Your fault!

Thinking blasphemous thoughts was nothing new to Dranko. How many times had he cursed his god beneath his breath while Mokad applied the scarring blade to his skin? When he had channeled for the beggar, he had felt—no, hoped, rather—that he and his god had reached an accord, that his roguish soul had been absolved. But no, it was all just more punishment. Delioch had given him a taste of what rewards might accrue to the devout, only to yank them away when it truly mattered.

"We need to stay focused," said Aravia. There was no emotion in her voice. Gods, how could she be so calm?

"Focused on what?" snapped Grey Wolf. Was his anger more about Ysabel's death, or Dranko's failure? "The job? Screw the job! As far as I'm concerned, Abernathy just murdered Ysabel. He can take his magic portal and shove it up his arse."

"That's not an option," said Aravia. "We promised we'd perform this task, and Abernathy didn't want us to waste any time. I'm sorry about Mrs. Horn, but we can't bring her back."

"How can you be so cold?" said Ernie, probably more loudly than he'd intended. "Mrs. Horn just…We can't keep going like nothing happened. What are we going to do? Shouldn't we bury her? And head straight back to Abernathy to tell him that…that…"

"No," said Aravia. "We should investigate the ruins and learn what we were sent to learn and *then* go back. Morningstar? Kibi? Don't you agree? Tor?"

Morningstar was staring at Mrs. Horn's corpse, and her voice was distant. "Yes," she said with obvious reluctance. "I suppose so. We need to mourn her, but…in the meantime, it will help to have something immediate to do."

Kibi didn't answer at all. He had released Grey Wolf but not said another word. Tor nodded, dumbly.

"That's right," said Aravia. "She's not going to become more dead if we get back to work."

"Gods, Aravia," said Grey Wolf. "That's heartless."

Coming from the guy who had just kicked him in the ribs. You're all heart, Grey Wolf.

"Maybe," said Aravia. "But it's true nonetheless."

Dranko stayed quiet; his instinct to make pithy comments had fled. He thought he had pegged the reason for Mrs. Horn's inclusion in the group: she'd be the old, wise head to keep the youngsters in line. She'd be their source of compassion, their voice of reason. But not anymore. Now she was just a body, her soul doubtlessly ascending to the heavens. Why had she been included if this was to be her fate? Was she just an object lesson? A warning? Was the idea that they'd all be more careful now, take this monster-prison business more seriously? For Abernathy or Delioch or anyone else to sacrifice her on an altar of expediency was beyond the pale.

"Grey Wolf's right," he said quietly. "I suppose I'm a failure. We're *all* failures. I think we're done. I say we head right back to Tal Hae and tell Abernathy he can find a new band of flunkies. He promised Mrs. Horn that if she came with us, he'd help her find her husband. How'd that work out for her? Why should we think his promises to the rest of us will turn out any differently?"

"We should vote," said Aravia. "It's the—"

"Vote?" Grey Wolf snarled. "When did this become a Gods-damned guild council? No vote. I'm leaving. This was an idiotic idea from the start. A bunch of random nobodies from nowhere picked by a senile wizard to help him save the kingdom? Dranko, you may be a fraud, but you're right about this."

"No, you ain't neither of you right," said Kibi. "We oughta stick it out."

When did Kibi start having opinions? Not that Dranko wasn't grateful he had stopped Grey Wolf from delivering more angry kicks.

"And why is that?" snapped Grey Wolf. "I thought you didn't believe in fate. If there's no destiny for us to be Abernathy's saviors, then what's keeping us here?"

"Our promises," said Kibi. "Not to mention it's the right thing to do unless you think Abernathy was lyin' about all the trouble his monster's gonna cause. I don't think he was lyin'."

Ernie had stopped rubbing Mrs. Horn's dead hand but hadn't let go. "Kibi's right," he said through his sniffles. "Mrs. Horn wouldn't have wanted us to give up. And the last thing she said to me was 'stay positive.' For her sake we ought to see this through. At least, we should find Abernathy's magic doorway and carry out our mission. And we need you, Grey Wolf. And you, Dranko. Without

Mrs. Horn, we'll all need each other even more."

Grey Wolf threw up his hands. "Oh, for Pikon's sake."

You don't need me. Dranko didn't see a single damn positive thing. Delioch had turned out to be a sadist. Maybe the scarbearers were right after all, that Delioch was all about punishment and healing in equal measures. Only for him, it was all punishment. The healing had been a mirage.

"I know you're all angry," said Aravia, as if she could read his mind. "Anger is a natural reaction to shock and grief. It's normal for…for us to feel this way. But Ernie and Kibi are correct. Mrs. Horn would be appalled if we abandoned our quest the first time something went wrong."

"Something didn't 'go wrong,'" said Dranko. "Mrs. Horn got *killed,* by *monsters.*"

"Ain't nothing more wrong than that," said Kibi.

Grey Wolf let out a long, frustrated sigh, and the edge of anger in his voice was replaced by something like resignation. "Fine. But now I'm doing it for Ysabel, and not for Abernathy. You understand that? Kibi, when we get back, you may need to restrain me again if our boss comes to check on us." He rubbed his chin. "Ysabel told me on the road that I ought to be teaching you kids how to fight. We fought these, these gopher-bugs, like a bunch of idiot amateurs, which is what most of you are. Even you, Tor. From now on, every night between dinner and bed, I'll give you some lessons on fighting as a group."

"So what do we do now?" asked Tor. The boy couldn't tear his eyes away from Mrs. Horn.

Dranko gestured to the other bodies still sprawled about the commons. "We need to bury her. We need to bury *all* these people."

"And we need to search the rest of the inn," said Grey Wolf. "Come on, let's get moving."

CHAPTER NINE

Truth be told, Aravia didn't know *what* to feel.

Mrs. Horn was dead. For all the knowledge crammed into Aravia's head, she didn't know how she should react. She felt numb, but that couldn't be right. If anyone *was* to die, Mrs. Horn was the one they could best afford to lose, having no fighting prowess, no magical talent, only basic survival skills and some knowledge of herbs. In a way they had been lucky it hadn't been someone else, though Aravia knew not to speak those thoughts aloud.

Aravia had also known what buttons to push to get the others refocused on Abernathy's mission. Emotions were a thing she could puzzle out; she understood them just fine. She just didn't feel them much herself.

After a minute of reflection, and finally satisfied that things were back on track, Aravia sat at one of the tables and pulled out a book and quill from her pack. She began to scribble, her awareness of the others dimming as they moved about the Shadow Chaser calling to one another. During the altercation with the gopher-bugs, she had made an experimental tweak to *minor arcanokinesis* that had proved far more effective than she could have imagined, so she wanted to get all of her thoughts down on parchment while they were fresh in her mind. She had condensed her arc spell down to half a second—two syllables and a fixed digital glyph—which as far as she knew was unheard of...or at least unheard of by Master Serpicore.

Aim, calibration, transfer of momentum, all of those had been adequate, and the little monster had been dispatched, splattered against the wall like a ripe tomato. It was gratifying to see results outside of Serpicore's testing room. Her mentor had strongly discouraged her improvisation (and in fairness, she had caused no small measure of havoc and destruction in his home with her experiments), but this was exactly *why* she was endlessly tweaking the few spell formulae Serpicore allowed her. *Minor arcanokinesis* was a slow telekinetic, and had she stuck to the original, Ernie would have had his face chewed off, and there'd be two dead members of their group instead of one.

It was sad, truly, about Mrs. Horn. She ought to feel *more* sad, but what good would that accomplish? Master Serpicore had told her, often, that emotions were the enemy of arcanism. They spoiled concentration and prevented objective analysis. Serpicore had commented more than once that her outstanding abilities were largely attributable to her ironclad management of her feelings.

Her vision was blurry, and she was more drained than a typical arc should leave her, so there was that to work on. Accelerating the spell had sucked out more than its fair share of her arcane potential. But that could be mitigated, perhaps if she incorporated her left hand into the glyph or worked on the subtleties of inflection in the syllables. Even with such a compact variant, there was ample room for tinkering.

She scribbled for another ten minutes, until the mere effort of writing and thinking so hard nearly made her black out. On instinct she reached down to scratch behind the ears of her cat, Pewter, but of course her beloved feline wasn't there. Pewter had been left behind at Master Serpicore's house, and she missed him terribly, like a little piece of her soul was absent.

Was it odd that her feeling of missing Pewter was greater than her grief over Mrs. Horn?

She set down her pen and looked to see what the others were doing.

Ernie and Morningstar had searched the kitchen behind the bar. The little monsters had been helping themselves to the food stores, but all of them had flown out to attack when fresh humans had showed up. Kibi and Tor were just coming down from the second floor.

"Two more bodies up there," said Kibi morosely. "Both in the hallway, like they knew somethin' was up but couldn't escape in time. Also a dead flyin' thing they squashed before it got 'em. Oughta bury 'em all, I suppose, like Dranko said."

Aravia returned her notebook to her pack and wrinkled her nose. She felt badly for the dead patrons, she truly did, though like Mrs. Horn they immediately became objects of low priority once deceased.

"There could be more monsters," warned Grey Wolf. "In the other buildings or still flying around outside. Whatever we do, we should stick together."

At least Grey Wolf was still thinking straight. That was important. The boys would follow his lead, and things were still at a delicate balance after Mrs. Horn's death. She'd need to look out for ways to keep the mission from falling apart.

Dranko said some sort of rites over the bodies of the dead. Aravia had been curious about Dranko's channeling powers and was disappointed not to have witnessed them even aside from the tragic consequence of his failure. Divine magics were a different beast altogether from arcanism as the power came from Gods rather than the air. Today's events had not disabused her of the belief that arcane magic was obviously superior, not being beholden to the changeable whims of supernatural beings.

Tor picked up one of the little furry corpses. "We killed monsters!" Then he blushed, probably realizing he shouldn't be gloating at a time like this. "Little monsters, sure, but monsters," he said more somberly. "Abernathy was right."

Ernie approached her. His face was still a mess, dust and grime sticking to his tear-streaked cheeks. He tried to smile, but it didn't work out very well. "Aravia, you gave me something to be positive about. You saved my life. Your magic is amazing."

Yes, that was true. "That was *minor arcanokinesis*," she explained. "My own compacted variant. Only a theory until just now, but it's nice to see it verified. I think I can make it faster."

"Er, yes…" said Ernie. His expression showed mild interest with little comprehension. When Serpicore had sent her into town on errands, she had seen that look on the face of everyone she chatted with. Alas, as much as she detested Serpicore's inflexible teaching methods, he was the only person she had ever met who matched her scholarly acumen. (Except for Abernathy, presumably, but she wasn't expecting a sit-down chat with *him* any time soon.)

Tor walked up to her and held out the body of the whatever-it-was. For some inexplicable reason she found it a charming gesture. "Aravia, do you know what this is?"

She had studied many disciplines, but monster-lore was not one of them. "I have no idea. But you should be proud of how you helped dispatch them."

Tor's face lit up at the compliment. "I was talking with Mrs. Horn on the journey here, and she said I ought to come up with a name for us. In the old stories, famous bands of heroes always had names."

"Are we a famous band of heroes now?" asked Dranko bitterly. "Will they tell the saga of how we let an old woman get killed by a gopher-bug?"

Tor fell silent. He was a good person, brave and idealistic. Aravia wouldn't deny that he was physically attractive, too; such a pity he was so hopelessly simpleminded. Not that most people she had met were up to her intellectual standards, but Tor was more like a puppy in the body of a man. Oh well.

"Speaking of those creatures," she said, "I'm reasonably certain that flying carnivorous gopher-bugs are not indigenous to the Greatwood. Where did these things come from? Why did they attack Verdshane? It's a near-certainty their presence here is related to Abernathy's magical prison door."

"And were we the first people to show up since the attack?" asked Morningstar. She was picking bits of chestnut fur from the flanges of her weapon. She hadn't said much since Mrs. Horn's death, but her eyes were damp and her jaw trembled.

"We don't know how long ago it happened," said Grey Wolf, "but the bodies look fairly fresh to me. Couldn't have been more than a few days. But let's say someone showed up since then, what would they have done? Probably either run away, or stayed to fight and ended up dead. Hells, some of these poor sots might have come in just like we did and gotten chewed to death for their trouble."

"Abernathy's Company," said Tor.

The others looked confused, but Aravia knew right away what Tor was talking about. "What do you say?" continued Tor, looking around. "It was one of the last things Mrs. Horn and I talked about, and I really think we ought to have a name. Anyone have a better one?"

"Who cares?" said Dranko exasperatedly. "Sure, fine, if it makes you happy."

"I don't know," said Grey Wolf. "Abernathy's not my favorite person in the world right now."

"Then what about Horn's Company?" Tor suggested. "To honor her memory."

Aravia didn't care much one way or the other, but it would help the group move past their grief and get on with the mission if they felt like they still had some connection with the recently departed.

"I like it," she said. "Tor, that's a beautiful idea."

"Speaking of Abernathy," said Morningstar, "let's remember what Aravia said and not lose track of why we're here."

"Agreed," said Aravia. "But our destination isn't here, it's the ruins to the north, remember? It's already dark outside, but I can make us some magical lights."

She tried to sound confident as she spoke, but avoided making eye contact with anyone. She was loath to admit it, but after casting her enhanced *minor arcanokinesis* Aravia wasn't certain she could cast more spells today in a controlled fashion. Every spell took something out of a wizard, and only a full night's rest replenished one's energy reservoir. Though Tor immediately jumped to her side, raring to go, she was spared by Grey Wolf from having to test her readiness.

"We'll wait until tomorrow," he said flatly. "If there's something dangerous out there, I want to be able to see it clearly."

"I'm not going anywhere," said Dranko. "My channeling didn't work, but even the attempt took a lot out of me. I can barely stand up. Anyway, we can stay here tonight. It's an inn, isn't it? I'll bet there are real beds upstairs."

"True," said Kibi. "If you don't mind steppin' over the corpses in the hallway."

"We should move them outside then...shouldn't we?" asked Ernie.

Aravia shuddered at the thought but reluctantly agreed. "We should if we intend to sleep here," she said. "Corpses are vectors for disease, not to mention the stink."

Horn's Company spent the next half an hour hauling the eight bodies out to the woods behind the inn. It was a gruesome task despite the corpses being lightened by blood loss. All of them had suffered ugly, ragged bite wounds to the neck. Aravia and Dranko were spared the duty of lugging the cadavers; the others carried the dead, while the two of them kept a watch for gopher-bugs or anything else that might pose a threat. Once the bodies had been collected, they took turns with an old spade discovered behind the inn, digging shallow graves for the deceased.

"If some random traveler comes by right now," said Dranko, as Grey Wolf turned a shovelful of earth over one of the corpses, "we're going to have a hard time explaining this."

But no one came along, and as the moon rose above the forest the company finished its grisly business.

Dranko bowed his head as he stood over Ysabel Horn's grave.

"Delioch, I commend Mrs. Horn to the heavens," he said. "None of us knew her very well, but it was obvious she had a good soul and didn't deserve to die like this. And I'm sorry I wasn't a more worthy vessel for your divine inspiration.

Give her a place of honor in the afterlife; she deserves it."

* * *

Back at the Shadow Chaser, Aravia sat at one of the tables that wasn't close to a dried pool of blood. Dranko headed behind the bar. "Hey now," he said, seeing that she was watching him. "Since we cleared out their place of monsters, I'd say we deserve a drink on the house. And I'm *really* in the mood to get drunk."

No one else was paying Dranko any mind; the others were distracted by their own conversations, or had gone upstairs to inspect and air out the bedrooms. Dranko grabbed a bottle from a shelf behind him. He was unsteady on his feet, and alcohol seemed a poor choice for someone in his condition. Was the mechanism by which channeling attempts drained life force similar to the one she herself experienced when casting spells?

Even as she thought these things, Dranko stumbled and leaned heavily against the bar, dropping the bottle. It thudded to the floor, and Dranko leaned down out of sight to pick it up. Five seconds later he hadn't stood up again.

"Dranko?" When he didn't answer, she dashed to the bar, hoping that he had merely passed out and fearful that a heretofore undiscovered gopher-bug was chomping on his neck. But it was neither. Dranko was on his hands and knees, his head cocked, listening.

"The whiskey's draining into somewhere," he said. "You can hear it. And look." He pointed to where a pool of spilled alcohol was collecting in a narrow crack between two floorboards and draining out of sight. But more than that, the crack continued around to form a fat rectangle in the floor.

"It's a trap door," she said. "And that bit of rope there is the handle."

Dranko tugged on the loop of rope that stuck out from one floorboard, and the trapdoor came up about a quarter-inch, then stopped. "Locked."

"From below," added Aravia. "Which means someone is down there, right now."

Still lifting the trapdoor, Dranko leaned down and put his mouth to the gap. "Hello down there! Exterminators here! We dealt with your vermin problem, so that'll be ten talons fifty."

"What are you doing?" Aravia made herself sound shocked, but was privately encouraged that Dranko had recovered enough to crack wise.

"Isn't it obvious?" asked Dranko. "Whoever's down there is hiding from the gopher-bugs. I'm letting them know it's safe to come out now."

"I suppose that's likely. Let's at least get the others over here before I shatter the lock. Just in case."

She looked up to find the rest of the group drifting toward them anyway, no doubt curious as to what was going on behind the bar. Aravia cracked her knuckles and prepared to cast. "Dranko," she asked, "how sturdy a lock would you say that feels like?"

Dranko pulled on the rope handle one more time. "Pretty sturdy. Why?"

"Just wondering." Aravia had been itching to try her own improved variant of *minor lockbreaker*, a spell she had been calling *Aravia's lockbuster* in her head. She had nearly cast it in Abernathy's tower, and again to get into the Greenhouse, but both times she had been thwarted. Finally, here was a chance for a proper field test! Aravia twirled her fingers and uttered the words of *Aravia's lockbuster*. Alas that Master Serpicore was not there to see it; he had never let her try it in his own home.

The trapdoor burst its hinges in a violent explosion, sending up a shower of wooden shards. Dranko cursed and slapped his face as a splinter lodged in his cheek. From somewhere below came the sound of scattered metal pieces clanging on stone.

"Dammit, Aravia!" Dranko barked. "There's someone down there, remember? You could have just dropped a metal bar on their head. Let's not kill anyone else today, okay?"

She had held the long "a" syllables of the chant for a hair too long, which combined with the motion of her left ring finger to impart too much kinetic energy to the target. Probably a result of her fatigue. She would fix that next time. "Sorry."

Tor reached down for the rope handle. "I'll go first." He lifted the wooden hatch. Aravia looked around him and down into the darkness. Instinctively she cast *heatless light* on a mug, but this time exhaustion disturbed her execution too much, and the mug glowed brightly for only a second before collapsing into a heap of gray glass pebbles.

Maybe no more casting today.

Ernie brought over a lantern, which illuminated a steep stone staircase leading to a tiny storeroom. On the floor down below was the outline of a person, either asleep or dead. The foul smell of human waste drifted up.

"Careful!" said Ernie, as Tor descended. "There could be more gopher-bugs down there."

When Tor returned up the stairs, he had the body over his shoulder. He set her down on the bar, and Aravia saw he had rescued a middle-aged woman wearing a stained apron over homespun work clothes. She was barely breathing, and her features were gaunt, with sunken eyes and cracked, dry skin.

Dranko moved to examine her. "Dehydrated, I think. Probably barricaded herself down there when the monsters flew in and hasn't had anything to drink in days." Aravia grabbed a jug of water from a shelf behind the bar and handed it to Dranko, who in turn dribbled some drops into the woman's mouth. "When someone's incredibly thirsty, you don't just give them a huge glass of water. You have to let them sip just a little bit at a time."

The woman reflexively swallowed the proffered water but didn't regain consciousness.

"I'll stay up with our patient," said Dranko. "The rest of you get some sleep. Someone should be on watch all the time, though, so I'll wake one of you up in a few hours."

Aravia wandered upstairs with the others and picked out a room. It must have belonged to one of the victims because there was a duffel in the corner and the bed was unmade. She sat on the bed and reflexively patted it, expecting Pewter to jump up beside her, then sagged as she remembered her cat hadn't made the journey with her. Was Serpicore feeding him? Her old master had never liked Pewter, being so averse to the horrors of cat hair on his furniture that the gray feline had been confined to her own room at all times. When they returned to the Greenhouse, she'd have to press Abernathy harder about retrieving him.

The bed itself had a wool mattress, which was plenty good enough for Aravia given the rigors of the day, and though she thought she might stay up an extra hour taking additional notes on her spells, sleep swiftly claimed her.

* * *

The woman from the cellar was named Minya; she was the owner of the Shadow Chaser. Some color had returned to her face, but her eyes were still too deep in their sockets.

"What happened here?" Aravia asked her over breakfast. Ernie had made himself at home in the kitchen and had scrambled some eggs with onions and scallions from the root cellar.

Minya's voice was cracked and tired. She twined her fingers together as she spoke. "I wish I knew. Happened three, maybe four days ago. Lost track, hidin' out down there. Had a room full of customers, troupe of actors goin' from Minok to Tal Killip, couple a' carpenters from Tal Hae headin' the other way. Middle of a sunny day, heard the strangest noise, little bit like a thunderclap, but not exactly. Quicker, sharper noise than that. Not natural soundin'. Noise came from them creepy haunted ruins, and everyone got quiet for a minute, but that was it, and we just chalked it up to bein' thunder after all."

"The ruins are haunted?" asked Grey Wolf. "By what?"

"Hells if I know," said Minya. "I'm smart enough to stay away, and so's everyone else in these parts."

Dranko raised an eyebrow at that. "Then how do you *know* they're haunted?"

"Never mind," said Grey Wolf before Minya could answer. "What happened then?"

"Nothin'—for about half an hour," said Minya. "Then we heard a buzzin' like a swarm a' bees, and those eyeball critters came flyin' in through the windows and landin' on folks' heads and necks. Everyone was screamin' and runnin' around, but the little monsters just started chewin'…chewin' people's…"

She stopped her narrative, grabbed Dranko's mug, and took a deep drink before continuing. "I panicked, sorry to say it. Got myself right down in the cellar when I saw one o' them things flying at me, heard it thump a few times on the door. Heard the…the yellin' and runnin' around of folks dyin' and tryin' to fight back. When the noise died down, I tried peekin' out, but the air was full a' them buzzin' monsters, so I stayed put.

"Every few hours I'd take another look, but those things weren't leavin', and the noise of slidin' back the bar attracted 'em and brought 'em buzzin' right over, so I just settled down to wait. Should a' grabbed a water jug on the way down, I guess. And that's about it. Storeroom had some apples, but that was all the water I got."

"You need to rest and to keep drinking," said Dranko. He looked at his cup. "Water would be better, though."

"You folks can stay as long as you like. You saved my life, no mistake about it. Don't know how I'm going to repay that."

Aravia was impatient to get to the important part of this conversation. A thunderclap from the woods where Abernathy's monster-prison was located?

Followed by an attack of unnatural creatures? She had learned to be highly skeptical of coincidence. "We won't be staying long," she said. "Tell us more about the ruins."

"Oh. Well, I only been there once, when I was a girl. You go about a half mile north a' here, you'll start seein' 'em. Used to be some great city out there hundreds a' years ago, but not much is left now 'cept a bunch a' crumbly walls. Didn't stay long. The whole time I was explorin', I had a feelin' like I wasn't supposed to be there, that somethin' was watchin' over my shoulder. And there weren't much to see, so I only went the one time."

Aravia sighed. "Anyone else here in town know anything about them?"

"Doubt it," said Minya wearily. "Those ruins are bad news, and everyone knows it."

* * *

Maybe someone else in Verdshane would have had more to say about the ruined city to the north, but they soon discovered that gopher-bugs had ripped through the rest of the village like a plague of deadly locusts, leaving no survivors. In the woodshed of one of the homes set back from the road, the company found the bodies of a young couple along with three crushed gopher-bugs. A heavy blood-spattered spade lay on the ground beside them. A hurried tour of the remaining homes revealed similar gory scenes. If any had survived the monster attack, they were either still in hiding or had fled down the Greatwood Road.

The forest north of the village was thick and difficult. The elms, pines, and beeches grew close enough together that navigating their territory was like winding through a wooden-walled maze. There were no game trails, let alone man-made tracks, to make the journey easier, and the trunks were thick enough that even Tor and Grey Wolf couldn't hack a path through them with their swords. Aravia silently cursed Master Serpicore for so severely restricting her access to his spellbooks.

As if reading her mind, Tor turned to her as they bushwhacked. "Hey Aravia, do you know any spells that would make this easier?"

"I know *of* plenty," she answered. "There are teleporting spells like the one Abernathy used to bring us to his tower. There are spells that change your substance to vapors, so you could slip between the trees like mist. There are spells that let people fly, so we could go *over* the trees. But Serpicore never let me see the books for them. Someday I'll learn them all, but that doesn't help us right now."

"That's okay," said Tor. "The spells you know have been great so far."

Aravia blushed, just a little. Then she thought about Abernathy's library and the spellbooks he had promised her. What would be in them? What great heights of arcane learning would she achieve with the collected formulae of an archmage at her fingertips?

Distracted by these thoughts, she was surprised to find herself suddenly in among the ruins. The remains of a stone wall, twenty feet at its highest point, rose up among the towering pine boles. Chunks of rock were scattered around the wall's base, and vines curled up and across its weathered stones.

Aravia peered into the morning haze rising from a carpet of last autumn's leaves, and everywhere now among the trees were the husks of a long-dead city, the remnants of its walls and towers and roads resting in mossy silence beneath the forest that had conquered it. The Company crossed what was once a wide avenue, marked now only by a few brave paving stones reaching futilely out of the moldering underbrush. Then another enormous decaying wall loomed before them, the seams between its stones sprouting with moss and rough brown lichen. In the days when it was strong and whole, it would have blocked their path, but time and the woods had conspired to fill it with gaps.

"How long ago do you suppose people lived here?" asked Dranko. "Or more to the point, how long ago did they *stop* living here?"

"Hundreds a' years," said Kibi. The stonecutter had his fingertips on the stone and had the oddest expression on his face. "For hundreds a' years, these stones've lived in silence."

Grey Wolf snorted and gave a curt laugh. "They tell you that, did they?"

Kibi didn't answer.

"I couldn't care less how old these ruins are," Grey Wolf said to the others. "What did Abernathy say we were looking for again?"

"A building with no way in," said Aravia. "And a door with a bear's head."

"That don't make no sense," said Kibi. "If there's a door, ain't that a way in?"

"And *all* of these buildings have a way in," said Morningstar. "Inasmuch as one could call them buildings at all. They're just foundations."

Kibi still had his hand upon the crumbling wall. Was the bearded man doing magic? She remembered his exact words from their first night in the Greenhouse. "It don't feel like magic," he had said. "Just feels natural-like."

She moved closer to him. "Kibi, how do you know the wall is that old?"

Kibi turned red and looked at his boots. "Oh, jus'…jus' a feelin', is all."

"Is this what you were talking about?" she pressed. "You've learned some kind of rock magic?"

"No, no…" Kibi took his hand from the wall and fidgeted with his thumbs. "I ain't never learned no magic, I promise you. Rocks sometimes give me a sense of 'em, but I ain't no wizard like you are."

No, he wasn't. Kibi was a quiet, kindly man but obviously not a great thinker, and wizardry demanded formidable intelligence. Whatever he was talking about, real or imagined, it wasn't going to be relevant to her studies, career, or ability to perform her new duties.

Now that the ruins surrounded them, there was no need to push on in any particular direction. Spreading out would accelerate the search, but Grey Wolf was quick to point out that splitting up would invite disaster if there were any more gopher-bugs buzzing around. Not that there had been any sign of them, nor of any other animals for that matter. Aravia hadn't spent much of her life in the woods, but she had read about them. In her books, forests like these were teeming with life—birds, squirrels, chipmunks and the like. But there was none of that: no birdsong, no animal tracks, no rustling of rodents or telltale bear droppings, none of the signs Aravia expected to see.

The animals knew better. Like *they* should know better. An unsettling realization fell upon her, as though she had just recalled an important but forgotten errand. She fought down an urge to stop and turn around.

Ernie put a voice to Aravia's anxiety. "We don't belong here. I think we should go back."

"We can't go back now," said Tor, though his voice carried little of its usual exuberant conviction.

"Ernie may be right," said Dranko. "This place is making me tingly and not in the good way."

Grey Wolf stopped. They all stopped. Aravia wiped sweat from her brow. A feeling of something akin to dread was growing in her mind—nothing overwhelming or panic-inducing, but a persistent, niggling fear that they had strayed into a place not meant for them.

"Maybe Abernathy was wrong to send us here," Grey Wolf said slowly.

Kibi walked forward until he was up at the head of the group, next to Grey Wolf. "What're you all talkin' about? I don't feel nothin' tingly. We've come all this way. How are we even *thinkin'* 'bout stoppin' now? You want Mrs. Horn to have died for no good reason?"

Aravia fought against the worry. A part of her mind had retained its clarity and was swiftly forming a hypothesis. "It's an enchantment. At least, I think it is. But I take it as a sign we're getting close to our goal. Minya said the ruins were haunted and no one comes here. I don't think they're haunted at all. I believe a subtle magical suggestion drives people back. Abernathy probably put it there himself to keep people from blundering into his monster-prison, but in his haste neglected to tell us. We have to fight through it."

Grey Wolf grunted nervously. "Let's keep on, then. Abernathy said the building we're looking for is intact, right? Everything else has been just bits of buildings, so something with four unbroken walls and a roof shouldn't be too hard to find. We'll walk in a group, but everyone pick a different direction to focus on, and we'll see what we see."

Half an hour later it was Kibi who spotted it. Despite her knowledge that their unease was artificial, Aravia found it hard to concentrate, and she kept looking back toward Verdshane. She caught the others stealing sidelong glances southward, or looking worriedly at their feet when they should be alert for Abernathy's building. But Kibi showed no sign of concern, and it was he who shouted, "Hey, I bet that's it over there. Dang, but it's huge."

The building in question would have looked immense just by dint of being surrounded by smaller fragments of its fellows, but its apparent size was augmented by its placement in a wide clearing. Also, it really was huge, a great stone rectangle topped with an enormous dome, the apex of which must have been a hundred feet off the ground.

The two sides in view had many window-like depressions, but these were filled in solid with stone blocks. There were no doors, marked with bears or otherwise, so Grey Wolf led the company around clockwise. On the far side, in the center of the wall, they found what they sought: a small door carved with the face of a snarling bear. (Calling it a "door" was not quite accurate; it was a door-shaped indentation, but there was no handle, no hinges, no keyhole, and no crack to show how it might open.)

"Abernathy said to close our eyes and walk through it," said Aravia.

"That sounds easy," said Tor. The boy closed his eyes, covered them with one hand for good measure, and stepped into the wall of stone. He passed through the "door," melting into it before vanishing entirely. His voice came from the other side. "Come take a look at this! It's amazing!"

Aravia was not at all practiced in illusions, but she could recognize a well-formed magical effect when she saw one. Her heart raced. Maybe she could convince the others to give her time to study it, after they'd checked out Abernathy's body-in-the-field.

While she stood admiring the illusion, the others phased through it, their bodies swallowed up with nary a ripple in the fake stone. She hurried in after them, only remembering at the last moment to shut her eyes. (Though was that truly necessary? She'd read the theory, that with a strong enough surety of disbelief, one could pass through illusionary barriers while observing them. She'd have to try it on the way out.)

The interior of the building was one gigantic chamber, the flat sections of its ceiling supported by soaring squared columns, and every surface—the walls, floor, columns, even the interior of its central dome—was of uncracked white marble. That alone would have impressed her. But in the building's center, on the floor directly beneath the dome, was a fifty-foot high hemispherical cage made of a glinting silvery metal. Its curved bars were thin and widely spaced; it wasn't a cage that could contain anything smaller than a bear. She looked closer. There were additional hemispheres of decreasing size, nested one inside the other, and in the center of them all was a glowing blue light. More detail than that she couldn't make out from where she stood, other than a large bundle of rags on the floor, just outside the blue radiance.

A ringing hum came from the metal bars, like the noise from a tuning fork that hadn't quite stopped oscillating. Magic was emanating from them, a magic so thick and powerful it almost had taste and smell. Here was a place of immensely powerful enchantment, just as Abernathy had promised her at the Greenhouse. Yes, her primary motivation had been to get her hands on his magical library, but almost as compelling had been his assurance of the wonders she would witness in his service. "My dear girl," he had said. "Working for me, you will see practical magic, out in the world, of a type and magnitude you will not find in your old master's house. There are old magics in our kingdom that most people have never seen. But you will."

She was certainly seeing some now! She walked forward while the others stood and gaped. The white marble floor was drab and dusty closer to the "door," but the slabs beneath the metal hemispheres were pristine and polished.

She stopped twenty feet in, at the edge of the outermost cage. She didn't recognize the material. It was the wrong color for either silver or iron, its shiny gray surface gleaming with a bronze-ish cast. The metal ribs were round, about four-inches in diameter, and so far apart from one another that she wouldn't even have to duck to step inside the cage.

"Aravia," said Grey Wolf, "do you think it's safe to get closer?"

"I'm slightly out of my depth," she admitted. "But I doubt Abernathy would have told us to get close enough to measure something in the middle of all this, if it *weren't* safe."

"Really?" said Grey Wolf. "Because I don't doubt that for a minute. He didn't mention anything about these metal bars. He might not have even known they were here."

Tor answered the question by stepping past both of them, crossing the perimeter himself, and turning to look at her. "It's fine. Come on."

They passed through three more curved metal cage walls, progressively smaller, and by the last of these Aravia had to crouch down to get through the shrinking gaps between the bars.

That's where she stopped, with only the innermost cage before her, and stared, puzzled.

"Uh oh," said Dranko.

"Aravia," said Grey Wolf slowly. "Do I remember right, that there's supposed to be a person suspended in that blue light, and our job is to measure how far off the ground his foot is?"

"Yes," said Aravia. "That's what Abernathy asked us to do. But…"

The innermost hemisphere was indeed filled with a soft blue glow, a magical field just as Abernathy had said. The hum of the metal bars was louder here, and the field was charged with vibrating energy.

There was also a person, a man with ruddy skin and golden hair, wearing baggy brown clothes of an unfamiliar style. The problem was, the man wasn't in the blue light at all. He was what she had mistaken for a pile of rags, lying in a pool of blood that had dried black on the white marble tiles. His neck had been torn open.

Hovering in the volume of azure radiance were about a dozen gopher-bugs, their insect wings frozen in mid-flap. They looked like museum pieces, perfectly still, single eyes open. Saliva glistened in their mouths. The closest of the creatures was nearly at the outer edge of the blue field, while the others formed a loose cloud of furry vermin that extended back to the very center of the concentric metal hemispheres.

Dranko frowned at the body. "So, zero inches off the ground then. That will be easy to remember."

Aravia stepped forward until her nose was only inches from the edge of the blue radiance—an edge that was crisply defined, like the curve of a colored glass bowl. The nearest gopher-bug was at eye-height, barely a foot away, a specimen pinned to nothing. "It's a stasis field," she whispered. "Time isn't passing in there."

"Really?" said Tor. "What would happen if I put my hand inside it?"

"Don't!" she barked. "Abernathy said not to touch it. I haven't made a great study of stasis fields, but my guess is that any part of you that went inside it would be permanently stuck there. We'd have to cut your hand off."

Tor took a step back.

"But what *happened*?" asked Grey Wolf. "Why are there gopher-bugs in there?"

"Let me think."

Thinking, of course, was what Aravia did best. In less than a minute she had it figured out. "I have a theory. Two theories, actually." The others watched her expectantly.

"Theory number one: the stasis field is part of the lock on Abernathy's door." She pieced the last few puzzle pieces together in her mind as she spoke. "The door itself is probably in its center, a magical portal, invisible. If anything manages to get through, it gets stuck in the stasis, a bug trapped in amber.

"That man, he's been in there for a while. Abernathy expected him to still be suspended, but something happened, and time started up again just for a second or two, and he escaped. But the gopher-bugs were waiting for him, and killed him before he could get very far. Then the stasis reactivated while the gopher-bugs were still flying around, and these were caught in it. That means someone *knew* the stasis field was going to drop, and had sent those monsters to kill the man before he could escape. It was only incidental that some of them found Verdshane and went on a rampage afterward."

The others just stared at her. She'd explain all this to Abernathy later; he at least would understand it.

"That's the *less* likely theory," she went on. "Theory number two is similar, though. Maybe Abernathy's monster has figured out a way to turn off the stasis for a very short period *and* get through the actual door, but didn't want to try itself, in case it didn't work. So it sent the gopher-bugs as a test. Maybe the man was from a previous test, I don't know. But the stasis snapped back on before all the gopher-bugs could escape its area."

Kibi scratched his beard. "So his test worked, then. And if he knows it worked, I'm thinkin' next time he might decide to try it himself."

One thing was certain: they had to report to Abernathy without delay.

CHAPTER TEN

Tor sure was glad Aravia knew what all that stuff with the metal cages was. What would they do without her? It was like having a smaller, prettier version of Abernathy traveling with them, and would his hand really stick in that blue light? Couldn't he just pull it out again? Why was it blue?

The others were leaving the building, which wasn't good because he should be in front in case anything happened—that was his job, to be in front, to catch any approaching perils before they could menace his friends—so he dashed ahead and went through the not-really-there doorway right after Grey Wolf.

Good thing he did that, too, because when he emerged in the big clearing there was someone waiting, watching, a person maybe thirty feet off at the edge of the woods with blue paint all over his face and no hair. There was a long, awkward pause while he and the blue-faced stranger stared at each other, and just as Dranko said, "Who's that?" the mystery man turned and bolted into the woods.

So Tor did the logical thing and took off after him because Blue-face must be up to no good to have fled like that, and Abernathy would want to know what he was doing there, so of course Tor had to give chase, and if he caught up and there was a fight, well, he was a great swordsman, and better it be him in case the man was dangerous because one person in their group dying was enough. And the others would be close behind if he needed help. And what if he *wasn't* up to no good, and maybe Blue-face was just scared of them, scared of a bunch of armed folk popping out through a solid panel of stone like that? But in that case Tor still wanted to talk to him and let him know they were friendly, and maybe the stranger knew what was going on with the gopher-bugs. Or was it her? If it was a woman maybe he shouldn't fight her even if she were hostile because you didn't fight against women. That's what Master Elgus had taught him back at Castle Firemount, though his father had scoffed at that and said that if a woman ever came at him with a blade, just worry about the blade.

He was in the woods now, slaloming through the trees and ruined foundations and keeping his quarry in sight and hearing the shouts of his friends behind him. Had they not seen Blue-face? They must have. He thought he was gaining.

Tor burst through a net of thick branches and into a small clearing, and there was the strange blue-faced person, and it was definitely a man, and it wasn't paint, it was just the color of his skin, so maybe this was Abernathy's monster? Something that powerful wouldn't be running away, but maybe coming through the what-was-it-called time-stopping field had weakened him, and now was the perfect time to strike, maybe the only time!

He and Blue-face drew swords at the same time, and both from sheaths over their backs, which was pretty funny and so he smiled at the man even though it looked like they were about to do battle, but Blue-face didn't smile back.

"We don't have to fight," said Tor. "We're the good guys. I just want to know what—"

Blue-face rushed him, raising his elbow in a classic feint before swinging low to slash Tor's leg, but Master Elgus had taught him that one; he blocked it, side-stepped, and aimed for Blue-face's exposed wrist: numb the wrist, he drops the sword, fight over.

But Blue-face was too quick for that—Gods, but he was *very* quick, dancing out of the way and hopping back in a kind of tilted pirouette, landing in a perfectly balanced crouch. Tor wasn't going to win on agility alone, but fortunately he was taller and stronger than Blue-face, and hadn't Master Elgus always taught him, figure out your opponent's strength and don't let him play to it? He could turn this into a brawl with swords. He advanced. Who was this person? *What* was he? Not a human, exactly. Or maybe a human who had undergone some strange skin-dyeing ritual? Was it the dye that made him so quick? Could Abernathy or Aravia make them magic dyes so they'd be better in battle? Though if he had come through the blue field, maybe *that* accounted for his color.

"Why is your skin blue?" he asked, even as he took a ferocious overhand hack.

Blue-face didn't answer but slipped gracefully out from Tor's swing arc, spinning and springing up to his left. Tor jumped back to avoid a whip-quick slash at his midsection but wasn't quite fast enough; his enemy's blade sliced open the front of his shirt and drew a stinging red stripe across his abdomen.

"Hey!" shouted Tor. "I liked that shirt!"

It was possible that this person was a better fighter than he was, but Tor stayed confident. His failure in the Shadow Chaser was weighing on his mind, but that only meant that Blue-face here was the perfect opportunity for redemption, and during his sparring lessons at his father's castle Tor had only practiced against other people, or man-sized dummies, so his style of fighting wasn't well suited to swatting at one-eyed furry oranges that zipped about like dragonflies, but Blue-face was a foe he could figure out. And Tor always remembered what Master Elgus told him once as they toiled in the castle's sparring yard. "Darien, you have more natural ability with a blade than any man I've seen in thirty long years of teaching swordplay. Your destiny may lie on a different path, but the moment you sit the throne of Forquelle, it will be a tragic waste of material."

Waste of material. Of all the compliments Master Elgus had paid him during his childhood, that was the one he remembered most vividly, and from that day forward, every stultifying lecture from his tutor Master Cawvus about math, reading, heraldry and laws had withered his soul another fraction, every moment he sat listening to his tutor's mind-numbing drone was a waste of his fantastic potential.

But look at him now! Dancing in the woods with an obvious enemy of the kingdom, making a difference, achieving that potential, and now would be a good time to strike, so he launched a violent flurry of diagonal blows, most of which Blue-face dodged or parried, but one of which sliced his enemy's upper arm. Ha! Take that! Blue-face hissed and executed an amazing riposte maneuver, a kind of springing leap with a mid-air strike in there somewhere, and there was the painful heat of another cut, this one on his thigh, and deeper than the first one.

Could he be losing? Preposterous! Blue-face was panting a bit, which was good because Tor was in great physical condition and his enemy's combat style looked exhausting, which meant he just had to survive long enough for that to become the deciding factor, maybe go on the defensive a bit while the strange man wore himself out. He crouched low, holding his sword before him, as Blue-face paced and circled, looking for an opening.

Quick as anything, Blue-face leaned forward and aimed a swing at Tor's neck. Tor parried, counterattacked, missed as the man danced backward. His leg hurt.

"I see them, over there!"

It was Grey Wolf's voice and not far away. Blue-face looked over Tor's shoulder, finally smiled, and sprinted away into the woods. Tor instinctively gave chase but fell to one knee, the pain from his thigh bringing spots to his eyes. Maybe he should sit down. He already was sitting down. The woods down at ground level had a rich, leafy smell that he quite enjoyed. Too bad Blue-face got away. Next time he'd win.

Then his friends were standing over him. Ernie was wide-eyed with worry, and Grey Wolf berated him for running off like that on his own, while Dranko squatted next to him and examined his wounds.

"Good news, Tor." Dranko pulled out some bandages and ointments from his pack. "Superficial cuts are my specialty. Bad news is, this stuff is going to make you itch something awful. Beats infection, though. Oh, and we should wait until tomorrow before letting you spend a full day walking."

Tor sat quietly while Dranko cleaned his wounds, stitched them up, smeared on three different salves, and wrapped them up in cloths.

"Dammit, Tor," said Grey Wolf while Dranko did his work. "You couldn't have waited for the rest of us? We had the advantage of numbers, and you squandered it. After what happened to Ysabel, we need to *think*. We need to work as a *team*. Use your brain next time!"

Tor hung his head. Grey Wolf was right, as usual.

* * *

Horn's Company spent the remainder of the day in Verdshane, helping Minya bury the remaining dead and clean up the Shadow Chaser. Dranko insisted that Tor rest and recover, which meant Kibi and Grey Wolf did most of the heavy labor. Grey Wolf had something funny happen to his stomach again like when they were on the way here, and Ernie was sure it wasn't food poisoning, which made sense because none of the others were having any trouble. Grey Wolf described it a funny way, that it was like someone had tied a rope to his insides and was trying to lead him somewhere by it, but it was obviously uncomfortable, so Tor didn't laugh at the image. Grey Wolf even said he felt faint, like everything was growing bright and translucent at the same time, and Dranko said he was probably dehydrated, so Minya got him a cup of water.

Tor had been certain Minya wouldn't want to stay. Everyone else in the village had run away or been killed! Who would she talk to? Who would tend the local farms? But the innkeeper had insisted, telling them proudly how she had bought the Shadow Chaser almost twenty years ago and over time had transformed it from a dilapidated, filthy flophouse to a clean and thriving inn and restaurant, catering to just about every traveler traversing the Greatwood Road between Minok and Tal Killip. She wasn't about to abandon her home and business. She could resupply from Minok, she said, and there'd still be just as many folk on the road needing food and lodging. Also, judging from the number of bodies they found in town, almost half of Verdshane's population still was unaccounted for.

"If those that fled return, we'll get this place goin' again. And if you ever come back this way, food and beds'll be on me."

Morningstar had tried explaining what they had found in the ruins—that there were more gopher-bugs, and no guarantee they'd stay trapped in that magical light forever. But Minya had been adamant. "Tell you what," she had said. "When you get back to Tal Hae, you tell 'em what happened here. With luck the mayor'll send some soldiers to see what's what and protect us from them flyin' critters."

So they departed first thing the next morning, leaving Minya to fend for herself. Tor admired her bravery, and it was likely that things would turn out well for her. She was a survivor, and the world could always use more of those.

CHAPTER ELEVEN

Aravia enjoyed the quiet during the walk home; it was a somber journey, a funeral march, and so no one talked much. This gave her uninterrupted hours to ponder how one would set up a stasis field, and mentally compile a list of questions for Abernathy. From time to time she wondered when her own sadness would set in, but it never did.

Ernie went out of his way on several occasions to point out flowers or cloud formations Mrs. Horn would have liked, and cried himself to sleep more than once. Tor tried a couple of times to strike up actual conversations, but they faltered and went nowhere. Grey Wolf and Dranko stayed as far apart as possible. Still, Aravia was confident that the time on the road was blunting the sharp edge of the others' grief. She worried about what would happen when they next talked to Abernathy, but she was also eager to share her hypotheses with him about what had been going on in the ruins.

They returned to Tal Hae after a week of travel, just an hour before sunset. The temperature had been dropping throughout the day, and a nettling sleet was falling as they reached the Greenhouse front door. The others dropped their packs in the foyer, then either slumped into the living room and fell into the couches, or headed upstairs for baths. But not Aravia.

"I'll let Abernathy know we're back." She shed her damp boots and cloak, bounded up the stairs, and entered the room with the crystal ball. "I wish to speak with Abernathy."

The ball fogged, and the face of Mister Golem appeared.

"Greetings! Abernathy is indisposed at the moment, but I would be pleased to convey your message to him."

Drat. "Please tell Abernathy that we're back, and have important news from Verdshane concerning his prison door. I'm sure he'll want to talk with us right away."

"I will convey your message to Abernathy at his earliest convenience. Is there anything else with which I can assist?"

"Yes. Please remind him that he has promised me access to his spellbooks, and also that I'd like him to see about having my cat, Pewter, delivered from Master Serpicore's house."

"I will convey that message also. Is there anything else with which I can assist?"

"No, that is all."

She stared disconsolately at the empty crystal ball for a minute, then realized just how dead-weight weary she was. A bath in her magical hot water tub would do her good. She had herself a long soak and nearly fell asleep, but the smell of roasting meat roused her. She dressed and headed downstairs. Perhaps Abernathy was already there, ready to hear her report.

The others (without the archmage, alas) were all gathered by the fireplace; someone had dragged an extra sofa over so that everyone could bask in the fire's warmth. Before preparing their dinner, Eddings had stacked their boots at the edge of the hearth to dry and had hung up all of their wet cloaks. He brought Aravia a mug of hot cider before she could even sit down.

"Dinner will be ready in a few minutes, Mistress Aravia. I have used the Icebox for venison and cider, but am still preparing a vegetable soup upon the stove." The butler's voice was unusually somber and he looked crestfallen; it took Aravia a moment to figure out why. The others must have told him about Mrs. Horn while she was up having her bath. She gave him an encouraging smile, settled into a sofa, took a sip of cider, and wished Pewter were there to jump up on her lap.

Eddings turned to Dranko and removed an envelope from inside his jacket. "Master Blackhope, this arrived for you two days ago. My apologies for forgetting it until now."

Dranko took the letter. "Maybe it's a summons by another archmage. Gotta climb that ladder..." He tore the letter open and read, eyes scanning rapidly back and forth. It was a long letter, written across several small sheets of paper. His smile faded as he read, and by the time he finished, he was practically shaking.

"Son of a bitch!" he shouted.

"What happened?" Aravia asked.

"Did your church send you a bad letter, like Morningstar's?" asked Tor.

"No," said Dranko. "I mean, yes. Well, in a way. Dammit!"

They all waited for him to continue. Even when Dranko stormed out after his tiff with Morningstar, he hadn't been this upset.

"Back when I lived in the church, I had one measly friend. One! She was the only one who didn't treat me like...like a goblin, and now she's run away because she uncovered some corruption that Mokad was part of."

"Who's Mokad?" asked Aravia.

Dranko answered by pulling up his sleeves. "All these scars? On my arms, my face, my back, my legs, my..." He stopped and looked up at her. "And a few places I won't mention with ladies present? Mokad is the one who put them there. It's part of church discipline, and Mokad loves to dish it out."

"Where is your friend now?" asked Morningstar.

"She didn't want to say. She's afraid for her life."

"Can you read it out loud?" asked Tor. "Maybe there's something we can do to help."

Dranko stared at Tor for a second, but instead of delivering some unkind words about the suggestion, he hunched forward on the sofa, reshuffled the pages of the letter, and began:

Dear Dranko,

I've run away from the church. I think I didn't have any choice, and there's something really bad going on there. A couple months back Tomnic got sent off to Hae Charagan, and a bunch of others with him—you remember Wister and Palinaya, they never liked the scarbearers much. Mokad and his bunch have been having lots of secret meetings, so I snooped around Mokad's bedroom and got caught which earned me seven scars and a week in the closet.

When I got out things were worse. A couple other scarbearers I don't like got brought in from Minok and one day Sirus was gone, the nice old priest, and no one would say where he was. So this time I broke into Mokad's office, which wasn't easy because he always keeps it locked, but I still remember how you showed me to pick locks so I broke in while he was in morning prayers. Well, you know I was never as sneaky as you, and I got caught again, but I'm fast and slipped by and ran out of the church, and now I'm hiding and I can't go back.

I found a bunch of papers in Mokad's office and I was caught before I could read everything, but I still remember what was on some of them. It was weird. Some of it was gold crescent counts, and they were high, in the hundreds I think. There's some kind of expensive project going on in the desert near Sand's Edge that they think might go for weeks yet, but they're not sure. Dozens of people are working on it. I guess they're using church money for it, but then why are they making it all a secret and having sneaky meetings in Mokad's room? And the papers mention something about the "Black Circle" a couple of times, like it's something important, and there was a letter that was signed with a circle instead of a name. It's weird, and I don't know what it is.

I guess this means I might not ever be a full priestess, with me running away from the church before my elevation. You're probably the only one who really understands how much that hurts. But if I learned something from all the teachings and sermons, it's that Delioch will see me through as long as I'm doing the right thing, and I am.

You were always my best friend, Dranko, and I wish you'd have visited sometime. I don't want to say where I am yet since this letter might get stolen. I'll write again if I find out more, and maybe we can meet in person.

Your friend,

Praska Tellenhien

Aravia shook her head. "I'm sorry about your friend, but it's not germane to our current assignment, is it? And it's not terribly surprising. Master Serpicore always says that churches are rife with corruption, and questions why the Gods don't do something about it."

Ernie glared at her. "That's awful, Dranko!"

"If we had a way to get in touch with her, she could stay here with us," said Tor.

"She knows Dranko's here," said Aravia. "How else would she have known where to send her letter? Eddings, has Dranko's friend come calling while we were gone?"

"She has not," replied Eddings.

"The thing that gets me," Dranko said, "is that if I hadn't agreed to work for Abernathy, I could go try to find her, or go to Sand's Edge to discover what Mokad is up to. Not that I mind all of your sparkling company, but now that we've done our job for Abernathy, maybe he can spare me for a couple of weeks."

"That depends," said Abernathy. "What exactly are you talking about?"

Aravia leapt to her feet, and everyone whirled to look toward the foyer. Abernathy stood in the entryway to the living room, bedecked in his white robe and outlined in the same azure glow as when he had visited her room and promised her access to his library. A gold chain hung around his neck, from which dangled a bright red ruby in a silver hoop. The wizard looked even older than he had the first time they had met, his back more bent, his face more creased, and his voice was tired, spent.

Abernathy took short shuffling steps toward them and leaned on his staff like a crutch. "I thought I owed you a visit. I understand you have some news from Verdshane."

Eddings hurried forward and helped ease Abernathy into an armchair, then fetched him a mug of cider. The old wizard's magical projection into the Greenhouse was fascinating. Somehow he was physically both in his tower *and* in the Greenhouse at the same time.

"Mister Abernathy," said Ernie. "We have some awful, awful news. Mrs. Horn...she died. We were attacked by monsters, it was terrible..."

He described the events at the Shadow Chaser, his narrative punctuated with stammers and sniffles.

"Why did you summon her?" Grey Wolf demanded when Ernie was done with his tale. "If she was just going to die the first time we went anywhere? Why? Abernathy, I don't care much that you're a powerful wizard, and I don't care if you can turn me into ten different kinds of frogs. As far as I'm concerned, you're as responsible for Ysabel's death as if you'd planted a knife in her chest with your own hand."

That was the sort of confrontational outburst Aravia had been afraid of. She hoped Abernathy had a satisfactory explanation. Abernathy didn't react immediately; he stared into the fireplace.

"I'm sorry," the old wizard said eventually. "Grey Wolf, I summoned her for the same reason I did the rest of you. My spell *chose* you. I didn't know if..." He shook his head. "There was a reason, even if we can't know what it was."

"That's ridiculous," said Grey Wolf angrily. "There wasn't a reason. She died because you sent her to a dangerous place an old woman shouldn't have been allowed anywhere near!"

"And I accept that responsibility," said Abernathy, his volume rising. That was the first time he had sounded even slightly angry. "Let me shoulder the blame. But take away the lesson, also. There may be fate at work here, in some fashion, but it's not going to save any of your lives. The world is dangerous, and it's only going to become more so in the coming months and years."

"That's not good enough!" said Dranko. "There has to be something more to it than that. Mrs. Horn was not a lesson. She was a person. A damn fine person who had her doubts right from the start about why you had picked her for this job. And she was right. You shouldn't have picked her. For that matter, you shouldn't have picked *me!* My religion forbids me from striking with a weapon, but it turns out I can't channel, either. Is it too late for me to opt out of this group, so you can find a real channeler? And you say, 'My spell did it' like you didn't have a choice, but it was *your* spell. How can we trust anything you tell us? Which one of us is going to be next?"

Abernathy frowned, the firelight casting his eyes in the flickering shadows of his brows. He touched his steepled fingers to his lips. Was he contemplating some kind of magical compulsion, sensing his team might be breaking apart?

"It is not too late," said Abernathy. "I promised you I would not use force, or a threat of force, to make you stay. I intend to keep that promise. But before any of you decide to leave, please, tell me about the rest of your journey and what you found at Verdshane. If your news is good, perhaps I will not need your services any longer."

"Sir," said Aravia, "we went to Verdshane as you requested and found the ruins there. We even found your building with the blue magical field. But the person—"

"Was dead," Dranko interrupted. "And on the ground. Little flying rodents killed him, just like they killed Mrs. Horn."

Abernathy clutched his mug. "Are you certain? And was he…was the body still in the field?"

"No," said Aravia. "He had walked or crawled a few feet away from it."

Abernathy stared again at the fire, and the shadows it cast upon his old features made him seem older still. "Too soon," he muttered. "We're not ready." Before Aravia could ask what he meant, Abernathy let out a huge sigh. "How do you know what killed him?"

"If I may," said Aravia before anyone else could answer, "I figured out what happened. Tell me, sir, is that blue field a sort of temporal stasis?"

Abernathy nodded. "Very good, Aravia."

She spent the next few minutes sharing her hypotheses with Abernathy. It pleased her to see the others listening raptly. Here she was, talking shop with an archmage!

"That is an excellent and accurate supposition," said Abernathy when she was finished. "For someone with so little practical experience, your ability to draw conclusions from evidence is remarkable."

She flushed with pride and wished desperately that Serpicore were there to see her praised by such a magical luminary as Abernathy.

"But the facts themselves are deeply troubling. We were expecting that the stasis field would not suffer that kind of failure for...well, not for a long time. And that the enemy could have cracked the door of his prison sufficiently to let out a swarm of skellari means our time is shorter than we imagined. We can adjust the wards to compensate, but now I fear our long vigil has become little more than a doomed holding action."

"What about the man with blue skin?" asked Tor.

Abernathy's eyebrows shot up. "What? Blue skin?"

"Outside the building with the magic field in it," said Tor. "There was a bald man with blue skin, and I chased him into the forest and we had a duel. He ran away before we could finish it even though he was a fantastically skilled warrior. Do you know who he is?"

Abernathy rubbed his temples with wrinkled fingers. "Yes, I think I do. That man is a Sharshun."

"A what?" asked Tor.

The aged wizard let out another long sigh, this one ending with a wheeze. He glanced at the ruby on his chest. "I think I need to give you a little more background regarding my life's work. The being we have trapped is the son of King Naloric the Monstrous. Do any of you recall your history lessons?"

Aravia had memorized every history book in Serpicore's house. She opened her mouth to answer, but Tor beat her to it.

"Sure!" said the boy. "Naloric the Monstrous was king of Charagan many hundreds of years ago, and he used to be called Naloric the Just, but overnight he became some kind of horrible villain, and nobody knows why."

"Very good," said Abernathy. "Indeed, King Naloric Skewn went from being a benign and beloved sovereign whose only fault was a mild obsession with collecting butterflies, to becoming a merciless monster who authorized a slave trade, imprisoned and tortured his political rivals, raised taxes to an unconscionable level, and committed other atrocities far too numerous to mention. Naturally the dukes revolted, and there were years of civil war. According to legend, Naloric was nearly killed in single combat by the Duchess Daynell Kalkas, but there was some fell power in him that resisted death even after suffering what should have been a mortal wound. Soon enough he had put down the rebellion and turned Charagan into a nightmare realm of abused slaves and terrified peasants, all toiling under his soldiers' whips while they were forced to build his mines and pits."

"Had a thing for holes, did he?" said Dranko.

"Indeed," said Abernathy. "At first we thought mining was his goal, but in many places he dug unfathomably deep holes for no reason that was ever discovered. Perhaps he was hoping to unearth something specific, but if he was, he never found it, for he never stopped digging. Countless thousands of workers died from accidents or fatigue in the process."

"So what happened to Naloric?" asked Morningstar.

"For a long time, nothing," said Abernathy. "Whatever had transformed him gave Naloric Skewn an unnatural longevity. His tyranny lasted over a hundred years. But though he was immune to the ravages of time, he was unable to forestall the doom of complacency. A resistance took root and grew, a resistance that included most of the powerful wizards of that era. Armies were gathered in remote places overlooked by Naloric and his cadre of warlords. The leaders of the resistance called themselves the Spire, which was the name of Daynell Kalkas's castle before Naloric had it razed.

"Finally the Spire struck, and once again there was war in Charagan. Despite all of our power and preparations, the Spire *still* could not kill Naloric Skewn; his power was too great to be quenched by any means we possessed. But we were able to banish him to a prison world, another world from which any escape could only be back into this one."

Aravia knew that one. "Sir, are you talking about a Prison Pair?"

"You continue to impress me, young lady. Yes, I am. The only way to leave the second Prison Pair world is by first traveling to the primary world. In most other cases passage between worlds, though difficult, is well within the powers of wizards who achieve certain echelons of skill and knowledge. Naloric was trapped in a room with only one door, as it were, and the most accomplished wizards of the Spire closed and locked that door behind him."

"I'm pretty sure I can guess where this is goin'" said Kibi. "I'll bet that Naloric fellah, he's figured out how to get back through the door."

"You're close," said Abernathy. "Happily, what happened to Naloric is that he *was* killed, in the end. Less than a year after his banishment, he contrived to kick the door in, to continue the metaphor, and emerge back into Spira. But the tremendous effort needed to make that ingress had weakened him, and the combined might of the Spire's greatest heroes was sufficient to slay him at last…though not without terrible loss. Our three most powerful wizards were killed in the battle that brought about Naloric's downfall: Typier, Parthol, and Alander. That all happened about five hundred years ago.

"But even that turned out not to be the end of it," Abernathy went on. "For Naloric had a son, named Naradawk, who had also been banished to the prison world. When Naloric broke free and was killed, his son Naradawk wasn't with him; he had stayed behind. We're not sure why. Perhaps Naloric was keeping him in reserve, not expecting that the Spire could seal up the breach between the worlds again so quickly. I think it more likely that Naradawk *expected* his father would be killed and chose to stay behind on purpose, knowing that one day he would be strong enough to make the attempt himself.

"Following Naloric's jailbreak, the remaining archmagi, along with the apprentices of those slain, vowed to become ever-vigilant, to guard ceaselessly the single portal that links our world, Spira, with Volpos, its prison-paired world. I myself was one of those, having been apprenticed to Alander all those years ago."

"And the portal to the other world where Naradawk is trapped," said Aravia, "that's near Verdshane, isn't it? That's why you have a stasis field set up around it—so that if anyone does break through, they'll get caught in it."

"Precisely," said Abernathy. "That man you saw has, until recently, been suspended in the stasis. Naradawk was able to squeeze him through the portal in the early days, before we had strengthened the spells we use to keep it closed. We've always assumed he was a prisoner, or at least someone Naradawk was willing to sacrifice. But since the day the man became trapped, the stasis field has also served as an early warning system, and by your account of it, it's gone off."

Ernie fidgeted as he spoke. "Er, in that case, sir, shouldn't you be guarding the, uh, portal instead of chatting with us? Not that we don't appreciate it…"

Abernathy nodded. "I should," he said. "But for the moment some of the other archmagi have taken over my portion of the ongoing spell we maintain to keep the portal shut."

"If Naloric could be killed, then there *must* be a way to kill his son," said Tor.

"As I mentioned," said the archmage, "we were unable to kill Naloric the first time, which is why banishment was the only option. His subsequent breach of the portal between worlds took so much of his strength and power to effect, the Spire was able to destroy him, but even weakened he killed our three greatest wizards. His own impatience was his undoing, but Naradawk has been biding his time now for centuries, gathering strength and only carefully probing for new weakness in the portal. None of the present generation of wizards, myself included, can approach the might of Typier, Parthol, and Alander. We're all older than you can imagine and very, very tired."

"How old, exactly?" asked Aravia. "If Alander was killed hundreds of years ago, and you were his apprentice, then you must be hundreds of years old yourself. How is that possible?"

"Correct, my dear," said Abernathy. "All of us have lived well beyond our normal span. The…the place we go to maintain the spell that keeps the portal sealed is constructed in part from a magical alloy called gartine, which slows the passage of time. It's the same metal we used to frame the stasis field in Verdshane. As such, all of us—myself, Salk, Fylnia, Grawly, and Ozella—we are all of us hundreds of years old."

Aravia immediately spotted a discrepancy. "Serpicore taught me there were six living archmagi. Did one of you die? Or is he wrong?"

Abernathy raised an eyebrow at her questions. "This Serpicore fellow is remarkably well-informed. I suppose technically there are six of us, but the sixth is a recluse named Caranch. He doesn't join us, and we've never actually met him, though he contacts us from time to time with remarkably savvy advice. There's something strange about him that none of us can put a finger on."

Aravia's heart was beating unusually fast given that she was perfectly still. King Naloric was a well-known figure, a historical villain who, like all such villains, had burned hot and dangerous for a time before being swept from the board of history by the inevitable ascendance of the just and heroic. The history books said that Naloric had been banished, permanently, to a place that was never quite spelled out. But there was nothing about his subsequent break-out, or his death, or a son still trapped in a prison-paired world, hungry to get out and avenge his father.

"I'm guessin' this has somethin' to do with Tor's blue fellah?" asked Kibi.

"Ah. Right," said Abernathy. "That 'blue fellow' was a Sharshun. Whatever malign power or substance infected Naloric the Just, and which we assume he passed on to his son, was used to create a cadre of dangerous servants called the Sharshun. We thought they were all wiped out in the decades following Naloric's ill-fated escape, and none have been seen for centuries. We know little about them, save for the fact that they were skilled warriors, and obsessed with the Seven Mirrors."

"Oh!" said Ernie. "I know about those."

Aravia felt a bit miffed; she had never heard of them.

"The Seven Mirrors aren't far from White Ferry," said Ernie. "They're a ring of tall obelisks out in the wilderness. They flash once a year, and some of the villagers make a sport of running out into the middle of them when they do. Flashing Day is like a holiday for all the surrounding villages."

"Why did the Sharshun care about them?" asked Aravia.

"We don't know," said Abernathy. "But they're connected in some way with a set of gemstones called the Eyes of Moirel, which the Sharshun were trying desperately to collect. The Sharshun believed that if they ever gathered all seven Eyes and brought them to the Seven Mirrors, they would win the war almost instantly."

"Too many names!" Dranko complained. "Sharshun? Mirrors? Eyes? Naloric and Naradawk? If you want us to stick this out, keep it simple!"

Aravia chuckled. "Relax," she told him. "I'm keeping track of everything." She tapped her head.

Abernathy looked right at her and smiled. "Good, good," he said. "Aravia, it gives me great comfort to know my spell chose you."

She flushed with pride.

"Say," said Dranko. "Since Aravia's got everything covered, I don't suppose you can spare me for a couple of weeks? I have a friend who's gotten into some trouble, and there are some strange goings-on at my old church. Something to do with Mokad and embezzlement and a black circle."

Abernathy's eyes grew wide. "Black Circle? Are you certain?"

"Read for yourself." Dranko handed over the letter from Praska.

Abernathy grabbed the letter and read the whole thing in about thirty seconds. When he was done, he handed the letter back without a word and stood stiffly, using his staff for leverage. Slowly, slowly, he walked around the living room, putting out one hand to touch the walls.

"Do you know why I summoned you?" he asked, addressing none of them in particular.

"You said you needed field agents," said Aravia. "Because the danger to the kingdom had become more imminent."

"Yes, and that's true," said Abernathy. "But only *since* I've summoned you has the *degree* of that danger become apparent. I cast the summoning spell because…"

The old man looked at them, looked at Aravia in particular. "Because I *felt* that I should. As though the world were whispering to me that now, after hundreds of years with nothing changing, events were about to become calamitous. You might say I summoned you on *faith*. That it was *destiny*."

Kibi grunted. "Don't believe in destiny, never have," he said. "M' ma always told me we make our own destiny, Gods or no."

"Yes, well, whether it was fate, Gods, or something else entirely, I seemed to have called you to the brink of a cliff, in a manner of speaking. The Black Circle…it is…an object of worship. Not a God, not exactly, more of a concept. A symbol of knowledge obtained through dark magic. Naloric venerated it, as did the Sharshun. But like the Sharshun, there has been no whisper of the Black Circle cult or its followers in several centuries. Now, all at once, we find that at least one Sharshun is still alive and interested in Verdshane. And that the Black Circle has infiltrated the Church of Delioch and is active with some project. And that Naradawk, so long banished, has figured out how to squeeze something, however small and relatively weak, through the door to his jail."

"We'll stop them all!" said Tor.

Abernathy swept his gaze across them. "Do the rest of you feel the same? Have I convinced you now of how badly I need you? Vent your anger at me, your frustration, your grief, if you must. I feel your loss and fully agree that Ysabel's death was a great tragedy. But our kingdom is sorely beset. I do not exaggerate when I say that Naradawk Skewn, if he escapes to our world, will be both willing and able to kill or enslave every single citizen of Charagan. If you will not serve me, then serve the kingdom. Serve the hope that this can all be avoided."

"I'm with you," said Aravia. She looked around at the others, and knew exactly what she should say. "Like Ernie said, we should do this for Mrs. Horn. But also because it's *right*."

Ernie nodded. "For Mrs. Horn."

Morningstar showed a grim smile. "I don't have a choice. The Ellish church has ordered me to stay."

Aravia looked expectantly at Grey Wolf and Dranko.

"Fine," said Grey Wolf, looking none too happy. "Fine. I'll stick with it. Probably never get another job anyway."

"And you, Dranko?" asked Abernathy.

Dranko ran his lips over his tusks. His tongue was a coal gray color. "If we can do something about the Black Circle, root them out, then Praska will be able to come back to the church." He showed a tusky grin. "Also, where else am I going to find a magic box that produces free wine? Yeah, I'm still in."

Tor turned to the wizard. "Then Mister Abernathy, tell us what you want us to do."

"What I want you to do is find the Crosser's Maze."

Aravia held up her hand when Dranko opened his mouth to protest. "I'll remember it," she told him. "Abernathy, what's the Crosser's Maze?" A strange curiosity filled her, a need to know more that was almost fierce.

"A legendary magical device whose function is to seal up rifts between worlds. If the stories are true—and some of my colleagues are convinced they are—we could permanently seal the portal to Naradawk's prison world. It would solve all of our problems."

A smile leapt to Tor's face. "We'll get it for you! Where is it? What does it look like?"

"We're working on it," said Abernathy. "There are some complications with acquiring it that some of the other archmagi are still puzzling over. But for the moment let's not worry about that. I'm going to set you to dealing with our shorter-term problems."

Why? Why was he setting aside the Maze? Surely she could help with those "complications." The surge of curiosity within her was almost frightening—but Abernathy was talking again.

"Dranko, this should please you. I want *all* of you to go to Sand's Edge and find out what the Black Circle is digging up out in the desert. It would not surprise me in the slightest if the Sharshun have located one of the Eyes of Moirel. See if that's the case. If it is, get it back for us. Hopefully the timing should work out afterward for visiting the Seven Mirrors on Flashing Day. It troubles me greatly to know the Sharshun are abroad again, and given their obsession with the Mirrors and the Eyes, there's a good chance they have some plan in the works. Sadly, what I most lack right now is intelligence, and you can—"

The ruby on the chain around Abernathy's neck flared to crimson life.

"Bother," he said. "Go to the desert, immediately. Find out what the Black Circle is up to. Good luck!"

Aravia called out, too late. "But Pewter, and your spellbooks…!"

Abernathy winked out.

Damn.

CHAPTER TWELVE

It was difficult for Ernest Carabend Roundhill to set aside his sorrow, but he did his level best. Always in his mind were Mrs. Horn's final words, so he tried hard to look at things in a positive light. He reminded himself that his time with Horn's Company was exhilarating, providing all sorts of new experiences and opportunities for self-discovery.

He had discovered that for all of Old Bowleg's competent instruction, there was always something new for Tor or Grey Wolf to teach him during their now-daily sparring sessions.

He had discovered that after a week of walking, his legs and feet toughened such that a ten-hour day of hiking barely caused him discomfort.

He had discovered new campfire cooking techniques, new words from Aravia to describe magic and its mysterious workings, and even more new words from Dranko that Tor suggested he not use around his parents.

And if you had asked Ernie four days ago, he'd have said a ship voyage sounded wonderfully exciting. He'd never even seen a map that showed beyond the borders of Harkran, and he had only a vague notion that Nahalm was another island duchy somewhere to the south.

But what Ernie was discovering right now was that he had little love for sailing ships, and less for the tumultuous rebellion they fueled in his guts. He stumbled across the deck on landlubber's legs and heaved his breakfast into the ocean. Tor was at his side quickly with a water-skin. "I was hoping you'd be used to sea travel by now," said his tall friend, and Ernie appreciated the sympathy, though he was already wondering if there might be a way for them to return to

Tal Hae afterward on foot, via some stretch of land previously overlooked by the kingdom's cartographers.

When *Brechen's Brow*—a merchant ship whose captain had been willing to take on seven unusual but financially sufficient passengers—finally put into harbor, Ernie dashed down the gangplank and kissed the ground.

"Aravia," he said. "Before we leave, I beg you, learn some teleport magic. I don't think my stomach can handle a return voyage."

"Oh, how I wish I could," answered the wizardess.

* * *

Sand's Edge, Aravia told him, was named for its proximity to a vast desert with the ominous name of the Mouth of Nahalm. The city was a sprawling mess, its white clay buildings arranged in haphazard fashion, with narrow dirt roads winding snake-like through the jumble. The air was hot and achingly dry, though this was ameliorated by public wells every fifty yards beside the busier streets.

As they meandered westward along the city's looping avenues, following Grey Wolf (who seemed to have an idea where he was headed), Ernie couldn't stop staring at the ragged children who rattled their cups at him. Where were their parents? And what was that sour, gritty smell, so unlike anything he had encountered in White Ferry?

"Don't do it," Dranko warned him when he reached for his coin pouch. "Once word spreads that you're a sucker, every wide-eyed waif for a dozen blocks will be on you like fleas on a dog, begging and pleading until you've given away everything but your hair. Not to mention it'll mark you as a target for however many pickpockets are watching us right now, which by my count is at least five."

"But we can afford it!" Ernie protested. "These people are suffering!"

"Do yourself a favor," Dranko answered. "Don't make eye contact, and if you have to indulge your sense of charity, do it on the way *out* of town."

Dranko's cynicism was appalling, but Ernie felt like a hayseed and followed his advice. Wanting to take his mind off his surroundings, he jogged forward until he was walking next to Grey Wolf at the head of the group. "Where are we going, exactly?" he asked.

Grey Wolf didn't break stride as he answered. "Dranko's friend said the 'secret project' we're looking for is in the desert near the city. I want to take a look at the famous Mouth of Nahalm myself. I spent some time talking with the captain of our ship about Sand's Edge. Just west of the city limits is a line of tall cliffs, which he described as being like the side of an enormous cook-pot. The Mouth of Nahalm is down in the pot, a desert at the bottom of a steep-sided crater. I figure if we stand on the edge and look out, maybe we'll see some activity out there, and if not, the project may have a base of operations set up at the edge of town. Either way, if whatever's going on is employing dozens of people, we just have to find some of them."

Thank goodness they had Grey Wolf to take charge of things! He never seemed scared or worried.

It took nearly an hour for them to reach the city limits of Sand's Edge and walk the hundred additional yards to the edge of the Mouth of Nahalm. That final stretch of land was uninhabited and uncultivated, as if the townsfolk were worried that the Mouth of Nahalm—or something in it—might devour anyone who came too close.

There was no fence, no hedge, no barrier at all to prevent someone from falling from the cliffside into the desert. Ernie crept as close as he dared and peered down. It was a twenty-foot drop to the sands below.

Dranko came up to stand next to him. "I bet you could just jump in. Want to see who sinks in the furthest?"

Ernie blanched. "No thanks."

Dranko fished a torch out of his pack and tossed it over the edge. It spun end over end as it fell, and Ernie expected it would land on the surface of the sand or maybe sink half-way into it. But the desert swallowed up the entire thing as surely as the sea would have done. The sand was more akin to dust.

"Yeesh," said Dranko. "I guess when local crime bosses need to get rid of bodies, they have a pretty easy time of it."

"Will you cut that out?" Ernie demanded. "It's bad enough imagining we may have to go out there ourselves."

Tor squinted into the setting sun. "Is that an island? I think it's an island!"

Ernie looked toward the horizon, across the flat sands of the Mouth of Nahalm. There was something looming out there, like a great steep-sided hill rising up out of the desert, though it was impossible to gauge its size or distance.

"It's one of the Wandering Islands," said Grey Wolf. "The captain told me there are dozens, drifting around in the sand. No one knows much about them, and they're all uninhabited."

"It's likely that Praska's secret project is on one of them," said Aravia.

Ernie stared down at where Dranko's torch wasn't. "But we can't just walk out into the desert. For one thing, we'd sink. For another, it could take weeks or months of wandering about before we found the right island. And that's assuming Aravia's guess is true!"

Grey Wolf spit down into the dust. "It's already getting dark. Tomorrow we'll split up and hit the streets, see what we can discover. Dranko, these punishers from your church, Mokad and his friends, how worried should we be about them finding out we're here to spy on them?"

"Pretty worried, I guess," said Dranko. "Mokad is a cruel bastard. I wouldn't have thought he'd want to go causing trouble outside the church, but if he's willing to embezzle hundreds of crescents to fund a bunch of evil cultists, he wouldn't bat an eye about dumping our bodies in the sandbox if it came to it."

"Then we'll just have to be discreet. Nobody mention the Black Circle directly. Just say you've heard rumors about something going on out there in the desert, and see if anyone knows what you're talking about. Find out everything you can without doing anything stupid."

Grey Wolf looked right at Tor as he said this, but his friend didn't seem to notice he was being singled out. Ernie envied Tor. How much better to be oblivious but confident, than a coward who worried about every last thing.

* * *

With their funds running low, they opted to forgo even the cheap guesthouses in the seedier parts of Sand's Edge. They filled their water skins before camping out on the barren strip between the city and the desert.

In the morning, Ernie prepared himself for several hours of fruitless wandering, sure to be made worse by the need to be circumspect about what he was asking about. It was already uncomfortably hot by the time they finished breakfast, and the sun shone down unhindered by cloud or haze. He pitied Morningstar, who kept her hood up and sleeves down despite the temperature. Before fifteen minutes had gone by, Ernie needed to stop and refill his water skin at a roadside well.

As he stood in a short line waiting his turn, his gaze fell upon a placard nailed to a door on the far side of the street. He couldn't read the smaller print, but the word "dig" was clear enough. After replenishing his water he scurried over for a closer look.

STRONG MEN WANTED

to serve as miners, diggers, and haulers for an

ARCHAEOLOGICAL DIG.

GOOD PAY for HARD WORK

on the Wandering Islands of the Mouth of Nahalm

TRAVEL KITS provided

Ernie could hardly believe his luck. He recalled Grey Wolf's admonition—find out everything he could without doing anything foolish. A voice in his head suggested he turn right around and come back later with the others, but then he thought about what Tor would do, and the respect he would earn when he came back with good information. He pushed open the door, summoned up what courage he had, and stepped into a spacious high-ceilinged room. It was mostly empty; near the back was a long table, and off to the side were wooden shelves stacked with large cloth-wrapped bundles. Three disreputable-looking men sat in chairs behind the table and talked in low voices, while a fourth man, skinny and stoop-shouldered, and with a shock of curly red hair, inspected the bundles.

"I'm…er…I'm here to inquire about working on your project," said Ernie.

The men behind the table stopped talking and watched him approach. All three were broad-shouldered and thick-necked. The biggest of the bunch, a flat-nosed brute with a jutting chin, graced him with a smile—not a nice smile—while another snickered and whispered something to the third.

"Check the sign again, boy," said the flat-nosed man. "Strong men are what we need, not children. Come back in five years when you've put some muscle on those bones." The other two laughed, and all three resumed their conversation as if he had already gone.

They were probably right, but Ernie fought down an instinct to walk out with his tail between his legs. Instead he raised both his chin and his voice. "I'm stronger than I look. What exactly is involved, and how do I prove I can do it?"

The men stopped talking again, and Flat-nose stood up. He was much taller than Ernie, and a sword was sheathed at his belt. He gave Ernie a look of amused indulgence, then gestured to a row of barrels set against the wall opposite the shelves.

"Let's see you pick those up, boy. Start with the smallest. Wouldn't want you to hurt yourself."

Ernie strode with purpose to the barrels, inwardly pleading with Pikon that he not make a fool of himself. He squatted in front of the smallest barrel, wrapped his arms around it, and stood up. From the sloshing sound and the shifting weight, he guessed it was about a quarter full of water, but he stood up without great difficulty. A childhood spent hauling bags of flour for his parents had prepared him well for this test.

Seeing the skeptical looks he hoisted the barrel up onto one shoulder. "You want it on the table?" he asked. He was trying his hardest to act how Grey Wolf or Tor would. Confidence!

"No, no," laughed Flat-nose. "Just put it down. You were right; you're stronger than you look. Try the third one."

Ernie set down the barrel as gently as he could and moved to the third. This one was larger, and the primary difficulty would be getting his arms around it sufficiently far. But he assumed a straight-backed lifting position, stretched his shoulders, and with some difficulty heaved it up to chest level. He held it there for several seconds. He could feel his face redden and his muscles burn but was unwilling to drop it.

"Okay, boy, you can set it down, gently if you please. Don't want to smash it now, do we?"

Ernie found this part the hardest, and the wide barrel nearly slipped from his arms. While his back protested, he managed to place the barrel down in a more or less controlled fashion. Then he tried his best not to pant from the exertion.

"Well?" he asked.

This time one of the other two men spoke, a bald brute with a dagger tattooed on the side of his head. "Stronger than you look and strong enough are two different things, kid. No dice."

"I'm also an excellent cook!" Ernie said, hoping this might be relevant.

"Cooks they got," said Flat-nose. "We appreciate you coming in, but now you're just wasting your time and ours. You can show yourself out."

Ernie's heart sank. How would Dranko handle this? He surely wouldn't walk out empty handed. He gulped down the lump of anxiety rising in his throat.

"Are there any other digs going on out in the desert that might be hiring?"

"Doubtful," said the bald man. "But also not our business. The harbormaster hires day-laborers; why don't you try down there?"

"Good idea." Ernie turned to go, then turned back. "Oh, but can you tell me why they're called 'wandering islands?' I'm from out of town."

"'Cause they move, obviously," said Flat-nose. "The islands out there aren't anchored to anything, so they just drift around in the sand."

"Then when you hire men who are strong enough, how do they find the right one?"

The men looked at one another. Was he coming across as too inquisitive?

"The islands move real slow," said the bald man with the tattoo. "You got a reason for all these questions?"

"Er, yes, I do. I may not be what you're looking for, but I have some friends also looking for work, and they're bigger and stronger than me. I want to tell them enough to make them interested. They'll also want to know who's sponsoring your dig, and what's the pay."

"A private investor wants to dig up some old junk on one of the islands," said Flat-nose. "As for pay, it's ten silver talons a day, but the foremen might decide to dock you if they feel you're not pulling your weight. Payment at the end of each day, out at the site."

"And how far out is the place, anyway?"

The third man spoke for the first time. "Boy, if we decide to hire on one of your friends, we'll tell them what they need to know. But since you're not going, none of this is your business. We've answered enough of your questions. Now scram."

There was something disturbing about him, the sharpness of his gaze, the oily disdain in his voice. Ernie hustled out the door.

CHAPTER THIRTEEN

Tor dashed to their agreed-upon rendezvous, and while he hadn't learned anything specifically relevant about a secret project out in the sands, he *had* scrounged up some information about the desert itself and also found a street vendor selling candied dates, a particular favorite of his, so the morning hadn't been a total loss, and everyone else would be pleased that he had bought a date for each person in Horn's Company, and surely someone had had more luck regarding their actual mission.

He was the last to arrive, but before he could hand out the dates Ernie started talking.

"I found it! I found a place where they're hiring folks for a dig out on one of the islands in the desert. That must be what we're looking for!" The baker described his experience at the recruiting house.

Tor beamed at his friend. "Well done, Ernest! Let's get over there and lift those barrels and get hired and out in the desert and see what those Black Circle cultists are digging up!" He was already forming a plan; he'd impress the recruiters with his great strength and then insist that all of his friends be allowed to join him as a condition of his taking the job.

Grey Wolf scowled at him, made a shushing gesture with his finger, then turned to Ernie. "How do you know this is the right operation?" he asked. "You didn't name-drop the Black Circle, did you?"

"Of course not!" said Ernie. "But how many ventures like this could be happening out there?"

"Ernie's right," said Tor. "I asked a bunch of locals about it, and if there's one thing they agreed upon, it's that *no one* goes out into the Mouth of Nahalm. They laughed at the idea of someone bothering to walk as far as the nearest island."

"From what I hear," said Dranko, "you couldn't walk across the desert even if you wanted to. As we already discovered, the sand is more like dust, so fine that you'd sink in up to your arse, or further."

"The sign on the door said 'travel kits provided,'" said Ernie. "I saw a bunch of bundled up packages in the recruiting hall. They must have figured something out."

Grey Wolf scratched his stubble. "They're not being very secretive, are they? You'd think an evil cult would be more hush-hush if they were trying to hide some unscrupulous plan."

"They're hiding in plain sight," said Morningstar. "By making it look like a legitimate business venture, no one will think twice about it." The Ellish priestess had her hood drawn so close around her face, not even her nose was sticking out. Was the heat as uncomfortable for her as light, given her upbringing?

"And I didn't see any signs of these Black Circle people," said Ernie. "The recruiters seemed like normal folk to me, if a little brusque."

"They probably don't even know who's sponsoring it," said Dranko.

Tor slapped Ernest heartily on the back. "Lead on!"

* * *

The recruitment house wasn't far, and Tor was ready to walk right in, but Dranko grabbed his arm. "Hold on," he said. "I think I shouldn't go in with you."

"Why not?"

"The traitors in my church may have sent out a warning that they've been compromised. If that warning got here before us, my lovely complexion could set off some alarm bells. Better I wait out here."

"Agreed," said Grey Wolf.

The remaining six walked into the recruitment office. The three men Ernie had described were there, tearing hunks from a loaf of bread on their long table. They all stood as Tor and the others walked toward them.

"I see you brought your friends, boy," said the tallest of the three. He walked from around the desk and looked down at Tor, who was unused to being looked down upon, literally or otherwise. This must be the one Ernie called "Flat-nose."

"So, you want to work on our little dig?"

"Yes, sir!" said Tor.

"We all do," said Grey Wolf.

"We're only hiring men," said the bald fellow. "You'll have to leave your women behind for as long as you're working for us."

Aravia made to protest this characterization, but Grey Wolf put a hand on her shoulder.

"Fine," said Grey Wolf. "You want strong backs? Our backs are strong, and we need coin. Tell us how this works."

"First we see if you're worth our time," said Flat-nose. "You, man-child, let's see you lift the third barrel in that line."

Tor looked at Ernie, who stared back at him pointedly. Oh, right! Was "man-child" meant to be an insult? "My name is Tor," he said proudly. "Tor Bladebearer." Tor walked to the barrel, bent down, grabbed it with both hands, and lifted it above his head. It wasn't very heavy.

"Impressive," said Flat-nose. "Put it down slowly, then lift the…how about the eighth one. Third from the end."

The next barrel was much heavier, and there was no way he could get it higher than his chest, but he muscled it up that far and held it there. All three men were watching now, and the bald one nodded in appreciation.

"You've got the chops, kid," he said. "Let's see what your friends can do, and then we'll talk specifics, find out if you still want the job."

Tor put the barrel back down, and Grey Wolf took his turn. He could only lift the sixth barrel in the row, but the recruiters found that sufficient. Then Kibi stepped up and walked straight to the last of the ten barrels. Its lid leaked sand.

"Not that one," said Flat-nose. "Nobody's been able—"

While the man talked, Kibi cracked his knuckles, squatted a couple of times, and grabbed the sand-filled cask. With a grunt he lifted it up off the ground. The three recruiters stared, eyes wide. Tor himself was a bit shocked, and delighted. Who knew that Kibi was so strong? Being a stonecutter must really build up one's muscles!

"You're not from Sand's Edge," said the third man, who had not spoken before now. He was barrel-chested and shorter than the others, and most of his fingers sported thick silver rings. His voice was oily and sibilant. "Where do you folks call home?"

"Tal Hae," said Tor, and he immediately cast a glance towards Grey Wolf. Maybe he should have made up something else, but it was too late now.

"And tell me, Tor Bladebearer, did you come all the way from Tal Hae just to do hard manual labor in one of the most dangerous places in Charagan?"

"Er…no, not exactly…"

"Curious." The man stared at Tor with beady and unblinking eyes, his gaze disconcertingly intent. His two confederates frowned and became inexplicably tense. "Haske," the bald man asked the man with the rings, "do you think—"

"Quiet," said Haske. "I'm sizing this one up. I'm thinking he could be foreman material."

Tor smiled, relieved. "You'll find I'm more than capable of—"

"These are the ones," Haske said abruptly, but before Tor could figure out what he meant, the man added, "Kill them."

Tor was certain he misheard. While he tried to work out what the man had *actually* said, Haske flicked his hand towards the door and it slammed shut by itself and a conspicuous *thunk* came from its lock and now Tattoo-head and Flat-nose were drawing swords from their sheaths while Grey Wolf was doing likewise and Morningstar pulled her mace from her belt. Ernie bolted for the door while Kibi tried to ready his pick, but it became caught in his shirt.

"What are you doing?" Tor cried, staring at Haske. "We just want to—hey!"

Haske's two thugs moved to bracket Grey Wolf, who was sidestepping rapidly and moving toward Morningstar, but Tor had to return his attention to Haske himself, coming swiftly at him. "Bad luck, boy," Haske hissed, but it wasn't bad luck at all; he had a sword and his enemy did not, and he was full of confidence despite the pain in his leg from the wound he suffered during his altercation with the Sharshun, though that reminded him that he hadn't actually *drawn* his sword, so he did that. But as his blade came free of its sheath, Haske spoke a few quick syllables and waved one hand at him; his sword was wrenched from his hand, stinging his fingers, which wasn't fair at all, and the weapon slid rapidly across the floor and came to rest beneath the shelves of travel kits and when he looked back a dagger had appeared in Haske's other hand.

"It's locked!" Ernie shouted from the other side of the room. "Aravia, can you open it?" Tor risked a quick glance over Haske's shoulder; Morningstar and Grey Wolf had arranged themselves back to back, fending off flurries of sword blows from Flat-nose and Tattoo-head.

"Dropped something important?" Haske chuckled, advancing with the knife.

His opponent knew what he was doing, moving the way Master Elgus moved back in the training yard of his father's castle, so Tor backed up, and maybe he could make his way over to where his sword was, but didn't dare take his eyes off his enemy, and Haske lunged, and he hopped back out of the way. Haske stepped quickly toward him a second time and slashed again, and this time he also spat a syllable while his off-hand made a swift gripping motion, and when Tor tried to leap away something pulled hard on his collar and the knife cut a gash right across his arm above the elbow. Blood quickly soaked his shirt.

If only he could hold on a little longer, his friends' superior numbers should become decisive. Ernie was returning from the door holding Pyknite, and Kibi had finally gotten his pick sorted out. But Haske quickly disengaged from Tor, backpedaled, and made a throwing motion with his left arm. The large table tipped itself over and slid across the room, smashing into Kibi and Ernie both as they tried to join the melee, sweeping them into the wall with the line of barrels. Tor lost sight of them, while Tattoo-head took advantage of the distraction to open a bleeding nick on Grey Wolf's cheek.

Tor focused again on Haske, just in time to see the dagger flashing toward him, and though he leapt to one side he was not quick enough to avoid the strike and it punctured his side just above his hip and the pain was searing. It was going to be tricky regaining his own blade because Haske was maneuvering him to the wrong side of the room, and while this man wasn't quite as skilled as the Sharshun person he fought near Verdshane, him having a weapon while Tor didn't was going make this a difficult fight to win. He fought down the tiniest upwelling of doubt, as this was his third battle as part of Horn's Company and he hadn't exactly covered himself in glory in either of the previous two and this one wasn't going so well either, and could Master Elgus have been exaggerating about how good a swordsman he was?

"It's nothing personal," said Haske, making a feint with the dagger. Tor dodged nimbly, arms extended, trying to block out the pain of his injuries. Should he try grabbing his attacker's wrist or moving in to grapple? Though he and the others had been practicing their sword-fighting on the road, wrestling was a discipline out of his experience, and Master Elgus had warned him of the folly of engaging an armed attacker without a weapon of one's own, but it was now past the moment when that advice would be useful. Worse, this man had both a dagger *and* wizardry at his disposal.

"What do you think we know?" he asked, thinking maybe he could distract his enemy until one of his friends could help. Grey Wolf had been knocked to the ground, scalp bleeding, but Ernie had limped from behind the magicked table to engage Flat-nose while Morningstar fought Tattoo-head. There was no sign of Aravia or Kibi. He hoped Aravia had gotten the door open and gone for help.

"I don't *think*," said Haske. "I *know*. The squealing brat from Tal Hae sent you."

Haske feinted and stabbed; Tor spun away, but the pain from his wounds was slowing him, and his foot nearly skidded on his own blood. They might be losing.

Gods, he thought. *I wish I had my sword.*

And his sword appeared, hovering in the air by his right hand, and how amazing was that? He grabbed the hilt and swung, and this time it was Haske who leapt back, barely avoiding the blade.

Tor was exultant. Adrenaline flooded through him, dulling his pain. He could make wishes! *I wish this man's feet were rooted to the floor,* he thought. But Haske ignored his plea to the supernatural, took another step back, crouched, mumbled, and waved. Tor's sword tried to free itself again from his grasp, but this time he was ready, and his grip was stronger, and even though his hand was getting slick with blood dripping from his arm, he held on, then stepped up to attack. This was the kind of fighting he was trained for! Haske fell back, startled, which gave Tor a good view of Tattoo-head driving Morningstar back toward the wall. Tor made a feint of his own toward Haske, then spun and rushed toward Tattoo-head, who barely turned in time to put his own sword up to block. But that left him wide open to Morningstar, who planted her mace in his chest.

One down, two to go! Flat-nose was hammering his weapon down upon Ernie, who was reduced to using Pyknite as a shield. "Morningstar, help Ernie. I'll take care of the wizard."

Gripping his sword as tightly as he could, Tor returned his attention to Haske. The man was standing fifteen feet away, looking straight at him, mouthing incomprehensible words and spiraling the fingers of his left hand.

Tor's muscles all seized up at once. He couldn't move. He couldn't even blink! Haske shook his head and appeared slightly dazed, like Aravia when she had cast too many spells at Verdshane, but he was well enough to stumble forward, knife out.

I wish I could move!

It was no good. Tor was well and truly paralyzed by some fancy magic, and now Haske was going to slice him wide open. Grey Wolf was regaining his feet, but Morningstar and Ernie were occupied by Flat-nose, and he couldn't see Aravia or Kibi anywhere, and there was nothing but a foot of air between Tor's chest and the point of Haske's dagger.

We did better this time. I hope everyone else survives.

Haske was drawing back his elbow, blinking rapidly, when one of the testing barrels soared into Tor's field of vision and caved in the side of Haske's head with a sickening crunch.

"Nice throw, Kibi!" he called. Kibi must be the strongest person he had ever met, which was strange because the stonecutter had never mentioned it, and if Tor were that strong, he'd want everyone to know so they'd realize they could rely on him even more.

Flat-nose, seeing that Haske was dead, dropped his sword and raised his arms.

"I surrender! Don't kill me, please!"

* * *

Dranko rushed into the room; having unlocked the door, Aravia slipped outside and returned ten seconds later with the placard seeking recruits, then closed the door quickly behind her. But when she moved to join the others, she stumbled and sat down awkwardly, clutching her head between her hands. Tor limped to her side.

"Are you okay? What happened?"

"Just been overdoing the magic," she said weakly. "First the *lockbuster*, then arcing your sword to you, then arcing the sign off the wall, all within a minute or two. And those last two were quite difficult; your sword is heavy, and the sign had about twenty nails in it."

"My sword…that was you, then?"

Aravia raised her eyebrows at him. "How did you *think* your sword got from the floor to your hand?"

Tor realized how ridiculous his first guess had been, but couldn't bring himself to admit it. "I…I wasn't sure. Everything was happening so fast…"

"Tor, lie down. Gently." Dranko stood before him, appraising his wounds.

Tor did as he was told, and Dranko knelt to examine his injuries more closely.

"You win," Dranko told him. "You're the worst off. The arm is superficial, but the hip will get serious if we don't take care of it."

"Could you try channeling again?" Tor asked.

"Yeah, maybe, but not until *after* I've taken care of you the traditional way. Just in case."

Tor lay still, trying not to flinch while Dranko applied his salves, stitched his wounds, and wrapped him in bandages. His cut from the Sharshun had reopened during the fighting, so Dranko took care of that one too.

While Dranko attended to the hurts of the others, and Kibi finished tying Flat-nose to a chair, Tor lay there on his back, ignoring the pain and replaying the battle in his mind. It was exhilarating, and he could easily set aside that he was the one who kept getting injured. The wizard, Haske, would have killed at least one of his friends if Tor hadn't been the one to engage him. That was his job—to find the most dangerous person in the room and take him on. Protect his friends. He had let the team down in Verdshane, letting Mrs. Horn get killed. He wouldn't make that mistake again.

His father, Olorayne Firemount, the baron of Forquelle, had once explained to him what life would be like once he had inherited the throne. Back then, before he had been rescued by Abernathy, his destiny had been to succeed his father as baron, when he would rule Forquelle, wasting his days with a daily torture of diplomacy, economics, ledgers, taxes, and various affairs of state. His sword would have grown rusty, his back bent over a desk covered in contracts and agreements, and his *true* destiny would have gone unfulfilled.

"A sword is a plaything," Olorayne had said. "The true weapons of a ruler are wisdom, knowledge, and guile. A sharp bookkeeper will be of more value to you than a sharp blade. Though," he had added with a chuckle, "ruling a barony is just as bloody a business as fighting on the battlefield."

Tor looked around at the red-splattered aftermath of their fight and severely doubted it. But by the Gods, he was better off here than safe in his palace back home.

CHAPTER FOURTEEN

Morningstar gripped the handle of her mace. "Let's start with the basics. What's your name?"

Grey Wolf was pressing Haske's knife to the man's neck. Morningstar had never done anything like this before, but she was damn near certain that, possibly excepting Grey Wolf, she was the only one in their group who would have no qualms about following through on threats.

"Why should I answer?"

Morningstar hefted her weapon, the spikes of which still glistened with blood. "Because if you don't, I will cause you great injury. Is withholding your name worth finding out if I'm lying?"

"Tig," said the man. "I'm called Tig."

"Well, Tig, I have several more questions for you, and as long as you keep answering them to my satisfaction, you stay healthy. Do we have a deal?"

Tig tightened his lips and said nothing.

Morningstar pointed to Haske's body. "That man over there. How did he know who we were?"

Her prisoner stared straight ahead and did not answer.

"Fine," said Morningstar. "Tor, untie his right arm, and you and Kibi hold it down on the table. That way, if he doesn't answer the next time I ask the question, I can smash his hand to a pulp."

Tor unwound the rope. She knew the boy was only complying because he thought she was bluffing. Kibi offered her a questioning look, which she ignored.

"One more time," said Morningstar. "How…?"

"He read your mind," said Tig quickly. "I don't know how. Some wizardry he knows. I've seen him do it before. Part of the recruitment process. He warned us something like this might happen, but you're the first people he ever told us to snuff."

"I don't believe you," said Morningstar. It was far more likely that these men had received warning from Tal Hae after Praska had escaped, as Dranko had feared. As soon as Tor admitted where they were from, Haske had decided to take no chances.

Tig looked down nervously at his pinioned hand. "Believe what you like, but it's the truth."

Morningstar changed her opinion slightly. Tig probably *thought* his confederate could read minds.

"Was your mind-reader in charge of this whole archaeological project? And if not, who's he working for?"

"Haske was in charge of finding muscle for the dig. But he didn't tell us who's calling the shots."

Ernie approached and whispered in her ear. Morningstar nodded. "My friend here says that when he first came in, there were four of you. Where's the fourth man?"

"Beats me," said Tig. "Don't even know his name. He was the guy who made and delivered the survival kits."

"Are you expecting him back again anytime soon?"

"Dunno. You'd have to ask the guy whose head your friend smashed. Too bad he's dead then, huh?"

Morningstar inwardly winced. This *would* have been much easier if they had taken Haske alive, but she could hardly fault Kibi for hurling his barrel.

"Then tell me what you people are digging for out there."

"Look, sister, the only stuff I've seen is what happens in this room. We screen for men who seem like they can swing a pick and haul rock. When we're satisfied, Haske lets them each take a survival kit, and tells them where and when to meet a guide who will take them out to the dig site. But what they're looking for, I have no idea. Really, I don't."

"And in all this time, have you ever overheard Haske or anyone else talking specifically about how one *gets* to the dig site?"

Tig shook his head, but only after a telltale pause.

"I'm guessing Haske chose you for your sword arm and not your skill at lying," she said. "I'll ask more directly this time. How do you get to the dig site?"

Tig glared at her but didn't respond.

"Last chance," said Morningstar. "How do you get to the dig site?"

"Go screw yourself, Ellish witch."

Morningstar sighed. She had hoped it wouldn't come to this. The others were bound to object. "Fine," she said evenly. "I see you've opted for the hard way. Tor, Kibi, make sure he doesn't move his arm."

"You won't do it," Tig spat.

"I will." And before any of the others could stop her, she lifted her weapon and smashed it down hard on the back of Tig's right hand. Her captive's eyes went wide as blood splattered and bones crunched. He opened his mouth to shriek, but Morningstar put her face right up to his. "If you scream, the next one goes in your eye."

Tig whimpered, tears streamed down his face, and he obviously tried very, very hard not to look at his mangled hand.

"Morningstar!" gasped Ernie. "What have you done?"

"Nothing that Dranko can't undo," she snapped, keeping her eyes locked on her subject. "You promised to let me do this, so please, don't interrupt me."

"But we don't know if Dranko—"

"Ernie, shut up!" This was hard enough without getting an earful of Ernie's misplaced pleas for mercy. "Tig, listen to me. My friend over there is a Deliochan channeler who can fix up your hand as good as new. But he'll only heal you if I ask him to, and I'll only ask him to if I hear the truth. Now, how do we get to the dig site?"

Technically she was correct; if Dranko wasn't lying, he *was* a channeler, albeit one who might have trouble fulfilling his part of the bargain. Tig glanced down at his crushed hand and bit his lip. He looked like he was about to pass out.

"Dranko," Morningstar snapped. "Do you have anything in your bag that dulls pain?"

Dranko came to her side. He looked down stoically at Tig's hand, but if he disapproved, he wasn't showing it.

"Yeah," he said. "Hold on."

Tig started to scream as Dranko dripped some thick purple liquid over his hand, but Grey Wolf pressed the dagger to his throat and he bit his lip instead.

"Better?" she asked.

Tig blinked tears from his eyes, but no longer seemed about to faint. "Promise...promise me that if I tell you, you'll ask your friend to heal me...please."

"I promise, but only if I think you're not lying to me." She let go of her weapon, leaving it standing at a diagonal, its spiked ball holding it upright by dint of being embedded in both Tig's hand and the wooden table beneath it. Arms crossed, she waited for Tig to talk.

Tig swallowed and kept his eyes off the table. His voice wavered, no doubt from the extreme pain he was in despite Dranko's goop, and his gasped sentences came quickly. "If you walk south out of the city...twenty minutes, along the edge of the desert...boulders right up against the edge. They've got...pulley system set up. Overnight...head straight west from there to the first island you see. Sleep during...the day. When...sun goes down again...walk northwest...four hours until you see another island. That's...the one."

"Thank you," said Morningstar. "Now, please wait there while I talk with my friends about what we should do next."

The expressions of her companions showed that she had an uphill climb ahead of her. Aravia was nearly as white as Morningstar herself and was staring at Tig's ruined hand. Tor was still obediently holding Tig's arm in place, but he was obviously conflicted and his complexion was a bit green. Kibi had let go when she had slammed down her mace and was looking away from the scene entirely. Ernie was red-faced and furious. Dranko and Grey Wolf were the only ones who weren't either disapproving or sickened by what she had done. Grey Wolf stood behind her, his body tense, but he nodded when she gestured for a group meeting in the far corner of the room.

They hadn't made it that far before Ernie exploded. "Morningstar, what in all that's holy was that? That's...that was torture! You tortured information out of that man!"

"Do you mean the fellow whose friend would have run you through given another few seconds? That man? I did nothing to him that he wouldn't have done to us in a heartbeat, and nothing that we wouldn't be patting ourselves on the back for, had we done it in the middle of the fight."

"But we're not in the middle of the fight!" cried Ernie. "He surrendered! You can't keep smashing someone after he surrenders!"

"The fight is still going on," she answered coolly. "This is just a different part of it. He only surrendered because he knew we'd have killed him otherwise, and

I gave him plenty of opportunity to talk without making me resort to violence. I even warned him of exactly what I would do if he didn't cooperate."

"And what now?" asked Ernie. "Dranko, can you heal him?"

"I don't know," said Dranko. "I can make sure he doesn't die of infection, maybe even without chopping off his hand. But if you mean channeling, I...wouldn't bet on it."

Morningstar didn't much care. Men like Tig had, as far as she was concerned, renounced any claim to mercy or compassion. She'd just as soon kill the prisoner and be done with it, but she had a good idea what Ernie would say to that.

"Time is important," she said. "We don't know who else might be coming here or what happened to the fourth man you saw. There's no way to hide the bodies or get them out the door without people on the streets watching us. What do we do if someone knocks in the next five minutes?"

"Hide the bodies?" Ernie was incredulous. "That's...not a thing people do! We just killed two people! We should be notifying the authorities, not figuring out how to...how to get rid of evidence."

"That wouldn't be wise, Ernie," said Grey Wolf, and Morningstar was glad to have someone at least nominally on her side. "What do you suppose a magistrate would say, given the evidence?"

Ernie looked around at the bloody carnage of the room and went pale. "But...but Abernathy..."

Grey Wolf shook his head. "Dammit, Ernie, Abernathy's name isn't some kind of password we can use to deflect the law! No one would believe us, or care much if they did. At best we could turn this into a stalemate of accusations, but we'd be passing the time in jail while justice sorted itself out."

Kibi was looking at everyone but her. "Now that we know where we're going, shouldn't we go there? If someone might be comin' back here, and some other a' these bad folk figure things out and chase after us, seems we want as big a head start as we can get."

Morningstar agreed. "Then what should we do with our friend when we leave?"

"We have three choices," said Aravia. "We can leave him here, alive. We can take him with us. Or we can kill him."

"That last one is *not* a choice!" Ernie squeaked.

"I disagree," said Morningstar. "In fact, it's the best choice. If we leave him here, he'll speed up any pursuit from the bad guys. If we take him with us, he could cause all sorts of mischief, possibly slowing us down or sabotaging our mission altogether. Ernie, you have to think practically right now. There's a—"

"No!" Ernie shouted, and he stomped his foot as he spoke. "I don't care how…how evil our prisoner is, or that he and his friends tried to kill us, or that he's part of some old evil cult. We are *not* going to be the sort of people who accept a man's surrender and then put him to death. If we do that, we'll be—"

Morningstar cut him off. "Please. 'We'll be no better than they are?' Is that what you were going to say?"

"Er…yes, something like that," Ernie stammered.

"Rubbish," said Morningstar. "The moment they decided to kill us without provocation it became impossible for us to be 'no better than they are.' That man relinquished his right to mercy when he lifted his sword against us. It won't reflect badly upon you to treat him the way he deserves."

Ernie hesitated, and for just a second Morningstar thought she had beaten down his resistance, but the baker's son showed annoying stubbornness. "Yes, it will!" he retorted. "How we treat other people is *exactly* what makes us good or bad people ourselves. Morningstar, believe me when I tell you, I don't *like* that man over there, and I think he deserves justice. But we are not the law, and I will not stand by if you or anyone else in this room tries to murder him."

It was inevitable. While she was gratified that her new teammates treated her as a respected equal, and even more so that they were all decent, competent, and (excepting Dranko) pleasant to be around, they were far too sentimental for their own good. The Ellish religion was, at its heart, devoted to protecting the innocent from predators, and its tenets left little room for interpretation about the complete lack of forgiveness predators were due.

She had the feeling that of all of them, Grey Wolf included, she alone was treating her new responsibilities with the hefty gravitas they deserved. Abernathy had made it clear before they left; the kingdom was under attack, severely, unexpectedly, and from multiple quarters.

"I suppose we'll need to be a guild council after all," said Grey Wolf with a sigh. "Let's vote on it." Though Morningstar knew how this would go, she was still glad enough not to continue the argument.

"All in favor of killing the prisoner right now?" Grey Wolf asked. Morningstar was the only person to raise her hand; not even Grey Wolf was siding with her. Maybe she was destined to be the outcast yet again.

"All in favor of leaving him here?" Kibi and Aravia raised their hands.

"Then I guess that's settled," said Grey Wolf. "He comes with us."

"There might be another option," said Dranko. He turned around and called across the room to their whimpering prisoner. "Hey Tig, is there a shrine to Delioch here in Sand's Edge?"

Tig nodded his head.

Dranko turned back and spoke quietly. "We can take him there. They may have a better channeler, and even if they don't, they'll be able to take care of his hand better than I will."

Morningstar shook her head. "And what if he starts screaming bloody murder the moment we walk out of this building?"

"I don't think he will," said Ernie. "Not if he wants to go through the rest of his life with a mangled sword-hand."

"We need to split up anyway," said Grey Wolf. "Tor is in no condition to hike across the desert."

"Neither are you," said Dranko. "You need at least a day before you do anything strenuous."

Grey Wolf shook his head. "I've had worse," he grumbled.

"Sure," said Dranko. "And when you had worse, you spent the day recovering in a tavern with a drink in your hand, not dragging your sorry arse across the Mouth of Nahalm. You should stay here with Tor and the prisoner. And Kibi…sorry, but speed will be more important than strength on this trip."

Morningstar had to admit that the goblin was making sense. "I'll go with you," she said with a sigh. "If we'll be traveling at night, my darksight will be useful. Aravia and Ernie, you should come too if you're up for it."

"If we wait until tonight, I'll be fine," said Aravia. "Though I may not be much good for spellcasting until tomorrow morning."

"I'm good too," said Ernie. "Kibi took the brunt of the table."

"What're you plannin' to do out there?" asked Kibi.

"Scout the place out," said Dranko. "Maybe send in someone who's good at sneaking, to steal whatever it is they're digging up. That's assuming we can find someone like that."

He grinned that ugly tusky grin.

Dranko fished a bag of coins from his pack. "Grey Wolf, take what we have left. The priests will want a donation in return for their attention. Pay them extra if it'll get them to channel for Tor. Pay a little more, and they may decide to keep their patient an extra day or two. Just leave enough to buy us passage home."

"Are we all set?" asked Morningstar. She didn't relish a journey across the desert with Dranko, but it was the best way to salvage the situation. "Let's go."

CHAPTER FIFTEEN

The last thing Dranko did before leaving the Black Circle's recruitment office was to rifle through the pockets of their fallen foes. The bald guy had only a pouch of coins hanging from his belt, but Haske was a different story. While the others looked on, probably shocked by his attention to detail, Dranko discovered three items of particular interest besides the several rings on the dead man's fingers. One was a folded piece of paper with a crude map of the desert and the closest few wandering islands. Each such island was marked with a wide circle showing its likely positions, and a small darker dot showing a specific location, probably where it was when the map was drawn. Judging from the arrows and small scrawled notes, Tig's description was spot on.

The second item was the key to the door, which was good because it would buy them some time.

The third item Dranko found hanging from Haske's neck, tucked beneath his shirt. On a slender metal chain was a small black ring like a spoke-less wagon wheel, only an inch in diameter. It was of some smooth metal, and though it looked innocuous, Dranko found it oddly discomfiting, as if it were an eye staring at him and wondering what he was up to. If nothing else, the presence of an actual, physical black circle confirmed that they had not stumbled across some *other* nefarious archeological project by mistake. He stuffed the little talisman into his own pocket with a thought to show it to Abernathy when they next returned to the Greenhouse.

He decided not to try channeling, even though Tor was in rough shape. Whether or not he succeeded, it would take too much out of him before a hike out into the Mouth of Nahalm. In addition to patching up his friends, he treated Tig's mangled hand as best he could. Morningstar had really done a number on the poor guy, and if there were no channelers at the Shrine of Delioch, he'd be lucky to ever hold a sword again. But those were the breaks. You get into bed with evil cultists, you don't complain when you get screwed.

The promise of magical healing was enough to convince the thug to remain docile as they casually exited the building. Dranko used the pommel of his dagger to snap Haske's key off in the lock. Tor, Grey Wolf, and Kibi escorted Tig away, while he and the others walked out of town and along the edge of the Mouth of Nahalm to the Black Circle's put-in point.

A simple block-and-tackle arrangement had been constructed behind (and in places bolted into) a cluster of large boulders massed near the lip of the desert's bowl, while the sands whispered twenty feet below. They waited three more hours in the shade of the boulders; it would be sheer idiocy to try walking through the desert in the baking afternoon heat.

Only when the sun was well on its way to the horizon did they get moving again. Each of them had brought one of the survival kits from the recruitment hall, and these included large paddle-like shoes that served the same function as snowshoes. Without them, anyone who tried to set foot in the Mouth of Nahalm would sink swiftly beneath its surface. One by one Dranko lowered the others on a little wooden platform attached to the ropes and pulleys, until only he remained on the higher ground. He locked the rope in place and came down hand over hand.

While the setting sun glared balefully across the desert, the four of them marched into the Mouth of Nahalm toward the single island in view. Even with the sand-shoes, Dranko's feet sank an inch or so with each step; Ernie said the desert's powdery grit reminded him of baker's sugar. The tiny breeze-blown particles soon found their way into Dranko's boots, his clothes, his mouth, his nose, his hair.

Luck was with them; the moon was full and the sky perfectly clear. By the crystal blue moonlight, they could just make out the rising hump of the wandering island. It wasn't going to set any records for speed; from this distance, it didn't seem to be moving at all.

The Mouth of Nahalm was flat; the sands didn't drift into hills and valleys the way Dranko had imagined. The breeze was constant but light, and once the air had cooled he found walking was less onerous than he had feared. But he would have given his left tusk to be able to sit down whenever he wanted. In the desert sitting took teamwork: three stood around the edges of a sheet and stretched it taut so the fourth could sit without sinking. Any other approach meant vanishing into the sand—which a stumbling Ernie had nearly proven early in the march. And resting one at a time was almost too tedious to be worth the delay.

So, with fewer rest breaks than any of them would have liked, they marched slowly across the desert. (Early on Aravia thought she had figured out a way to jog safely, and within five seconds the only visible parts of her were her sand-shoes and one flailing hand. Ernie, next in line, pulled her out, and she was coughing and sneezing out little clumps of sand for an hour.) But even at their cautious pace they arrived at the wandering island an hour before sunrise.

The island was an imperfect hemisphere of rough brown rock rising up out of the sand, its sloping sides curving upward and out of sight. Its size was difficult to judge, but having been walking towards it for hours, Dranko guessed it was at least a hundred yards across and thirty yards high at its rounded peak.

"Do we sleep on top?" asked Ernie. "What if I roll off while I'm sleeping? I'd be dead before I woke up! And how can we possibly get up there?"

Dranko stared up at the island's summit. "When we were on the road to Verdshane, I grumbled to Mrs. Horn that there were always tree roots under my bedroll. She told me to imagine the most uncomfortable night I'd ever spent and how pleased I would have been to have a nice bed of roots to sleep on. Perspective, she said. Always have perspective."

Ernie wiped sweat from his brow. "She was right. I guess this won't be so bad."

"And look on the bright side," said Dranko. "Everyone hopes they'll die peacefully in their sleep, right?"

"Dranko, that's—"

"Look in your travel kit," said Aravia. "That netting is a hammock, and the spikes must be for holding it to the side of the island."

Ernie let out a relieved breath. "Oh."

Each survival kit came with a rope-net hammock, a dozen metal spikes, a mallet, two spare water skins, a roll of beef jerky, and a thin but strong white sheet, in addition to the sand-shoes. Dranko, seeing that the rock surface of the island was rough and irregular, briefly toyed with the idea of climbing to the top and taking a look around the desert, but the thought of taking an inadvertent dive into a sandpit of death was enough to dissuade him.

Dranko settled down into his hammock. "Morningstar, you must love this," he called out. "Going to bed at sunrise, getting to sleep all day long, and then marching at night. What could be better, right?"

"Almost anything would be better," she said. "We're spiked into the side of a floating island in the middle of a desert, and I feel like I have sand in every place it's possible for there to *be* sand."

"Really? Even in your—"

"Yes, Dranko, even in my nose, which is what I'm sure you were about to ask. Now be quiet and go to sleep."

Dranko chuckled inwardly and thought some suppressed laughter came from Ernie's hammock as well.

Going to sleep was unlikely to be a problem, given how long and exhausting a day (and night) it had been. The four of them had trudged through the desert for nine hours. So severe was his exhaustion, Dranko knew that despite the sand that scratched his skin nearly everywhere, he'd be out the moment he let his eyelids droop.

But he had a small task to perform before calling it a night. Though it was tricky, wriggling in an undersized hammock staked to the curving vertical wall of the wandering island, he fished a small bottle, hardly more than a vial, from his pack. The note was already stuffed inside. *Dranko was here.* He had purchased a half-dozen such containers before they boarded the ship to Sand's Edge, thinking his travels for Abernathy might afford new opportunities, and had sealed one of his notes in each. He had already thrown one of his signatures overboard somewhere in the Middle Sea.

This was admittedly a long shot. He had no idea if objects ever "washed up" on whatever shorelines the Mouth of Nahalm might have elsewhere along its hundreds of miles of perimeter. Was it a steep-sided bowl all the way around? Or might some traveler far to the west stumble across his signed jetsam, taking the bottle and showing it, amazed, to his friends?

Who knew? He let the bottle fall, and it vanished beneath the sands like a stone dropped into a still pond. Satisfied, he turned his body to face into the rocky wall of the island (so the rising sun wouldn't shine into his eyes) and tried to sleep.

* * *

Breakfast was a challenge. They munched on whatever they could easily retrieve from their packs while staying in their hammocks, then carefully put on their sand shoes, lowered themselves down, and checked their gear a final time.

Trudging through the desert by the failing light of the setting sun, Dranko pondered what he would do when they reached the next island, the one where these Black Circle bastards were digging up Gods-only-knew-what.

"Here's the plan," he said. "In a few hours we're going to arrive at Black Circle central. When we're about half an hour away, you three will stay back while I go on ahead to spy things out."

"By yourself?" asked Ernie.

"Of course by myself. I'm sneaky and can climb, and while the rest of you were making honest livings before our current situation, I was learning how to not be noticed in places I wasn't supposed to be. There's a decent chance I can find out what's going on up there without being spotted. Meanwhile you just relax and enjoy the breathtakingly flat scenery and wait for me to come back. We've seen how it's safer to travel in a group, so we should plan on heading back together after I'm done scouting."

"Yes," said Aravia, "but if you get caught or something happens to you, how will we know you need rescuing?"

"You won't," said Dranko. "Before I go, we'll work out how long you give me before writing me off and heading back to Sand's Edge."

"We can't just leave you!" said Ernie.

"Sure you can. Look, they've probably got dozens of men up there, all specifically chosen for being able to smash things with their beefy arms. And they may have a few more spell-slingers like Haske, not to mention those blue-skinned guys."

"The Sharshun," said Aravia.

"Yeah, them. Point is, we're not an army. Going in force is a fool's game."

"I think it's a good plan," said Morningstar. "The rest of us would only increase the chances of one of us being observed."

The others nodded their agreement. Dranko, having expected his teammates to need a little more persuasion, wasn't sure if he should be flattered or…or whatever one feels when your friends think you're expendable. He went with the former.

"Great. Then let's keep moving before one of you figures out a reason to talk me out of it."

* * *

The moon had set by the time Dranko approached the second wandering island, which was good because if there was one singular feature the Mouth of Nahalm lacked, it was cover. Even better, he could see the island well before anyone on it could possibly see him because of the dozens of torches burning high on its surface. Unlike the rounded dome they had camped upon the previous day, this one was more like a mesa. But as his slow sand-shoe steps brought him closer, Dranko saw he'd have one unusual difficulty: the island was visibly wandering.

Aravia had speculated that the Mouth of Nahalm was a deep layer of sand floating on actual water far below and that the islands extended all the way down, such that whatever currents moved through the aquatic substrata swept the islands slowly along with them. Either that, she said, or the islands were powerfully magical. But now those currents, natural or otherwise, were carrying this particular island away to the north. He kept altering his course to keep the mesa in front of him, and prayed to Delioch that it wasn't out-pacing him. Dranko had great faith in his own sense of balance, but there was no one to rescue him right now should he make a false step. He quickened his strides as much as he dared, trying to calculate an angle of approach where he'd cut the island off before it could escape.

At last he drew close enough to make out detail. The nearest arc of the enormous hill was covered with complex scaffolding, a tangle of ropes, pulleys, platforms, hanging lanterns, and baskets the size of cows. That must be how supplies and workers were brought up to the top of the mesa, well over a hundred feet above the sand. Though it was hard to judge now that the moon was down, this second island was at least half again as big as the previous one.

With only a final twenty yards to go, it became apparent that the wandering island was *not* outrunning him, but he was not gaining on it very quickly. The first tough decision was upon him: boldly approach the "front door" and get a lift on one of the platforms, or scale a different side of the island to arrive unseen and unnoticed. He had talked a good game about sneaking around and staying out of sight, but he guessed that anything worth seeing would be heavily guarded and inaccessible.

No, he had another idea in mind, one that played just as much to his strengths. Even his scars could work to his advantage.

Dranko circled around to the left, allowing the island to slide past him. Only once he had hiked around to the far side from the scaffolding (and there didn't appear to be any other "official" ways up) did he spot the serious flaw in his plan: he couldn't climb while wearing his sand-shoes. If the island were stationary, he could unstrap them but still stand upon them, then reach down and grab them after he had secured purchase on the rock face. But the motion of his climbing wall made that nearly impossible; his shoes would get left behind the moment he stepped out of them.

"Screw it," he muttered. "Everyone up there must have sand-shoes. I'll just steal a new pair before I come back down."

Climbing the side of the wandering island was barely a challenge; the strange gritty rock was rough and pitted, offering plenty of finger and toe holds. The only tricky part was at the beginning; he had unlaced the shoes and had to wait for a likely looking entry point to slide past, then hope he didn't screw up and end up plunging into the dust. His experience with climbing onto moving walls was understandably limited. But having succeeded at that, he scrambled up the side of the island without any slips, all the while trying hard not to think about the consequences of losing his grip. The higher he went, the gentler was the angle of his ascent. After ten minutes of steady progress, the slant of the island's flank pitched forward abruptly, turning his climb into more of a steep walk for a good fifty feet before mostly flattening out entirely.

The rock plateau—at least the part he could see—was covered with canvas tents of varying size and dozens of torches on extremely tall poles. The tent city was awash in flickering shadows, but the ground sloped gently up towards the center of the island, so Dranko couldn't see much beyond twenty yards. While no people were in view, there was a distant clink of metal against stone in an uneven syncopated rhythm, as well as a cacophony of shouts, exhortations, songs, and general chatter coming from farther in, toward the middle of the island's flat head.

Before going any further he retraced his steps back to where the angle of his climb had changed. There he hammered one of his hammock stakes into the rock (timing his strikes with the rhythmic clinking to mask the sound), then uncoiled his longest length of rope and tied it fast, letting its slack length fall down and away into the darkness. He prayed to all the Gods that he wouldn't have to use it, but it never hurt to have an escape route ready.

A tent city lit only by torches was about as perfect a sneaking environment as

Dranko was ever likely to see. Unhurriedly he slipped from shadow to shadow, always moving toward the center of activity in the middle of the plateau. Within two or three minutes he started to see people, some trudging between tents hauling heavy sacks, some carrying large picks or oversized hammers. One rolled a sloshing barrel in a barely controlled stagger, weaving between the tents. There wasn't any standard uniform in play, which gave him one less thing to worry about.

On a hunch he took Haske's pendant from his pocket, draped its chain around his neck, and tucked the little black metal circle inside his shirt. There was always the possibility of using it as credentials. He still felt an ambiguous unease about the thing—maybe Delioch was expressing displeasure at him wearing the talisman of an evil cult?—but after his failure to channel at Verdshane, he and his god weren't really on speaking terms. Then, having made up his mind about how to approach this, he strode boldly out from the shadow of a tent and approached the nearest worker.

"You there," he barked. "Come here."

The man, a towering brute with a neck bigger around than Dranko's thigh, was walking slowly, clutching a bowl and spooning gruel into his mouth. He held up his spoon. "I'm on lunch break."

"Then I'll be quick," said Dranko. "The sooner you answer my questions, the sooner I'll give you leave to go."

"What's this about?"

"My people are paying for this dig," said Dranko. "I'm here to make sure our money is being well-spent. What's your name?"

The man glanced around in confusion. "Uh…I'm Romas. But shouldn't you be talking to Khorl? Or Lapis? I'm just here to—"

"I know why you're here, Romas," Dranko snapped. "And I'll be talking to the others soon enough. But first I want to hear how things are going from someone else, someone lower down the chain of command, in case your superiors try to blow smoke up my arse. Now, tell me, between Lapis and Khorl, who would you say has more authority here?"

"Lapis does. She's in charge of everything. Khorl's just my foreman."

Dranko whipped out the paper map he had filched from Haske's corpse and made a show of looking at it. "Interesting. And how is the dig progressing? What have you found so far?"

Romas scratched his head. "Are you sure you should be asking me? Khorl told me we shouldn't—"

"I don't care what Khorl told you. Frankly, we're not entirely certain Khorl is cut out for this operation, and that's part of why I'm here. Now answer my questions…or do I need to tell Lapis that you've been uncooperative?"

"No, I—"

"Good. Now I'll ask again. What have you unearthed so far?"

Romas squinted down at Dranko, and Dranko returned a look of impatient expectation.

"My team ain't found nothin,' but Khorl says we're still digging for…" He scrunched up his face in concentration. "For sec-on-dar-y re-lics."

Dranko picked up on the operative word at once. "Still? Have any of the other teams found something important?"

"Well, yeah. Day before yesterday I heard they finally found the big statue we've been looking for. Now they're trying to figure how to get it out."

"Excellent," said Dranko. *Looks like Abernathy was wrong about this operation being about finding an Eye of Moirel.* He tried not to let any emotions show besides a muted satisfaction. "Show me."

"Uh…what?"

"Show me where the statue is. I need to see it for myself."

"I don't think I can do that. We have to keep to our own site. Boss's orders."

"That's fine. I'll make a note to commend your discipline. Can you direct me to where they've found the statue?"

"Uh…no, sorry. I don't know which dig it got found at."

"How many dig sites are there?"

"I dunno. Maybe twenty?"

Dranko sighed. He could keep edging inward, shanghaiing random workers until he found one with satisfactory clearance, but each person he tried to bluff increased the chances that one of them would call him on it and raise a ruckus. And it was likely to wind up in the same place anyway, so he decided to raise the stakes sooner rather than later.

"Romas, thank you for your time. One last thing before you go back to your lunch—can you find Khorl and ask him to meet me here? Tell him one of the investors wishes to speak with him, but don't mention that I've already interviewed you."

"Uh…sure."

The man lumbered into the shadows and disappeared around the back of a large tent. If his luck continued to hold, this Khorl fellow would be exactly the sort of mark he was hoping to find—someone with enough authority to get him where he needed to go, but not enough to realize that Dranko was spewing one hundred percent horse manure.

He rehearsed what he'd say, the attitude he'd strike, the names he'd be willing to drop. As long as he maintained the illusion that he could call down Lapis's wrath, he could wangle his way just about anywhere. For an evil cult of forbidden knowledge, these Black Circle people weren't particularly…

"What is going on here? Who are you?"

Three figures stepped out of the darkness and into the pool of light thrown by the nearest torch. One was his good friend Romas. To the bulky gentleman's right was a middle-aged man with a black beard and a scowl—probably Khorl. And to Romas's left was a tall, hawk-faced woman wearing baggy gray trousers and an unbuttoned black jacket over a gray blouse. From her neck hung a black circle pendant, twin to the one Dranko had stripped from Haske and which was now tucked into his own shirt. A small silver ring pierced her right nostril.

She was completely bald, and the torchlight flickered over her indigo face.

"That's him, Lapis," said Romas. "He says he's the man paying for everything."

Oh, crap. Dranko had more than half a mind to run. He could lose himself in the shadows, dart around the tent city until he found a pair of sand-shoes, and bolt for his escape rope. Fighting was out of the question; the use of weapons against people was forbidden by the Church of Delioch.

But Lapis herself forestalled any panicked moves on his part by launching into a tirade of her own. "This is outrageous!" she practically shouted. "We could not have spelled this out any more clearly. Your only role in this is to supply the money for our operation. Under no circumstances were you and your scar-faced brethren to get involved, let alone come out here yourselves! I should consider this a breach of contract."

Dranko saw the opening and lunged for it, praying that his grasp of the situation was accurate.

"Mokad does not see it that way," he said, watching her face as carefully as possible for her reaction. And react she did; her face stiffened and her breath caught. "He is dissatisfied with your progress, and asked me personally to inspect the premises."

"Dissatisfied? It is not Mokad's place to express his opinion! He should be more than pleased with his end of the bargain."

Dranko desperately wanted to know what that was, but it was the sort of question that could disrupt this delicate dance.

"That's as may be," he said, making a show of choosing his words carefully—and that was not difficult, given how fast his mind was racing. He forced himself into what he called his "fancy pants mindset," where he dropped his usual crude speech patterns and tried to sound as snobbish and effete as possible. *Pretend you're Aravia.*

"But Mokad and his associates are beginning to run a risk of discovery, so large are the sums involved," he said. "He might be obliged to, how shall I say this, turn off the tap, should he not be satisfied. That would be a shame, don't you think? Though not as much as the particulars of all this becoming common knowledge."

Lapis's eyes grew wide. "Are you blackmailing me?"

"I am merely conveying Mokad's *opinions* on your agreement. But, no, I am not blackmailing you because we want nothing except for some visual confirmation of your progress."

He leaned forward just slightly and in a more conspiratorial tone added, "I understand that you have found what we've been looking for."

Lapis said nothing for a second, her face a twisted blue mask of rage. If she wielded any magic, like Haske, she might just blast him to smithereens and sort things out afterward.

"And who are you, exactly?" she asked, her voice calmer, though her eyes flashed fire.

"My name is Pietr," said Dranko smoothly. "I am the man Mokad turns to when he needs something done properly."

"And how is it that Mokad never mentioned you, Pietr?"

"He keeps me in his pocket," said Dranko. "It keeps me out of harm's way until my services are required. Mokad considers me an irreplaceable asset."

"I see."

Lapis mastered herself and looked directly into his eyes, which made him recall Morningstar's interrogation of Tig—specifically, the part where Tig claimed that Haske could read minds. If Lapis could do likewise, he was in deep, deep trouble. Her gaze was steady now, her eyes narrowing, and she swallowed as she stared. For the tiniest moment Dranko felt something like a feather brush over his mind, soft little tendrils seeking access to his thoughts. Realizing that the game was up, Dranko focused all his thoughts on giving her the finger.

Beneath his shirt, the black metal circle grew warm against his skin. Lapis stared at him a moment longer, then let out a frustrated sigh.

"Tell Mokad that I will report this to my own superiors. Tell him he can be replaced. Tell him…tell him the sage will not be happy with his behavior."

Dranko nodded, entirely uncertain how or why this was playing out the way it was. Who was the sage? But she was believing his lies, and he had one more card to play.

"Mokad had another message for you," he said, pitching his voice low. "But *only* for you." He glanced at Khorl. Lapis shooed the foreman a short distance away and stepped closer. Her lips were almost black, and her breath carried a whiff of something indescribably foul.

"Tell me," she hissed.

"Mokad said to tell you, he *may* have a lead on an Eye of Moirel. If he's pleased with the outcome of this operation, *and* his investigations prove out, he *may* be willing to share what he knows."

Lapis straightened suddenly, as though someone had goosed her with a pike. Her eyes and mouth both opened comically wide.

"Listen to me, Pietr," she whispered menacingly. "If Mokad knows about an Eye, he will tell us everything, even if all we dig up here is a rusted bucket. He is playing a game for which he is not ready. Tell him I'll be talking to him as soon as I'm off this Circle-forsaken rock, and if he holds anything back, I will tear off his face and see what kind of scar it leaves."

She took a step back and smiled at him. "Khorl, please escort Pietr here to site nine and show him what we've found. Then see him to the platforms and get him off my island."

"Yes, Lapis."

* * *

Dranko wasn't sure what he was looking at.

No, that wasn't entirely true. He knew it was a statue, half again as tall as he was. He knew that while it was humanoid, it wasn't human; no man or woman or goblin-touched had fangs that long, or claws that sharp, or eyes that far apart, or a chin that long and pointed, or wings neatly folded behind its back. And he knew that it was made of rock, some kind of striated marble as orange and luminous as a harvest moon.

But he also knew that this thing was more, and that it was worse, and that he wanted as little to do with it as possible. Its deep-socketed eyes, two blood-colored marbles with cat-slit pupils, were like windows into the Hells, and something looked out of them, eager, hungry. Though it was just an inert stone sculpture, inanimate, incapable of causing him harm unless it fell on him, Dranko had to fight down his flight reflex from the moment he laid his eyes upon it.

"As you can see," said Khorl, "the artifact is entirely unharmed, and the greatest care has been taken to preserve it in its original condition." The bearded man sounded bored.

Dranko wanted to make a dash for the elevator and scream for the pulley-men to haul him back to the surface. He forced himself to speak. "Impressive. But since you've found it, why is it still down here? What is the delay?"

"You may have noticed that the rock of the wandering islands is not of any kind found elsewhere on Charagan. The greatest care must be taken to avoid cave-ins and rock falls. We are doing everything possible to make sure that when the artifact is extracted, there are no accidents that might damage it."

"And how long do you anticipate that will take? We're paying for every hour you spend, after all."

"I think I heard another three days," said Khorl.

"Acceptable," said Dranko. He forced himself to look at the orange monster, and though the marble statue hadn't moved an inch, Dranko would have sworn on Delioch's name that it was not only looking back at him, but planning to murder him, to sink its claws into his guts and eat them, slowly.

Dranko edged away from it ever so slightly. He could hardly bear to look at the statue's cruel features, but he feared that if he took his eyes off it, it would choose that moment to strike. "Once you have it safely removed, where does it go next?"

He asked the question with all the nonchalance he could muster, but Khorl still gave him a narrow-eyed look. "I don't know," he said. "And I was under the impression that all of the post-operation details were none of the investors' business."

"That's fine," Dranko said quickly. "I only asked out of personal curiosity. Khorl, thank you for your time. I think we're done here." Maybe he could squeeze some more information out of the foreman, but he'd be damned if he was going to stay one more minute down here with that orange devil silently plotting his death.

As the pulley-men hoisted the platform that brought Dranko and Khorl to the surface, miners were still working all around them, widening the shaft that led down to where the monstrous statue had been unearthed. Khorl had already told him it had been found in its hollowed-out rectangular gap, buried deep in the gritty rock that composed the wandering island, with no sign of how it had been placed there.

The farther the elevator took him away from the statue, the more relieved and optimistic Dranko became. He stepped off the platform and onto the island's surface and breathed in the cool desert air, only now realizing how hot and dusty the chamber had been down below. He turned to Khorl, thinking that he might risk another few carefully couched questions before heading back to the desert to find his friends.

Two thoughts came to him immediately. One was that he had no good sense of how far the island had moved since his arrival, which would make locating the others a dicey proposition.

The second was that he needed to leave *right now*. Over Khorl's shoulder, some thirty feet away and standing in the direct light of a torch, Lapis was listening to an animated man who was vigorously gesticulating as he talked. He was tall, stoop-shouldered, and his frizzy red hair glowed in the firelight.

Lapis turned and looked directly at Dranko. She raised her hand to point at him just as he decided to run like the Hells, and even as he dashed away leaving the bewildered Khorl behind, the scaffolding holding up the array of pulleys and the elevator platform burst apart in a spray of beams and spiraling ropes.

Shouts and commotion erupted in his wake, but Dranko never looked back. He sprinted through the tent city, keeping his eyes open for any sign of where anyone kept their sand-shoes. He saw none. He should have asked Romas. More to the point, he should have had a less suicidal plan from the start.

It didn't take him long to leave the torchlight and scattered tents behind, and find himself on the steepening downward slope at the island's edge. Praying that his sense of direction wouldn't fail him in his panic, he turned to his left and started to run around the island's perimeter, barely able to see in the faint light from the nearest torches. Dranko knew there was a good chance he'd miss his rope in the darkness if he ran too fast, but as soon as Lapis got things organized, there would be search parties out in force.

After five minutes of a frantic jogging search, Dranko convinced himself that he'd gone too far and turned around. From the tent city came more cries and barked orders, and clusters of men with torches were floating free of the busy center of the island, heading toward the edges. How much time did he have before he was spotted?

Not long, it turned out. Less than a minute after he had changed directions, he found his rope because the metal spike was gleaming in the torchlight. Unfortunately, the torch in question was held by a large bearded man not more than thirty feet away.

"Found him!" bellowed the man! "He's here!"

New plan. He'd rappel down the side of the island, cling spider-like to the wall lower down, scuttle sideways along it, climb back up at a different point along the island's circumference, sneak into the tent city again, find sand shoes, then climb down again, all before the sun came up.

It was a stupid plan. Its chance of success was essentially zero, but there was no time to devise another.

Dranko needed to rappel downward as fast as possible, in case the man who found him pulled up his stake. He gave himself as much of a running start as he could, sprinted down the steep slope letting gravity assist as much as possible, and launched himself out into the air. The rope slid through his fingers, burning away the skin of his palms until he grabbed hold. As soon as he secured his grip, he swung back toward the island and slammed into it about fifty feet down, bruising his right shoulder, his right knee…Hells, every bone and muscle on the whole right side of his body. He'd probably broken something, but he could figure out what later.

He rappelled downward, wincing in pain, kicking off the island wall with his left foot, feeling his right shoulder burn like it was on fire.

He was still thirty feet above the desert floor when the spike gave way, either loosened too much by his initial jump or pulled out by someone up top. It hardly mattered. His brain suggested that he try to land spread-eagled, but long before his battered body could act on the idea he fell in feet first.

The sand offered little resistance; the Mouth of Nahalm swallowed him whole.

CHAPTER SIXTEEN

Morningstar cast her gaze westward into the darkness. The island was a purple-gray hill outlined against the night's starry black. Dim orange light flickered on its top, which made sense; if the Black Circle cultists were working on the mesa, they'd have torches or bonfires lit. Assuming the island was the same size as the one upon which they had camped, it should be about a half-hour's trudge away.

They had agreed to give Dranko three hours, but Ernie grew fidgety after twenty minutes.

"Maybe we should follow him," he said. "Make sure he gets there okay."

Morningstar shook her head. "We should stick to the plan. If we get too close, it's more likely we'll be noticed."

They had spread out one of their sheets over the sand, and Aravia was taking the first turn lying down. The wind had calmed, stilling the restless powdery sand, and the only sound was a tiny rhythmic clinking coming faintly across the desert.

"But we could be closer than this," said Ernie. "If it's dark out here and light up there, they wouldn't see us unless we were practically on top of them, right?"

"Maybe," Morningstar conceded. "But what does it matter? If he gets caught, are you proposing we mount a rescue? How would we even get up there? Dranko says he can climb, but I know I can't. We'd be throwing our lives away after his."

Throwing good lives after bad.

Not that she specifically wished death upon Dranko; he was vulgar and lacked redeeming qualities, but he was part of the team, and she'd look out for him if it came to it. Still, there were limits to the risks she'd take to save his life.

"Aravia," asked Ernie, "do you have any spells that would help?"

The wizardess thought for a moment. "I could try arcing one of you high enough to crest the angle of the island wall, but I'd have to improvise. I'd give it about a one in ten chance of working, and if it missed, you'd bounce off and fall back into the…"

"So, no," said Morningstar. "Ernie, I understand you're worried, but Dranko will either get caught or he won't. There's no wind tonight, so he can follow his footprints back here easily enough. Let's give him time to work, and minimize the risk."

"I guess." Ernie sounded unconvinced.

Morningstar tried to imagine what Dranko would do when he reached the island. Would there be places for him to hide? If the enemy had sentries posted around the perimeter, he'd be spotted almost immediately. And if he were captured, would he give them up? They were sitting ducks out here, should any sort of armed expedition be launched from the island.

She didn't trust him. Dranko was a confessed criminal and had lied about being a Deliochan channeler. (If not for his scars and his admittedly expert field-medic skills, she wouldn't believe he was a disciple of Delioch at all.) But he *was* risking his life already, and, begrudgingly, she decided he wouldn't betray them.

She stared out at the distant island with its crown of lights. Dranko would be arriving there any minute.

"I hope he's okay," whispered Ernie.

"He can take care of himself," said Morningstar. "Stop worrying and—"

She blinked and refocused her eyes. Was the desert air playing tricks?

Oh no.

The island was moving.

"We have to go," she said sharply. "Now!"

"Is Dranko coming back already?" asked Ernie.

"It's the opposite. He's getting farther away. The wandering island is wandering away from us." She kept talking as she and Ernie hoisted Aravia to her feet. "If it moves far enough, Dranko won't be able to find his way back here. We need to follow it, so that when Dranko gets off the island I can see him. We'll follow *our* tracks back to Sand's Edge. Come on."

They marched as quickly as they could. The only sounds were the rasps of their paddle-shaped sand shoes sliding across the sand, and their soft grunts of exertion. Morningstar's legs were already sore. As they moved, she became more and more convinced that Dranko was going to fail. If ever there lived a man whose bravado outdistanced his abilities, it was him. And sneaking around one's home city was one thing, but infiltrating an enemy camp was something else entirely. He had probably already been captured.

"Are we catching up?" gasped Ernie.

Morningstar had to stop walking to be certain. "Yes. It's not moving very fast, but it's still angling away from us. No more stops until we get there."

There was nothing else to do but to keep slogging. They plotted an indirect course, which was made easier when the island veered a bit *toward* them and picked up speed.

"The optimal plan is not to get too close *too* fast," Aravia explained. "We don't want the island to go shooting past an hour before Dranko decides to leave. The goal is to approach at an angle, keep it within your sight for as long as possible."

Now they were close enough to see individual torch fires, though soon those would be eclipsed by the island's steeply dropping sides. Morningstar was relieved to see that the firelight didn't wash onto the desert floor around it, so they would be effectively invisible until they were close. An irregular pattern of staccato clinks, metal on stone, came from high up.

The island continued to accelerate, probably caught in a fast-moving current far beneath the sands. It was going to pass them on a diagonal in only a couple of minutes, so they adjusted their route yet again. Now they were fleeing from it, so that it would glide by more slowly.

A sudden burst of shouts came from the island-top.

"They've seen us!" hissed Ernie.

It sounded like quite a commotion, dozens of men yelling to one another. What could they do? If the Black Circle cultists had noticed their arrival, the three of them might have even put Dranko's life in jeopardy, stirring up a hornet's nest while he was trying to hide somewhere.

The island was now quickly sliding past them, not more than fifty feet distant. A voice from above shouted, "Spread out and find him!" So was it Dranko who had the operation in an uproar? Or had the cultists seen Morningstar and her friends, which had prompted Dranko to do something rash? Either way, what could they do to help him?

She gauged the island's speed at maybe thirty feet each second; soon it would be past them, taking Dranko with it.

"Found him!" someone roared. "He's here!" The shout came from the rear of the island, as figured by its direction. She looked up, and even as the moving mountain swept past her, a person rappelled wildly out over its edge on a rope, then swung down and crashed hard into the rock wall. He squirmed, rotated his body, and kicked off with his left foot, sliding down another dozen feet before tightening his grip and bouncing again into the island's side.

Morningstar squinted. "He's there! And he's not wearing his sand-shoes. I don't know what he thinks he's—"

The rope gave way, and Dranko fell. In the second before he reached the desert floor he twined the rope around his left arm, and then he vanished into the sand. The rope followed him down like a snake escaping into its hole, but a good length of it remained resting on the surface.

"Goddess! Come on, quickly!"

The three of them hurried over while the island retreated. For the moment at least, none of the cultists were inclined to follow Dranko over the edge. They probably assumed he was a dead man.

Not if Morningstar could help it. With Aravia and Ernie following, she went for where the rope lay twitching. That was good; it meant Dranko was still alive. It took the three of them a minute to work out how they could all haul on the rope at once; it involved laying out one of the sheets for them to stand upon. This was because they couldn't apply the necessary leverage to extract Dranko from the desert without toppling over themselves. Slowly, painstakingly, they pulled on the rope, praying that Dranko wouldn't release his grip. Ernie was the strongest; without him, she and Aravia would never have managed it. But after another minute of straining and heaving at the rope, Dranko's arm surfaced, followed soon by his shoulder and his head. His grip was loose; Dranko's instinct to wrap the rope around his arm was what saved him. They grabbed his unconscious body and dragged it onto the sheet.

"Is he alive?" asked Ernie anxiously. "What do we do?"

Morningstar crouched next to Dranko, wondering the same. She pried his mouth open and scooped damp sand from it with her hand, and after two handfuls an instinctive cough racked his chest. A plume of dust escaped his lungs.

"Alive," said Aravia. "Good."

But he didn't regain consciousness. Aravia suggested turning him on his side and pounding his back, to get as much sand out of him as possible, but when Dranko's coughs became less and less productive, they stopped thumping him.

"We need to drag him," Morningstar said. "We need to get back to the first island before the sun comes up, and there's no way to know how long he'll be out. Come on. We'll make the sheet into a triangle. Ernie, you and I will pull on the front corners for a start."

Ernie looked skeptical. "I don't know if we'll—"

"Ernie! We don't have a choice. I don't like it either, but this is what the Goddess wills. Grab a corner and let's move. We need to hurry."

And so the three of them began a long, painful trudge eastward, hauling Dranko's flour-sack body across the night-dark sand.

* * *

Goddess, whatever were my sins, surely you have burned them away.

It was approaching noon, and only now was the city of Sand's Edge in sight, a blurry mirage swimming in the haze, two hours away at least. A significant part of her mind was convinced she had died and gone to the Hells, but still she shuffled her feet. One, then the other, then the other, then the other. Beside her Ernie trudged in a daze, the corner of Dranko's sheet bunched in his sweating hands and slung over his shoulder. Behind, Aravia was wheezing or coughing with each step. But Morningstar had suffered the most. The sun had scorched her like an avenging spirit of fire, punishing her for a lifetime spent hiding from it.

Their water had run out hours ago, despite their miserly rationing. It had been right around the time they realized the first island had wandered far enough out of their path that they'd be better off marching through the morning, sunlight be damned.

But it's I who have been damned.

Everything hurt. Her skin was a mottled canvas of leathery white patches and angry red welts. Her muscles screamed obscenities. Her thighs cramped. Sweat soaked her clothes. She glanced back at Dranko, willing him to wake up and take a turn. He lacked sand shoes, but she'd give him hers and let him drag her sweat-damp body the rest of the way. But he was still out, and so they had to endure.

My soul is on fire, you wretched goblin pickpocket. You'd better be alive when we get to

Sand's Edge. If you die, I will hunt you through the afterlife.

How many hours had they walked since pulling Dranko out of the sand? Ten? Twelve? It felt like a month, counted out in seconds of pain and thirst.

For another hour the sand whispered its mockery while the sun bludgeoned them, but she would not let them defeat her. She would not fall, not let the desert have her withered, dehydrated body. Ernie had fallen twice, but both times he had stumbled backward onto the sheet and so had survived. Aravia walked with her face slack, eyes distant, her mind probably far away from this open-air oven. The details of the city became sharper. It was a wonder that her eyes still worked; they were hot marbles in her skull, dry and brittle.

Some people were standing on the lip of the desert, waving their arms. She hoped it was Grey Wolf and the others, but if it were a contingent of Black Circle cultists waiting for them, what was there to be done?

One step, and then another, and then another. And then…the scaffolding, and arms under her shoulders, and ropes, and she was lifted, and a water skin was put to her lips. She would have cried, but her tears had long since dried up and blown away.

* * *

She didn't remember much after that. There was Grey Wolf, propping her up. There was Kibi with Dranko slung over his shoulder, and Tor helping Ernie and Aravia. There was a gangplank, and a ship, and a ladder, and the blessed cool of a dark hold.

Thank the Goddess for the holds of ships.

She slept for a time but was woken by the pain; her skin felt like burnt paper. She sat up and found herself seated upon a sack of grain. The ship rocked gently, her companions resting quietly nearby. Aravia was reading a book; Grey Wolf was sharpening his sword with a strop.

Five feet away, lying on a jury-rigged cot of bedrolls and packing crates, was Dranko, asleep. His chest rose and fell.

"You're awake!" Ernie's skin was an angry color, but there was relief in his smile.

She nodded but couldn't stop staring at Dranko. "We're going back to Tal Hae?"

"That's right," said Grey Wolf. "Cost us the last of our money. We're lucky we had enough after paying the healers to patch up Tor and fix Tig's hand."

Grey Wolf's various wounds were still wrapped in bloody bandages. *He* hadn't been the beneficiary of any channeling. Morningstar would have just as happily lopped Tig's head off once he had served his purpose, but the Goddess only knew what Ernie would have said to that.

"What about *him?*" she asked.

"Not sure," said Grey Wolf. "Been in and out of sleep. Hasn't said anything."

For two hours she stared at Dranko, trying to reach a state of inner peace. It was difficult with her skin on fire. It hurt where her clothing brushed it. It hurt when she moved. It hurt just from sitting there watching the goblin snore. She couldn't decide if her pain and anger were fairly directed at him, and she didn't much care.

Finally Dranko coughed and his eyes opened. He tried sitting up, failed twice, and gave up. "I always thought the afterlife would smell less like a bait-house," he croaked from his back.

"Welcome back to the land of the living," said Grey Wolf. He paused while Dranko coughed some more.

"We're on a ship," Dranko said when he had recovered.

"Observant as ever," said Grey Wolf.

"Last I remember, I was suffocating to death. How is it that I'm still alive?"

"Morningstar is how," said Grey Wolf, looking at her with a grim smile. "You should start thinking now about how you're going to thank her. She saved your life."

Dranko attempted again to sit, and this time he succeeded, though it precipitated another long hacking fit. She looked at him, at his hideous scarred face, and said nothing.

There aren't enough thanks in the world.

Dranko looked back at her. "She did, huh?"

Morningstar shrugged, and her shoulders burned. Goddess, but it hurt even to shrug.

"I remember falling into the desert. How could you possibly have found me, let alone dug me up? The moon had set, and the sky was clouding up, so there wasn't even that much star-shine."

Morningstar sighed. "I see in the dark, remember?"

"The rest of us couldn't see anything," said Ernie. "But Morningstar saw your flying leap, and your rope come loose, and your fall into the sand."

"How did you get me out?" asked Dranko. "I must have fallen in twenty feet at least."

"More like ten," said Morningstar. "But you helped save yourself, wrapping your rope around your arm like that. I saw the rope sticking out of the sand, and we used it to pull you out."

"I did? I don't remember doing that, but it's the sort of clever thing I'd have thought of."

"The hardest part was getting you back to Sand's Edge," said Ernie. "You were out cold the entire time, and barely breathing. We rigged up a litter using the sheet from Morningstar's kit, and the three of us each took a corner and hauled you along the surface of the desert."

Aravia looked up from her book. "And that wasn't the worst part. The first island had drifted too far away from the straightest-line path back to Sand's Edge. We ended up dragging you for fourteen hours, and more than half of that was after sunrise."

Could Dranko understand what that desert march had done to her? The Mouth of Nahalm had breathed its relentless light and heat over her, the sun searing its mark on her like a flaming brand. What Ellish part of her could have survived? Was the Goddess punishing her, just as She had punished her with her hair and her name and her skin? Dranko had made the argument that Ell must have a higher purpose in store for her, but what if this constant punishment *was* the purpose?

She stared into Dranko's eyes, showing him her pain, and he closed his own.

"Look," he said, "I'm beyond grateful that you came to rescue me. And I don't doubt that hauling me across the desert was about as fun as sticking your head in a forge. There were about three different times out there I thought I was a dead man, but here I am, thanks to you, with nothing more than sand in my lungs."

Morningstar listened as Dranko told his tale, the goblin pausing every minute or two to cough and gulp down more water. When the story reached the moment where Dranko had been lowered into the main vault, he stopped. Grey Wolf leaned in, impatient. "What? What did you see?"

"I don't know exactly. It was a statue. A big statue of a…I don't know, a demon, maybe? About ten feet tall, wings, claws, fangs, the works. All made out of red-orange marble. But it was more than that. It was…horrible. The whole time I was in there with it, I got the sense that it was about to come to life and tear me apart. A literal sense. This was *real*. That statue is magical, a bad, bad thing, and now bad people have it. We have to tell Abernathy."

Abernathy. Oh, how Morningstar hated him right now. If not for the wizard's meddling, she'd have walked out on this collection of misfits and not looked back. Instead, she had been backed into this accursed sunlit corner. But the practical bit of her mind still had some say, and she agreed that Abernathy might know what the statue was and what it portended.

"Dranko, let me see if I understand you." Grey Wolf's voice brimmed with contempt. "You were down in the vault with this…thing. And you thought it was dangerous. And you were about to flee for your life. Couldn't you have tried to smash it or something?"

Dranko coughed out a harsh laugh. "I forgot to borrow Kibi's hammer and chisel. And no, I couldn't have. I could barely make myself look at it. If I had dared lift a finger against it, it would have…would have…I don't know. Something awful."

"It was a statue," said Grey Wolf. "Did it show any *actual* signs of coming to life, or were you just afraid that it would? Dammit, Dranko, we'll have put two weeks into this trip, not to mention all the blood and the sweat and having to sleep in a Gods-damned ship's hold, and all we've gotten from it is that you discovered they were hauling out a statue from a floating rock?"

Dranko opened his mouth to protest, but Grey Wolf wasn't finished.

"You are so Gods-damned worthless!" he raged. "You're a coward, a drunkard, and the one time we really needed you, you sat there like a drooling idiot while Mrs. Horn bled to death. At least she found herbs to help Morningstar while you were laughing off her pain and telling us you were saving your miraculous channeling for something more serious. Remember that, goblin? It should have been you with your Gods-damned neck bitten."

As much as Morningstar hated Dranko right now, she was shocked at Grey Wolf's venom. Dranko stared back at him. "Are you done?" he asked.

"I don't know. Have you screwed anything else up that you haven't told us about?"

"Grey Wolf, go easy on him, will you?" said Ernie, his voice crackling like he was about to cry. "I…I believe him about the statue. It was certainly the whole point of these cultists being out there in the first place! It could be valuable just to know about it."

Ernie would bend over backward to see the best in just about anyone, which was a charming but not particularly useful trait.

"What about Eyes of Moirel?" Morningstar asked. "Abernathy thought they might have found one. Did you see anything that looked like a magical gemstone?"

"No, just the statue. I might have snooped around some more, but I kind of ran out of time." Dranko smiled bitterly at Grey Wolf. "My good friend Mr. Wolf here can think what he wants, but I wasn't 'about to flee.' While I was down in the vault, that fourth guy you saw back at Sand's Edge showed up. He must have found the carnage we left in the recruitment office and force-marched himself out to the island to warn Lapis. Who's a wizard, by the way. She nearly blasted my head off with some kind of…whatever it is that Aravia does. Arcing."

"I'm glad you're alive," said Ernie.

"Me too," said Dranko.

"Still wasn't worth it," said Grey Wolf. "You saw what they were up to, but now they know someone's on to them."

"Oh, come on, Grey Wolf." Dranko had finally cleared his lungs out. "They already knew. It was Praska who outed them. If anything, these Black Circle people should be pissed off at Mokad now. Especially after I told Lapis that Mokad was holding out on her about an Eye of Moirel."

Dranko lay back down and closed his eyes.

* * *

That night, asleep in a makeshift hammock that rocked to the ocean's sway, Morningstar dreamed a Seer-dream that made no sense.

She floats high above the ground. Below her are seven giants arrayed in a circle, their arms locked together. They are massive, steady creatures, disinclined to move. But they are weeping, their tears falling silently to the dust.

Morningstar descends to see more clearly. The giants mourn for seven dead mice, their bodies lying broken and still in the center of their circle. She senses the giants' immeasurable sadness as they stand their silent vigil.

All at once a brilliant light shines from the giants' eyes, and Morningstar does not flinch. The seven mice spring to life and run in a little circle of their own, a circle within a circle. The giants rejoice, but their eyes flash again and the mice drop dead, dead a second time. Their bodies become dust. The giants close their eyes and turn to stone, their watch ended at last.

CHAPTER SEVENTEEN

E rnie found a large wooden crate waiting for him at the Greenhouse.

"I bet it's from my parents. They promised me care packages once I got settled in."

Not that he was feeling very settled. He had been nervous enough on that first day, when Abernathy had summoned him. But the things that had happened since…Pikon's pancakes, but it had all been so horrible. Poor Mrs. Horn, dying in a pool of blood, and all the dead bodies in Verdshane. The terrifying fight against the cultists in Sand's Edge. And then, almost as awful as Mrs. Horn's death, there was Morningstar's decision to mutilate a prisoner to get information. He had been standing *right there!* If he closed his eyes, he could hear the sound of Tig's finger bones breaking.

And Morningstar hadn't shown any remorse, even afterward! She considered it just part of the business of saving the world, and maybe she was right, but it made Ernie squirm to think about. They were the Heroes, and torture was the practice of Villains. But Grey Wolf and Dranko, they didn't have any problem with it, and neither did Tor and Aravia, not really. Sure, it made them uncomfortable, but they were happy to let Morningstar be the heavy. Among his companions, only Kibi properly shared his distress. Not that the stonecutter had made a big deal out of it. Kibi was quiet and tended to keep his opinions to himself. But Ernie had seen the shock in his eyes, the color draining from his face, when Morningstar had brought down her mace.

Maybe something from Mom would cheer him up. He dragged his package into the living room and levered off the lid with Pyknite. The others were sitting and relaxing, most of them with wine glasses, while Eddings fussed and made sure everyone was comfortable. Tor was stretched out on a couch, a thick white bandage still wrapped around his thigh and over his wounded hip. Dranko said he was a fast healer. Aravia had gone to the secret room straight away, but the crystal ball was answered by Mister Golem, so now there was nothing to do but wait for Abernathy to get back to them.

Grey Wolf chuckled. "Mommy send you a blanket?"

Ernie reddened and pretended not to have heard. He found a piece of paper resting atop the straw padding that protected the crate's contents.

"Let me guess," said Dranko. "You're secretly a priest, and someone from your church has ominous news. That seems to be the pattern around here."

Ernie scanned the letter. "No, I was right, it's from Mom and Dad. They sent me some wool socks, and an extra jacket, and Mom copied some recipes down for me." (There was also a thick woolen blanket along with his favorite stuffed bear, Bumbly, but he wasn't about to admit to those in front of Grey Wolf.) "But she said they got the golden ring off that statue of me in Murgy's basement, and it's in here somewhere."

"Your what?" asked Dranko.

"Didn't I tell you about that?"

"You told us there was a mysterious statue of you in a neighbor's cellar," said Dranko. "But what's this about gold?"

"Oh. There was a gold ring around one of my fingers," said Ernie. "I mean, the statue's finger. Murgy said he'd have it sent to me once they figured out how to get it off without damaging the statue. I guess they did."

He rummaged around near the bottom of the crate and found what he was looking for in the folds of the blanket. It was a golden band, a fat gold ring sized for a giant, but to Ernie it seemed perfectly suited as a bracelet. There were tiny runes etched into its polished surface. He held it up.

"Hey, hey!" said Dranko. "Looks like Ernie's acquired us some additional capital. Good thing; we're out of cash."

"Where did you get that?" Kibi leapt from his chair, spilling his wine, and stared at the golden circlet with an expression of utter bewilderment. "How…how in the Gods' good names…"

It was shocking to see Kibi so distraught. He had always seemed so calm, so soft-spoken. Had he raised his voice even once since they met? This was by far the most emotional Ernie had seen him; his reaction to the gold bracelet was shock bordering on panic.

Ernie lifted the piece of jewelry and held it out to Kibi with a puzzled expression. "Do you know what this is?"

"'Course I do!" Kibi practically shouted. "I seen that piece a' gold every day a' my life! It belongs to my mother, and it's got to stay with her! How did it come to be here?"

That made no sense. "It can't be," Ernie said.

Kibi put out his hand, and Ernie handed over the bracelet. "It is!" Kibi cried, running one hand agitatedly through his hair. "Same size, same crazy runes, and not a scratch on it. I don't know what it was doin' in your hometown, Ernie, but I got to get this here back to my ma."

Ernie took the bracelet back. "Kibi, it can't be the same one. This wasn't just 'in my hometown.' It was on a statue that must have been buried underground for hundreds of years."

"There must be two of them." Aravia stood and walked over to join Ernie and Kibi. "Either identical or close enough that you couldn't tell them apart. What do the runes say?"

"How should I know?" said Ernie. "They aren't normal letters."

Aravia leaned in and scrutinized the thing while Ernie held it out. "I don't recognize them either," she admitted.

Kibi was so distraught he tugged on his beard, but Aravia must be right about there being duplicates. "If this *did* belong to your mother, why is it so important that she get it back?"

"Well, that's a strange thing now," said Kibi. The stonecutter looked almost imploringly at Aravia, surely hoping the wizardess was correct, but his voice remained agitated. "The way my father, Bim, always tells it, is that he was up in the high hills, clearin' the trail between Eggoggin and Marhold. There'd just been an avalanche, see, and trade was fairly well stymied. Anyway, my father was leverin' rocks and trees off the trail when he looks down into this valley, and there was a young woman in a green dress, just sittin' on top of a pile a' debris, calm as anything, and beautiful as a polished emerald. Dad figured she must a' fallen down there from the trail, so he clambered down to help her out. He was always a gallant one for the ladies, to hear him tell it.

"The lass was fine, no injuries, not even dust on her dress. But she couldn't remember nothin' about how she got there, or who her family was, or anything about anything. Just her name—Gela. And she had a golden bracelet on her wrist. Said she didn't know what it was, but that is was vital that she never take it off. Said she'd die if she weren't wearin' it, though she couldn't say what made her think it.

"Dad figured she got knocked on the head, probably out walkin' during the avalanche. He took her back to Eggoggin and took care of her, waitin' for her memories to come back. But they never did, and no one ever came along who knew who she was. Somethin' had erased all her memories of her past, but it never seemed to bother her none. Eventually she and Dad got married, and she became Gela dun Bim, and they had a son, who you all are lookin' at."

He pointed at the golden bracelet in Ernie's hand. "And every day a' my life, that there bangle has been around my ma's wrist. Or maybe, like Aravia says, and what I hope more than hope, one that only looks just like it."

"What were the chances of that?" Tor exclaimed. "Abernathy's spell picks a bunch of random people, and two of you have the same circlet? It seems impossible!"

"No," said Aravia. "I think it was quite likely. You're just confusing causality. Abernathy's spell picked Ernie and Kibi *because* of that connection. That piece of jewelry must have some great significance. We just don't know what it is yet."

Ernie turned to Eddings. "Mr. Eddings, can you send a letter to Kibi's parents, asking if they still have his mom's gold circlet?"

"If I know the address, then certainly, Master Roundhill."

Well, wasn't that interesting! The arrival of the statue's ring had prompted Kibi to reveal more about himself in two minutes than he had in three weeks. Ernie felt a sudden camaraderie now with the bearded gentleman, a shared mystery about their pasts. Someone had placed the gold band on the statue; was it the same person who had given Kibi's mom its twin? And Abernathy may not know anything about why a stone likeness of Ernie was buried beneath his hometown, but magic, as he was learning, worked in mysterious ways. Now at least he had a possible explanation for why he had been chosen, an old secret, an enigmatic artifact, and a connection to a stonecutter's family.

The shrieking warble of the crystal ball sounded from upstairs.

"Gods," said Dranko. "You'd think the most powerful wizard in the world could find a more pleasant sound for that."

"Why would he want to?" asked Aravia, as the whole group sprang to their feet and headed for the stairs. "Look at the hurry we're in to make it stop."

Dranko did most of the talking for the first few minutes, taking Abernathy through his discoveries atop the island that drifted through the Mouth of Nahalm. Abernathy's pale and anxious face grew downright ashen as Dranko described the disturbing statue being unearthed by the Black Circle. Ernie gulped, not enjoying the thought of anything that would worry an archmage like that.

"Do you know what the statue was?" he asked when Dranko was done.

"And who is the sage?" added Dranko. "Lapis sure made it sound like that's the person in charge."

Abernathy's face tightened, as though he was remembering something unpleasant. "Remember, I've not been keeping up on recent events. I don't know who the sage is. But the statue sounds like a Blood Gargoyle. We thought they had all been destroyed but…it's…well, it's beyond your ability to handle. Also I doubt it's meant for you, so don't worry any more about it."

Abernathy gave what appeared to be a reassuring smile, but Ernie knew better. Ernie knew that expression because of how often he made it himself. Abernathy was putting on a brave face, but inside he was terrified. Which in turn made *him* terrified.

"Listen carefully," said the old wizard. "Thanks to Dranko's gambit with Lapis, not only can I make some preparations regarding the gargoyle, but we also know the Sharshun are still keenly interested in the Eyes of Moirel. My next task for you is to go to the Seven Mirrors in time for Flashing Day, which is just over a week away. It's a near certainty the Sharshun will try something, especially if they think Mokad has an Eye. Be ready for anything."

Abernathy paused, though he obviously had more to say. His lips moved as if he was rehearsing a speech, and he took a deep breath. "At our last meeting I mentioned something called the Crosser's Maze, which I and some of my associates feel is our best bet to make Naradawk's prison a permanent one. What I did not tell you is that the primary impediment to retrieving it is that it lies on a continent called Kivia, on the far side of the accurately named Uncrossable Sea."

"I can see how that would be a problem," said Dranko.

"But there *is* a way across it, or at least there was, long ago," said Abernathy. "During Naloric's long reign of terror he acquired allies from Kivia, armies of fire-worshippers, and these did not cross the sea. Rather, their forces had arrived through a large enchanted archway hidden in the forest near the very tip of the Balani Peninsula. We surmise that the archway has a twin in Kivia, and that the Kivians had a way of activating them such that they connected the two kingdoms. But by the time we found the arch on our side, it was inert, no more than a free-standing sculpture in a large trampled-down clearing.

"The Kivian Arch was the subject of much study and scrutiny in the following years, but our finest wizards and sages could not figure out how to turn it back on. After the war King Garos had a significant military detachment stationed nearby, should the Kivians attempt a second invasion, but King Argis after him disbanded that force. Claimed it was an unnecessary drain on the treasury.

"Over the years, one of my fellow archmagi, Ozella, has had agents of her own down there on the peninsula, just to keep an eye on the Kivian Arch. The most recent of these is a fellow named Levec who's been living in the town closest to the arch, a peaceful little hamlet called Seablade Point. Levec sent Ozella brief updates like clockwork, once every month for more than a hundred months in a row—until two months ago."

Ernie's voice was almost a whisper. "What do you think happened to him?"

"I don't know," said Abernathy. "But it's possible that there's been some development involving the Kivian Arch itself, and that Levec is either still investigating it or has died as a result of it. Given the confluence of current events, with the Black Circle and the Sharshun emerging just as the portal in Verdshane has started to crack, it's possible that the forces of evil, such as they are, have also opened the Kivian Arch or are in the process of opening it. If there's someone masterminding all these efforts, perhaps they are trying to coordinate Naradawk's arrival with military forces from Kivia."

Ernie was utterly bewildered by all of this, not to mention terrified. What in all the Gods' names was he doing smack in the middle of such tumultuous, world-threatening circumstances? The weight of so much responsibility was going to crush him.

"After you have gone to the Seven Mirrors," said Abernathy, "it is possible that I will be...unavailable to debrief you. In that eventuality, I want you to go next to Seablade Point and determine what, if anything, is happening concerning the Kivian Arch. If our enemies are activating it, we may be able to use that to our advantage. Oh, and be discreet. Don't mention the Spire, or the involvement of archmagi, unless absolutely necessary."

"For how long will you be unavailable?" asked Aravia. "And I'm still waiting on those spellbooks, when you get the chance."

"I don't know how long," Abernathy sighed. "I have now shared with you most of the known details about the perils the Kingdom of Charagan faces. You may need to show some additional initiative in the coming days or weeks, in case I find myself preoccupied."

Ernie could read between the lines and found the idea unsettling. "Uh, sir? We're not really world-saving heroes." He cast an apologetic look at Tor, who had opened his mouth to protest. "Don't you have anyone better?"

"I'm afraid not. During the years of peace that followed Naloric's death, the Spire faded away to almost nothing. Once we counted the King of Charagan among our number, not to mention the dukes, several generals, priests from most of the Travelers and Pikon, and assorted other heroes of the realm. But you can keep a coalition together only for so many decades, during which meeting after meeting consists of aging wizards telling a room full of important people that there's nothing new to talk about. Our gatherings became fewer, our membership dwindled.

"When King Garos died, his son King Argis decided that the Spire was no longer worth the trouble and expense. Oh, he understood, I think, the importance of what we wizards were doing, keeping Naradawk locked away in his prison world. But the Spire itself...King Argis felt it was a threat to his sovereignty, an organization that could act on its own and make decisions for the good of the kingdom even if the king personally disagreed with those decisions. So he ordered the archmagi to continue their work and disbanded the Spire.

"Now it's just the five of us, and we spend all our time in our towers, keeping Naradawk out. Levec, our one outside agent other than yourselves, has stopped sending reports. I don't mean to make you feel pressured, but right now the world is in danger and you seven represent our best opportunity to measure that danger, and possibly stop it."

Ernie felt faint. "But—"

"With all due respect, your wizardliness," Dranko interrupted, "that still doesn't make sense. Spire or no Spire, we're just...just some people. Tor's a great fighter, sure, but there must be some Stormknights of Werthis who are better. And Aravia's just an apprentice; that Serpicore guy she keeps talking about must be a more powerful wizard. And Delioch knows, you could have put on a blindfold and picked a better channeler than me. If Charagan is about to go to the Hells in a kingdom-sized hand-basket, why are you giving all the responsibility for it to a bunch of nobodies?"

"It's a fair question," said Abernathy. "My spell picked you, for reasons—"

"Yes, yes, you told us already," interrupted Dranko. "For reasons you don't understand. But where did that spell come from? Who told you to cast it? What are you not telling us?"

Abernathy's face was oddly bulbous in the crystal ball, and it was hard to tell whom among them he was looking at, but Ernie thought the old wizard's gaze flicked over to where Kibi and Aravia stood at the end of their semicircle. His bearded face crinkled into an apologetic smile.

"I don't...I can't tell you that, Dranko. You'll have to believe me when I tell you that each and every one of you has a vital role to play in the days to come."

Ernie couldn't keep silent. "Even Mrs. Horn?"

Abernathy looked at them sadly but said nothing. Then a chime echoed from somewhere behind Abernathy, its sound floating out from the crystal ball. Ernie guessed by now what it signified—that Naradawk had his hands on the bars of his cell and was rattling them with extra vigor.

"The Seven Mirrors, and Seablade Point!" cried Abernathy, and the crystal ball went dark.

"Dammit, but I wish he'd stop doing that," said Grey Wolf.

"That was ominous," said Dranko.

"He was scared," said Ernie. "Abernathy was scared."

"No great puzzle 'bout that," said Kibi. "Man's been keeping Charagan safe for Gods know how long, and now it's comin' apart on 'im."

"But he's got us!" said Tor. "We'll put things to rights, I know it."

"I'd like to know what a Blood Gargoyle is," said Grey Wolf. "I don't suppose any of you have heard of it. Aravia?"

Aravia shook her head no, obviously irked that she didn't know.

"My sisters might have information," said Morningstar.

Ernie stared at her, surprised.

The Ellish priestess shrugged. "I suppose it's not betraying a secret. It's just that we don't often have cause to discuss the inner workings of our sisterhood with outsiders. The Ellish Chroniclers maintain extensive historical libraries. The Temple of Ell has a presence in most major cities of Charagan, and I've heard the shrine here in Tal Hae has an extensive collection. I could send a letter, or go visit in person I suppose, and ask the Chroniclers to see if they have knowledge of a Blood Gargoyle. Or the Eyes of Moirel, or the Seven Mirrors, or even Abernathy himself."

Grey Wolf frowned at her. "How come you haven't mentioned we had that sort of resource at our disposal?"

"Because 'we' don't," said Morningstar sharply. "Ellish archives are not public. Even now I'm not certain that I'm comfortable asking the Chroniclers to do research for the benefit of a wizard's agenda."

"But Abernathy's protecting the kingdom!" said Ernie. "Surely your sisters will understand how important this is!"

"The Ellish temple is not known for its trusting nature. I can ask, but the Chroniclers are going to want to know *why* I want this information, and there's a good chance they won't believe anything I say about Naradawk and his otherworld prison." Her face grew taut as she added, "And if any of my reputation has leaked across the bay from Port Kymer to Tal Hae, it's not going to help our chances."

"Morningstar, you're a practical person," said Grey Wolf. "We've seen that recently. You'll still ask them, won't you?"

Morningstar nodded, her face neutral. "Yes, I'll ask. I'll go over there tonight. The worst they can do is…well, they can laugh and shut the door in my face. And tomorrow morning we'll have breakfast, wave at the sun, and pay these Seven Mirrors a visit. Don't want to miss Flashing Day, do we?"

CHAPTER EIGHTEEN

Temples to the Goddess Ell, large or small, shared a distinct architectural style that went beyond their monochromatic color scheme. Yes, they were painted uniformly black, such that persons not raised in darkness would perceive them as disquietingly featureless. But with her darksight, Morningstar could see that oversized upside-down triangles embellished the side walls, along with impressive pointed tympana speckled with smaller triangular adornments. The point-down black triangle was the holy symbol of the Ellish religion, representing the shield of darkness that would protect the innocent from nocturnal dangers.

No lamps or torches burned around the Tal Hae cathedral's exterior, and its position in the city, nestled among other tall buildings, shielded it (quite intentionally) from more distant ambient light, but its detail was clear enough. Its familiar designs gave Morningstar comfort; they confirmed her time with Horn's Company had not diminished her darksight.

The triangles might also have reminded her that the dictates and will of the Goddess were a constant, no matter the petty judgments of the sisters who served Her. But after the Mouth of Nahalm, she suspected more than ever that the judgment of Ell Herself had already been passed against her.

As she approached the dark front door and knocked, her apprehension grew. Had her reputation arrived here before her? She breathed deeply and sought for inner calm.

The door opened. A young novice stood in the doorway, black hair cut short.

"Good midnight," said Morningstar.

"And to you." The girl, no older than fifteen, stared at Morningstar, puzzled. Morningstar was wearing her Ellish robes but probably looked like an imposter with her snow-white hair and sunburned skin.

"I am Sister Morningstar from Port Kymer. I am here to speak with the Chroniclers. May I enter?"

The novice looked distinctively uncomfortable. "Oh, yes, forgive me. I am Sister Adriana. Please, sister, come in. I am sorry that you have missed the start of the midnight service, though you are welcome to attend what remains of it."

Morningstar stepped into the darkened narthex and instinctively let her fingertips trail along the walls. Like the Ellish buildings in Port Kymer, the cathedral here featured tactile artwork at elbow height, black-on-black but textured so it could also be "seen" with one's fingertips.

"I would be honored," she said. Morningstar couldn't help but feel nervous. On the one hand she might be better accepted after taking part in the temple's holy traditions. On the other, being seen by more sisters increased the chance that she would be recognized, or at least be made an object of unwanted curiosity. Sister Adriana led her into the back of the nave, where she sat as unobtrusively as possible on a short padded bench. To her left, high up in a loft, was a choir three times the size of the one at Port Kymer. Its sound was hauntingly lovely, the hymn a traditional chant on a common theme: venerating Ell and Her role in allowing the Traveling Gods to escape the Great Adversary.

According to scripture, the Traveling Gods had fought a long and terrible war against the Great Adversary, in which most of the Gods had been slain. Only six survived, but those half dozen were able to imprison the Adversary before fleeing across the universe to the world of Spira. Ell's role had been to weave a net of impenetrable blackness about the Adversary's head, so that He stumbled blindly into His prison while the other Gods gathered Their mortal flocks for the journey. Afterward those six Gods—Ell, Brechen, Werthis, Delioch, Corilayna, and Uthol Inga—arrived on this new world and reached an accord with Pikon, god of the fields, who already claimed the native mortals of Spira as His own.

Morningstar found the notion of warring Gods to be hopelessly abstract, but there was a disturbing parallel between Abernathy's locked-up monster and the Gods' imprisoned Adversary. She shook her head. It was extremely unlikely that the archmagi had, literally, a God-killer held captive.

There were more than three dozen sisters attending the midnight service, and some of these had turned around on their benches to look at her. Now two were leaning and whispering to one another. She sat up straighter. So what if she attracted attention, she decided. Let them think what they would.

When the songs had been sung, the prayers uttered, the devotions made, and the service ended, Morningstar stood and stretched while the sisters dispersed. A tall woman approached, appearing from a transept. She was older, perhaps in her early forties, and wore a disapproving frown.

"Sister Morningstar?"

Morningstar sighed at the undisguised contempt, but she retained her poise.

"I am," she said. "The service was lovely. I'm impressed by the chorale. Our singers at Port Kymer are not half as well trained."

"I'm sure your sisters back home will enjoy your criticisms," said the sister.

"I'm sorry," said Morningstar. "We haven't been introduced."

"I am Sister Corinne. Adriana tells me you are here to speak to the Chroniclers. Might I know your business with them?"

"I wish to learn about a certainly legendary creature," Morningstar said cautiously.

"Being one yourself?"

Morningstar blinked. "Excuse me?"

"What happened to your face? It almost looks as though you have been out in the sun."

You have no idea. But I'm not about to share anything with you, Sister Corinne.

"Yes, it does look that way."

"I know who you are, Morningstar. I have heard the tales from Port Kymer of the White Anathema. We had hoped you would never come here, bringing the disfavor of Ell with you. I hope your stay is short."

Morningstar's emotional armor held. She thought again of her blistering march across the Mouth of Nahalm and what it meant to suffer truly the disfavor of Ell. She smiled thinly. "I hope so too. If you could point me toward the library, I can make my own way, and you need not suffer my presence any longer."

Sister Corinne gestured toward a door near the left side of the narthex. "Through that door, down the stairs. The library is in the basement. Ask for Sister Previa." Corinne turned her back and strode off without any of the customary parting words or gestures.

* * *

The Tal Hae archive lived up to its billing; it was enormous, stretching nearly the entire length of the cathedral, several dozen arched vaults connected by short stone walkways and miniature flights of stairs. Morningstar inhaled the scents of dust and parchment as she wandered through the vaults, and it was several minutes before she found a librarian.

"I am looking for Sister Previa." She kept her voice polite but braced for the inevitable.

"You have found her." The woman was slight and plain-faced, her black hair tied up in a bun skewered with a pair of ebony sticks. She peered at Morningstar with obvious curiosity.

"I am Sister Morningstar of Port Kymer," she said. "I wish to commission some research."

Previa smiled at her. "You are the infamous Sister Morningstar? Have you come to throw me into the sun?"

"No," said Morningstar, taken aback. "The sun is much too far away for that."

Previa gave a little laugh. "Thank the Goddess." She looked Morningstar up and down. "From the stories, I expected the White Anathema to be brandishing unholy fire and threatening us with curses. I'm disappointed."

The Morningstar back at Port Kymer wouldn't have known how to react to someone sharing a friendly jest, but her time with Horn's Company had given her some practice.

"I make it a point to not bring unholy fires into libraries," she said.

"A wise policy," Previa agreed.

Morningstar glanced back toward the stairwell. "I met Sister Corinne after midnight services. From her attitude, I thought I might find myself unwelcome to everyone here."

Previa smiled again, a wide, warm smile. "Only to the small-minded among us. We've all heard about Sister Morningstar, the White Anathema of Port Kymer, but the rumors only made me think there must be a poor white-haired sister there with a great deal of patience. I apologize for any mistreatment you endure here in Tal Hae, but I assure you it won't come from me. Now, how may the Chroniclers be of service to you?"

In Port Kymer, other than her Shield trainer Clariel, the sisters had all been either coldly distant or overtly disdainful. Could she have found a true ally among the Ellish sisterhood?

"I find myself in unusual circumstances," she began. She hadn't intended to share any more about herself than was necessary, but faced with such plain acceptance, the words spilled forth before she could stop them. "The High Priestess Rhiavonne has given me dispensation to walk beneath the sun and ordered that I work under the Archmage Abernathy for the good of the kingdom. In that capacity, I am here to learn about some topics that have arisen."

She stopped and bit her tongue. Previa was staring at her with wide eyes. Had she ruined this nascent could-be friendship by admitting too much truth?

"Goddess," Previa breathed. "I've never…I mean, I can't imagine…"

"It's every bit as unpleasant as it sounds," said Morningstar.

Previa shook her head. "For what it's worth, I'm sorry."

"Thank you."

"I'm sure that's not doing your reputation any favors," Previa added.

"I haven't told anyone else within the sisterhood," said Morningstar. "And I'd prefer it stay private, if you don't mind."

Previa looked at her thoughtfully. "Of course. Interesting times we live in, no?"

"Previa, I've been out of my temple for some weeks now. What do you mean?"

"Of course, you wouldn't know then. The Dreamseers have been having the same recurring Seer-dreams of late, of some huge object, like a meteor, streaking out of the sky and smashing into Spira. In some of these dreams the object is a deadly, decidedly non-Ellish black, and in others it is blindingly white. The Seers also argue about whether these are augurs of the future or visions of the past. No one knows what to make of it."

Morningstar almost blurted out that she too had been recently made a Dreamseer, but she had shared enough secrets already.

"It's interesting," Previa continued. "I've never heard of a sister granted full permission to walk in daylight, but here you are…"

"You think I'm the white meteor?"

"The thought did occur to me. But if you are, don't smash up my library. Now, please, how may I help you in my official capacity?"

Morningstar started with only two requests: that Previa find out what she could about Eyes of Moirel and Blood Gargoyles. Previa showed immediate and keen interest and promised she could dig something up within days.

"I'll send what I find to the Greenhouse," she promised. "And you should feel free to return here, either for more information or just to talk. This is your home as much as it is mine, Morningstar of Ell. Don't let the Corinnes of the world convince you otherwise."

CHAPTER NINETEEN

I t was a pleasant enough week's walk from Tal Hae to the Seven Mirrors, but Kibi usually fell behind. That didn't surprise him any; he was always a slow hiker, slow but steady, rolling along like a boulder. The long hours didn't bother him, and he enjoyed the lush countryside, greening peacefully in the spring sunshine. The road was muddy in places, enough that it was quicker to walk instead through the damp grass beside it.

On the fourth day out from the city, when Kibi was lagging a bit after lunch, Ernie slowed his own pace and dropped back to walk next to him. Good lad, that Ernest Roundhill. The boy had a good heart and worried whenever one of his companions suffered. Not that Kibi was suffering, but each time the others got too far ahead, Ernie would check on him, making sure he wasn't cramping and reminding him to drink every few minutes.

"I'm fine, son," he said as Ernie fell into stride with him. "Jus' walkin' an' thinkin, like usual. Always had heavy legs, my ma would say, but I'll get as far as the rest a' ya 'fore the day's out."

Kibi never went out of his way to seek company. It wasn't that he disliked people, but he couldn't ever think of what to say to them. Other folk moved through life too quickly, not just when they walked, but in how they acted toward one another or in seeking to meet their own needs and desires. It was hard to be social with folk hurrying past on either side. Life would always come to you, he found. No need to rush out and grab it.

"Strange, isn't it?" said Ernie. "About our gold circles. Did you really never find out where your mother came from?"

Ah, there it was. Kibi had wondered when Ernie would get around to starting this conversation. Between the boy's natural shyness and his own reticence, they hadn't talked much about their newfound connection.

Kibi smiled a little to let Ernie know he was being sociable. "Nope."

"Why do you think she has a matching ring to the one they found buried on a statue of me?"

That was a stumper all right. Kibi had let himself be convinced that they were two different rings, but that just raised a different set of questions.

"Suppose they must've been made by the same person, long time ago. My ma got hold a' one, and the other got put on your statue."

"And do you really think your mom would…that she needs to wear hers all the time? To keep her alive?"

Kibi shrugged. "She certainly seems to think so." He always found it odd that his father, Bim, a man ordinarily disdainful of Godless superstition, never challenged his mother about the gold circlet. His mother Gela had insisted, with a terrified urgency, that her bracelet needed to stay on her wrist every minute of her life. She could never explain why but said it was just as important to her as breathing.

"Kibi," said Ernie, "that night we were all summoned to Abernathy's tower, you said you had some kind of trick you could do with stone, that was kind of like magic but wasn't. What did you mean?"

Kibi's face flushed beneath his beard. Had he really said that? He must have been flustered by being in such a strange circumstance. What he did with stone was personal, a secret he had long kept. And it wasn't really a trick, anyways.

"Not sure I can explain it. Jus'…me and the rock, we got an understandin'. Ain't nothin' too special, I guess."

Ernie smiled. "I think you're being modest, Kibi. Is it something you can show me?"

He opened his mouth to tell Ernie he'd rather not, that it wasn't something he did in front of other people. But Mrs. Horn would have told him not to be so closed up about it. And besides, Ernie was so inoffensive, and now they had a strange connection, and surely it wouldn't harm anything. Everything was different now. He was on a team, had to work with people instead of stone.

"I guess. Ain't much, but I can show ya."

He bent and pried a rock from the mud at the side of the road, a chunk of brown chert the size of a plum. It had been in the ground here a long, long time, and had only worked its way up to the surface in the past fifty years or so. No one had ever picked it up before now.

Gently he kneaded the stone, and it became soft beneath his fingers. He pressed and squeezed it, shaping it like a sculptor, knowing by instinct where to apply pressure so as not to break it apart. Over the course of a minute he transformed the many-faceted, asymmetric piece of rock into a round flat disc. Then he ran his finger over its newly smooth surface, tracing the letter E, and the letter was carved upon the stone from just the lightest touch. When he was done, the rock was pleased with its new shape, and Kibi thanked it silently for its cooperation. He couldn't change a rock without its approval, after all.

He handed it to Ernie, who stood with his mouth agape.

"Ain't nothin' really," Kibi said. "And it ain't magic, not like what Aravia does, or Abernathy. It's jus' me and the rock reachin' an agreement a' sorts. Can't explain any better'n that."

"I think it's incredible!" said Ernie. "Can I keep this?"

"Wouldn't a' put your initial on it otherwise."

* * *

The Seven Mirrors rose like upthrust fingers out of the grass, jet-black obelisks reaching for the afternoon sun. They formed a perfect seven-pointed ring nearly a hundred feet across, and each massive plinth towered a hundred feet in the air, a dark giant casting a long shadow over the plains.

Kibi worked his way through the crowds to get a better look at them; after walking a week to see this place, he had built up some high expectations. Ernie said the nearest town was over ten miles away, but Flashing Day attracted throngs of commoners from all the regional villages: Tal Inniston, White Ferry, Greentree, even from Tal Werek over thirty miles distant. It was a tradition hundreds of years old according to Ernie; men, women, and children gathered at the circle of stones, pitched tents, made picnics, danced and sang songs, and treated the whole thing like a festival holiday.

"My father used to bring a cart from White Ferry and sell bread," Ernie said, "though we haven't been back in several years. It got to be too much of a bother, coming all this way."

As Kibi came closer, he felt a hum, a resonant vibration almost too faint to discern, coming from the ring of standing stones.

"You feel that?" he asked Ernie, who walked beside him.

"Feel what?"

"Feel that deep thrummin' from the Mirrors."

Ernie stopped and made a show of listening. "No."

That didn't surprise him. Nobody else felt the things Kibi felt, or heard the things he heard.

Back in Eggoggin, the village of his birth and all his life until this strange wizard business, he had done his best to downplay his odd affinity for stone. The masons and architects he worked with knew something was amiss, but Kibi had been careful not to do his...oh, he hated to call it magic. It wasn't magic. It was too natural for that. Beneath his fingers, stone melted, became malleable, workable like clay. He could suggest a new shape, and if the stone had no objection, it became what he wanted. As far as he knew, no one had ever witnessed him plying his unique skill until he had shown it to Ernie on the journey here.

If it were only that, he might have explained it to someone, even showed it off before now. But it was also deeply personal. The earth was like a friend who was cripplingly shy around anyone but him, but who trusted him implicitly. It *wanted* to be worked, shaped, but it was nobody's business but his own. And Kibilhathur knew that because, in their own lugubrious way, the stones spoke to him.

That had first happened when Kibi was seven, as he toiled in the fields beside his father. They were clearing away rocks from a new half-acre intended for rye, and Kibi had been tasked with carrying out the biggest ones he could lift. As he struggled to flip over a wide slab of granite a feeling had come to him, seeping into his fingers through the stone. *Too heavy.* Not words, exactly, but he understood.

He had stood quickly and looked around. There was his father, ten feet off, smashing up a boulder.

"Father, can the stones speak?"

Bim, grunting with the effort of his labor, brought down his pick. "'Course they can. This one here's sayin', 'I give up!'"

"No, I mean it," Kibi had insisted.

His father had puffed a few breaths, leaning on his pick handle and smiling at his son. "Get yer head out a' th' clouds, boy. No, rocks don't say nothin'. And if they did, what would they say? They're jus' rocks."

Kibi had nodded and looked back down at the granite slab. *I'm sorry*, he thought to it. *Father's going to break you up to get you out of this field.*

But the stone didn't mind.

In the intervening years, the stones had spoken to him many times over, in their vague, doleful way. And the bond held in both directions; the earth trusted him, trusted him to treat it with respect, to understand its watchful, solitary existence.

As an apprentice stonecutter, he had refined the ability to knead and shape stone with his hands, always in small ways, improving his work, strengthening it. By laying his hands upon a slab, he knew exactly how it should be cut, how it *wanted* to be cut, where to place the chisel, how hard to strike, so he never lost so much as a flake. On his off days he collected rocks the size of his fist and carved them cunningly using his gifts (but never so well that others would suspect how he achieved such fine detail). He sold these to a peddler, who said there was great demand for such ornaments in the city of Hae Kalkas.

And so he continued for another decade, absorbed in his work, keeping largely to himself, knowing that his reputation as a solitary eccentric was well deserved. He just went on about his business, until the day it became a wizard's business.

* * *

Kibi stopped when he reached the perimeter of the circle formed by the Mirrors. It was clear how they got their name; though the outward-facing surfaces of the obelisks were rough-hewn, their inward-facing sides were flat and polished to a reflective black shine. Kibi walked clockwise until he stood immediately beside one. The deep rumbling in his innards grew stronger. There was strength in these stones; they were ancient, forbidding, and yet anticipatory, as if they were built for a purpose that had not yet been realized.

Though the cautious part of his nature warned against it, Kibi reached out and placed his palm against the rough plinth. A jolt of energy shot through him, not painful, but it set his arm to trembling. An overwhelming power resided here, a power that thrilled and terrified him, a power that was his, or that could be his, though these towering menhirs were not meant for him.

Kibilhathur. Your time is long past, but it has not yet come. Abide, and return.

He pulled his hand away. The voices of stones had always been heavy in his mind, but the words of the Mirror had been like deep-rumbling boulders rolling through his soul, shaking him nearly senseless. And they were words! Not just feelings and moods that his mind interpreted, but speech, true speech. Kibi stumbled; Ernie held him up.

"Are you okay, Kibi?"

"I think I might ought a' sit m'self down," he said dizzily.

The others had dispersed soon after arriving at the Flashing Day fair. Dranko and Tor were now haggling at a cluster of little carts, out of which some enterprising craftsmen and farmers were selling foodstuffs and souvenirs. Morningstar was sitting in the lengthening shadow of the easternmost Mirror, talking animatedly with Aravia. Grey Wolf was moving casually through the crowd, looking for anyone or anything suspicious; he had admonished the rest of them to do the same, though Flashing Day's big moment wasn't until noon tomorrow.

Kibi and Ernie walked to a stretch of grass a little ways removed from the bulk of the crowd and well outside the area circumscribed by the Seven Mirrors. Kibi took a long pull from his water skin and waited for his quivering bones to quiet. The skull-rattling subsonic vibrations eased the farther he removed himself from the huge obsidian standing-stones.

A cluster of children appeared nearby, tussling and jostling one another, all staring at him, some with poor enough manners to point. The oldest, a girl of thirteen years or so, took a few steps toward him.

"Why'd you do that, mister?"

She looked pointedly at the closest Mirror.

His mind was still wobbly, but Kibi made himself smile at her. "You mean touch that thing? Dunno, really. Why?"

"Bad luck," said the girl. "Don't you know it's bad luck to touch the Mirrors?"

"No," Kibi admitted. "I didn't. Why is it bad luck?"

"Just is. My momma's been bringing us here since I was five, and she says not to touch the Mirrors. Never seen anyone do it all this time, but you did."

"What did it feel like?" asked a boy, maybe eight or nine.

"Like rock," Kibi said, smiling. "Bit cold, given the sunshine, but nothin' strange about it."

"Did it eat your soul?" A second boy asked this odd question, a boy a year or two older than the first, but less bold. He hung back, just behind the shoulder of the older girl.

"Doubt it," said Kibi. "I'd be dead, wouldn't I?"

"My dad says the Mirrors eat your soul if you touch them," said the boy. "Make it so you never even existed at all."

Kibi turned to Ernie, who was smiling uncertainly at him. To the children he said, "Well, you seem a bright lot a' young'uns. I'm sittin' right here. Do I exist, or not?"

None of the children answered, and faced with such superstition-dispelling evidence the bunch of them turned inward toward one another before dashing back into the crowd. But now a number of men and women were looking his way, talking and gesturing toward him. Damn, but maybe setting his hand to the Mirror was a bad idea. They were there to keep a lookout for something the bad guys might want to keep secret, and here he was calling unnecessary attention to himself.

As if to drive this point home, a man detached himself from the edge of the crowd and sauntered towards them. He was whippet-thin and carried a rapier at his side, though Kibi's attention was mostly drawn to his perfectly manicured salt-and-pepper handlebar mustache, curled up at both ends. A long loaf of bread was tucked beneath his arm, and he gave Kibi and Ernie a broad, friendly smile as he approached.

"First time at Flashing Day?" he asked.

"Not for me," said Ernie. "My family used to come most years. But this is the first time for my friend here." Kibi nodded though his head still buzzed.

"My name is Sagiro," said the mustachioed man, his voice formal and soft. "Sagiro Emberleaf. Whom do I have the honor of addressing?"

"Ernest Roundhill at your service. And this is Kibi. But I don't remember seeing you here before, and your mustache would be hard to forget."

Sagiro smiled, stroked his handlebars, then tore off two hunks of bread and handed one to each of them. "I used to come quite often, but I have not been back to this most remarkable place in almost a decade."

Kibi knew he ought to be more sociable, but even now at a farther remove from the Mirrors, the brain-numbing vibrations, not to mention the deep earth-bones earthquake voice that had sounded in his mind, had left him with a powerful bewilderment. He was happy enough to let Ernie do the talking.

"What made you come back now, then?" asked Ernie.

Sagiro rubbed his clean-shaven chin. "I'm not entirely certain. I always found Flashing Day to be a fascinating phenomenon, but life becomes so busy, it can be hard to find the time for little forays into the countryside. But what of your friend? Kibi, is it? Back when I used to come every year, visitors had a superstitious aversion to touching the Mirrors, but I saw that you had no such compunction. Is there basis to the fears of the crowds, would you say?"

Sagiro bit off a piece of bread, seemingly content to chew while waiting for Kibi to answer, but Kibi's stone-affinity was a private thing, and he never did think much of nosy folk.

"Nah," he said. "Things are just big ol' stones, aren't they? Seems funny to go through all the trouble a' polishin' 'em up."

"It helps with the flashing, I imagine," said Sagiro. He gave Kibi a thoughtful look, then turned back to Ernie. "Have you ever run the Mirrors?"

Ernie laughed. "No. My parents always said it was a foolish thing to do. 'Don't get mixed up in magic you don't understand,' they told me, and I was a good son and listened to their advice. I saw a couple of people do it when I was younger; Dad said it all came of too much ale, but nothing bad ever seemed to happen to anyone who ran out into the lights. But what about you, Mr. Emberleaf?"

Sagiro looked out at the obelisks. The band of children was playing rag-ball inside their circle, laughing as they kicked a wad of bound-up old cloth back and forth across the grassy spaces between the Mirrors.

"No," he said. Then he looked back at Kibi and Ernie. "I'm not so foolish as to get mixed up in magic I don't understand."

The mustachioed gentleman bowed before them. "It has been a pleasure meeting you both. Kibi, as I'm sure your friend here has already told you, the Flashing will occur at noon tomorrow. I'm certain you will enjoy the spectacle."

Sagiro took one more bite from his baguette and wandered back into the crowd.

* * *

Kibi's headache had subsided by the next morning, but the hum of power radiating from the Mirrors had taken up a permanent residence inside his skeleton. The words the Mirror had spoken still rang in his memory. *Abide, and return.* But a night's sleep had not granted him any new insight.

More travelers must have arrived overnight, for the size of the crowd had swelled, and new pilgrims were arriving every hour.

"We should spread out," said Grey Wolf. "Everyone find a different vantage point, so we'll have the greatest chance of seeing whatever Abernathy thinks we might see. Keep a sharp eye out for Sharshun." He squinted up at the sky. "Probably less than half an hour. There aren't any hills nearby, so we'll just have to work our way towards the front of the crowds."

"People don't usually get much closer than twenty feet from the Mirrors," said Ernie. "Unless they're running them, of course."

"But what if what we're looking for takes place back in the crowds somewhere?" asked Morningstar.

"There are too many people here for us to watch them all, *and* the Mirrors too," said Grey Wolf.

"I can work the crowd," said Dranko. "Each of you pick a spot near the front, and I'll mosey through the spectators, keeping an eye out for anyone acting oddly, or baldly, or…blue-skin-y."

Grey Wolf assigned each of them a location, as the mass of onlookers formed their own secondary ring surrounding the circle of obsidian obelisks. Kibi dutifully pushed through the crowds, ignoring the glares and protestations, until he had obtained a front-row seat barely fifteen feet from the nearest Mirror. Much of the audience was sitting on the grass, but Kibi chose to stand; he should be ready if anything interesting happened.

"Are you ready for the big moment?" Sagiro Emberleaf had appeared silently beside him.

"I suppose," said Kibi. Being this close to a Mirror had set his teeth buzzing and raised goose-flesh on his arms; how much of his physical discomfort was showing on his face, in his body language? He fought an urge to walk over and see what more it might have to say.

As the shadows of the black pillars shortened, the crowd became quieter, and many people swiveled their heads around, probably wondering who, if anyone, was going to dash bravely out into the center of the stones when the lights came on. Kibi found himself becoming unusually nervous. Sagiro had gone quiet, his eagerness to witness the spectacle written clearly on his face.

The sun reached its zenith, and several things happened with such unexpected speed, not to mention sensory overload, that Kibi had trouble piecing together a coherent narrative afterward.

First, there were the lights.

Ernie had already explained what "flashing" meant in the context of the Mirrors, but Kibi was not prepared for the reality of it. From each standing stone, a tall blade of white light leapt silently from the mirrored inward-facing surface, sheets of dazzling radiance that shot across the interior of the ring as though walls of pure luminescence had sprung into existence. The Mirrors were angled such that these planes of light instantly formed a crisscrossing seven-sided star. Though the sun shone down unobstructed, these rigid curtains were bright enough to appear nearly opaque.

Where the seven walls of light intersected, they formed a smaller seven-sided shape in the center of the Mirrors. Each face of that heptagon shimmered with a different color: red, orange, yellow, green, blue, indigo, purple.

Kibi absorbed all of these visible details, but only barely, because his body had become a sieve through which some molten energy was being forcibly strained. The Seven Mirrors contained something like a pure concentration of Kibi's natural affinity for stone. Standing so close to the perfect slashes of light slicing out of the shining black pillars was like enduring the roaring impact of a mile-tall waterfall.

And yet, for all of that, Kibi kept enough focus and sense of his surroundings to see that someone was, in fact, running the Mirrors. A tall figure in a long dark robe, his face hidden in its deep hood, was sprinting toward the confluence of light curtains. Something clutched in the runner's left hand was trailing an emerald light; streamers of green flowed from between his fingers like glowing ribbons.

From the corner of his eye Kibi saw that Sagiro was leaning forward, intently watching the runner in the robe. But Kibi's attention was quickly diverted by a *second* runner, a tall youth with a sword strapped to his back. He was dashing in from a different side of the circle, a quarter-turn farther around clockwise.

It was Tor.

The two were converging, which was inevitable given that they were both sprinting for the middle of the same circle. But Tor moved faster, and in another handful of seconds Kibi could see that he was *not* headed for the rainbow-colored heptagon, but was rather on a trajectory to intercept the man in the robes.

Ten feet shy of the multicolored center, Tor leapt and bowled over the other man with a perfectly executed flying tackle. Both tumbled to the grass, and as the robed man put out his hands to break his fall, he let go of the glowing green object. It was the size of a large walnut and clearly visible as it escaped the man's grasp, trailing green fire. But away from his grip its emerald glow faded and it lost itself in the tall grass.

As for the man himself, the hood fell away from his head, and though the color of his skin was impossible to tell in the harsh light of the Mirrors, his head was as bald as a melon.

Next to Kibi, Sagiro gasped and sucked in a quick breath, and *he* bolted for the center. Kibi instinctively gave chase but felt something akin to drunkenness from having endured the relentless outpouring of power from the Mirrors. Sagiro was weasel-quick and easily outran him, but the rest of the company was already rushing to Tor's aid from all around the ring. They arrived nearly at the same time, but while Kibi's friends concerned themselves with Tor and the Sharshun, Sagiro himself dropped to his hands and knees and searched in the grass.

Kibi's progress was painfully slow, as though he were fighting a massive headwind, but when he passed through the invisible perimeter described by the Seven Mirrors, everything changed. The deep-earth power of the Mirrors still raged all about, but it no longer troubled him. Quite the opposite; Kibi was nearly overcome by a surge of psychic clarity. There was a magic in the earth, and it was *his*. It had always been his, a power that came from below, from the earth-bones of the world, and the Seven Mirrors were fingers dripping with magic from that megalithic source.

It all came to him, the obvious clear truth. The Sharshun had been carrying an Eye of Moirel—an emerald, most likely—and now Sagiro was searching for it while the rest of the company concerned themselves with the man who had dropped it. But Sagiro was looking in the wrong place. Kibi could tell because the prize the man sought, the jewel dropped by the Sharshun, now appeared to his eyes as a fiery green star. While his friends struggled with the bald man, Kibi walked forward calmly, reached down into the sawgrass, and picked up something like an enormous emerald, smooth, round as a plum and as big as a baby's fist.

GREETINGS, KIBILHATHUR. IT IS A PLEASURE TO SEE YOU AGAIN.

The emerald spoke directly into his mind, sharp and crystalline, not the melancholy voice of a granite hillside, nor the earthquake-voice of the Mirror. Kibi couldn't remember having a previous encounter with a magical gemstone, and thought it likely that it was speaking on behalf of all the stone in the world.

"Are you an Eye of Moirel?" he asked it.

WE WERE NEVER HERS TO COMMAND.

"What would've happened had that man carried you to the center of the Mirrors?"

MINOR, TEMPORARY DISPLACEMENT. I LACK TWO WILLING BROTHERS.

"Two other Eyes of Moirel? How many of you are there?"

THERE ARE SEVEN, KIBILHATHUR.

"How do you know my name?"

ALL THE STONES KNOW YOUR NAME.

Time was up. The sheets of light slicing from the Seven Mirrors all vanished at once. Bereft of their ambient light, the Eye in Kibi's hand lost its green color and now looked like a spherical diamond. He brought it close to his nose and peered into it; at its center was a little dot of black, no larger than a pea, a sphere within a sphere.

"May I see that for a moment?"

Sagiro's request was made so casually, so reasonably, that Kibi nearly handed it over on instinct. But he stayed his hand and took a step back.

"I don't think I oughta," he said warily. "You ran out here awful quick to grab it. Why?"

"I'm a collector," said Sagiro. "Gems that large and…unusual…are quite rare, wouldn't you agree? But what about you? Why did your friends rush out to attack the man who held it?"

Kibi glanced over to where his six companions were standing up. On the ground by their feet was the man Tor had tackled; tall, hairless, and with skin the color of a ripe blueberry. The Sharshun lay on his back, eyes staring up lifelessly, a red froth oozing from the corner of his mouth.

"I don't see how that's your business," said Kibi.

Sagiro looked down upon the Sharshun. "To all appearances, your friends have murdered that poor fellow. How will you explain it, I wonder?"

Kibi ignored that problem for the moment. "Who was he?" he asked.

The mustachioed man abruptly turned to face the crowd of onlookers, which had been slowly shifting forward to see what was happening with the company and the blue-skinned Sharshun. Even to the last, Kibi expected that Sagiro would offer some sensible defense on their behalf, but the façade of friendship crumbled as the man spoke.

"My fellow citizens of Harkran!" Sagiro shouted. "These people have done foul murder! It is your duty to detain them, so that they may answer for their heinous crime. I will ride quickly for Tal Inniston, to fetch members of the local constabulary." So saying, Sagiro dashed away, parting the startled crowd, to where a horse waited patiently, tied to a tent stake.

Kibi cursed himself for misreading his new acquaintance so badly. To his companions he asked, "Is he dead?"

Aravia nodded. "Yes, but he killed himself. I think. Some kind of poison…"

"To make sure he couldn't be captured and interrogated," said Morningstar.

The masses of onlookers, several hundred people at least, milled about uncertainly. Some were armed, and Kibi knew there was little to be done if the mob turned hostile. Not even Morningstar would be willing to fight and possibly injure or kill innocent citizens, citizens who'd think they were doing a good deed.

A few of the braver and more physically imposing individuals were looking at one another, waiting to see who would make the first move. Kibi figured that any minute now, someone would demand that they drop their weapons, and start asking questions about how the Sharshun had died and why they had attacked him in the first place. Kibi sure hoped his friends had good answers. Maybe Dranko could talk them clear.

"Ernest? Ernest Roundhill?" A large and elderly woman pushed her way to the front, and those near her made plenty of room, looking relieved that someone was taking charge. The seven of them *did* make a formidable-looking squad.

"Mrs. Appleford?" Ernie stepped forward with an anxious smile. "I promise we didn't kill that man. You know I'd never be part of something that…that criminal."

Mrs. Appleford shook her head. "I wouldn't have thought it, but then what just happened here? That boy." She pointed to Tor. "He knocked that fellow to the ground, and you all ran out to help him, and…is that person truly dead? Why is his skin such a strange color?"

Ernie opened his mouth, closed it again, looked around nervously. The truth was going to sound ridiculous, but Kibi knew that Ernie was so honest, he was unlikely to offer up anything else.

"He killed himself," Ernie managed. "He…I don't think he wanted to be questioned…"

Mrs. Appleford and the rest of the Flashing Day crowd waited for something more definitive. Ernie glanced at Dranko, took a deep breath as if he was about to try a standing broad jump across a pit of snakes, and said with a shocking amount of conviction, "That man is part of an order that was trying to destroy the Mirrors! That's the whole reason we were sent here—to stop him from carrying out his evil scheme. Our goal was to simply subdue him, and to learn more about his organization, but he—"

"He poisoned himself," said Aravia. She had been examining the Sharshun's mouth, which had continued to foam even minutes after his death. "It appears he had a poison sac lodged in the roof of his mouth, which he broke open with his tongue."

"Mrs. Appleford," said Ernie. "I left White Ferry about a month ago, remember? Tell all these people why."

The woman's eyes went wide as she pieced together the puzzle. She turned to face the crowd behind her. "Young Ernest here was summoned to Tal Hae by a powerful wizard."

Ernie indicated his friends. "We all were. And this is why we're here today. The archmage of Tal Hae sent us to stop that man."

"It's true," said a tall man in a straw hat. "I even seen the letter myself, from the wizard-upon-high who lives in the big city. Ernest Roundhill here is as honest a young gentleman as you are ever likely to meet. We've known his family since he was born, and if he tells you him and his friends didn't kill nobody, and that there dead fellow was up to no good, you can be darned sure it's the truth."

Ernie's face turned beet red, but the murmur in the crowd changed noticeably in tenor, from tentatively hostile to relieved and congratulatory. Several people came forward to shake his hand and look with disgusted fascination upon the body of the Sharshun as it lay at the foot of the northernmost Mirror.

Kibi slipped the Eye of Moirel into his pocket.

CHAPTER TWENTY

Most of Master Serpicore's library of six hundred volumes were histories, treatises on magical theories, or essays explaining proper mental exercises and techniques for improving one's focus as an arcane caster. A smaller number were biographies of famous wizards and scholars of decades long past. About a dozen were novels, poorly written, some containing scenes of surprising prurience given Serpicore's buttoned-up sensibilities.

But on the library's back wall, on high shelves that Aravia was forbidden to approach, were Serpicore's seventy-nine books containing full magical formulae for more than two hundred different spells and variants. According to Serpicore it was one of the finest collections of arcane formulations ever assembled, and Aravia had no reason to doubt it.

On four different occasions over her two years of apprenticeship, Aravia had made plans to sneak into the library and steal a look at those seventy-nine tomes. The fourth time she had actually tried it, and in so doing learned that Serpicore had not been bluffing about the magical safeguards he employed to prevent unauthorized access. Her fingertips had been numb for almost a week afterward.

Knowledge and its accumulation were the most important things in her life. Knowing that she shared a house with seventy-nine spellbooks that she was forbidden to read was like working in a bakery and being denied the bread.

From the moment she had appeared in Abernathy's tower and realized that the invitation had not in fact been a puzzling hoax on the part of her teacher, Aravia had hoped that her archmagely patron would share *his* spellbooks with her. Surely one of the greatest wizards ever to put on a robe would have a library at least as impressive as Serpicore's. When he had made his plea that she join his team that first night in the Greenhouse, he had promised to grant her access to a library he had described as "impressive, if disorganized." But since then, Abernathy's distracted nature and constant attendance to Naradawk Skewn's prison had conspired to prevent him from following through on his promise. Now, as Grey Wolf turned his key in the Greenhouse door, she resolved that this time she would not let him put off the subject any longer.

She need not have worried. The oversized living room bookcase, empty since they had taken up residence, was now jammed with tomes.

Eddings walked in from the dining room. "Welcome home, good sirs and madams. I trust everything went well in your latest travels?"

Aravia was far too distracted to answer. She rushed to the bookshelf and pulled down a volume at random. Its title page announced *Formulae and Variants on the Casting of Spontaneous Levitation.*

"Ah, yes," said Eddings, as the rest of the company dropped their packs and hung up their cloaks. "Abernathy delivered these books the very evening that you departed. He asked me to convey his regrets that his available lending stock was not more extensive, along with a warning that as a relative novice, you may find his personal style of transcription and note-taking to be opaque."

Not more extensive? There were easily five hundred books here, and if even half of them contained spell formulae, it would be nearly triple what Serpicore had on his shelves. She flipped open the book on levitation to one of its opening pages.

It was full of gibberish. It wasn't in a foreign language—the words themselves were legible and in Chargish—but they didn't follow any of the standard protocols and known forms for spell recipes.

She scanned ahead six pages. More gobbledygook. She skipped to the end, and on the final page, beneath a large inscrutable diagram, were the words "*More experimentation is warranted, but I believe the previous chapters adequately summarize the primary variants on both area-based and object-based levitation.*"

Two more books, one on rapid short-range teleportation and the other on synchronizing the visual and aural aspects of simple illusions, were similarly impenetrable. Given enough time she could puzzle through Abernathy's dense and mysterious magical dialect, but it would be easier if she could ask him a few general questions first.

Aravia returned the books to the shelf. "We should report in." Abernathy would want to know about the Seven Mirrors and Kibi's Eye of Moirel, which was sufficient pretense for bothering him about the spellbooks.

"I'll say," said Dranko. "We need to thank him."

Dranko had emptied a sack of small red and white rocks out onto the table. Eddings walked over next to him. "After delivering Aravia's books, Abernathy retrieved that bag of gemstones. He was in a great hurry by that time; something in his tower was alarming him severely. But regarding them he left another message: that he had remembered an old stash of opals he had always meant to use as ritual components, and he hoped they would be adequate as a fresh source of funds."

Dranko laughed and held one of the opals to his eye. "These are adequate in the same way that an entire cow would be adequate for dinner." He turned to Grey Wolf. "Do you forgive Abernathy for summoning us now? We get to see the world, fight against evil, live in a ritzy house, and get paid handsomely for it. What's not to like?"

"I don't know," said Grey Wolf dryly. "Why don't we ask Ysabel Horn that question? My recollection is that Abernathy summoned her, and she died a meaningless death. Do you remember that, Dranko? When you claimed you were a channeler? Do you forgive Abernathy for summoning *her*?"

Dranko turned red, looked away from Grey Wolf, and said nothing.

Aravia had nearly forgotten about Mrs. Horn. Did that make her a bad person? She didn't think so. Serpicore had counseled that a successful arcanist harbored no regrets; like all emotions, they were only distractions, impediments to forward learning. Either way, this sort of exchange served no good purpose. "So, Abernathy!"

She bounded to the foyer and up the stairs while the others followed. Inside the secret room, the crystal ball filled with mist, and within seconds the metal head of Mister Golem filled its round interior.

"Dammit," she muttered.

"Abernathy is unavailable under any circumstance," said the tinny voice.

"But what if it's an emergency?" Aravia blurted before she could stop herself.

"It's not, is it?" said Ernie.

"Abernathy is unavailable under any circumstance," repeated Mister Golem. "Please carry out his previous instructions."

"What do you think happened to him?" asked Tor. "Do you think he's dead?

Did Naradawk get out?"

Aravia tried to keep the keen disappointment from her voice. "No. He warned us this might happen, remember? My guess is that Naradawk is making a push to escape, and Abernathy needs all of his focus and concentration to thwart that attempt."

"Then let's leave him to it," said Grey Wolf. "We'll get a good night's sleep, and tomorrow morning we'll find a ship that can take us to Seablade Point. We'll see if Abernathy's magical archway is working."

Aravia would just have to puzzle through Abernathy's dialect on her own. The others would take care of the mundane details of planning and preparation for the trip to Seablade Point, while she made a start on the books. In the living room she scanned the shelves, looking for anything that looked like a primer, and though she failed to find one, there *was* a thin tome whose spine read *On Locks*. Lacking any better method of teaching herself Abernathy's opaque style of spell transcription, she could start with something she already knew and work sideways. She slid out the book, scratched her cheek, grabbed another three books that seemed interesting, and carried the pile to a chair by the fireplace.

She was still on the first page of *On Locks* when Kibi sat in the chair next to her.

"Aravia," he said in his deep, slow voice. "You got a minute or two to chat?"

She was tempted to say no, so great was her impatience to read, but with a sigh she set the book on her lap. "What is it, Kibi?"

"It's about...magic."

Well, she could spare a minute or two.

"I never did fancy myself a magicker," said Kibi, "what I can do with stone and all."

Oh, that. His not-really-magic. "I remember you telling me, in the woods near Verdshane. What exactly *do* you do with stone?"

"I...I understand it," he said slowly. "I can shape it with m' fingers, kind a' tell it what to do. And sometimes it tells me things, too." He shifted uncomfortably in his chair, looked away, looked back again. "When you do your spells, how does it work? What does it feel like, if you get me? Is it all book-learnin', or is it a deep-down kind a' thing?"

"It's both," she said. "Most people cannot perform magic under any circumstance. Whether you have the potential is mostly luck, though family inheritance plays a part." Seeing Kibi's confusion, she clarified. "I mean if your parents were wizards, you have a better chance of being one yourself."

"Oh. Were your parents wizards then?"

"My mother was, in an inconsequential way. The only thing she ever learned to do was make weak magical lights. She was not…well-suited for the rigors of training. See, that's the other part. It's not enough to have the gift. You also have to work extremely hard, studying and memorizing and practicing every day for hours, week after week, month after month. And even then, to be more than a hedge-wizard, you need to have a knife-sharp mind. Which, fortunately for me, I do."

Kibi just stared at her for a moment, and she hoped, having answered so thoroughly, that he would wander off and leave her to her books.

"I'm only askin'," said Kibi, his words coming in slow motion, "'cause them Seven Mirrors, they…"

The stonecutter stopped, closed his mouth.

"They what?"

Kibi produced the Eye of Moirel from his pocket. During the kerfuffle with the suicidal Sharshun, only Kibi had noticed that their bald adversary was holding a gem in his hand, a gem the stonecutter had claimed was trailing a green fire, though she hadn't seen it. He had shown it to the rest of Horn's Company on the walk back from the Mirrors. Now he held it in his palm, a large, smooth diamond, perfectly round, with a marble of jet lodged impossibly in its center.

"They're a source a' some kind a' powerful magic, is what I'm sayin'. And I think I could do somethin' with it, if I could figure out how, but it ain't nothin' I got any experience with. Heck, this here Eye a' Moirel feels like it's getting antsy. It talked to me too, when I first picked it up, but only when them crazy lights was flashin'. And then the Mirrors talked to me on top a' that, though they didn't make no sense. I ain't told no one 'bout that part yet."

"Kibi, I can't figure out what you're asking."

"Right. I guess I ain't sure yet, what all I need to know. Maybe now that you've got all them magicky books, one of 'em could help figure out what this here Eye is for."

"I don't know. Maybe. Serpicore mentioned that there were spells for identifying the properties of enchanted objects but that there was little point in learning them since such objects were so scarce."

Her books beckoned, but the notion of a magical talking gemstone *was* intriguing. She reached out to take the gem from Kibi, but it hopped from his hand to the floor, like a cricket aware it was about to be captured. The two of them stared, startled and fascinated, as it rolled quickly across the floor toward the foyer.

"Guess we should get after it," said Kibi.

Aravia sprang from her chair and the two gave chase. The Eye of Moirel turned sharply before it reached the front door and bounced up the stairs two at a time like a children's ball come to life. Aravia and Kibi scrambled to keep up.

"You get back here!" Kibi cried, but the diamond paid no heed. By the time Aravia reached the upstairs hallway, it had rolled twenty feet down and stopped in front of Ernie's door, glinting in the light of Abernathy's heatless torches.

Kibi puffed up behind her. "What's it doin'?"

"I don't know."

It rolled sharply into the bottom of the door, struck, and bounced off.

"Come in," came Ernie's voice.

The Eye of Moirel vibrated on the wood floor of the hallway, its rapid tapping sounding like chattering teeth. Just as Aravia took a step forward for a better look, it blasted *through* the door like it had been shot from a ballista, with such force that it left a nearly perfect round hole with only a few ragged splinters. A startled yelp came from inside the room.

"Ernie!"

Aravia dashed down the hall and turned the handle of Ernie's door. It wasn't locked; she pushed it open. Ernie was sitting on the edge of his bed, a journal in one hand and a quill in the other, but he wasn't writing. He was staring open-mouthed at the crate that his parents had sent, pushed up against the wall. Like the door, the crate had a small round hole in it.

Aravia's mind surged with insight, her subconscious taking it upon itself to connect the dots. Kibi had some rapport with the Eye of Moirel, and a golden circlet had been found on a statue of Ernie that matched one Kibi claimed belonged to his mother. The Eye, she knew, must be attracted to the circlet in some way, and thus its surprising journey to Ernie's room. She held her breath.

Oh…there was Ernie's circlet, resting on his bedside table on the opposite side of the room. So much for insight.

Something climbed out of the crate.

It was a stuffed bear. But unlike most children's toy animals, this one was missing one of its button eyes, and in its place was a pulsing emerald glow. The bear was dirty, one leg was a bit longer than the other, and little tufts of wool poked out through its parted seams, but it was surprisingly limber. It swung itself up and balanced on the lip of the crate.

Kibi arrived in the doorway. "Is that a stuffed animal?"

"My mom sent it to me," said Ernie faintly. "It was my favorite when I was little, and she thought…well, you know how moms are. But…what is that in its eye? What just happened? Why is my bear…alive?"

HELLO, ERNEST. YOU ARE LOOKING WELL.

"Pikon's pancakes!" Ernie squeaked. "Did…did Bumbly just talk? To me?"

The bear's voice was deep and resonant—an almost comical effect, coming as it did from a cuddly little toy. Even as it spoke, a green crystalline rime crept from its glowing socket and spread like a quick frost across its face.

USE THE CIRCLE, COME FULL CIRCLE, BREAK THE CIRCLE.

"What does that mean?" asked Ernie. "And why is your eye glowing like that?"

KIBILHATHUR, KEEP ME SAFE.

Aravia grew impatient. "Eye of Moirel, tell us, what is your purpose? How are you connected to the Seven Mirrors? Who are the Sharshun, and why are they trying to find you?"

MY PURPOSE IS TO TRAVEL, NOWHERE. BRING CARANCH'S GIFT.

"But what…" Aravia began, but the Eye spoke one more time.

THE SHARSHUN WILL UNMAKE THE WORLD. YOU MUST KEEP US FROM THEM. BRING ME MY BROTHERS.

The green light vanished like a snuffed candle. The crystal coating, which had spread almost to the bear's stuffed belly, sublimated into a vanishing mist. The Eye of Moirel dropped out to the floor, while Bumbly flopped backward, lifeless, into the crate.

Ernie's voice was shrill. "What is going on?"

Kibi reached down and plucked the Eye of Moirel from the floor. Aravia didn't know what was going on, not yet, but she'd figure it out. As the most powerful wizard available, she'd have to.

CHAPTER TWENTY-ONE

T o Morningstar, Shield, from Previa, Chronicler,

Having been authorized to pursue research on your behalf, following your earlier visit to our temple, I am pleased to offer you the following summary of our findings so far:

The name of Moirel appears in a particularly old legend of questionable veracity, in which she was a wizard who appeared many hundreds of years ago (exact date not known) in the middle of the circle of standing stones known as the Seven Mirrors. She was carrying several magical diamonds, each cut round, but she was disoriented and subsequently robbed of her jewels by bandits. Moirel spent the rest of her days searching for the jewels without success, though she was driven mad with the desire to find them. These diamonds are almost certainly the Eyes of Moirel since in a second account, as she wandered the countryside in her lunacy, she "asked all she met to give her back her Eyes, so she could go home." The specific purpose of the Eyes is not mentioned, but it might be surmised that they were integral to Moirel's supposed appearance.

The Seven Mirrors themselves are well known and documented: seven obelisks arranged in a circular pattern, far from any human habitation, approximately one hundred miles southeast of Tal Hae. Once every year, at the end of the fifth week of spring, they "flash," as cascades of light appear in the center of their ring. We have no records of who built them, or why, or what purpose the flashing serves, but when considering my findings on the Eyes of Moirel, it is reasonable supposition that the Eyes and Mirrors combine to effect a form of magical transport.

A Blood Gargoyle is a semi-mythical creature whose existence seems to be in dispute among scholars. The only historical account is vague; the gargoyle is described as both powerful and malevolent, and as having wiped out an entire city (not specified), including hundreds of trained *soldiers, before it was defeated and smashed by one of the Archmagi (unnamed). It is physically described as "an orange devil, bat-winged and relentless."*

It was a pleasure meeting you, Morningstar, and I hope you can endure the burdens of walking in light that the Goddess has given you to bear. If the Chroniclers can be of more assistance, I would be happy to oblige.

May the Goddess guide you.

A messenger had delivered the letter just after midnight, and Morningstar read it aloud to the others over breakfast the next morning. *It was a pleasure meeting you…* She read that sentence again in her mind and smiled. That first night in the Greenhouse, Abernathy had suggested that her new companions would see her as a friend, and she couldn't deny the truth of it. Kibi and Tor were certainly friendly toward her, and dour Grey Wolf (if nothing else) respected her practical outlook. It had crept up on her, this feeling of fitting in, and it startled her to realize she had started to take it for granted.

But such congenial words from a fellow priestess gave her an even deeper hope that her place in the world might change for the better. Was there a Previa out there for every Corinne?

"No wonder Abernathy was worried about the blood gargoyle," said Ernie. "I bet those Black Circle people are planning to bring it to life somehow."

Morningstar didn't see the point in speculating. "If it wiped out a city and hundreds of soldiers, there's not much the seven of us can do about it. Abernathy had plenty of time to warn the other archmages, or the king, I suppose, before he…became unavailable."

"Archmagi," said Aravia. "The plural of 'archmage' is 'archmagi.'"

"Whew," said Dranko. "That was a close call. We nearly forgot how smart you were!"

"We should get going, then," said Tor. "To Seablade Point!"

Ah, Tor. Always to the point. She shook her head at his impetuosity, but at least he kept things moving forward.

"But what about the Sharshun unmaking the world?" Ernie was wringing his hands. "I'm more worried about that!"

Aravia shook her head. "Perhaps, but we have no leads to follow. The Eye of Moirel said to bring him his brothers, but we don't know where any of them are. Abernathy was very clear about our next assignment: investigate the portal-arch near Seablade Point, since it's our only possible means of finding the Crosser's

Maze."

"Our ship leaves at noon, so we have a few hours," said Dranko. "After we've eaten, I'll pass out everyone's windfall from Abernathy's opals."

Morningstar was still irritated with Dranko, in general because he provoked anger as a hobby and in specific because of how her whole body chafed. Her skin was recovering with unexpected speed from her march through the desert, but the burned patches were peeling and itched with a fury.

The rest of breakfast was quiet. Aravia scarfed down her food, finished her meal in five minutes, stood, and practically ran for the living room.

Tor laughed. "She loves her books!"

"Let her read as much as she can," said Ernie. "Every new spell she learns could be the one that keeps the rest of us alive later on."

An increasingly loud sound of heavy footsteps came from the basement stairs, and Kibi entered the dining room looking a bit nervous.

"Basement is full a' closets, and each closet has an iron trunk. Put the Eye in a trunk, locked it, locked the closet door. Eye said to keep it safe, and I can't figure out how to get it any safer. Hard to say if it could blast through iron or not."

* * *

Dranko had booked them passage on the *Goldfish*, a small single-masted merchant's cog. The Royal Strait threatened ships with a perilous maze of reefs and shallows, its dangers compounded by capricious crosswinds. Smaller and more nimble ships had an easier time making the abrupt course-changes necessary for safe passage. Once clear of the strait, it would be a few days' sail down the eastern coast of Lanei to the tiny hamlet of Seablade Point.

The hold of the *Goldfish* was cramped and had no good space for hanging hammocks; Morningstar found a niche among padded crates of glassware to stuff her bedroll. As the ship's captain had forbade any open flames in the hold, Aravia conjured up two magically-lit copper chits to help the others get settled on the first night at sea.

Aravia kept one of these lights for herself, sequestered herself in a small nook formed by a stack of boxes and the protruding hull ribbing, and was alternately poring over books and scribbling manically in a notebook. Her pack was so heavy she could barely lift it, as she had stuffed as many of Abernathy's spellbooks into it as she could manage, not to mention another half-dozen she had convinced Tor to carry.

"Hey Aravia," said Ernie. "Are you working on teleport magic? Ships make my stomach do backflips."

Morningstar found them quite comfortable. It was not uncommon for Ellish sisters to travel this way, when they were obliged to make multi-day journeys. But poor Ernie was not meant for ships; his complexion was unnatural.

"Yes," said Aravia. "But it's complicated, and Abernathy's bizarre notational patterns aren't making it any easier, so I could do without interruptions."

"Fine," said Grey Wolf. "The rest of us will…uuuungh." He doubled over in obvious pain, gripping his midsection with both hands. "Not again…"

"Dranko," Morningstar snapped. "Can you do something?"

Dranko chuckled. "Like what? He's not wounded. Maybe he has a parasite."

The goblin's flippancy towards Grey Wolf's suffering was in exceedingly poor taste.

"Gah!" Grey Wolf barked. "It feels like someone's trying to drag me around by my intestines, just like before. Maybe some…"

And he vanished. No lights, no smoke, no magical effects. Morningstar rubbed her eyes, but it was no trick; the others were just as shocked. Grey Wolf had simply disappeared.

"Aravia!" Morningstar snapped. "What happened? Was that magic?"

Aravia looked up. "Was what magic? What are you talking about?"

"Grey Wolf!" Ernie shrieked. "He was having that weird stomach pain again, and then just disappeared, like he teleported away!"

Morningstar gestured to Aravia's book. "You said you were studying how to teleport. Could you have accidentally cast it on Grey Wolf?"

"It doesn't work like that," said Aravia. "I was just reading, not casting. And when you teleport, you can't send someone *else* away without going along with them yourself."

"Then what happened?" asked Tor. "Where could he have gone?"

"Maybe he's still on the ship somewheres," said Kibi. "First thing we oughta do is search for 'im."

Lacking a better alternative they did as Kibi suggested, scouring the ship both below and above decks, but Grey Wolf was gone without a trace. They gathered an hour later in the hold, all of them nervous, perhaps wondering who would be next. Morningstar sensed they needed someone to take charge. She didn't want to do it herself, but no one else was likely to step up.

"We can't let this change anything," she said. "We have our job to do, so let's keep our focus." It was hard for her to put conviction into her words, rattled as she was by Grey Wolf's disappearance. He had been a strong guiding presence, not to mention the oldest member of the group since Mrs. Horn had died.

"But what if someone's attacking us?" asked Ernie. "Abernathy's put us in a dangerous position. What if someone in the Black Circle did this? Or a Sharshun? Or…oh, I don't know."

"Doubt it," said Kibi.

Morningstar looked at him. "Why is that?"

"'Cause he first complained 'bout his stomach on the way to Verdshane, 'fore we had done anythin' or even heard a' all these bad people."

"Then what do you think happened?" asked Ernie, his voice still wavering.

Kibi rubbed his beard. "Ernie, you and me, we got picked by Abernathy's spell 'cause of our strange connection, that's what Aravia here said, and I got no cause to doubt it. Seems to me, Grey Wolf has somethin' odd about him too, what with his stomach and all. So maybe his vanishin' is part a' what got him picked to be one of us in the first place. Maybe he was supposed to disappear."

That was a stretch, but Kibi's words gave the others at least a sliver of comfort. "It's a good theory, Kibi," Morningstar said. "Since there's nothing else we can do about it, at least until Abernathy wakes up and we're home to tell him, let's carry on with our mission. We should refocus. Why don't we review everything we know about what's going on."

The others shifted uneasily and looked at one other for a long, uncomfortable moment. Then Dranko spoke.

"As I see it, we've got three things to worry about, besides whatever made Grey Wolf disappear. We've got the Black Circle cult that infiltrated my church and dug up a horrible monster in the desert that has Abernathy shaking in his wizard boots. We've got the Sharshun, who are looking for Eyes of Moirel gemstones that have some connection to that rock circle—"

"The Seven Mirrors." Aravia had her nose back in her book and didn't look like she was paying attention.

"Thanks, Miss Library," said Dranko. "Right. And Ernie's stuffed bear thinks the Sharshun want to make the world end, which would be a serious inconvenience because then where would I buy my cigars? And we've got the monster-emperor kicking down his prison door at Verdshane. Am I missing anything?"

"There's the guy with the big mustache that was at the Mirrors," said Kibi. "He was awful quick to jump in when the Sharshun dropped his Eye of Moirel. Good bet he's up to somethin'."

Aravia still didn't look up from her book. "Sagiro Emberleaf. Hey, does someone have a handful of chits?"

Dranko produced the coins. Aravia took the chits one at a time, each time murmuring quickly and flexing the fingers of her left hand. One by one, the coins lit up.

Ernie jumped to his feet. "Why are you all so calm about this? Grey Wolf is gone, and you're…you're messing around with coins and talking about things like nothing happened! We need him!"

Morningstar sighed. Hysteria would get them nowhere. "Ernie, what do you propose we do? We've searched the ship; he's not here. Of course we're all worried, but do you think it will help to panic?"

Ernie reddened and looked down at his toes. "No. It's just…"

"It's okay, Ernie," said Tor. "But Morningstar's right. We're still doing our job for Abernathy. We'll just have to hope that Grey Wolf's okay, and will come back safely from wherever he went."

"Done," said Aravia. In her hand, all twelve chits were glowing like little torches. "Best of all, if I understand Abernathy's book properly, these should stay lit for a month. Just keep one or two in your pocket, and pull one out when you need light. By working on Abernathy's variants of spells I already knew, I think I'm figuring out the best way to learn his dialect."

Morningstar looked at the pile of glowing copper coins in Aravia's palm, impressed. Then the shock came. She'd been staring into the cluster of lights for a good ten seconds with only the barest of squints. Before Abernathy's summons, she'd have been squeezing her eyes shut to avoid the pain and blindness from something so bright, but now…

"Ell, forgive me," she muttered.

* * *

There was a young boy, lost in the woods.

The trees grew so close together as to form solid expanses of silver-gray, turning the forest into a high-walled labyrinth, dark and full of an eerie rustling. The boy's bare feet crunched on a carpet of dead leaves.

Morningstar was in the dream as well, a Seer-dream of startling clarity; the moonlight etched the edges of every leaf and branch, and the shadows cast upon the ground were knife-sharp. She held her morning-star mace.

The boy walked toward her down a corridor of oaks, slowly, fearfully. "I'm lost," he said in a small voice. "Where am I?"

"You're dreaming," said Morningstar, and this was peculiar because dreamers of Seer-dreams could only observe. They could not talk, or move, or influence the dreams, but were granted a place inside them by Ell to better understand the workings of the world.

This was something new.

She took a step forward, marveling at the tactile sensations of her bare feet on the leaves, the feel of her robe against the pale skin of her arms.

"But something's after me," pleaded the boy. "I'm in trouble!"

"No, child," said Morningstar soothingly. "No harm can come to you here. This is only a dream."

"Do not lie to the boy, Dreamwalker."

A man stepped out into the forest path, emerging from a gap in the tree wall that Morningstar couldn't see from her straight-on vantage point. He was clad foot to neck in gleaming blood-red plates, but his movements were fluid, troublingly unencumbered. A sheathed blade hung at his belt, and a helmet, red to match his armor, was tucked under his left arm. A goatee covered his chin beneath a wicked grin. This newcomer stood between Morningstar and the boy.

It was the man from her first Seer-dream—the one whom Tor had bull-rushed off the tower-top.

"Plenty of harm can come to you, boy," said the man. Casually, with his one free hand, he picked up the child by the collar of his shirt and tossed him toward Morningstar, effortlessly, like a man scattering bread crumbs for pigeons. The terrified child crashed into Morningstar, sending them both sprawling. The boy wailed in shock and pain; blood ran from a freshly scraped elbow.

Morningstar struggled to one knee. "Wake up, child," she implored. "Wake, and all of this will be forgotten."

The red-armored warrior walked slowly forward.

Morningstar filled her voice with urgency. "Wake up! You must wake!"

The boy looked back at her with wide eyes and a trembling lip. Tears gathered on his lashes.

At the sound of a sword being drawn she risked a glance upward. The warrior was only ten feet away.

She closed her eyes and tried to will *the boy from the dream. "Awaken!"*

The boy vanished. A pair of gleaming red greaves moved into view. Morningstar looked up at the red-armored man looming above her and scurried back, regaining her feet as she moved. The man took another step forward, unhurried.

"He told me there might be some Ellish roaches crawling around inside your world's dreams. I didn't expect to have to step on one so soon."

A good part of Morningstar's subconscious was yammering at her to wake up, flee the dream. The warrior's sword was like a shard of black ice, glistening with a dark liquid that oozed over its metal surface. But this was a Seer-dream (wasn't it?), and Ell would not have put her here if she was meant to flee. She raised her mace in defiance.

"You don't belong here," she said, surprising herself with the steadiness of her voice. "Get out, before I drive you out."

The man chuckled. "Roaches all have one thing in common," he said. "Shine a light upon them and they scurry away. Begone, little bug."

He held up his off-hand, and a ring on his finger blazed with a furious white light. Morningstar flinched but held steady.

"Is that supposed to put me off?" she asked, standing her ground though her eyes burned in the glare. "You have a lot to learn, though you've figured out cowardice well enough, tormenting a defenseless child. What is your name, coward?"

A flicker of doubt and surprise passed over the man's face; he had expected his light to be more enervating, Morningstar was certain. But he regained his composure and his sneer.

"I am Aktallian Dreamborn. Remember that, so you can answer those who ask who sent you to the afterlife."

Morningstar's weapon vanished from her hand; somehow her enemy had willed it away. No, more than that, he had altered the dream so that she no longer held it. Aktallian laughed, stepped quickly forward, and thrust his sword into her stomach. She screamed, the fire of the wound burning her guts. Clutching her abdomen as he withdrew the blade, blood pouring out in a torrent through her hands, she dropped to her knees.

"Speed you to the heavens, Ellish roach." He spat upon her, and she fell.

* * *

Morningstar woke, screaming, in the hold of the ship. Relief shot through her, but only briefly, before it was replaced by a terrible agony from her belly. She tried to sit up but her muscles didn't respond; just the attempt made the already indescribable pain even more intense. She screamed again, more loudly, and around her in a pain-dimmed haze she became aware of lights and voices.

Aravia was there first, shining a lit coin upon her. "Dranko!" Aravia shouted. "Get over here now! Wake up! Dranko!"

Morningstar feebly raised her hands from her stomach; they were soaked with gore, and more blood was pooling all around her. How…?

"Ernie, Tor, something attacked Morningstar. Something's in here with us; find it! Dranko, hurry, she's dying!"

The pain faded, replaced by a numbing cold. Aravia's light was fading away.

"Keep your eyes open!" shouted Aravia. "Can you talk? Morningstar, look at me. Keep looking at me. Dranko, is there anything you can do for her?"

Then Dranko was above her, his face darkening at the extent of her wound.

Goddess, please, don't let that goblin face be the last thing I ever see.

Dranko spoke quickly, words of entreaty spilling from his lips, and for a second the pain surged back into her legs, her belly; her throat opened and fresh screams poured out. But then the pain was gone, replaced by warmth and light and now she would sleep, and was it a terrible blasphemy to ask for dreamless slumber?

Her wish was granted.

CHAPTER TWENTY-TWO

Dranko awoke covered in blood, drying but still sticky, and this made him grumpy. His thoughts were slow and mushy, like someone was stifling his mind with a pillow. Mild nausea stirred his stomach, probably from the gentle rocking of the ship, and that wasn't helping matters.

The others were already awake, sitting against the shipping crates, talking quietly and drinking from water skins. If the blood were indicative of some imminent or ongoing emergency, he would have expected more activity and shouting, so that was a relief.

"Whose blood is this?" he demanded. "And why is it all over me?"

"It's mine," said Morningstar. The Ellish priestess wasn't talking or drinking but sat with her eyes closed even as she spoke. "You healed me about an hour ago."

Maybe this was one of those dreams where you think you've woken up, but it's a sham and you're still dreaming. "I…what?"

"You were still half-asleep yourself," said Aravia. "You channeled, Dranko. You saved Morningstar's life and fell right back asleep."

Dranko shook his head, but this did little to clear it.

"I channeled? Really?"

"Really," said Ernie. "Your hands glowed yellow, and Morningstar's stomach healed right up."

Why don't I remember that?

"Good for me," he said. "But what happened to Morningstar's stomach? And why is no one else still worried about it?"

"I was attacked," said Morningstar. "And I'm plenty worried. But none of the rest of you are in danger, I think. I was attacked in a dream."

That didn't make sense. None of this did. He hadn't even *tried* to channel since the disaster with Mrs. Horn at Verdshane. He had convinced himself that the beggar had been a fluke, a one-time thing that had pushed his limits too far, left him a broken vessel unworthy of Delioch.

No. That's not it. You're terrified of the price Delioch demands for His grace. If you can't be honest with the others, be honest with yourself at least.

But unless the others were playing an extremely tasteless joke, he had channeled a second time. He wished he could recall what it was like.

"You...what? Is that possible? How can something hurt your actual body while you're dreaming?"

"I don't know." Morningstar sounded frustrated, dejected, and scared in equal measures. "I was having what I thought was another Seer-dream, but there was...there was an armored man there with a black sword, the same man I saw in my first Seer-dream, the man who Tor tackled from a high ledge."

In fits and starts, Morningstar described the entirety of her experience, right up to when she woke and found that the sword wound inflicted upon her in the dream had also done its damage to her waking body.

"So," said Dranko, when Morningstar was finished, "any idea what it all means?"

Morningstar shook her head. "I've never heard of a sister having Seer-dreams where the dreamer had agency, nor of any case where a dreamer suffered real injuries from anything that happened while asleep. But I do remember one thing clearly—this Aktallian made a comment that he had been sent by someone else and had been warned about 'your world's dreams.'"

Dranko tried to shake the cotton stuffing out of his head; he ought to be making some connection. Of course Aravia put it together immediately.

"I think Aktallian is from Naradawk's prison world, and it was Naradawk who sent him," she said. "Though it's possible he's come from some other world entirely."

Dranko had been imagining that Naradawk's prison was more like a big room, out on a little island in the ocean somewhere, cut off from the rest of Spira. But other worlds? He was just going to have to ask.

"Aravia, for the sake of those of us who weren't taught at Serpicore's Wizard School for the Insufferably Gifted, could you maybe explain a bit more about other worlds?"

"Dranko," said Aravia with mock disapproval, "you've often talked about the education you received at the Church of Delioch, before you…left."

Dranko grimaced. "You can say 'before you were kicked out on your arse' if you want."

"Didn't they teach you about the afterlife and where the Gods live before you were kicked out on your arse?"

Dranko tried to sound as professorial as possible, adopting the formal tones of his one-time teachers. "Of course. The Gods occupy the Heavens, and each maintains His or Her own celestial realm. When someone dies, their soul ascends to the realm associated with their chosen deity, assuming they've been diligent about following that God's teachings. And bad people go to the Hells, naturally."

"So you *have* learned about other worlds," said Aravia. "The Heavens and the Hells are real places, you know. You just can't visit them unless you're dead."

Dranko had spent more than his fair share of time thinking about the Hells, given the steady litany of warnings from Mokad that he was destined to wind up there should he continue his malcontented delinquency. Some of the scarbearers' descriptions were gruesomely detailed: souls forced into the forms of monsters fated to prowl the fiery plains; souls returned to human bodies, the better to experience an eternity of anguish, and impaled on stakes; souls immersed in rivers of boiling acid; that sort of thing. But so absurdly horrific were these portraits of the netherworld that Dranko had eventually concluded it must all be a kind of tortured (ha!) metaphor, that no such place *really* existed.

In other words, it was mostly scare tactics.

"So this guy in the red armor," he said, "he may have come from the Hells?"

"No, probably not," said Aravia. "*Most* other worlds are like this one. Normal places with normal people in them. You can't travel between them the same way you could walk from, say, Tal Hae to Verdshane. They're not in the same dimension."

"I have no idea what that means," said Dranko. This would be a better conversation to have once he'd recovered a bit more.

"It doesn't matter," said Aravia. "Just take my word for it. There are potentially an infinite number of worlds similar to this one, but as a matter of course they never have anything to do with one another. But with the proper magic at one's disposal, one could travel between them."

Dranko rubbed his temples. "So the prison world that Abernathy's monster is trapped in, it's actually a whole world, like this one, with countries and people and trees and everything else?"

"Possibly. Oh, it's certainly a world, but it could be a barren wasteland, or one with thriving cities, or nothing but forest for thousands of miles. But if Naradawk is as powerful as Abernathy thinks, it's a good bet that he's running the place."

"And now he's sending thugs through Abernathy's portal to attack us in our dreams?"

"That's what I'm saying," said Aravia. "I suppose we should be happy that he's still unable or unwilling to come himself, but yes."

Dranko was still troubled. "Could Aktallian get himself into *any* of our dreams, then, and slice us up?"

"I don't know!" Morningstar said, probably more loudly than she intended. "I'm sorry, but...I just don't know. This is all out of my experience. Maybe Previa knows, or someone else at the Temple. I'll find out when we get back. But..."

She raised her arms in a gesture of helplessness, but she caught Dranko's eye, lowered her hands, and stared at him.

"Thank you, Dranko," she said quietly. "I admit, I've been...unhappy with you, about having to endure the Mouth of Nahalm after we rescued you. Walking in the sun all that way was not easy for me, and I blamed you for it. I still do. I don't like you. You're crude, abrasive, and not half as clever as you think you are."

Dranko gave a little laugh. "I'd hate to think how this conversation would be going if I *hadn't* just saved your life. Can we say three-quarters as clever and be done with it?"

Morningstar's face was unreadable in the shadows. "You did save my life. And you tried to save Mrs. Horn. I've often wondered why it was that Abernathy's spell chose you to help us safeguard Charagan, but it's become obvious, hasn't it? You truly are a channeler. Delioch favors you—though I cannot imagine why."

Dranko smiled at her. "You're terrible at apologies."

Morningstar rose without another word and climbed the ladder to the deck. The others shifted around uncomfortably, none of them looking at his face.

"What?" he demanded. "I just saved her life, apparently, and for that I get called all sorts of names. And I'm supposed to just sit here and take it?"

"You weren't there," said Ernie. "Not awake, at least. In the desert. She's been having a really hard time with this whole thing, Dranko. She feels like an outcast, *and* she's being forced to endure terrible physical hardships. Give her a break."

An outcast, huh? Physical hardships? He imagined the feel of Mokad's scarring blade against his skin. He knew how *that* felt. Without giving himself time to think too hard (and it was still too hard to think, anyhow), he heaved himself to his feet and followed Morningstar up the ladder. It was dark, the hour before sunrise, and the stars above the ship played hide and seek among the high moonlit clouds. Morningstar stood close at hand, eyes closed, leaning on the rail.

"I know how you feel," he said.

She didn't turn to face him. "I doubt it."

The ship rocked gently, water chuckling against the hull.

Dranko took a deep breath. "When I was eight, one of the other boys in the village threw a rock at me, right at my head. Chipped my tusk and gashed the side of my face. His name was Pietr Tock. Can't say I hated him more than any other kid, and it wasn't the first rock I'd had hurled at me. Usually I dodged 'em better.

"Everyone in town loved Pietr Tock. He was a fine, handsome, hard-working lad, and I was…well, when I got home and cried to Grandpa, blood and tears all over my face, you know what he did? He beat me for lying. Said 'Shame on you, Melen, shame for telling tales about such a well-mannered child.' That was my name back then, Melen, before I changed it. After giving me the belt, Grandpa smeared some old salve on my cheek and told me to stop wailing and to make dinner. Wasn't long before that was my first real scar, years before Mokad got his hands on me."

Morningstar didn't turn to look at him, but she asked, "Why did you change your name?"

Dranko almost told her the whole story, right there, but some of it he still wasn't ready to share. The abridged version would do. "It was just me and my grandparents. My parents had both died…when I was very young. Grammy Saramin loved me like her own son, but Grandpa, he blamed me for every bad thing that had happened to our family, and there were a lot of bad things. When Grammy died, Grandpa didn't wait two weeks before shipping me off to Tal Hae to be a ward of the Church of Delioch. Old bastard couldn't wait to be rid of me. I was fourteen years old by then.

"One of the things they let you do at the church is take a new name, if you want. So I looked in some books in the church library and found what I needed. I told Mokad I was changing my name to Dranko. It's a goblin word. It means 'unwelcome.'"

Morningstar's hands tightened on the railing, and now she looked at him. Her eyes reflected the starlight.

"Morningstar, maybe Abernathy's spell, or fate, or whatever it was, put us both where we are because we can understand one another's pain. I'm not asking you to like me, but when I say I know how you feel, it's because I know how you feel. I'll probably regret sharing all this with you, but now that we've taken turns saving each other's life, it seemed like a thing to do. Now I'm going back down to get some more sleep. Gods, but my head hurts."

CHAPTER TWENTY-THREE

Despite his own small town upbringing, Ernie found Seablade Point to be outwardly quaint. It was a tiny fishing village, bigger than Verdshane but only half the size of White Ferry. Clinging to the southern tip of the Balani Peninsula like a fixture of barnacles, its scattering of small buildings crouched low to avoid the constant crosswinds.

They had gathered in the commons of Seablade Point's only inn, the Old Keg, enjoying mugs of excellent beer that cost a mere copper chit each. Half the town's population must have been crowded in there as well, mostly fisherfolk who had ended the day early as a pounding rain pelted outside.

Dranko had suggested that before they interrogated the townsfolk, they should mingle and make friends. Now he was in his element, regaling the locals with tales of adventure, while Tor sat nearby interjecting dramatic flourishes to the narrative. A crowd had massed around them; even one stranger in town was rare, let alone such a motley half-dozen as Horn's Company. Dranko had already fielded a number of questions about both his scars and his tusks but didn't seem to mind. Now he was retelling the Battle of the Gopher-Bugs.

It was a good sign that they had come to terms with the awful events of that place and the death of Mrs. Horn. Even though they had only known her a week, almost every night now someone recalled a bit of wisdom she had imparted or a kindly remark she had made. The grief was still there, but it had taken on a soft glow. It was like a fire you didn't want to touch, but the warmth of which was almost a comfort. Whenever he was feeling timid or lost, he imagined her face, her smile, her encouraging words. *Stay positive, Ernest.*

A gale of laughter came from Dranko's table. Ernie admired his lack of self-consciousness about his appearance. Would Ernie be as outgoing if he looked like that, with tusks and all those scars? And yet there was something paradoxical about Dranko's behavior, where on the one hand he was crude and abrasive, always wanting to drive people away, while on the other he lapped up attention like a hungry cat at the milk bowl. Maybe he was just desperate to leave an impression and didn't care what kind.

Morningstar was sitting quietly at the end of their long table, ignored by the townsfolk, chin propped in one hand. Dark circles beneath her eyes betrayed a profound weariness; her encounter with Aktallian must be affecting the soundness of her sleep. He too would be nervous about going to bed, if a murderous warrior could show up in his dreams and skewer him like a sausage! But beyond offers of moral support, he wasn't sure how he could help.

Aravia was alone in a corner of the commons, nose in a book, one hand flipping pages back and forth while the other raced across her own notebook with a pen. She had been like that the entire voyage, studying Abernathy's books with a fervent energy that impressed him mightily. Ernie figured she had spent more time reading in the past week than he had done his whole life, unless you included recipes.

He still found it unsettling that his friends weren't fretting more about Grey Wolf's disappearance. Aravia in particular had barely reacted at all, as though people vanished out of ships' holds every other day where she was from. Yes, of course, there was nothing they could *do*, and Horn's Company needed to stay the course and learn about the Kivian Arch, but still. Surely there was *some* precaution they should be taking.

Ernie shook his head, took a long pull at his beer mug, and looked around the Old Keg one more time. He felt restless. They should be finding out what they could about the arch. Grey Wolf wouldn't be sitting around waiting for someone else to take charge, that was for sure! As Kibi was unlikely to strike up a conversation with strangers, Ernie took it upon himself to start the investigation. On the ship they had decided that there was little reason to be circumspect; Abernathy hadn't mentioned that Levec, or the Kivian Arch itself, was anything particularly secret.

He flagged down a serving woman.

"Excuse me, miss?"

A buxom, button-nosed lass approached, swaying and weaving between the close-set tables. She was near his own age, maybe a bit older, and she looked upon Ernie with a mischievous smile. "Yes, handsome stranger?"

Ernie flushed to the tips of his ears. "Uh, hello. I…this is excellent beer!"

"Thank you, good sir. Might I ask your name?"

"Ernest. Ernest Roundhill."

"Pleased to meet you! My name's Perri. Do you always carry a sword, Ernest Roundhill, and travel with such outlandish folk?"

Perri sat down into the chair opposite and brushed back a fetching strand of auburn hair from her face. "We see so few strangers here," she said before Ernie could answer her questions. "The supply ships come every couple of months, but the sailors are all the same. Boorish, flea-ridden, with bad teeth. But you're something different, I think. You're certainly better looking than most of them. Tell me, where are you from?"

Ernie was terrified of girls, to be honest about it. He had tended to freeze up when the lasses back in White Ferry tried to flirt, but this was…well, something different all right. Certainly none of them had come right out and told him he was handsome. Silently he thanked the Gods that Dranko was too distracted to have overheard, or who knew what sort of crude jests he'd be making right now.

"White Ferry," he said, before hastily adding, "That's near Tal Hae. On Harkran. It's, uh, far from here. On a ship. We came on a ship."

He forced himself to stop talking.

"I've never been away from Seablade Point," said Perri. "I've been listening to your friends' tale, and your life sounds so exciting!"

She leaned towards him, probably because it was so difficult to hear over the noise of Dranko's oration, which had the side effect, no doubt unintentional, of revealing even more of her cleavage than had already been evident. Not that he had noticed that! Ernie did the proper thing and maintained studious eye contact.

"Oh, it is," he said. "We're on an important mission right now, to, uh…"

Abernathy *had* suggested not mentioning the archmagi or the Spire during their investigations, but those limitations made it difficult for Ernie to properly convey the gravity of things. He groped for some word that would express the unimaginable import of their work, but came up empty.

"…to find an important person," he finished lamely. But Perri's attention didn't waver, and if anything she leaned a bit further in his direction. Eye contact!

"Who are you looking for?" she asked. "And why would an important person come to Seablade Point in the first place?"

"Well, there's a man who's lived here for a long time, and we were hoping to speak with him. His name is Levec. Perhaps you know him?"

Perri sat up straight, curtailing his view. Not that he was disappointed! "Oh," she said. "There was someone here called that, I…I think. But he left."

"I'm sorry to hear that. Do you know when he left, and where he went?"

Her eyes became unfocused, as though she were trying to dredge up a very old memory. "I'm not sure. Maybe…a year ago? And I don't know where he went. He just…went away."

Her coquettish manner had altogether vanished, which left Ernie feeling both relief and regret. She stared over his shoulder for another several seconds.

"Then maybe you can help me with something else," said Ernie. "We're also looking for a big stone archway, probably in the nearby woods."

She didn't reply right away. Ernie tried to place her expression. Puzzled?

"That does sound familiar," she said slowly. "But…no, an arch? In the woods? No, I'm sure I've never heard of it."

Ernie was puzzled as well. "If you're sure you've never heard of it, then why does it sound familiar?"

"I guess I was wrong. There's no arch here, Ernest. Not that I have ever seen. Enjoy your beer."

She retreated quickly, leaving Ernie bewildered and just a bit crestfallen. Not wanting to disturb Aravia, he wandered to the far side of the table where Kibi sat with his beer, eyes half closed.

He recounted his brief conversation with Perri, even including her possible interest in him as a physical specimen—though he added that last part only because the sudden change in her demeanor at the end was so peculiar. Kibi stroked his beard and looked Ernie up and down.

"Well, you are a right handsome fella, so I ain't surprised about that part."

"That's not the point!" Ernie nodded toward Perri, who had drifted to the far side of the commons to collect some empty mugs. "I think she knows something, but doesn't want to say."

"You want me to go have a chat with her?"

"No. I don't want her to think we've come to harass her."

Kibi pondered another few seconds. "Would be strange if you struck up a chat with the only person in town who wants to hide the truth. Maybe we oughta ask a few more folks and see if they all clam up the same way."

Ernie glanced over at Aravia, thinking maybe he would risk bothering her after all, just long enough to ask her advice, but she had already put down her book. The fingers on her left hand twiddled in a practiced gesture, and she moved her head slowly from side to side, taking in the whole of the Old Keg commons. Her right fist was clenched, but yellow light leaked out from between her fingers. Was she gripping one of her *heatless light* coins? Abruptly she stood, stuffed her books back in her pack, and walked straight to Morningstar. She whispered something in the Ellish sister's ear, upon which Morningstar rose and sauntered towards him while Aravia moved off to where Dranko and Tor were holding forth.

"Aravia says we should talk outside," Morningstar said. "She said she's discovered something important."

They regrouped out on the street. Ernie pulled his cloak's hood up over his head to ward off the rain, though the wind made that something of a fool's errand.

"Why aren't we having this discussion back inside?" asked Dranko. "It's dry and full of cheap beer in there."

"Because we can't trust them," said Aravia.

"Who?" asked Morningstar.

"Listen," said Aravia. "I've been trying to learn some simple utility magic from Abernathy's books, and one of the spells I've learned is called *aura sense*. It lets me detect anything that's magical—or has a spell cast on it—within about a hundred feet of me. I thought it would be useful in case we ended up tromping around the forest looking for a big magical archway."

"Makes sense," said Kibi.

"It worked exactly as I expected; the spell indicated a minor enchantment on a magically lit coin. Oh, and also on your sword, Ernie."

"Really? Pyknite is a *magic sword?*"

"Yes. The enchantment is not powerful, but your blade is certainly ensorcelled."

"And you had to drag us out into the rain to tell us?" Dranko grumbled.

"No, no, it's not that. It's not just my coin and Ernie's sword that are magical. *So is every single person in that inn.* All of them. It's a moderately strong enchantment mixed with an enervating vitamancy."

"What does—" Tor began.

"Life force," said Aravia. "Vitamancy is a school of magic that deals with life energy, typically by either bolstering it or draining it away. These people are all afflicted with that second one. Enervating."

"I was just talking to, uh, Perri," said Ernie. "One of the serving girls. It seemed like it couldn't hurt. But when I asked her about Levec and the arch, she got kind of confused."

"What does that mean, kind of confused?" asked Morningstar.

"Like…like she knew for a second and then forgot? Or maybe that she knew, but was afraid to tell me and so pretended she didn't know. She *did* say that Levec left town about a year ago, but didn't seem very sure of herself. I don't know exactly. I can go back and talk to her again." And this time he might manage not to babble so much.

"She's probably lying about Levec," said Aravia. "Abernathy told us he was still sending reports up until a couple of months ago. It's possible that the whole town is involved in something nefarious, so I'd suggest not talking to anyone else until we find out more."

"Maybe we should go searchin' for that arch," suggested Kibi.

Dranko blew rainwater from his lips. "Now? In this downpour?"

"We'll be camping out in the rain anyway," said Aravia. "The only place to stay in this town is where we just came from, and it's filled with people under the effects of unknown magic. We can't trust them."

"We still have an hour or two of daylight left," said Tor. "Why not check it out right now? Abernathy told us more or less where to look, and Aravia can cast her aura finder spell. And Levec could be at the arch right now. If he is, we'll have found both things we're looking for with just a bit of walking. Come on!"

At least it was a place to go. While none of the rest of the company seemed to share Tor's optimism, they all seemed wary of the Inn of Enchanted Villagers. Ernie certainly was, despite the lingering and pleasant memory of Perri's auburn locks. So off they marched, putting their backs to the southern end of the peninsula and heading inland toward the hilly forest where the arch was supposed to be. There was no road to follow, but a narrow weedy footpath along a low stone wall took them most of the way to the woods.

On the far side of the wall a farmer was out working in her field despite the rain, pulling up weeds from a row of young cabbages. She stood, stared, waved, then returned to her labor. Aravia slowed and dropped to the back of the line as she wiggled her fingers.

"She's the same as the others," she said, a bit breathless. "I wondered if maybe the Old Keg itself was the source of the enchantment, but my hypothesis now is that everyone in the town is affected."

The forest was sparse and easily negotiated but still offered decent protection from the rain. Ernie pulled the soggy hood of his cloak away from his head.

"So, Aravia," said Dranko. "Since it's going to be dark soon, can you do your magic thing and get us where we're going? I thought the whole point of you learning that spell was as an arch detector."

"Yes," said Aravia. "But I've cast it twice already in the last half an hour. I need a few minutes to recover. I'll be able to cast it again, but I'd like to get a little closer to where we think we're going before I do."

The forest was dim and growing dimmer by the minute. Ernie remembered he had one of Aravia's glowing coins in his pocket and pulled it out. It was still thrilling to hold an enchanted object in his hand, one created by a wizard that *he personally knew.* No, two objects—the sword Pyknite was magical too. Did it have hidden powers? Old Bowlegs had often said that his blade hated goblins; maybe he meant that more literally than Ernie had suspected.

"That's going to wash out my darksight," said Morningstar. "And give us away to anyone who might be watching."

"But the rest of us have to see," said Tor. "And if there's anyone out here, I say the sooner we confront them, the better."

Morningstar sighed. "We shouldn't be so quick to—"

"Excuse me," Kibi interrupted. He had also produced a shining coin and was peering at the ground ahead. "I'd say you can stop bickerin' since it's obvious where we're headed."

"Did the rocks tell you?" asked Ernie.

"Nope. I'm just noticin' all them footprints where we ain't been yet."

Out came more light-coins, until everyone but Morningstar was holding one and bending low to the forest floor. Sure enough, coming in from behind them at a slight diagonal and leading off into the recesses of the wood was a trampled down swath of churned mud. Many sets of footprints were evident, though most of them, where such detail could still be made out, had been made by bare feet.

"That's more than just a well-traveled path," said Tor. "It looks like dozens of people have been coming this way for months."

"There and back," said Aravia. "The prints seem evenly divided in which way they're facing."

Ernie stared at the ground. "I wish I knew more about tracking. Can any of you tell how fresh these are?"

Dranko crouched and leaned until his tusks nearly grazed the dirt. "Pretty fresh, I think. I can still make out individual toe prints."

"Then let's follow them," said Tor, and he bounded forward through the trees, leaving the others to either follow or let him go alone.

Ernie dashed to catch up. "Tor, remember what might be going on here. Abernathy said an army once invaded through the arch, and they might be trying again. Slow down and let's stick together, okay?"

"If there were an army out here, we'd hear them," said Tor. "Stop worrying so much."

Ernie flinched; that was the sort of thing someone would say right before a hail of arrows or a rampaging bear attack. But the only sounds in the darkening wood were from the boots of the company and the drip of water down from the trees.

They discovered the Kivian Arch only ten minutes later—so hardly more than a half hour ramble from Seablade Point—and Ernie was overwhelmed by its immensity. He gazed up in awe, light-coin held in his upraised hand. It stood watch among the trees like a silent giant. The keystone must have been forty feet off the ground, and his parents' house could have sat comfortably between the arch's legs.

"Freestanding, triumphal, unadorned entablature." Kibi, standing next to him, didn't seem to realize he was talking aloud.

Ernie was impressed. "What does that mean?"

"Oh," answered Kibi. "That jus' means the top part a' the arch is flat on top instead of curved, and ain't got no fancy carvings."

Dranko strode directly over to the nearest of the massive pylons. "I know this will shock everyone, but the footprints stop directly beneath the arch. So what we've got is, a whole bunch of townsfolk come out here pretty regularly in their bare feet, dance around under the arch, then go home again, and they don't want to talk about it with strangers. Must be one heck of a party!"

"Could they be going *through* the arch?" asked Tor. "Maybe it's already opened!"

"I doubt it," said Aravia. "The mass of footprints is all around the area under the arch, on both sides of it. If they were going through it to Kivia, most or all of their prints would only be on one side."

"No sign of Levec," said Kibi. The stonecutter had joined Dranko standing next to the closer of the arch's two squared pillars. He put his palm against it. "This ain't any kind a' ordinary stone I ever seen." He held up his light-coin. "And it's got metal in it."

Intrigued, Ernie moved to join them. The surface of the Kivian Arch was knobbly, rough-hewn from something akin to granite, but darker and veined with thin black streaks.

"Ain't natural," said Kibi. "And it ain't talkin', neither."

"It's almost certainly magical," said Aravia. "But it can't hurt to be sure."

That turned out to be an inaccurate statement. She twiddled her fingers to cast her magic-detecting spell, then with a cry threw her arm across her face before staggering backward and falling into the leafy mud. Ernie heard several others join him in his alarmed cry of "Aravia!" and Dranko was quickly at her side.

Tor hurried over. "Is she okay?"

Aravia groaned and sat up, one hand flat on the ground, the other rubbing her temples.

"I'm guessing that means it's magic," said Dranko.

Aravia seemed to try laughing; her shoulders shook a bit, but she was too weak to make much noise. Tor helped her to her feet, and she leaned against him, eyes closed, gulping air and coughing.

"I'll…I'll be all right," she croaked, smiling up at Tor. "Wasn't ready for that much magic. It was like having a room full of unshuttered lanterns aimed at my eyes at once. Not to mention I haven't worked on any refinements to make casting *aura sense* less draining, and that was my third one in less than an hour. Not the smartest thing I could have done."

Kibi stared at the arch, frowning, like he disapproved of it. "So what now?"

"I've got an idea," said Dranko. "Since it looks like a crowd shows up here regularly, we should find somewhere nearby where we can hide out and watch without being spotted ourselves. See what happens. Maybe they have a way to open it. Maybe they just hang out and drink wine. Either way, we'll learn more than we know right now."

"But we can't let them see us," said Ernie. "And in the dark, how are we going to see them?"

"They probably bring torches or lamps or something," said Dranko. Then he pointed to Morningstar. "And if they don't, we've got her."

Horn's Company searched around the forest for a good twenty minutes before finding a suitably hidden thicket, far enough removed from the Kivian Arch that discovery was unlikely, but close enough for Morningstar to make out reasonable detail. It was possible, of course, that whoever showed up here would first search the surrounding forest for spies, especially if they included any of the townsfolk who had met the company earlier in the Old Keg. But they didn't see any footprints near their hiding spot and did their best not to leave too many of their own.

Sunset brought with it a chorus of insect noises and the percussive brapping of bullfrogs. The night cooled a little as it deepened, and the rain stopped, though the cloud cover remained thick, blocking out moonlight and star-shine.

They ate an unsatisfying dinner of jerky and dried fruit, after which Aravia immediately fell asleep. Ernie sorely missed the Greenhouse kitchen, and sat in silence on a damp log, thinking about the pies he would bake when they got home. Presumably the Icebox would produce raw ingredients if he asked for them, and not just finished meals. How long would Icebox-conjured spices last? For that matter, some spices were rare and valuable, enough so that they could make a decent profit conjuring and selling things like saffron or asafetida. Eddings said the dishes vanished after a day, but did the food? He'd have to tell Dranko about his idea.

Ernie's eyelids drooped as these thoughts flitted through his head, and eventually, lying on his back with his head on a passel of damp leaves, he fell asleep.

Then Tor was shaking him. "Ernie, wake up. Something's happening."

"Whuh?" he managed.

It took a minute for his eyes to adjust to near-total darkness. The cloud cover had thinned a little while he slept, allowing the faintest dappled wash of moonlight to reach the forest floor, and while Aravia was still out cold, Morningstar, Dranko, and Kibi had inched forward to the edge of the thicket closest to the arch. They were lying on their stomachs with their heads all nearly together, so they could whisper to one another as quietly as possible. He and Tor tiptoed over and lay down too, squeezing in.

Seven people had wandered up to the Arch from the direction of Seablade Point, two of whom Ernie thought he recognized from the Old Keg. One held a swinging lantern and another a sputtering torch. All seven were barefoot and dressed in nightshirts or sleeping gowns, but they showed no sign of discomfort at the chill night air. They weren't talking to one another or communicating in any other way Ernie could see but milled about around the arch as if in a trance.

Over the next ten minutes another twenty-three people straggled into view, some by themselves, others in groups of two or three. Ernie's breath caught a little; one of them was Perri, wearing a long white nightgown, her disheveled hair glinting in the light of the various lamps and torches brought by the others.

"What are they doing?" he whispered.

"Who knows?" answered Tor. "Let's just keep watching."

The assembled townsfolk slowly arranged themselves into a straight line, directly under the arch, stretching between its two columns. Some were facing away from the company's hiding spot, while others were looking more or less straight at them. Thank Pikon their circle of light didn't extend to the hidden thicket! Perri's face was too far away for Ernie to discern anything of her expression.

All at once every light went out, plunging the Arch and its thirty visitors into blackness. But their eyes were pairs of little orange specks, hovering in a ragged line like a string of glowing beads, shining as though they were reflecting the light of a bonfire.

"That ain't natural," whispered Kibi.

The forest didn't remain dark for long. A bright flame-orange light sprung up beneath the arch, filling its inverted U and enveloping the thirty villagers. It cast all the trees around it in a flickering glow, almost as if they were on fire, and it was easy to imagine that the people had also been set aflame. But there was no sound, no fiery crackling or torch's hiss—just an enormous wall of light stretching the length and height of the arch.

Ernie nearly leapt from his hiding place, thinking that Perri and the rest were under some kind of magical attack, but Morningstar put a hand on his back and whispered harshly in his ear.

"We have no idea who else might be out there, and if we all go rushing out, we'll be leaving Aravia unprotected. We're here to gather information, so just watch and try to notice anything important."

The townsfolk, now a line of glowing silhouettes, remained stock still for several more minutes, transfixed by the arch-light. It was all very dreamlike, the surreal tableau making little sense, particularly since Ernie had only recently been awakened. Maybe he *was* dreaming.

"Am I dreaming?" he asked Tor.

"I don't think so."

Out went the arch-light, leaving behind the pin-prick fires in the eyes of the villagers, though as before there was nothing they might be reflecting. Then a few small flames leapt up as several of them re-lit their lanterns and torches. In a shuffling, shambling, voiceless pack, the barefooted and nightshirted citizens of Seablade Point moved off into the forest, heading back toward their homes.

When the sound of their departure had faded, Ernie moved to stand up, stretch, and have a drink from his water skin. But Morningstar whispered, "Stay down and stay quiet. Someone's still out there."

Ernie squinted and tried to see, but after staring at the solid wall of orange light his vision was blotted with pulsing afterimages. Nervous seconds ticked away; Tor on his right and Morningstar on his left were both holding their breaths.

"He's gone," said Morningstar, and the fact that she didn't whisper led to everyone else sitting up, exhaling, and generally creating a stir. Only Aravia stayed where she was, still asleep, snoring gently.

"So should we follow him?" asked Tor.

"No," said Morningstar. "Not with Aravia still out. It looks like we're dealing with someone with magic at his disposal, and frankly I want Aravia up and alert when we confront him."

"Who was it?" Ernie asked. "Someone we saw at the Old Keg?"

"No one I recognized," said Morningstar. "Tall, on the heavy side, bushy gray beard, red hair. Long red robes. And more importantly, he was walking with a purpose. Everyone else was stumbling around like sleepwalkers, but the fellow who stayed behind, he was wide awake. And unlike the others he didn't head back into town. I say we camp here tonight, let Aravia sleep off her spellcasting, keep watches in case anything else happens with the arch, and tomorrow morning we find our mystery man."

Ernie was shaking from a combination of adrenaline and cold, but at the words "camp here" a tremendous drowsiness overtook him. He lay down again on the spongy forest floor and tried to rediscover his dreams of apple pies.

CHAPTER TWENTY-FOUR

Tor had difficulty falling asleep.

In other circumstances he would have agitated for immediate pursuit of Morningstar's red-robed man because what if he was a villain in the final planning stages of something truly awful, and the only time he left himself vulnerable was on his late-night walks back to wherever he lived? Or what if the Arch was about to open? Or it could be the man was Levec himself, and his shenanigans with the arch were *preventing* a gateway opening to what-was-it-called, the other country across the Uncrossable Sea.

Whatever was going on, they needed to know the truth, and the sooner the better! After all, Charagan was in danger, and they needed the Crosser's Maze to stop the evil banished emperor from invading, but instead they had opted to wait until morning, which, he admitted, was the right call.

They needed Aravia. He rolled over and looked at her, sleeping, mouth slightly open, black hair matted and half covering her face.

She was the reason he couldn't sleep. She needed protecting, and he wanted to protect her, and if he fell asleep too, who knew what could happen?

No, that wasn't it. Wasn't all of it. He couldn't sleep because he was thinking about her, yes, but he was thinking all sorts of things about her, and it was very confusing.

At his father's castle in Forquelle, Tor's interactions with girls had been both limited and academic. His mother had a young lady-in-waiting who had smiled at him once, but his father had already warned him of the wily predilections and uncouth ambitions of the serving class. And a nobleman from mainland Lanei had brought his daughter on a state visit, a girl whom Tor was told might be a potential match for him in several years' time, but she was obsessed with dresses and combs and centerpieces, all topics on which Tor could not muster even a mild opinion without growing sleepy. Girls and their interests held little fascination for him, and besides, he had known for years that he would be running away eventually, and having to drag a girl along with him would have been much too complicated.

But who could have guessed that there were girls like Aravia in the world? She was fantastic! She wasn't afraid to say what she thought, and she didn't shy away from adventure at all, not like he was sure the baroness' daughter would have done, and she'd already saved his life at least once with her incredible magical powers.

The trouble, of course, was that she was so unbelievably smart. Tor was certain that Aravia was the smartest person he had ever met, except maybe Abernathy, but he was older and had lived longer, and Aravia would know just as much as Abernathy someday when she was an archmage, while Tor himself on the other hand...well, he was intelligent, his parents had always said so, but not in any way that mattered, and his memory was always spotty, and he knew he had trouble staying focused on things, and reading required spending too much energy thinking about only one thing at a time. The only pastime he found worthy of his focus was sword-fighting, and what could possibly cause Aravia to have any interest in a fighting man who didn't like to read?

The few times she'd spoken directly to him, it was mostly to correct words he mispronounced or facts he had gotten wrong. Not that she was mean or derisive or anything; it was just how she was—smart—and she was working so hard to learn more spells, he shouldn't distract her.

She was, if anything, even more beautiful when she was asleep, and he tried not to dwell on how his stomach lurched when he imagined what it might be like if he could hold her hand. Tomorrow, with Corilayna's blessing, they'd discover a bad guy to fight, and life would be simple again.

* * *

When Tor woke the next morning, only his mouth was dry. It wasn't raining, but there must have been an overnight squall sufficiently energetic to get through the trees, and his clothes were damp and pilled. That only bothered him for a moment; the others were up, including Aravia, sitting on soggy logs and eating a cold breakfast. She was well enough to have a book already open on her lap while she idly chewed her hardtack.

"New spell?" he asked.

Aravia didn't look up. "Yes. *Teleport*." She balanced the book on her knees and knit her brows in concentration, while her free hand executed a series of awkward slicing movements. "I almost have it, but I've got to get the gestural aspects just right, to redirect the aetheric counterforce."

"Oh. That sounds important. I'll let you concentrate."

"Thanks, Tor."

He didn't take the dismissal personally, though it would have been nice to talk with her. She was like that with everyone, and her magical abilities were Horn's Company's most important asset.

He had missed some discussion about whether to go back into town or follow the man who had been last to leave the arch. The rest of the company had concluded that town was too risky, that they should first try to find the red-robed observer of last night's strange ritual. Thanks to Ernie's brief, well-meaning chat with the serving woman Perri, at least one of the townsfolk knew the company had an interest in Levec and the arch.

Leaving Aravia in peace, Tor wandered over to where Morningstar stood, gazing out of their secluded thicket toward the looming Kivian Arch.

"So you know which way he went?"

Morningstar pointed southeastward. "He left between those two trees, the one with the two knots and the skinny tree with silvery bark. He went in a straight line until I lost sight of him, so that gives us a good lead."

Tor wolfed down breakfast and grabbed his driest clothes, but the others seemed to be taking their time. They should get moving! Though Aravia he could understand, since she was working hard on learning how to teleport. He wandered out into the clearing with the arch and stared up at its high crosspiece.

An idea popped unbidden into his head. "Hey," he called back, "maybe something will happen if one of us walks through the arch after last night's ritual."

And he did, the cries from the others coming too late to stop him. Maybe it was only his imagination, but the air felt warmer, and just a bit tingly, as he passed beneath its span.

Even Aravia had come running. Her eyes were wide. "Tor, you nitwit! What if that had been a trap? That man was probably a Kivian, and they worship fire. You could have gotten yourself roasted!"

Nitwit? Tor winced. She was probably right. She was staring at him with an expression that he couldn't decipher.

"But nothing happened," he said. "And we might have learned something interesting. Besides, all those people stood underneath it last night, and they were even in nightclothes, and they didn't get burned or anything. We're here to get information, right? *And*, if anything bad *was* going to happen, better it happen to me."

He realized as he said this that it sounded like he was bragging. But he *was* the strongest and toughest of the group, now that Grey Wolf was gone. (Kibi didn't really count; he was stronger, but not in a front-line-of-battle sort of way.) He had thought this through on the ship voyage to Seablade Point. Everyone else in the company had a clear purpose. Aravia was their wizard, and Dranko was their healer. Kibi and Ernie had some connection to the Eyes of Moirel and the Seven Mirrors, though Tor didn't understand what it was, and Kibi also had the ability to talk to rocks. And Morningstar had prophetic dreams.

So what was his purpose? Only one thing made sense. He was the protector, not just of Aravia but the rest of them as well. It was his job to put himself in danger so that no one else would have to. Which, he supposed, made him important too, and that satisfied him.

Aravia was still staring at him.

"I, uh, didn't mean to boast," he said. "It's just that—"

"Tor, shut up."

Now he understood Aravia's face; she was angry. He had never seen her angry. She always seemed so composed. "Next time," she said, "tell us before you do anything stupid, okay? That way we can talk you out of it."

"Sorry," he said, and he meant it. He still thought it had been worth the risk, but it pained him that he had upset Aravia so badly.

"Hey Tor," said Dranko. "Now that you've determined that the arch doesn't set you on fire, let's get moving."

They trailed behind Morningstar in a line, picking their way over fallen branches and scattered mossy rocks. Unlike the forest around the ruins near Verdshane, this place was full of spring bustle; sparrows and chickadees flitted from tree to tree, chipmunks poked curious noses out from the underbrush, and clouds of gnats clustered in sunbeams.

Forquelle had no woods like these, but Tor had come to love them. They brought him an inner peace, a sense of waiting and watching and absorbing the beauty of nature, filling him with the energy he'd need for the perils and adventures that were sure to come. He was meant for the great outdoors, just as he was meant for a life of heroics, far from the throne of Forquelle.

Less than a half hour's walk from the Arch the group broke free of the forest. A gusting and salty breeze slapped Tor in the face, while gulls wheeled and cried overhead, riding the wind. He stood at the bottom of a long grassy slope that rose to a wide cliff overlooking the sea, and when Tor shaded his eyes to block the rising sun, he saw a stone building perched there upon the bluff.

"It's a church of Brechen!" he said.

"Stands to reason," said Dranko. "It is a fishing village, after all."

"Why would a fire worshipper be heading toward a church of the Sea God?" Morningstar wondered aloud.

"'Cause he likes fish?" said Dranko.

Who knew what dangers could lie ahead? By unspoken agreement they trudged up the hill. Tor sped his stride until he was out in front, then drew his sword. No one objected.

The increasing grade of the slope forced them to veer away from the church building as they approached. They crested a final weedy rise and struck a wide gravel path that snaked away from the church, tip-toeing along the cliff top back toward the heart of the town.

The building itself was unassuming as churches went, solid mortared stone inset with small stained glass windows, predominately blue and green. The largest of these displayed a series of foam-topped waves, and from the tallest wave an arm was extended, gripping a sea-blue sword.

"Services to Brechen are at sunrise and sunset," said Tor. "My father..." He bit his lip. "I mean, since I grew up on an island, we revered Brechen most among the Travelers."

"Hope someone's still here then," said Kibi.

"Should we knock?" asked Ernie.

"Depends," said Dranko, keeping his voice low. "Are we charging in with weapons drawn, or is this more of a friendly social call?"

"We're here for information," said Aravia. "We can always resort to violence if we're pushed to it."

Tor struck the door several times with its teardrop-shaped brass knocker.

When no one came after two minutes, he knocked a second time.

"No one's home," said Dranko. He tried the handle, but the door didn't open. "Aravia, can you—"

A rasping sound came from inside, as of a bar being lifted. The wooden door swung inward. There, looking out, stood a tall, heavyset man with a coarse grey beard, just as Morningstar had described, though he was wearing a long sea-green frock over a light blue shirt. Ocean waves had been stitched up and down the panels of the frock.

His eyes fell upon Tor, who was still holding his sword unsheathed, and he took a quick step backward. His hands went up in a gesture of supplication.

"I've got no valuables here, good master!" he exclaimed. "But this house is protected by Brechen, the Seablade, Master of the Waves, so tread ye armed across my threshold at your peril!"

It took Tor a second to understand that he himself was causing this reaction. He quickly sheathed his sword.

"We aren't bandits!" said Ernie. "We only want to come in and talk."

The bearded priest lowered his arms and gave them a searching look. "You're not from the village, of that I'm certain, but in my long years here I've had no visitors such as ye. From where do ye hail?"

"We hail from Harkran, mostly," said Dranko. "That's a long way from here, and our feet are pretty sore, so we'd appreciate it if we could come in, sit down, and have a chat with you. Might we know your name, father?"

"Travelers are always welcome in the house of Brechen," said the man. "I am Father Hodge, humble servant of the Seablade. But if you would come upon His holy ground, I must ask you to leave your weapons outside."

"No offense," said Dranko, "but given that your God is called the Seablade, I'm sure He wouldn't mind us holding on to our stuff." He took a small step forward and inched his foot into the doorway. "Father Hodge, we need to talk to you about where you were last night, and what you saw, and we'd like to do it in as civilized a fashion as possible."

Tor was delighted that Dranko had cut to the chase so quickly. He expected one of two things to happen next: either Hodge would make a run for it, maybe to a hidden back door out of the church, or he'd launch an attack, probably with some kind of magical unholy fire, but instead Hodge stared at them for about three tense seconds before his expression nearly collapsed in relief.

"Are you sure ye weren't followed?" he asked, bending forward and speaking quietly. "The townsfolk…they…"

"Yeah, we know," said Dranko. "And no, we weren't followed."

"And you've seen it, with your own eyes?"

Dranko nodded.

"Then come in, quickly, and keep your weapons. I'd feel safer that way."

Tor's arm and back muscles relaxed. He had been fully prepared for a melee, thinking that Father Hodge was responsible for the strange ritual in the woods, but all things considered this was preferable. He followed Father Hodge into the church. The priest of Brechen poked his head outside one final time after they were in, then hastily closed and barred the door.

The church was nothing like the enormous shrine to Brechen in his father's castle back home. This one was mostly one room, small as naves went, with only a single line of wooden pews. The stained glass, attractive as it was, didn't admit much light, but six large hanging braziers had been lit along the walls. Hodge motioned for them to sit in one of the pews, and he stood in the adjacent row so he could face them.

"Are you here about the arch?" he asked.

"Yes!" said Tor, assuming that Dranko had already broken the ice on the topic. "Do you know what's going on?"

"Only what I've seen with my own eyes," said Father Hodge. "Every night the same. Thirty come from the town, a different thirty each time. They come a-wandering up to the woods in their nightclothes just afore midnight. Like sheep they are, sleepwalkers all, unmindful of cold or rain. The arch—you know about the arch—it lights up and throws off heat, but the folk aren't burned. When the light dies down again, the folk stagger back to their beds, and have no memory of it the next morn. But they're tired, weak. Whatever's happening, it's drawing life out of those poor people."

"And how did you find out this was going on?" asked Dranko.

Father Hodge started to answer but checked himself. "How do I know I can trust ye?" he asked. "Will ye swear on Brechen's name, under His roof, that you're not mixed up in this business? That you're not involved in what's causing this devil's work?"

"We swear!" said Tor. "On Brechen's sword, I swear we'd like to help those people and figure out what's going on."

"Good then," said Father Hodge. "I'll tell ye." He paused, looking at each member of Horn's Company as though trying to gauge their merit. "There was a man. He had lived in town a long time, a quiet man of middling years who came to services twice every week. Never thought much about him, but he seemed harmless enough. Nearly three months ago he stayed behind after sunset services and told me he had something urgent to discuss. I'd never seen him so distraught. His name was Levec."

"Oh!" said Tor. "We were hoping to find him."

Aravia sighed.

"I can't help ye with that, friend," said Father Hodge. "Levec, he told me that some powerful person had sent him to town years before, to keep an eye on an ancient arch in the forest. Said it had great magic and could be used to ill purpose. Now everyone in town knows about the arch in the woods, but it was just a curiosity from a forgotten age. We'd never seen anything magic about it. But Levec told me he had made some terrible discovery about the arch and needed to sail to Lanei to learn more. He urged me to visit the arch each night at midnight, stay well hidden, and observe everything I saw. Told me to keep a journal of which townsfolk visited each night, or as many as I could tell in the dark. Had me note how long that infernal glow stayed lit, and anything else I thought worthy of his interest. He'd be back, he said, soon as he could. Levec was on the next merchant ship when it departed, and that's the last I've seen or heard of the man. But I've been doing as he asked, night after night, and I guess ye know what I've seen out there. Do you know what devilry is cooking?"

There wasn't any reason not to tell Father Hodge everything they knew, and indeed Tor had already opened his mouth to start, but Dranko spoke first.

"Not exactly. In fact, it sounds like you already know more than we do. I'd love to see the notes you've been taking."

"And one question," said Aravia. "Why were you wearing red robes last night instead of something Brechenish?"

Father Hodge laughed. "A suspicious lot are ye, but I can't blame ye for that. The nights are chilly in the woods, as I realized after a few trips out for Levec. My religious raiment is not much for keeping a man warm." He grabbed his blue frock and rubbed its thin fabric between finger and thumb. "But afore she passed on, blessed be she now in the ocean's arms, my wife knit me a warmer set of robes, and her favorite color was always red. I pray that the Seablade be not offended, but I'll be no good to Him if I die of chill."

"I guess not," said Dranko.

"If you'll wait here," said Father Hodge, "I'll bring ye my notes. They're locked away safe in my office as I can't discount that one of my congregation is behind this strange business."

He slid himself out from between the two rows of pews and walked down the aisle to the sanctuary, then opened a small door there and disappeared inside.

"This is working out better than I expected," said Ernie. "He's the next best thing to Levec, I guess."

"I still don't trust him," said Dranko. "His story is too…too neat. And for someone so worried, he trusted us too quickly."

"I agree with Ernie," said Tor. "Dranko you should learn to…to trust—"

Another thought appeared in his head, the way thoughts sometimes did, a rabbit poking its head out of a hole. "Oh. Wait."

"What?" asked Morningstar.

"Just something I remembered about priests of Brechen. They're not allowed to be married. I don't even think they're allowed to have *been* married. Something about being married to the sea, and Brechen's wrath if—"

"Crap!" said Dranko. "I knew it. He's probably running away right now!"

The office door opened, and Hodge stepped out, holding a paper in one hand.

"Oh," said Tor. "Nothing to worry about."

"*Nifi Infernix!*" shouted Hodge.

All six of the hanging braziers erupted into blooming fireballs that roared upward to scorch the ceiling. Tor instinctively closed his eyes and shielded his face from the oven-blast of heat. When he opened his eyes again the air had become translucently orange, an effect not unlike what they had seen beneath the arch the previous night. Up on the top step of the sanctuary, Hodge was waving his arms and chanting.

"You were saying?" Dranko growled.

Tor only experienced the shame of poor judgment for a second before it was overcome with a jubilant realization of how simple things had just become. He reached to draw his sword.

He couldn't. His arm would hardly move, and for that matter his legs had become nearly paralyzed. All he could do was turn his head—barely—and doing so revealed that his friends were experiencing the same effect.

Also it was growing warmer, rapidly.

"Infidels!" Hodge bellowed. "I have long been ready for an intrusion such as this. Levec told me his full tale before his bones blackened for the glory of the

Burning God. There is no power in your tiny land to hinder our return."

The temperature rose further, drawing out sweat all over Tor's body, and even as he struggled to take a single step toward Hodge, he wondered if it might get so hot as to set him and his friends on fire, and the thought of Aravia dying that way filled him with rage, but his anger was useless against Hodge's spell; it was as if his whole body were immersed in a hot, thick glue that had nearly hardened.

"Great Lord Nifi, God of Fire and Destruction, I make of these foolish interlopers an offering. I pray they hasten our crossing as the prophecies foretell!"

Morningstar shrieked; she was trying to bring up her hands to cover her face, but her arms moved in slow motion, and the others were crying out, though Tor could barely hear them over the roaring of the braziers. The heat was most definitely increasing as Hodge continued to chant, and Tor attempted another step, and was strong enough to make a few inches of headway, but it was hopeless, he'd never escape the scorching light before he went up in flames, and his dreams of Horn's Company saving the world from the evil emperor were coming to an excruciating end. He had let everybody down.

Two arms grabbed him around the waist and lifted him off the ground. Someone was trying to make sure he couldn't escape the heat; he tried to squirm from their grasp.

"Hold still, Tor!"

It was Kibi! The stonecutter had lifted him up and was now staggering toward the end of the pew.

"Aravia says the braziers are focusin' Hodge's magic," Kibi gasped. Tor marveled that Kibi could move at all. Step by step Tor was carried toward the wall, and Kibi coughed and spluttered as he set Tor down beneath the brazier, but even as Tor struggled to raise his arms, he realized it was just out of his reach, because while in ordinary circumstances he could have easily jumped up to grab it, Hodge's miasma of searing air was too potent.

The ends of Kibi's beard were curling, but he picked up Tor again, this time wrapping his arms around Tor's thighs, and with what must have been a superhuman effort he hoisted Tor into the air, raising him over a foot off the ground.

"Grab it, lad! Tip the damn thing over!"

Tor raised his arms. His whole body was in hot, stinging pain, but he managed it, hooking the fingertips of both hands over the lip of the brazier just as Kibi's strength gave out, and gravity worked in their favor; as Tor dropped to the floor, the brazier tipped over and poured out several dozen tiny red stones, falling upon Tor and Kibi and burning like hot coals from a campfire, but as they spilled out of the brazier, the orange light that was baking him alive went out.

Master Elgus had often required Tor to swing a double-weight sword for several minutes before sparring because after growing used to an overweight weapon, his muscles would feel that much stronger once his real sword was back in his hand. Having had his limbs mired in Hodge's thick, burning light, Tor's entire body now felt powerful, buoyant, liberated, and putting aside the pain from his burns, he rushed down the aisle beside the wall, drawing his sword as he ran.

Hodge's expression had gone from jubilant to angry. The servant of Nifi raised his arm and launched a melon-sized ball of flames from his fingertips, so Tor kicked off the wall and dove down behind the second row of pews, hearing the fireball crackle overhead and explode against the wall behind him, and a shower of sparks fell sizzling into his hair and onto his clothes, but it had clearly missed, so undaunted he leapt to his feet, and there was Ernie dashing down the opposite aisle. Hodge turned and bolted for the door to his sanctuary, slamming it shut just as Tor and Ernie reached it together, and though Tor led with his shoulder, which should have busted it wide open, Hodge had barred the door from the inside, so Tor bounced off and the impact on his burned skin made him scream.

Even so, he was prepared to fling himself at the door as many times as it took to flush out Hodge, but that was not necessary. Aravia shouted from the back of the church and Hodge's office door exploded from its hinges. From the corner of his eye Tor saw Aravia flying backward through the air, landing awkwardly on a pew several rows back.

Filled with fury, he brought up his sword and stepped toward Hodge, who stood defiantly inside his small office.

"It matters not what ye do to me, lad," said Hodge. His right hand was glowing a cherry red. "It's set in motion as Nifi demands, and our armies will burn your toy kingdom to the ground."

"We'll see about that!" shouted Ernie, standing next to Tor with Pyknite in his hand. "There won't be any—"

Hodge punched the air in front of Ernie, and a blazing ball of light burst at the baker's chest. Ernie sailed backward out the door, trailing smoke.

"So shall suffer all of the Burning God's enemies!" said Hodge, turning to Tor. "His purging fires will cleanse the—"

Tor didn't wait to hear the end of the sentence; he jammed the point of his sword into Hodge's throat.

CHAPTER TWENTY-FIVE

Ernie's smoking body soared from Hodge's office. Tor emerged immediately after, blood smeared on the end of his sword. His skin was pink and raw, and looked as though it had been daubed with red paint in a dozen different places.

Kibi prayed that Ernie was still alive. He rushed down the aisle toward the front of the nave. "Is he—?"

"I killed him," said Tor, but the boy's voice was frantic. "Dranko! Ernie's badly hurt! Hodge hit him right in the chest!"

Dranko groaned. Like Tor his skin was blistered, but he stumbled into the aisle and hurried to the front of the church. Morningstar had curled into a ball on the floor, and Aravia was sprawled over a pew in the back. She must have miscast her door-busting spell and knocked herself silly. Hodge's fire had done a number, and no mistake.

Tor was right about Ernie. The baker had a horrific burn upon his chest, about as bad as Kibi had ever seen. Hodge's fire blast had seared a hole right through Ernie's shirt, and his skin was a sludgy black and pink mess.

"You can channel again, right?" asked Tor. "You have to save him!"

"I don't know!" Dranko barked. "Just calm down. When I…when Mrs. Horn died, Grey Wolf was right in my face and I couldn't concentrate. Give me some peace!"

Tor shut up right away. Hard to blame him for being in a panic, though.

Kibi looked on stoically. Mrs. Horn was dead, and Grey Wolf had been magicked away. If Ernie died, it would leave just five of them, and even he could see that was a poor rate of attrition. And he *liked* Ernie. The boy was a good soul, and on top of that there were the golden circlets that linked them together.

Dranko took out a silver pendant and draped it around his neck, then knelt before Ernie and put his hands right on the damp ruin of the boy's chest.

"Lord Delioch, I pray for your intervention. I pray for healing, that this man be made sound and whole."

Nothing happened. It was just like in Verdshane with Mrs. Horn. Kibi fought down an urge to say something encouraging. Tor bit his lip.

"Please, Lord, I entreat you," said Dranko. It was odd, hearing such serious, pious words coming out of Dranko's irreverent mouth. "Let Ernie be made sound and whole."

Ernie breathing was ragged, his eyes closed. There was no golden light shining from Dranko's fingers the way there had been on the ship when he had healed Morningstar. Dranko continued to pray, rocking back and forth on his knees, hands covered in Ernie's blood.

"Come on, Dranko…" Tor whispered.

Ernie stopped breathing.

Dranko lifted one hand from Ernie's chest and wiped his own brow with his forearm, as though his prayers were physically taxing. Maybe the pain he was in from Hodge's fire was keeping him from concentrating. He pressed his hand down again; gore oozed between his fingers.

"I know the price!" Dranko's voice was hoarse. "Damn it, Delioch, take whatever you need! Let Ernie be made—"

Light burst outward from Dranko's fingertips, spilling over Ernie and flooding down the aisle between the pews. Kibi was forced to close his eyes, so bright was the blessing of Delioch, and when he opened them again, Ernie's skin was smooth and unburnt. Dranko swayed on his knees but managed to steady himself with one hand against the floor.

"Burn cream," he slurred. "For the rest. Green stuff in the round jar."

And with that he toppled over, head falling onto Ernie's torso, and he immediately began to snore.

There was no doubt about Dranko, that was sure. For all his goblin blood and hard drinking and foul language, the man was right in Delioch's favor. Kibi rooted around in Dranko's pack until he found the salve, then divvied it up among the others. There wasn't enough, but a single jar was better than nothing. Morningstar was worse off than the rest. Though Dranko's healing had cured her of the burns suffered in the desert, her skin was still pale and sensitive to heat, so Kibi doled out an extra dollop for her. Same for Aravia, who still hadn't recovered fully from the sunburns suffered on her trek across the Mouth of Nahalm. She was staggered after blasting Hodge's door off its hinges. Tor was less badly off, more shaken up than injured, though his fingers were badly blistered from where he had grabbed the hot brazier. Ernie was in perfect health and was sleeping peacefully with Dranko on top of him.

Thank the Gods no one was burned *too* badly. He and Tor had cut short Hodge's ritual just in time. And as for himself, Kibi wasn't burned a bit, aside from his beard. The fires of Hodge had felt warm to him, but obviously nothing like what the others had experienced. He chalked it up to having been farthest away from Hodge when the man had done his magicking—that and a dollop of good luck. He said a quick prayer to Corilayna, Goddess of Fortune, and took stock of their situation.

"We got hours yet before sundown, but we oughta be well out a' here by then," he said to those companions who were conscious. "I ain't got no desire to try convincin' the townsfolk that we killed their priest a' Brechen because he was actually worshippin' some foreign fire god."

He thought some more. "Course, only way out is by ship, and the only harbor is by the town. But we'll work that out once you're all feelin' better. In the meantime I guess I'll see what Hodge has been keepin' in his office. Will you be okay restin' here?"

No one objected, so while everyone else recovered, Kibi ventured into Hodge's office.

The door had been wrenched out of its frame by the force of Aravia's magic, which was mightily impressive. Inside the place was in a bit of a shambles, not even considering Hodge's body or the pool of blood under it. Hodge had not been one for cleanliness or organization, leaving clothing, papers, and religious accoutrements out in untidy piles. There was a desk and a wardrobe, the former covered with various Brechenish holy books and some candle stubs, the latter filled mostly with Brechenish vestments, though with one long red robe forced all the way to one side.

There was nothing incriminating to be found, not in or on the desk, not in the wardrobe, and not in the large trunk pushed up against the back wall. The trunk was half-filled with intricate scrimshaw, which Kibi had not seen before, but it seemed like something an authentic priest of Brechen would keep. Hodge had been thorough in maintaining his pretense.

As Kibi closed the trunk, he felt an odd twinge. It was a jarring resonance in his bones, warning him of a mismatch between his observations and the reality of the room. He placed his palm against the cold stone wall. A whisper tickled his mind.

Behind the trunk.

He crouched down and shoved the trunk aside easily; the wall behind it was slightly discolored. Where two masonry seams met, the mortar was curiously indented. Kibi pushed the indentation with his thumb. There was a click, some hidden mechanism in the wall whirred and slid, and a large section of the wall pivoted on a camouflaged hinge.

Kibi whistled. "Nice bit a' work." He stepped through the revealed door into a hidden room, not much more than a glorified closet. There wasn't enough light in it to see, but when he had fumbled for his light-coin and held it up, he discovered a second trunk, an enormous redwood chest banded with gold. Kibi slowly lifted the lid.

Its interior was nearly full, packed with a variety of fascinating treasures. On the top was a two-foot-tall bronze statuette of a man with his arms raised, his mouth open in a scream, painted flames all over his body. Kibi picked it up, hefted it, grimaced at its lifelike expression of a person who was burning to death, and set it aside.

Kibi next withdrew a half-dozen bottles of dark red wine and a smaller flask filled with brandy. Beneath those was a collection of little pyramids made of a lightweight red-gold metal. Each was four inches to the edge. He wasn't familiar with the alloy. One by one he took these out of the trunk until he had counted twenty-seven.

Near the bottom was a red leather-bound book, its cover showing a burning man in the same pose and proportions as the bronze statuette. Kibi flipped it open to a random page, but the writing was in a foreign language. As he tossed it to the side, a single loose leaf of aged parchment fluttered out from just inside the front cover. This had only two short written paragraphs, and though the first was in the same unintelligible language, the second was in archaic but understandable Chargish. Kibi read.

As the Emperor was driven out, so were we also, for a long season, a bitter season and a cold. But in the Book of the Burning God it is so writ, of the land beyond the Churning Sea, a Ventifact Colossus will again walk the earth and three Stormknights will lay it low. Then, on the fingertip of lands once ours, the Gate will be open, forced ajar with souls, and the Children of the Burning God will return to conquer.

Kibi read this over several times and frowned. Aravia would be better suited to decipher its meaning. He slid the parchment back into the leather book and peered into the trunk to see what remained inside.

His thoroughness was well rewarded. Pushed up against the front panel of the chest was a small leather bag half-full of small rubies. Kibi didn't possess Dranko's ability to gauge their value, but he guessed they might fetch a couple dozen crescents all told.

Finally, rolled up at the bottom and pushed to the back of the trunk was an orange carpet tied up with three loops of red silk ribbon. Kibi figured that was a prayer mat, but he pulled it out anyway and stacked it with everything else. After leaning bodily into the trunk with his light-coin to make certain it was empty, he made several trips to carry the plunder out to the sanctuary, stepping over the stiffening corpse of Hodge each time. Tor watched him, and Kibi knew the boy would be happily helping him if his fingers hadn't been so scorched.

Aravia wobbled over and sat down next to Tor. "What's all that?" she asked, pointing to where Kibi had piled up the contents of Hodge's trunk.

"Hodge's stuff. Figured we'd take as much with us as we could. There's some kind a' prophecy you should take a look at."

Aravia stepped up onto the pew and looked out over the nave. "Looks like Ernie and Dranko are the only ones out. Kibi, I can get us straight home from here without needing a ship. We must get everyone together, in physical contact, and someone needs to be carrying everything we want to take with us."

It took Kibi a moment to work through all that. "Are you sayin' you can magic us all out a' here?"

"Yes. In theory. Teleporting. That's most of what I've been studying since we last left the Greenhouse. I'm confident it will work."

"You sure, missy? You look like someone's been beatin' you with a stick."

Aravia stood up a bit straighter. "I'm not sure. But I'm confident, and we don't have a choice. You're right about the townsfolk. Either they're unwitting dupes, in which case they'll think we killed their priest, or they're all in league, in which case—they'll think we killed their priest."

Kibi clicked his tongue. Gods, what a mess. He stuffed as many of the little metal pyramids into his pack as would fit, and was able to carry the book and the sack of rubies. Morningstar took the idol, and Tor held the rolled-up carpet.

They gathered in a circle around Ernie and Dranko, both still lying unconscious.

"Morningstar, make sure you're in physical contact with Ernie. Kibi, same with you for Dranko. You and Tor should also put a hand on my shoulder; everyone needs to be in contact either with me or with someone I'm in contact with. Even just touching them with your foot is fine, but I very much do not want to leave them behind. Everyone ready?"

Kibi shoved his foot under Ernie's shoulder to be certain and placed a hand on Aravia's shoulder as instructed.

"This should take about thirty seconds," said Aravia. "And I need to say a number of syllables quite quickly in that time, and perform intricate gestures with my fingers. Please don't distract me. Right?"

"Right," said Morningstar. Kibi just nodded.

Aravia cast her spell, speaking so quickly he couldn't begin to guess what words she was saying. Her fingers danced and twirled, her hand flexed, and…

Starry black flying vertigo darkness hurricane screaming shifting…

…and something even more uncomfortable happened at the end, as if he had been shunted, violently, about twenty feet to one side. It felt like the whole world had tilted quickly, then righted itself.

All of that took about five seconds, and he stood, blinking rapidly, in front of the Greenhouse door.

Morningstar looked at him with some relief. "There you are. I was starting to think you hadn't come with us."

Kibi couldn't focus on what Morningstar was saying; his innards were still swirling like water in a washtub.

"Oh," said Aravia. "The Greenhouse is protected from that kind of ingress. Should have thought of that. By the Gods, I'm tired. I think I'll—"

She lay down suddenly on the front path and closed her eyes.

Kibi looked around, impressed. The girl had done it!

"You go on ahead," he said to Tor and Morningstar. "I'll carry these three inside."

* * *

With Morningstar's assistance, Kibi set Aravia and Dranko down gently on couches in the living room and propped Ernie in a padded armchair. With many apologies Tor headed up to his room to immerse his hands in cold water. Morningstar likewise excused herself to lie down after all were inside. Only when everyone was settled in did Kibi stump upstairs, intending to wash away the soot and grime he had acquired during their encounter with Hodge. He found two things amiss.

First, the door to the secret room was open, and it had been closed when they had departed for Seablade Point. Maybe Abernathy had called and chatted with their butler while they were away, or Eddings had just been dusting in there and forgotten to shut the door behind him. He poked his head into the little room with the crystal ball and found it undisturbed. Well, no matter; he'd ask Eddings about it later.

His own room was the next down from that one, and there he discovered the second disturbing thing: Abernathy himself was sprawled out on his bed, face down, limbs splayed, as though he had gotten himself drunk and wandered into the Greenhouse by mistake before passing out. His body was outlined in that blue radiance that meant he was both here and still in his tower; Kibi never quite understood how that was supposed to work.

He hurried over and turned the old wizard onto his back, then drew away in shock. One side of Abernathy's face was badly burned, and the other had three oozing claw marks raked across the cheek. His torn, singed robes were spattered with blood and shimmered with tiny flakes of something like red-orange mica schist. It was as if someone had sprinkled him with rock dust.

Abernathy's eyes fluttered open.

"Kibi..."

"Mister Abernathy, what in the Gods' names happened to you?"

"Listen to me," Abernathy whispered. Kibi had to put his face all the way to Abernathy's to hear. "The...blood gargoyle. Attacked my tower. I was prepared to fight it off, thanks to your warning, but still...still..."

"Sir, you need help, but Dranko's out cold. What should I—"

"Listen! While I was...distracted fighting the gargoyle, something...new got through at Verdshane. Not...not Naradawk, but someone very dangerous. Salk...saw him as he made the crossing; a man wearing the...crimson armor...Naradawk's servant."

Even Kibi could add two and two. Morningstar's dream-assailant!

"Kibi..." Abernathy was gasping out his whispers now, his chest bucking with silent punctuating coughs. "I'll be...fine...eventually, but...we need the Crosser's Maze. Arch...Kivian Arch...counting on you..."

Kibi wanted to fetch the others but refused to leave Abernathy alone. "What about yer archmage friends? Can't they help?"

"Busy," Abernathy wheezed. "All they can do to...keep Naradawk out...has to be...has to be you."

Abernathy's eyes closed, and his coughing ceased. For a terrified moment Kibi was sure the wizard was dead, but the old man's chest still rose and fell, barely.

"Abernathy? We just came from the arch. It ain't open! And somethin' happened to Grey Wolf; he's gone missin'. You need to tell us what to do next. Abernathy!"

But the old wizard was comatose.

Kibi knew he should go tell the others right away, but he had to sit a minute. It was too overwhelming. Here he was, in a fancy house in a city far from his home, magicked there by the world's most powerful wizard and charged with protecting the kingdom from an ever-expanding roster of enemies—cultists, fire-worshippers, a locked-up monster king, a guy who could stab you in dreams—and now, here was that wizard, injured and unconscious, in his own room, having just reminded him that the survival of Charagan hinged on the efforts of him and his companions.

The Gods had made him strong, but damn if they weren't giving him a heavy burden to shoulder.

"I ain't cut out fer this," Kibi muttered. "Better warn the rest."

He turned to go, but something out of place caught his attention, something sitting on the lip of the water tub in the corner. He stared at it for a moment, his distracted brain a bit slow in recognizing it.

It was Bumbly, Ernie's stuffed bear, its head drooped low over its chest.

Kibi took a step towards it, and at his approach the head perked up and its left eye blazed green. Living crystal spread across the bear's face from its embedded gemstone, then down its body until the entire animal looked carved from frosted jade.

"Not now, you blasted bear!"

It wasn't enough that Abernathy was out cold in Kibi's room. He was tired and still woozy from being teleported, and this whole thing felt like a mostly bad dream, and now his mysterious talking green rock was coming to life again? Gods, it was too much!

I LACK TWO WILLING BROTHERS.

"You said that before!" Kibi shouted at it. "Just tell me what you want and stop with your stupid riddlin'!"

YOU MUST BRING MY BROTHERS. ONE IS CLOSE.

"Are your brothers more Eyes of Moirel, like you?"

IN THE YOUNG HILLS EASTWARD, THE WATER BENDS 'ROUND. A MOUTH OPENS. INSIDE IS MY BROTHER.

"Dammit, be more specific!"

HASTEN. THE SHARSHUN SEEK US, AND IF THEY FIND US, THEY WILL UNMAKE THE WORLD.

"But I don't..."

KEEP ME SAFE, KIBILHATHUR.

The Eye dropped from the bear's socket and clunked onto the wooden floor. Bumbly quickly shed its green coating into the air and toppled backward into the empty tub. Kibi picked up the Eye of Moirel, no longer colored, just a large round diamond with a tiny heart of jet.

"Guess Abernathy's trunk weren't good enough," Kibi said wearily to the diamond. "Not sure how to keep you any safer."

* * *

Kibi was unused to talking, but he had a lot to say.

Finally, two hours before midnight, everyone was awake at the same time. Kibi could have knocked over any of the company with a feather. It had been a long, trying day, a bloody day after a late night camping in the woods, but he knew he shouldn't wait until morning.

"I got some things you'll all want to hear."

The others became quiet in a hurry and stared at him. His face reddened beneath his beard at the notion they thought him worth listening to. He was still overwhelmed, but being in the presence of his friends helped to calm him.

First he told the others about Abernathy, currently convalescing in Kibi's bedroom. "Guess the gargoyle must a' come after him. He said 'cause of our warnin', he was able to beat it, but while he was dealin' with it, that's when that Dreamborn fellah showed up."

"I'll check on Abernathy as soon as I have the strength to get out of this couch," said Dranko. "Maybe next week or the week after."

It didn't seem like a joking matter, but that was Dranko for you. Next, Kibi reported what Bumbly had told him about the Eyes of Moirel and the Sharshun. "I think we oughta do what it says. We ain't got no new orders from Abernathy, and the world gettin' unmade sounds like a thing we oughta keep from happenin'."

On that topic there was unanimous agreement.

"One more thing," said Kibi. "I found this in Hodge's office back in Seablade Point."

He produced the scrap of prophecy and read it aloud. When he was done, Aravia asked to see it, and he handed it over.

"It's obvious, don't you think?" she said.

"Nope," he answered. He was never much good at riddles.

"Well, here, think about it. *As the Emperor was driven out, so were we also, for a long season, a bitter season and a cold.* Abernathy told us that Emperor Naloric had fire-worshipping allies during the war that ended with his banishment. Those would be the Kivians, Hodge's people, who came from the land on the other side of the Uncrossable Sea."

Kibi pondered. "So what's a Ventifact Colossus?"

"I don't know," Aravia admitted. "But according to Hodge's prophecy, it's going to get killed by three Stormknights, and that will signal, or herald, or otherwise coincide with the Kivian Arch opening up."

Stormknights, Kibi knew, were warriors who venerated Werthis, the God of War.

"And that's good, right?" Kibi hoped he was keeping everything straight. "We need that arch open so we can get to Kivia and find Abernathy's maze that will stop Naradawk."

Ernie's eyes grew wide. "But we just stopped them, didn't we? We killed Hodge! What if we needed him to keep doing his rituals, to open the arch for us?"

"There's still too much we don't know," said Aravia. "Mostly I wish I knew what a Ventifact Colossus was."

"Aravia, if you don't know what it is, no one does," said Tor.

"Previa might," said Morningstar. "I'll pay a visit to the temple before I go to bed. We'll see if there are any records of a colossus in the Ellish archives."

Once their conversation was over, the rest of the company went to sleep. Kibi was tired, too; though he had been spared the worst ravages of Hodge's fire spell (for which he still had no good explanation), he was bone weary and ready for sleep. Of course, Abernathy was in his bed, but he didn't mind taking the couch for a while.

But first he went to the kitchen for the heaviest cast-iron pot he could find. Into this he placed the Eye of Moirel, then wrapped the lid tight with a long length of rope. In the basement he chose a second iron trunk (since there was a hole blasted right through the metal of the first one he had used) and set the pot down inside it. Trunk locked, closet door shut, he wondered if there was anything more he could do.

CHAPTER TWENTY-SIX

E veryone ready to go?"
Morningstar stood by the Greenhouse door, tapping her foot. For all that Charagan was in peril, most immediately from world-unmaking gemstones, her companions showed a troubling lack of urgency. Was it because they were rudderless without specific instructions from Abernathy? Grey Wolf would have kicked everyone out the door by now. Where had he gone? Was he even alive?

"Almost!" called Aravia. She was cramming her pack—and also Tor's—with books.

Ernie came in from the kitchen and handed out loaves of bread. "Some things can't be rushed."

"Fine," Morningstar grumbled. She glanced at the sunshine streaming in through the window and squinted into it defiantly. Dranko was reclining on a living room couch, looking peaked. Before breakfast he had been to see Abernathy but could not wake the old man.

"Hey Aravia," said Dranko. "Now that you can cast *teleport*, why are we bothering to walk anywhere?"

"It doesn't work that way. I can only teleport to a place I've been. And the more familiar I am with the destination, the less likely it is that something will go wrong."

"Should I ask what kind of things can go wrong?"

"There are several possible failure cases," said Aravia. "We could end up missing the target by arbitrary yards or miles. Or we might mistakenly arrive in a place with superficial similarities to my intended destination—like I intend an arrival at the Old Keg but take us to the Shadow Chaser instead. Worst case is solid displacement, where we end up embedded in the ground, or walls, or trees, or even other people. That would be messy."

Dranko winced. "How messy?"

"Fatally messy."

"Right."

"Also, until I refine my technique and get a lot more practice, a single *teleport* will take nearly all of my casting energy, so I'd rather only use it to take us someplace we know is safe."

"Do you think we'll be in danger, going after another Eye of Moirel?" asked Tor. "It's just a gemstone, isn't it?"

Kibi shook his head. "The green Eye we got, it said them Sharshun fellahs were after 'em too, and you know from experience how dangerous they are."

"Right," said Tor with a grin. He probably relished the thought of a rematch.

* * *

Though the Eye of Moirel's instructions to Kibi had been cryptic, Aravia claimed they made perfect sense. To demonstrate, she drew by memory a detailed sketch of a region twenty-miles east or so from Tal Hae, where the Talflun River took a sweeping curve through a cluster of hills. As for "a mouth opens," she guessed that the mouth of a cave was the mostly likely interpretation.

After the long cross-country marches and multi-day journeys in the holds of ships, a two-day stroll across fields and meadows was more than welcome. Morningstar still found the sun too bright, and kept her hood drawn forward to shield her eyes, but it was tolerable. Had it truly been less than two months since her dispensation from the church to travel in daylight?

When all of this was over, how would the Ellish temple react to her acclimation? More and more, she found herself caring less and less. Her devotion to Ell Herself was not diminished, and her encounter with Previa had given her some hope that her sisters' rejection need not be universal. Either way, let the others think what they would; Rhiavonne had sent her into the blistering desert, and she had emerged burnished but no less a sister of Ell than before.

"It all looks so green," she said as they hiked alongside a burbling stream. "I can distinguish colors with my darksight, but they're different. Muted. I know it's blasphemous to say, but it makes me sad that my sisters don't get to experience how colorful the world is. They can only remember it from childhood."

"It's your destiny," said Dranko. "Why do you think Ell named you Morningstar and gave you white hair? You think She didn't know you'd end up tromping around outside looking for magic rocks?"

"It makes more sense now," she admitted. "And I try to be appreciative that I've been put in this position. But I'd always hoped that when I learned the reason I was born so different, it would be something that would make me *less* of an outcast among my sisterhood. But that was not to be. I suppose it doesn't matter."

"Believe me," said Dranko, "I sympathize. But look on the bright side. Someday, when we've saved the world, are famous heroes, and they're having parades for us through the streets, you can go back to your temple and tell them all where they can stick it."

Morningstar smiled but said nothing. Sometimes Dranko was almost tolerable.

After a few seconds' pause, Dranko added, "When I said 'look on the bright side,' that was just an expression."

"I don't want to be famous," said Morningstar. "A life without friends made me value simplicity. As much as learning to adapt to sunlight has been a transition, it's been just as trying, accepting that my life is never again likely to be simple."

"Are you kidding?" asked Dranko. "How much simpler can our purpose be than 'stop a world-conquering evil monster from busting out and killing everyone?'"

"But we're not doing that right now. We're—how did you put it—'tromping around looking for magic rocks.'"

Dranko grinned his tusky grin. "Stopping the world from being unmade by blue-skinned bald guys will have to suffice."

* * *

Morningstar had a dream that night. It was no ordinary dream, but not a Seer Dream either, or however one might describe her encounter with Aktallian Dreamborn. It was, she felt, the end of all that she had been, and the beginning of all that she might become.

Greetings, Morningstar of Ell.

All around her was starlight and grass, the air crisp with midnight chill. She was armored in a shirt of mail rings, and a triangle shield was on her arm. Her mace was at her belt.

The being who had addressed her was majestic and dark, an angelic woman wrapped in black robes, a sword upheld, her feet hovering inches above the turf. But Morningstar did not fear her—at least, not in the same way she feared Aktallian. Divinity shone from the angel's noble face, her holiness so spiritually effulgent that Morningstar shielded her eyes and fell to her knees.

Rise, Morningstar. Rise and be glad, for you are chosen.

Morningstar stayed kneeling, looking at the ground. She didn't understand but didn't need to. "I am not worthy of being chosen."

That is not for you to decide. Nor would it matter, were it to be true. Ell has chosen you. Look upon me, child.

With an effort of will that bettered any she had made in this life, Morningstar raised her eyes. The angel's face was stern but merciful, beautiful but perilous. It was *pure.* Morningstar was not looking upon the face of Ell, but on something that reflected a part of Her grace.

"What must I do?" she asked. "For what have I been chosen?"

You are a child of darkness, but you are the Child of Light and the Daughter of Dreams. Ell has made you a Dreamwalker, the first in a generation.

"I'm sorry…I don't know what that means."

All dreams have a place, and all dreams linger. Together they form an expanding tapestry through which some may walk. The Tapestry is many things to many dreamers, but for you, Morningstar of Ell, it will be a battlefield, and you must be ready to fight.

"Aktallian. Is he whom I must fight? I am not strong enough."

You will be. I will train you. And when the time comes, you will find others from your sisterhood to fight by your side.

Morningstar bowed her head again and still would not stand in the presence of this avatar of Ell. "How is this possible? The Gods cannot interfere directly in the mortal affairs of Spira. The Injunction forbids Them."

I am bending the rules. We are not on Spira. I will train you here, in the weave of the Tapestry that you have dreamed. Now stand, Morningstar of Ell."

Morningstar stood and looked upon the face of the avatar. "Is this my destiny?" she asked. "To throw down Aktallian? But what of my service to Abernathy?"

The future is a thousand roads to a thousand fates, and the Gods see them all, but they cannot tell which path you will walk. They can but set out lights to guide your way. Now I have talked enough. Morningstar, Shield of Ell, Child of Light and Daughter of Dreams, defend yourself.

The angel advanced upon her, sword raised, her blade shining bright beneath the stars.

* * *

Morningstar awoke the next morning with a soul-shivering thrill. She lay in her bedroll, looking up as dawn's spreading pink glow gently filled the sky.

I am a Child of Light and a Daughter of Dreams.

She felt refreshed and energetic, despite a clear memory of having sparred with the avatar for hours. Should she tell the others? Her experience with the avatar had been intensely personal. Her soul had been both humbled and uplifted, its most burning question given a gloriously terrifying answer.

At the temple in Port Kymer there had been no one close enough to share her heart's secrets. She had been grateful to those who merely showed her indifference and not the mingled fear and hostility that had become so commonplace. Faced with years of passive-aggressive resentment, Morningstar had set her life's trajectory towards solitude and simplicity, prayer and practicality. She tried mitigating her bitterness with meditation, with limited success.

All of that had been disrupted with Abernathy's summons. She felt a growing bond with her companions, naturally, and was still exploring the reality of having friendships, but there remained a part of her that was skeptical, fearing it was all ephemeral, an illusion. Were they truly friends or merely victims of the same circumstance? She would tell them about the avatar one day, sooner if it became relevant to their tasks, later otherwise, but not today.

Her thoughts were interrupted by Dranko sitting up and belching.

Definitely not today.

* * *

They ate a hurried breakfast. Morningstar did her best to move things along, to instill a proper sense of urgency. Grey Wolf wouldn't have tolerated any dawdling. She wondered again where he was. And yet, more than anything else in her mind, there was the dream and the avatar.

You are the Child of Light and Daughter of Dreams. Ell has made you a Dreamwalker.

Her spirits were lifted, albeit on a frightening updraft. Goddess, but Dranko had been right. She had so many questions, and no one to answer them. Was there precedent? First in a generation, the avatar had said. So what had Dreamwalkers done in previous generations? Should she announce this officially within the temple? Send word to the High Priestess Rhiavonne?

"We should only be an hour or two from the bend in the river," said Aravia, "but given the vague nature of our instructions, we should be on the lookout from the outset."

The hills were barely worthy of the name. They rose tentatively out of the farmlands, grassy even to their tops, though here and there some bare bouldery patches poked through their green flanks. The Talflun, a narrow and lazy river, carved its shiftless path through the hills, wandering along a shallow valley running southwest to northeast.

Just as the Talflun took a wide turn southward again, Dranko called out that he could see black spots on the hills ahead. Morningstar envied him his superior sight; her own vision was still uncertain during the day, especially when the sun was out. It was another five minutes before she could see what he meant; the slopes of the hills on both sides of the river became steep and barren, and riddled with crevices near ground level. Many of these were wide enough for a person to fit through, but only a handful were worthy of being called caves.

"That's a lot to explore," said Tor.

"Maybe one looks more like a mouth than the others," said Ernie.

In another five minutes they had reached the scattering of jagged black clefts in the hillsides. Fortunately the river here was shallow and its current weak.

"This'll go a lot faster if we split up," said Dranko. "But we should stay in pairs. I know there's been no sign of anyone passing this way, but I suppose there might be bears or…or tigers or something living in the bigger caves."

Morningstar looked at him and laughed. "Tigers?"

"This isn't really my area of expertise. Put me in a city and I'll be king of it soon enough, but all this nature…" Dranko scratched himself indelicately.

Tigers notwithstanding, the plan was sound, and it gave her an excuse to separate herself from Dranko. "We've got three who are trained to fight," she said. "Me, Tor, and Ernie. Dranko, you go with Ernie, and Tor will go with Kibi. Aravia, why don't you come with me? Each pair, make sure you stay within shouting distance of at least one other, and every half an hour or so everyone should leave the caves and make visual contact."

"So," said Dranko. "You're in charge, then?"

Morningstar sighed. "If you have a better idea, I'm all ears."

"No, no, it was more of a general question."

"Then here's my general answer. Yes, until someone else wants to be."

Dranko swept his arm toward the caves, palm up. "Ladies first."

Grouped as Morningstar suggested, Horn's Company combed through the hill caves. Morningstar and Aravia headed a hundred feet downriver, stopping to peer into a few openings too small for either of them to crawl through. First Morningstar would stick her head in (or put her eye up to the hole for the smallest ones) and check with her darksight. Then Aravia used a light-coin to inspect each cavity, hoping to catch the glint of a diamond, assuming all the Eyes of Moirel were the same.

It was difficult to concentrate. *Ell has made you a Dreamwalker.* She imagined confronting all of the sisters who had mistreated her over the years. *There was a plan for me all along. I am every inch the sister that you are, and then some.* But it shamed her to entertain those fancies. *This is the plan, or part of it. Keep your focus, Morningstar of Ell.*

After a half-dozen of the rocky holes proved empty, Morningstar looked back over her shoulder. Dranko and Ernie vanished into a large cave on the far side of the river.

"The Eye said, 'A mouth opens,'" said Aravia. "I'd say that points to a larger cavern, and that we're wasting our time with these little holes. Let's head to the big ones and worry about the small ones later if we need to."

"Agreed," said Morningstar.

They spent the next hour exploring two sizable caves, each larger than the spacious Greenhouse living room. Their search pattern stayed the same; Morningstar would first stand in the opening and sweep her gaze through the darkness, looking both for the Eye of Moirel and for anything that might pose a danger during a close-up search. Then Aravia would come in and shine her light around, and they'd both explore the cavern's entirety as thoroughly as possible.

Both caves came up empty, but there was a third they had spotted twenty more feet downstream. They picked their way over the stones and scrub until Morningstar stood in the entrance.

There was a man in the cave, asleep on its pebbly floor, tucked in a blanket with his head on a wadded up shirt. The remains of a small campfire rested inside an ad-hoc ring of stones close at hand.

The sleeper stirred and rolled onto his back, revealing his long handlebar mustache.

"Gods, it's Sagiro, the man from the Mirrors," whispered Aravia.

Sagiro opened his eyes. Morningstar drew her weapon. "Aravia, get the others. Quickly." Before the mustachioed man could even sit up, Morningstar strode forward and placed the sharp flanges of her mace against his neck. "Stay on the ground, Sagiro, and don't make any sudden movements. Do you understand me?"

"Of course," said Sagiro calmly. There was no trace of confusion in his voice as one might expect of someone just woken. "I do prefer that my neck remain unperforated."

"After what happened at the Seven Mirrors, I'm tempted to lean a little harder," said Morningstar.

"You mean when I called upon the people of our fair kingdom to apprehend a band of murderers? I believe the scales of morality are currently weighted in my favor concerning the events to which you refer."

"We didn't kill that…man. He killed himself, ingested some kind of poison."

"I watched you and your friends assault him unprovoked."

Her patience was fraying. "Why are you here, Sagiro? I already know, of course, but it would make me less inclined to make holes in your neck if you would just admit it up front."

"Very well. I am here seeking an Eye of Moirel, just as you are. I have had no luck searching in other caves and was taking a rest before setting out to explore this one."

"Tell me again why you are searching for it."

"Why would I not want to find a diamond worth hundreds of gold crescents?"

Ell's shadow, but he sounded so *reasonable*.

"And how did you know to look here for it?"

"That is information I am disinclined to share. Are you threatening to kill me if I do not speak?"

That was an easy one. "Yes, I'll kill you unless you tell me. How do you know where to find Eyes of Moirel?"

Sagiro looked up at her, seemingly relaxed, though the spikes of her mace pressed dimples into his skin. She did not feel moved to mercy towards those who attacked her, but Sagiro had not, as far as she knew, committed any evil acts. Still, the need for this information was worth a bluff.

"On that subject, I regret that I cannot disclose my sources, not even with my life in such peril," said Sagiro. "If you must kill me, there is little I can do about it."

Damn. Was he was calling her bluff or simply resigned to his death?

"However, I can promise that if you let me live, I will depart this place entirely and leave the search to you and your friends. I know when I am bested. Would that be acceptable to you?"

Aravia returned to the cave. "They're on their way."

Sagiro's rapier was leaning against the nearest wall. "Aravia, do you see Sagiro's weapon? Over there. Could you take it, please?"

Aravia did so.

"Also," added Morningstar, "if he makes any hostile moves, blast him or set him on fire."

She hoped Aravia would play along, and her faith was rewarded. Aravia wiggled her fingers. "I'd be more than pleased."

"Stand slowly," said Morningstar. "Collect your things, and don't do anything that might make either of us think you're up to something. When my friends are all here, we'll let you go, on the condition that you head straight back upriver. Agreed?"

"Will you return my weapon?" asked Sagiro.

"No chance. Letting you live will have to be enough."

"I have no wish to harm you, truly, but I understand why you are suspicious."

Morningstar removed the head of her weapon from beneath Sagiro's chin, and the wiry little man stood, slowly, keeping his hands in plain sight.

Ernie and Dranko appeared in the cave mouth.

"Well, look who's here," said Dranko. "The guy with the mustache who tried to frame us. You tried to frame us, I mean. Not the mustache."

"Sagiro was just leaving," said Morningstar. "He's agreed to give up his search and leave the area. We keep his weapon. Ernie, Dranko, why don't you help pack up Sagiro's campsite while I keep an eye on where his hands are."

Sagiro stood stock still while his belongings were stuffed back into his pack. Dranko made no attempt to hide that he was rooting through the man's possessions, going so far as to pull out a small leather pouch that jingled. "You don't mind if I take this, do you? I'm sure a man as enterprising as yourself won't be poor for long."

Sagiro did not reply. Dranko pocketed the pouch while Ernie tied up the bedroll.

"I hope someday we meet in better circumstances," said Sagiro. "Perhaps you will have learned the errors of your ways."

He took a step toward the cave mouth just as Kibi and Tor arrived.

"You!" said Kibi. "What are you doin' here?"

"Our friend has agreed to skedaddle," said Dranko. "We keep his weapon, he agrees to go back to where he came from and leave the searching to us."

Kibi was staring goggle-eyed at Sagiro. "You can't let him go! He's got an Eye of Moirel right there in his pocket! I'm lookin' at it right now, red as a rose."

Sagiro sighed.

The blood drained from Morningstar's face. How could she have fallen for such a simple ruse as that? "You've had it all this time?" she cried. "You...you little weasel..."

"You know," said Dranko, "I admire a man who runs a good con. But when your opponent can see the cards up your sleeve, it's a good idea to cut your losses."

Sagiro still acted unruffled. "Is that a colorful way of telling me you intend to take my lawful possession by force?"

"Yeah," said Dranko. "Though the less we have to hurt you, the happier we'll all be."

"We don't want to hurt you at all," Ernie added quickly.

"And I do not wish to be hurt," said Sagiro. "Nor do I wish any harm to you. It seems you have won the day again. I invite you to reach into my pocket, which apparently your friend Kibi can easily identify, and remove the object you seek."

Morningstar sensed a trap. "No." Dranko said "no" at the same time, probably thinking the same thing. She added, "Take it out of your pocket yourself and toss it to the ground, then back up."

Sagiro reached into his pocket and pulled out a round diamond, a twin to the one in the Greenhouse. He graced them with a rueful smile.

"Now would be a good time," he said.

Morningstar only had a second to wonder what the mustachioed man meant or whom he was talking to. A shockwave blast of red light pulsed from Sagiro's hand, lifting her slightly off her feet, as though she were floating in an ocean while a slow wave rolled past. Something like a blanket was thrown over her sense of self, and all went dark.

* * *

Slowly, slowly she regained consciousness. Her head throbbed, but nothing else hurt, so she sat up. Late afternoon sun shone in her eyes; looking away from it brought her friends into her field of vision. They were all out cold, though their chests were rising and falling.

It took her ten good seconds of hard thinking to remember where she was and why everyone was sprawled on the ground inside a cave. Sagiro! The man with the handlebar mustache had done something, attacked them with the Eye of Moirel. There was no sign of him now. She stood and walked gingerly to the cave mouth, but the only living creatures nearby were two deer drinking from the river. They spooked and bolted. Sagiro was nowhere in sight.

One by one the others awoke, groaning and rubbing their eyes. Only Kibi was still unconscious.

Dranko lurched to his feet. "Damn. Where's Sagiro?"

"Gone," said Morningstar. "I wonder why he didn't kill us all when he had the chance."

"Or at least rob us blind while we were out," added Dranko.

Ernie had propped himself up against a wall. "Because that's what you two would have done, right? Because we're Horn's Company, band of thieves and murderers."

"Relax, Ernie," said Dranko. "We're talking about someone who hasn't treated us very well both times we've encountered him." He grinned. "Also, yeah, of *course* I'd have looted him. It's strange you even have to ask."

"Sagiro did say he didn't want to hurt us," said Tor. "Maybe he was telling the truth."

"He just blasted us all into unconsciousness," said Dranko, "and that hurt."

"But Morningstar's right," said Tor. "He had the opportunity to kill us all and didn't take it."

"Could be Sagiro didn't know how long we'd be unconscious," said Aravia, "and getting the Eye away was all he cared about."

"So now what?" asked Tor. "Should we go after him?"

Aravia shook her head. "He's been gone for hours, and we have no idea where he might have headed."

Kibi was the last to wake. "What in all the Hells jus' happened?"

"Our mustachioed friend did some trick with the Eye of Moirel," said Dranko. "Kibi, you never told us those things were little magic weapons. We should stop keeping ours locked up and start carrying it around for emergencies!"

Kibi groaned and sat up. "I ain't got no notion of how that'd work. Sagiro must be some kind a' wizard."

"I don't think so," said Aravia. "Did you hear what he said right before he released the concussive blast?"

Ernie nodded. "He said, 'Now would be a good time.'"

"And who was he talking to?"

No one answered right away.

"The better question," Aravia amended, "would be '*what* was he talking to?' Because I think he was telling the Eye itself to cast its spell."

"And it listened?" asked Ernie.

"Kibi has talked to ours," said Aravia. "Even when it wasn't possessing your stuffed bear."

"But it just spewed out a bunch a' cryptic mumbo jumbo," said Kibi.

"'Course, it ain't been all that clear in the bear, neither."

"You should sit down and have a chat with it when we get home," said Dranko. "Promise it you'll give it a good polish every night if it'll let us carry it around and zap our enemies for us."

No one was saying the important truth out loud. Morningstar turned her back to the sunlight spilling into the cave. "What will it say when we show up without its brother? When we come back having failed."

CHAPTER TWENTY-SEVEN

Failed. The word should be making her angry, given the reactions of her companions. But it wasn't. Everyone else was so demoralized—not as much as when Mrs. Horn had died, but there was an air of inevitable doom hanging in the cave.

Aravia was intimately familiar with suffering setbacks. The Gods knew, during her apprenticeship with Master Serpicore, that her improvisations and experiments had not always been resounding successes on the first try. But every time she had accidentally set the workbench on fire, or turned a rack of valuable glassware into sand, or caused Serpicore's hair to disappear, she had used those…miscalibrations…to improve her techniques and knowledge of the arcane.

For all of Serpicore's faults, he had never stopped hammering home the importance of keeping a level head. "Being a wizard means being a failure," he had told her once. "A thousand times you will be a failure before every great success. But if you allow each botched attempt to dishearten you, you will never achieve your potential. There is no place in magic for your heart, and no place in your heart for magic."

But what *was* in her heart? She searched the memories of her childhood—a perfectly ordinary one, the daughter of two cartwrights in the city of Sentinel, though she spent more time reading and less time learning the family craft than her parents would have preferred. She remembered a presumably typical collage of young emotions: joy, fear, frustration, excitement, sadness. There was the time she had taken a dare from her friend Camilla to swing on a leafy vine across the narrow point of the Adderflun River. She could pick apart the memory, examine it from different angles, note the exhilaration of flight followed by the terror when she realized she wouldn't reach the far bank, and the relief when she had successfully swum to shore.

But all of that was in her mind, not her heart. The emotions associated with that memory were faded and gray, moved into a dusty cabinet seldom examined.

When Aravia was seventeen, her parents had crumbled in the face of the indisputable evidence of her genius and sent her to study arcanism with Master Serpicore. Though Serpicore was notoriously strict and only accepted students of a certain potential, he had admitted her after but a single interview, forgoing the usual battery of tests. He had even agreed that she could keep Pewter, though he detested pets.

Her heart beat faster when she thought of her cat, left behind with Serpicore. She missed her Pewter, and that was real. She wasn't sure she could put him in the danger that so clearly was part and parcel of working for Abernathy. But if she discovered that Serpicore was mistreating him...

There. *There* was something that made her angry.

Morningstar and Dranko began to bicker, which jarred her from her reverie. She understood that she should try to cheer the others up, make them see that there was success on the far side of this failure.

"There's another one, right?" she asked Kibi. "Another Eye?"

"Well, I guess so. The Eye we got at home, it said, 'You must find my brothers. One is close.' Maybe it'll tell us where to find another one, sure. Come to think of it, at the Mirrors, it told me it lacked 'two willing brothers.'"

"We're oh-for-one so far," said Dranko. "And Sagiro has at least one. How many are there altogether?"

"Seven," said Kibi. "The green one we got said there was seven."

"That makes sense," said Aravia. "Magic is full of symmetries, and there are seven Mirrors as well. Kibi, you said the Eye Sagiro just took was red, didn't you?"

"Yup."

"And the one we have at home turns green when it's...active. Now, remember that when the Mirrors flashed, they formed a seven sided light-structure where each side was a different color. I'd say there are seven Eyes, each one corresponding to one of the colors at Flashing Day."

"Brilliant!" Tor exclaimed. "That has to be right. And there are still five more, and we only need two of them."

She smiled at the boy. His attitude flew right in the face of Serpicore's teachings. He was never discouraged, but he achieved that state not through any intellectual rigor or practiced self-discipline. He was *all* heart, and it kept him boundlessly optimistic. That was boosted, of course, by the fact that he was incapable of dwelling on anything negative long enough for it to color his worldview. Nor was he ever likely to become a wizard.

"But we don't know how many Sagiro already has," said Ernie. "Or the Sharshun."

"More importantly," said Morningstar, "we don't know what the Eyes *do*."

"They unmake the world," said Tor. "Do we need to know the details?"

"Knowing *how* they unmake the world might help us put a stop to it," said Morningstar.

Aravia knew they weren't going to find any answers standing around in a cave. "Then let's go home. Maybe Abernathy has woken up, or Bumbly will have more to say. Gather round, and I'll teleport us back to the Greenhouse."

* * *

She cast her spell, the cave vanished, and there was the Greenhouse door. But just like before, something tugged at the magic, as though it was taking its effect only reluctantly.

"It happened again," said Ernie, looking around. "Where's Kibi?"

"Running late," said Dranko.

As when they teleported the first time, the stonecutter appeared five seconds after the rest of them. He stumbled a few feet sideways.

"I feel like I been stuffed in a barrel and rolled down a hill," he said. "Aravia, any way you could make your teleportin' a mite less dizzifyin'?"

Aravia frowned at him. "It should be a seamless translation," she said. "Did any of the rest of you experience any discomfort?"

"Not me," said Tor, and no one else had either.

"You're also showing up a few seconds late," said Aravia to Kibi. "For some reason the spell isn't working quite right with you."

"I'm startin' to get the sense that all magic goes wonky where I'm concerned," said Kibi. "Though I suppose there's more good than bad in that if that's why Hodge's crazy fire didn't bother me."

"But Sagiro's attack with his Eye of Moirel knocked you out, longer than any of us," said Aravia. "We'll have to experiment on you to know for sure."

Kibi crossed his arms. "We won't have to do any such thing."

"Have it your way. But if it were me, I'd want to know as much as possible about my resistance to magic. And that reminds me. Kibi, I want to check all the objects you brought back from Seablade Point, to see if they're enchanted. I don't have much magic left today after teleporting, but one *aura sense* before bed shouldn't be a problem."

Aravia strode inside, but her sense of purpose slid away when she saw Eddings at the stairway, shaking his head.

"Abernathy has still not regained consciousness, though his breathing is steady and he suffers no fever."

Aravia was happy the old wizard was alive but impatient all the same. "Dranko, can't you wake him up?"

"I've taken care of his burns and cuts, and he's not injured in any other way I can see. He's going to have to wake up on his own."

"Fine. In that case let's find out if Hodge had any enchanted goodies stashed away."

Tor helped her make a pile of objects on the living room table, which included the twenty-seven little metal pyramids, red leather book, bag of rubies, and rolled-up carpet from Hodge's trunk.

"You want me to fetch the Eye of Moirel from the basement?" asked Kibi.

"That's not necessary," said Aravia. "I'm confident our little green diamond is the most magical thing in the Greenhouse right now. Once I've taught myself the spell that identifies the *properties* of magical objects, then we'll see what I can learn about it."

Aravia cast her spell and gazed upon the pile. "No magic on the gemstones or the book, but the pyramids all have a medium-grade enchantment upon them. So does the rug."

"Ooh!" said Tor. "Maybe it's a flying carpet! My mother read a story to me when I was little where a young girl discovered a flying carpet and used it to rescue her grandmother from an evil prince. I've always wanted to fly on one!"

"Unlikely," said Aravia. "I expect its purpose, as well as that of the tetrahedra, was as part of the rituals Hodge was going to use—or maybe already had used—to activate the Kivian Arch."

Aravia took a lurching side step and steadied herself on the table. "I think I'll lie down. Teleporting took more out of me than I thought." Of course, having discovered that some of Hodge's belongings were enchanted, she itched to know the details.

Tor hurried to her side and helped her to a couch. "Just take a rest," he told her. "Eddings almost has dinner ready, but I'll bring you out a plate so you don't have to get up. What's a tetrahedra?"

"It's a fancy word for pyramids. And thanks, Tor. You're so sweet. While you're up, would you mind grabbing the thin green book out of my pack? I might as well get some reading done while I eat."

Whatever else you might say about Tor, he was a gentleman. Aravia had grown up an only child, and though she was older, he was like the big brother she never had.

Tor blinked. "What? Oh, are you sure? You look pretty pale."

"I'll be fine," Aravia insisted. "It's the book with the spell that determines what our magic stuff does. It's a straightforward spell; I just haven't prioritized it before now."

Tor brought her the book, then hurried off to fetch her stew, but before he returned, her eyes grew heavy and sleep took her. When Eddings gently shook her awake at midnight, all the others had already gone to bed.

* * *

Aravia expected to be the first down to breakfast. Her brain had woken her up from a sound sleep, insisting that she get an early start studying, and her stomach, displeased at having missed dinner last night, had chimed in demanding sustenance. But though it couldn't yet be five o'clock in the morning, there were already two seated at the dining room table.

Well, technically, one of them was *on* the table. Bumbly the bear sat at one end, slightly flopped over but mostly sitting up, the Eye of Moirel wedged into the fabric of its left eye. It was not moving, or talking, or glowing.

Morningstar sat at the far end, a piece of paper in her hand, and she was looking intently at Bumbly as though engaged in a staring contest with it.

"It was already here when I came down, but it hasn't done anything yet. It could be waiting for Kibi or Ernie."

Aravia took a closer look. The Eye was heavy enough to cant Bumbly's head to the left, lending the bear an almost thoughtful pose. "Why are you up so early?" she asked.

"I…had a dream," said Morningstar.

"Oh. A Seer-dream?"

"No, not exactly. It was—I'm sorry, I don't think I'm ready to talk about it yet. But it's nothing bad. When it ended, I woke up and couldn't get back to sleep."

Aravia was curious but didn't press. "And what is that?" she asked, pointing to the paper.

Eddings came in from the kitchen, polishing a large bowl with a rag. "That was delivered for Morningstar at one hour after midnight."

"From Previa," said Morningstar. "She and her Chroniclers were able to find—something—about the Ventifact Colossus. I was going to share it with everyone once you were all awake, but here. According to Previa it's a scrap from a work called *Gleanings of Romus the Mad,* a compilation of predictions and proclamations from a half-crazed diviner several hundred years ago. One of Previa's assistants remembered having read it before, since the prophecy in question is so strange. She copied it down as precisely as she could, including…well, it's easier to see for yourself."

Aravia took the oversized sheet of parchment. The lettering leaned every which way, as though a child had penned it, and the spelling was appalling.

Th' Ventifact Giant wyl wayke besyde th' city o' Ganit Tuvith, when th' red tresspass'r wynds the Chelonian Horn from th' highest tow'r o' Tuvith an' calls th' Colossus forth. Th' grayte Ventifact Turtle will plod th' streets o' Ganit Tuvith and smash haf the city, but as th' Stormknytes wyl a' byn warn'd, three o' their number wyl smyte th' beest, an' rytely so; for if the turtle is allow'd t' live, it wyl call t' its kyn, an' wayke an army o' turtles to conquer the kingdom. Gods help us then! The Turtle Army! Verily it wyl sweep 'cross th' land, ARMOR-PLAYTED AN' STONY-EYED, AN' WHO IN HYS RYTE MYND WOOLD NO' FLEE FROM SUCH MYTE! RYVYRS WOOOLD FLO' WITH TURTLES, YE GODS HELP US, AND VERILY WOOLD THEY DANCE ON MYE HEAD! Heavyns, I need mye elyxyr, my poor hed.

Aravia read through the page of prophetic ramblings, frowned, and read it again. The skewed letters actually grew bigger as Romus had written, as if he we wanted to make sure readers took him seriously. "So the Ventifact Colossus is a *turtle?*" she asked. "One big enough that it will take three people to kill it?"

"I'm thinking of my Seer-dream. The one with a turtle walking towards a toy city and threatening to step on it."

"Right, I remember," said Aravia. "But then Eddings killed it with a letter opener."

"What if the city was life-sized?" said Morningstar. "What if the Ventifact Colossus is really that big?"

Aravia read the prophecy one more time. "Hmm. Remember this was written by someone known as Romus the Mad. This could all still be symbolic. Or, worse, a bit of misleading lunacy that means nothing." But her mind was picking apart the details of the page, turning them over, analyzing.

"Summoned by the red trespasser," said Morningstar. "Which could be Aktallian Dreamborn, with his red armor." She frowned. "But…isn't that good? We want the prophecy to come true, don't we? So that the way to Kivia gets opened? And in order for that to happen, the Colossus needs to get called so that the Stormknights can kill it."

"I suppose that…"

"But what if the Stormknights *don't* kill it?" Morningstar continued. "Then it will lead an army of giant turtles that will lay waste to the kingdom. Maybe it would be better to stop it from being summoned in the first place."

"*If* Romus is correct, then yes, we'll have to figure that out," said Aravia. "But right now this isn't enough to go on. At the very least we need to find out where Ganit Tuvith is. I don't recall that name." She pictured the map of Charagan in her head and mentally scanned its various islands but came up empty. "It's not on my map. Can you ask Previa if she can look that one up too?"

"Yes, of course."

"Or maybe Abernathy knows."

"He's still out," said Morningstar. "I checked on him before I came downstairs."

Aravia sighed. This saving-the-world business was stressful enough knowing there were wise and powerful wizards steering the ship. Now they were adrift. "Ask your sisters about Ganit Tuvith then. I'm not sure what to do next, and the more information we have, the better decisions we can make."

* * *

YOU MUST SECURE MY BROTHER.

Bumbly had flared to emerald green life once all six of them had come down for breakfast. They crowded around the little bear, allowing Kibi to stand the closest.

"We tried that," said Kibi. "But someone else got there first and nabbed it."

HARD BY NORLIN'S HEADWATERS, A KEEP CRUMBLES. TIME AGAIN IS SHORT. WHEN THE WORLD IS UNMADE, YOU WILL NEED MY LAST BROTHER. WITHOUT HIM, NOTHING MATTERS.

"Last?" Ernie said. "You mean our enemies have all the others? Sagiro, or the Sharshun?"

"Dammit," said Kibi. "Can't you speak plain? What does that mean?"

KEEP ME SAFE, KIBILHATHUR.

The Eye of Moirel clunked on the wooden table, leaving Bumbly looking as confused as the rest of them. Kibi let out a growling bellow. "Safe from what, you confounded rock? I ain't got nowhere safer to keep you, but you keep blastin' your way out!"

"Maybe it just means the Greenhouse," said Ernie.

Kibi gave a helpless shrug. "Tell you what else. Did the rest of you notice? Bumbly said 'when.' 'When the world is unmade.' Not 'if.' Made it sound like somethin' we ain't gonna prevent."

"Maybe," said Aravia. "But the Eye clearly prefers to speak in obscurities, so we shouldn't get hung up on the niceties of its vocabulary. And it still strongly believes we need to find a second one, which wouldn't matter if the world is going to be unmade no matter what we do."

"So, great," said Dranko. "We have something else to keep us busy until Abernathy wakes up. Hey Map-girl, where are Norlin's headwaters?"

Aravia raised an eyebrow. "Map-girl?"

"It's a compliment."

"It's on Nahalm, same duchy as Sand's Edge. In fact, it's the Norlin River that empties out into the Sea of Storms just north of the desert. But the river starts about a hundred miles north of there, in the Norlin Hills.

"What about the turtles?" asked Morningstar.

The others looked at her curiously.

"Oh. Right. Look at this."

Morningstar passed around her excerpt from the *Gleanings of Romus the Mad*.

"I'd be inclined to chalk this up as meaningless ravings," she concluded. "Except for two things. One is my Seer-dream about a turtle crushing a city. The other is Romus's mention of a 'red trespasser,' which sounds like Aktallian. We don't know where Ganit Tuvith is, but I'll see if Previa can find out."

"Do the Stormknights even know they're supposed to slay this enormous turtle?" asked Dranko.

"Who knows?" said Morningstar. "Probably? Romus predicts they'll have been warned."

"Maybe by us!" said Tor.

Aravia had little to add; she expected that the turtle was a symbol that would become clear in time. But there was something else on her mind.

"In a little while I'll know what all our magic stuff can do. Another hour with the spellbook for *identification* should be enough; it doesn't look particularly complex or taxing."

She read over breakfast, barely aware of what she was eating. Even a relatively simple spell (and *identification* was one of the easiest in Abernathy's library) took concentration and discipline, not to mention a good deal of tricky memorization, but she knew she'd be up to it.

When the meal was done, the company adjourned to the living room, where the table was mostly covered with Hodge's metal pyramids. There was also his prayer mat, and Ernie placed his sword Pyknite down as well. Aravia added the Eye of Moirel, and Dranko fished his Black Circle pendant from around his neck and tossed it in with the rest.

"Wait!" said Ernie, before Aravia could begin. "Let me get the bracelet they found on my statue." He dashed upstairs and soon returned, placing the golden circlet onto the table.

Aravia began to cast. *Identification* was a three-minute spell, its syllables spoken slowly and gestures repeated in sets of five. As she neared the end, a tiny voice in the back of her mind warned that she might be misinterpreting Abernathy's notes on vocal inflection, but she pressed on nonetheless.

As she spiraled her thumbs to end the spell, the objects on the table began to glow and rise, just a few inches. Ernie's sword tilted up hilt first until it was balanced on its point.

Hmm. If the spell had worked properly, knowledge of the magic items' history, purpose, and function should have appeared in her head, as though she had just read full descriptions. But that hadn't happened, and the glow was getting brighter, and the objects were jittering and bumping against the table.

Now that she thought a bit harder about it, Abernathy's notes on thumb spirals were ambiguous, particularly regarding the base energy types. Had she inadvertently invoked a kinetic component *inside* the oral divinatory shell?

Uh oh.

One of the metal pyramids flared with white light and bounced nearly to the ceiling. Then another one hopped and thumped *against* the ceiling, ricocheting off at an angle toward the dining room.

"Everyone down on your stomachs, as flat as you can, and shut your eyes tight!" Aravia shouted. "Now!"

She flung herself down, half under the table, just as the living room filled with a cacophony of clattering metal and hard *thunks* as the pyramids smashed into the walls and ceiling. Through her closed eyelids came pulses of light like flaring suns, and she hoped the others had heeded her warning lest they be blinded.

Someone let out a cry of pain.

"Down!" she yelled. "Stay down!"

For a short while the living room sounded like an enclosed archery range with fifty amateur bowmen aiming while blindfolded. When it was over (and it couldn't have been more than ten seconds), Aravia opened one eye and then the other, sat up, and smacked her head against the bottom of the table.

"Is everyone...?" She meant to say "okay," but a torrent of knowledge chose that moment to rush through her brain like a raging river, physically knocking her over with its intensity. Information about Ernie's sword, the metal pyramids, Hodge's rolled-up carpet—everything except the Eye of Moirel—was deposited in her mind like shore-silt from a retreating wave. She groaned.

"Gods, but that smarts!"

The others were slowly standing, except for Kibi who remained on his stomach. Most of the little pyramids were embedded in the wooden walls, a few had been driven into beams near the ceiling, a few more had failed to find purchase and lay strewn about the floor...and one was lodged point down in Kibi's left buttock. It was obviously painful, but Aravia couldn't stifle a snort of laughter. Dranko stood over Kibi and rolled up his sleeves.

"I'll heal you, on the condition that no one ever mentions this outside the Greenhouse."

"Seems like we get attacked 'n awful lot in this business," said Kibi from the ground. He was trying to smile but his face contorted into a pained grimace when he spoke. "You better get yourself used to puttin' your hands on anyplace we get hurt."

"Sorry about that," said Aravia. "I guess my understanding of Abernathy's magical dialect could still use some fine tuning."

Dranko looked pointedly at Kibi, then up at the ceiling where Pyknite still quivered, jammed point-first into a wooden rafter. "We have our front-runner for understatement of the week."

While Dranko tended to Kibi's unfortunate injury—using conventional medicine, as he was disinclined to channel—Aravia sifted through the knowledge that her spell had placed in her head. It was like recalling from memory a set of facts she had read in a book only minutes before.

"First thing, the Greenhouse itself is overwhelmingly enchanted. It has so many layers of arcane protections and abjurations infused into its construction, I can't even keep track of them all. That's both encouraging—that Abernathy should have gone through so much trouble—and worrying, that he felt we'd need such extraordinary protection."

She turned to Ernie. "Your sword Pyknite was forged with three drops of goblin blood 114 years ago. A wizard named Ellivia enchanted it as it was hammered, so that it will carve through goblins like blocks of soft cheese. The potency of the magic is tied to the confidence and skill of the wielder."

Ernie gave a worried little smile. "I wonder if Old Bowlegs knew that."

"The pyramids are hundreds of years old, but the spell didn't give me an exact age. They are critical secondary components in a complex ritual meant to open a direct portal between two gartine-infused arches."

"We guessed that already, didn't we?" asked Morningstar.

"Sort of," said Aravia. "They're secondary because they're only meant to augment the efficacy of the primary ritual. Hodge was softening up the target, but someone else is performing the ritual that will activate the arch. That's good news, since it implies we didn't shut down Hodge's plan in its entirety."

She pointed to Ernie's circlet. "That's still something of a mystery," she said. "It's something called a Talisman of Stability, and one of its effects is to prevent the wearer from traveling between worlds. There's more, but the spell didn't provide any additional detail. And as far as my spell is concerned, the Eye of Moirel isn't magical at all. Something about its nature defies arcane scrutiny."

She picked up the Black Circle pendant they had taken from Haske in Sand's Edge. "This thing shields minds, mostly to prevent them from being read, but it will also protect you from other magical spells that can affect your brain."

"Are there a lot of those?" asked Dranko.

"Sure, though they tend to be extremely difficult to cast, not to mention the ethical concerns. There are spells that can compel a person to take certain actions or *not* to take them. There are also spells that can erase or modify people's memories. Serpicore mentioned once that that class of magic is illegal in Charagan, and so he had no plans to teach them to me."

She held up the red rug. Tor was going to love this. "As for the prayer mat, it's not a prayer mat. It's a flying carpet."

Tor's face lit up like a sunrise. He grabbed the rolled up carpet from Aravia and dashed to the back yard. A minute later his voice shouted, "How do I get it to fly?"

Aravia and the others joined him on the lawn. The carpet was small—barely five feet long and maybe three feet wide, thinly woven from red and gold silk threads. A gaudy fire motif was prominently featured in its design, and a row of orange tassels lined one of the shorter edges. Tor had it rolled out on the grass and was sitting cross-legged on its center.

"This carpet is called Vyasa Vya in the ancient tongue of a people called the Delfirians," she said. "That means 'Burning Sky.' It was used several times for reconnaissance during a war against Bederen, a kingdom bordering Delfir, but a Delfirian scout flew too low and was killed by crossbow fire. Bederen and Delfir must be places beyond the Uncrossable Sea. The spell didn't tell me how it ended up in Hodge's trunk."

Tor gave her an impatient look. "But how do you make it fly?"

"I was getting to that. Someone seated on the front center of the carpet can control and steer Vyasa Vya by gripping the orange tassels and issuing mental commands. It has magical safeguards to prevent you from—"

"You mean I just have to *think* about flying?" Tor gripped two tassels in front of him, and before Aravia could explain that the carpet would default to hovering if the tassels were released (unless the driver had issued specific instructions to the contrary) or that kinetic buffers would prevent someone from falling off during all but the steepest banks, the carpet had shot upward fifteen feet and zipped to the far side of the lawn. It flew speedily but not outrageously so—maybe half as fast as a galloping horse—and trailed intertwining snakes of dark gray smoke behind it.

"Not much use if you need to be stealthy," said Dranko.

"It's a *flying carpet*," said Aravia, smiling at the sight of Tor zooming around the yard. "How can you possibly complain?"

Tor let out a whoop and flew higher, until he was above the yard's lone tree, a thirty-foot maple. Was there an altitude above which Abernathy's magical screen wouldn't prevent the rest of Tal Hae from noticing the carpet, even if it was flying directly above the property?

Tor brought Vyasa Vya down in a steep dive, smoke streaming from its back edge like a tail of fuzzy ropes, and pulled up where he started, not more than eight inches above the grass. He didn't rock forward despite his sudden stop, as the carpet magically siphoned away his inertia. Surely there were practical lessons she could learn from its function, particularly vis-à-vis flying or levitation spells.

Tor leapt from the carpet and wobbled a little on his feet. "That was amazing! And think about how much easier this will make our lives."

"It's too small for all of us to ride at once," said Aravia. "If more than four people sit on it, it won't fly."

One by one they took Vyasa Vya for short flights above the back lawn. Ernie never went higher than the top of the fence, and muttered something about not caring for heights. Only Kibi abstained, grumbling about a general mistrust borne of magic's muted effects on him. "Last thing I need is for that crazy thing to malfunction while I'm flyin' twenty feet off the ground."

Aravia found it trickier than she expected when she took her turn. The carpet more or less obeyed her mental commands, but her unusually keen mental focus proved an impediment. Every time there was the slightest discrepancy between what she wanted the rug to do, and what it *did*, she would think about the minute series of adjustments that would correct the problem. This caused Vyasa Vya to jitter and twitch beneath her, creating a feedback loop of correction and overcorrection that the carpet seemed to resent.

The carpet's speed and maneuverability were the same with four passengers as with one, but with five Vyasa Vya refused even to lift from the ground. Tor was far and away the most accomplished at controlling their new toy, and by unspoken agreement he was allowed to roll it up and tie it onto the bottom of his traveling pack.

Aravia did some quick distance and travel-speed calculations. "If we don't mind being separated for a bit, a single driver can shuttle us in two groups. As long as the carpet goes faster than three times the speed of our walkers—which it does—we can get to the Norlin Hills in a day and a half.

Kibi looked distinctly displeased. "How's that work?"

"Tor can fly three of us northward for an hour, drop us off, and fly back. He'll pick up the other two and bring everyone together. We'll keep repeating that until we've arrived."

"Do you need to rest before we set out?" asked Morningstar.

Aravia was confident that all would be well. "No. I know my last spell went spectacularly awry, but it wasn't very taxing. And I remember that spot at the edge of the Mouth of Nahalm where we lowered ourselves down, well enough to get us there. We waited there for hours."

"I seem to recall you using the phrase 'fatally messy,'" said Dranko. "Not that I didn't enjoy your flying caltrop extravaganza just now, at least until Kibi ended up with a holy Kivian ritual object lodged in his arse. But 'at the edge of the desert' sounds suspiciously close to 'out over the desert' if you miss. What are the odds of that?"

Aravia ran through the likely scenarios in her head. "Minimal."

"But not zero," said Dranko.

"I know what I'm doing! Also, do you think it was a coincidence that Sagiro just *happened* to beat us to the punch by a day or less, after the Eyes of Moirel had been scattered and lost for centuries? Whatever source of information Bumbly has been tapping into about where his brothers are, Sagiro has it too. He's probably on his way to the Norlin Hills right now. The Green Eye just told us time was short and implied that failure would result in the world being unmade, which sounds just as bad as it being conquered by Naradawk Skewn. We can't wait until tomorrow."

CHAPTER TWENTY-EIGHT

I f anyone was likely to wind up head-down in the Mouth of Nahalm, it was
Kibi. Thus far he had been afflicted with an unaccountable time delay each
time Aravia had magicked the group from one place to another, and who
was to say a similar thing couldn't happen in terms of a landing spot? He asked
Aravia if maybe she didn't have a more inland place she recalled well enough.

"Sorry, Kibi," was her answer. "From now on I'll make a point to memorize
the details of places we may want to teleport to someday, but I wasn't thinking
about that during our stay in Sand's Edge. *Maybe* I could get us into the
recruiting hall where we were attacked, but the risks would be even greater. My
mental map of that room isn't as sharp, and there might be people in there who
want to kill us."

In the end they put it to a vote, and though Kibi argued that Aravia should be
as rested as possible, he was outvoted four to two. Only Ernie agreed with his
caution.

"Then pack up!" said Dranko once the matter was settled. "Looks like
another day on the job for Abernathy's Magic Rock Collectors."

"I got to do one more thing before we head out," said Kibi. He borrowed the
Greenhouse's second-sturdiest iron cook-pot, and this time filled it with water
before dropping in the Eye of Moirel. Then he scooped up some sandy soil from
around the back door and filled the pot until the Eye was in the center of a
sludgy mass. After securing the lid he dropped the pot into a third iron trunk in
the basement, apprehensive at the rate he was inviting the Eye to punch holes
through their collection of chests, not to mention the closet doors.

"Now stay put!" he admonished. "I'm tryin' to keep you safe like you keep askin' for, but this is the last time I'm goin' to all this trouble. Next time you get yourself loose, I'm just gonna toss you in a cheap vase and have done with it."

* * *

They checked on Abernathy one last time before they departed, but the wizard was still out cold. The old man's face was healing (Dranko having cleaned his wounds and applied ointment to his burns) but served as a grim reminder of how dangerous their lives had become. Eddings was keeping him watered and promised to keep a constant eye on him while the company was away. Aravia gathered everyone, and Dranko suggested that they rope themselves together.

"Just in case Aravia's off by a few feet, and some of us end up over the edge," he explained.

"That's extremely unlikely," said Aravia. "Just relax."

Dranko was talking good sense. "I'll be more relaxed if I'm tied on to the rest of you," Kibi said.

They did as Dranko suggested while Aravia rolled her eyes, which set Kibi to worrying that making Aravia impatient wasn't improving the odds of a safe landing. But the wizard lass did her hocus-pocus and all was well. There was a jarring displacement and unnerving sense of being unhinged from the world, and then he stood, solidly, at the lip of the Mouth of Nahalm. No one was dangling over the edge.

"You get lost again?" asked Dranko.

Kibi glowered. "That'd be more funny if it didn't feel like someone steppin' on my stomach."

"Let's get moving," said Aravia. "The best way not to get lost would be to head due north until we strike the Norlin River, then follow it up into the hills and look around for a ruined castle."

Kibi looked on uneasily as Tor unfurled Vyasa Vya with a deft snap. "I volunteer to go in the second group," he said quickly. Even though they had agreed that the carpet would fly close to the ground (unless they needed aerial reconnaissance for some reason), an unreasoning terror gripped Kibi's heart when he imagined rising up away from the solid earth. Could the others see how nervous he was?

Morningstar offered to keep him company. Ernie, Aravia, and Dranko climbed onto the back of the carpet while Tor took the pilot's seat and gripped the tassels. Kibi's stomach lurched just watching the damn thing rise up three feet and hover, rippling like a wind-blown sheet hanging on a drying line.

"I'll be back for you two in an hour," said Tor. He was grinning back at them even as the carpet sped away. The last thing Kibi heard was Aravia admonishing Tor to watch where he was going, and in minutes the only sign of his departed friends was a lingering trail of charcoal-colored smoke.

"Guess we might as well walk after 'em," said Kibi. "Shave some time off the trip."

Morningstar nodded and the two began to march. The terrain was dry and brown, flat brown earth and stunted brown scrub stretching on for miles. The few straggly white clouds did nothing to dim the sun, and Morningstar tugged her hood forward to shield her face.

"As the year gets on," said Kibi, "you're gonna start bakin' in that black robe. Oughta get yourself a sun hat."

"Good idea," said Morningstar curtly.

Kibi didn't have much experience with Ellish priestesses. There weren't any in Eggoggin, and not that many in Hae Kalkas either, the nearby city where he picked up supplies now and again. He'd heard all sorts of rumors, of course, about them secretly being evil witches and drinking blood and such, but never put much stock in them.

Morningstar wasn't very talkative, which suited Kibi just fine. He wasn't much for conversation himself and didn't know what to say that Morningstar would find worthwhile. But Morningstar had been unusually withdrawn the past day or so, like she had gotten word that a relative had died. Maybe she'd received some new piece of bad news from her church. As they kicked their way through a rocky field of weeds, she looked almost dazed.

"Anything botherin' you, Morningstar? Seems like you got somethin' on your mind. We got some time to kill before Tor gets back."

Morningstar didn't answer or break stride or give any other sign of having heard him. He could take a hint and didn't press, but she spoke up a minute later.

"Kibi, you've said a few times now that you don't believe in destiny. Why is that?"

"That's an easy one," he replied. "What on earth did the Gods put us here for if our choices are decided ahead a' time? Seems more likely they let us live our lives out the way we want."

Morningstar smiled, though only the corner of her mouth peeked out from her black hood. "I *do* believe in destiny, but not that it's an immutable future that we're forced into. I think destiny is more like a...a place, a city on the horizon where the Gods want us to wind up. And if we make the best choices, our lives will finish there, even if we didn't realize that's where we were headed the entire time."

Kibi thought back to the Seven Mirrors, when he held the Eye of Moirel in his hand. *All the stones know your name.*

"But that ain't destiny then," he said. "That's more like the Gods making a wish and then hopin' it comes true. But you must know as well as anyone that the Gods can't muck around with our lives down here, not directly."

Morningstar smiled again. "Kibi, can I tell you something in confidence? Something I don't want the others to hear just yet?"

The question made Kibi feel distinctly uncomfortable. "I suppose, but why me?"

"I don't know," said Morningstar. "Maybe because I want to tell *someone*, and you're...well, you're..."

"I think I get it. I'm quiet, and I ain't interested in gossipin' like some a' the others. And we ain't talked much since we all got together, so I ain't got no basis to judge you. Is it somethin' like that?"

Morningstar stopped walking, looked at him, and laughed. "You are quiet, but when you do decide to speak, it's worth listening to. You should tell us what you think more often."

Kibi blushed. "If there's one thing our little band don't lack, it's opinions. Figure it's better to keep mine to myself unless I think someone ought to hear it."

"I admire your attitude," said Morningstar. "So may I share my secret with you?"

"All right."

Morningstar started walking again, quickly, and Kibi hustled to keep up.

"Ell showed me my destiny a couple of nights ago."

Kibi patiently said nothing.

"She sent an avatar to my dreams. The avatar told me I had been chosen to be a Dreamwalker, something that hasn't happened in many, many years. It's complicated, but when people dream, they leave behind the places that they dreamed. The red-armored man who nearly killed me, he's made himself at home there, and I'm supposed to do battle with him. The avatar is training me, since battle there is…strange. She called me Child of Light and Daughter of Dreams."

Kibi rolled that around in his head. "And you're certain that weren't just an ordinary dream, where you dreamed it weren't ordinary?"

"Yes, I'm sure. The avatar returned last night. And yes, I know you think I may have dreamt that as well, but trust me, I understand dreams."

Kibi didn't doubt Morningstar believed what she said, but he couldn't help but wonder.

"Did your avatar friend tell you anything more specific? Like when your battle is gonna happen? Or what mischief he's gonna get up to if you don't beat 'im?"

"No, not yet. But it explains so much. Why I was born so…different. Why I was called to the sisterhood when no one believed I would be. Even why I'm so mistrusted. Child of Light would sound like a heresy to the sisters of Ell."

Kibi scratched his head. "Why don't Ell just send dreams to everyone, then? Lettin' 'em all know that you're a Dreamwalker, up to somethin' important, and they shouldn't hold it against you?"

"You said it yourself. The Gods don't meddle directly. Ell gives some of us Seer-dreams, but those are ambiguous foretellings, not directives. The avatar is already treading a thin line with me."

"So you're a Dreamseer *and* a Child of Light? Sounds like Ell has heaped a lot a' responsibility on your shoulders. Guess it's a good thing Abernathy put you someplace with friends to help you out."

* * *

Tor returned for them three miles out from Sand's Edge. Kibi spotted the carpet flying high overhead, hundreds of feet up it looked like, a tiny orange kite with a smoky tail. What happened to staying close to the ground? The boy descended with alarming speed and landed deftly just a few yards away.

"Hop on!"

Morningstar climbed up, but Kibi balked, terror rising in his throat.

"I ain't sure I can do this," he muttered.

"Come on, it's fun," said Tor.

Kibi could think of a hundred words he'd choose before "fun," and Tor's enthusiasm only increased his discomfiture. The boy should be thinking about caution, not fancy flying maneuvers.

"You promise to keep as low to the ground as possible?"

"If you're sure that's what you want."

Kibi stepped onto the carpet, heart hammering crazily. "Yeah, I'm sure," he whispered. As his back foot left the ground a vertiginous wave of nausea swept through him. His head pounded in time with his thumping heart. Morningstar's voice sounded far away. "Just go, as quickly as you can. And stay low, like Kibi asked."

Vyasa Vya lurched and sped. Kibi kept his eyes closed and curled himself up on the back of the carpet. He fought down the instinct to roll off on purpose, thinking that the pain of his landing would be far preferable to the horrible revulsion of being so removed from the ground.

As the wind rushed through his hair and fluttered his beard, he tried to recall having this kind of sickening sensation in the past. As a stonecutter he had spent a decent amount of time up on ladders, or on the high roofs of buildings, without suffering any of the ill effects of vertigo. But the ladders and buildings, they had always been on the ground themselves. Unlike the carpet…

"Are you going to live?" Morningstar was talking loudly over the wind.

"Yeah," Kibi forced himself to say. "But I ain't enjoyin' livin' just now."

* * *

Kibi had to endure five more trips like that before the journey's first day was over. Each time, when Tor brought the carpet to a stop, Kibi rolled off and hugged the ground like his own mother come to embrace him. Dranko asked if he needed healing the first time, and the others gathered around him in concern, but only the blessed touch of the earth brought him peace. He knew he'd have to endure it; the alternatives would be to slow everyone else down or let them leave him behind. He wouldn't accept the first, and his friends wouldn't allow the second.

His sleep that night began with a predictable nightmare. He was back on the carpet, but Tor had lost control of it, the rug spiraling upward into the vast blue ocean of the sky. Kibi gripped the carpet, bunching its fabric into his sweaty fists, only to feel it unraveling in his fingers. Beneath him were islands of clouds;

the solidity of Spira was lost to him.

Morningstar was there with him on the carpet.

"Be at peace, Kibilhathur. This is only a dream. Spira's surface has not abandoned you. Close your eyes and let your demons go."

The dream became misty and lost its cutting edge of dread. Kibi shook his head and looked up at her.

"Morningstar? Are you really here, or am I just dreamin' you?"

"It doesn't matter. Look again, Kibilhathur."

He peered over the side of the unwinding carpet and found he was back on the ground. Of its own volition his body rolled sideways until his shoulder blades pressed into the dirt.

His eyes snapped open. A million stars blazed across the sky, but it was a sky far away, and its glittering expanse did not trouble him. Several feet away Morningstar slumbered in her bedroll, a tiny smile on her lips.

* * *

Morningstar didn't want to talk about it the next day, and she reminded Kibi she preferred to keep the subject a secret from the others. He still insisted on thanking her and marveling at what she had done.

"You talk to rocks and work stone like clay," she said quietly. "And I am learning to walk inside dreams…and mold *them* like clay, in a manner of speaking. I don't see that one is more astounding than the other."

Kibi endured the day's carpet rides with a tad less panic, and it helped that there were fewer of them. An hour before noon they reached the stubby Norlin Hills, at which point Tor took the carpet on a solo flight to scout. Morningstar had argued that if Sagiro was already there searching, the carpet's smoke trail would give away the company's arrival. But the prevailing opinion was that speed was their highest priority, and finding the "crumbling keep" could take days of wandering in the hills if they didn't avail themselves of a bird's-eye view.

That decision paid off quickly, as Tor returned within the hour announcing that he had spotted the decaying ruins of an old hill fort. "We can be there in two hours if we keep shuttling people on the flying carpet. There's even an old path leading to it, blocked with boulders in some places and washed out in others."

"And did you see any sign a' Sagiro?" asked Kibi.

"I didn't see anyone, and I flew over it a few times checking. I'm pretty sure it's abandoned."

Kibi suffered three more brief carpet rides before they had all gathered at the edge of a narrow but deep ravine, at the bottom of which swift and frothing rapids swept southward to join the Norlin River. On the far side of the ravine, not more than twenty feet distant, were the remains of a time-ravaged fortress. There had been a drawbridge once, but the chains had rusted through and the planks must have long since dropped into the river. Tor confirmed that there was no other point of entry, as the old fort perched atop a steep-sided and solitary hill. Someone standing on the ramparts and jumping down into the courtyard would fall only twenty feet, but a leap *outward* would result in a hundred-foot plummet into the river (if you were lucky) or onto sharp rocks (if you were not).

Much as Kibi hated the carpet, he was glad of it now. With Vyasa Vya the absence of a drawbridge was no impediment, and soon all six of them were standing on the weedy hard-packed soil of the fort's main courtyard. Around them moss and vines had covered most of the remaining walls, both the parts that were standing and the crumbled blocks, patchy with grime and lichen, that lay tumbled about like children's toys.

The fort was of a plain, uninspired design, just four walls, tall square towers at each corner, and a once-strong keep in its center. The gatehouse was small, its single iron portcullis rusted away. A building that might once have been a stable had collapsed in a sagging ruin against the south wall. The entire interior wasn't more than fifty yards on a side.

"After we're famous," said Dranko, "we should ask for this place as a vacation home. Little fixing up and it'll be fit for a king. Or a knight, or whatever they make us once we've saved the kingdom. We can call it Castle Blackhope."

The others fanned out to search, each choosing a different heap of rubble, but Kibi stayed put. A vibrating thrum sang in his bones, a radiating power from somewhere nearby that reminded him strongly of the Seven Mirrors. The Eye was close! He took two long steps to a waist-high chunk of fallen rock and put his hand upon it, and while it offered no direct advice, the keen sense of a deep-earth heartbeat grew stronger. When he concentrated, he perceived the source of that power and was drawn to it, as a hungry man to the scent of a hot home-cooked meal.

"Hey!" he shouted. The others stopped their searching to look at him. "It's in the keep, up on the second story."

After their previous encounter with Sagiro, none of his friends asked him how he knew. Kibi found that gratifying. His own meager abilities to shape stone had never been as impressive as Tor's martial prowess, or Dranko's street smarts, or Aravia's wizardry. The Eyes of Moirel had revealed in Kibi an unusual area of expertise, but it remained to be seen of what use the diamonds would be. His mind went back to his talk with Morningstar from the previous day, in particular on the subject of destiny.

He shook his head. "Don't mean nothin'," he muttered to himself. "You got a gift, is all, and Abernathy's spell picked you 'cause of it. Nothin' more to it than that. A general will pick his best warrior to lead a charge, but that don't make it destiny he'll win the field."

The keep was more intact than its surroundings, though its walls were pocked with holes and a corner of its roof was caved in. It even had a door, half-rotten and leaning loosely against its frame. Kibi went through first, though Tor was quickly by his side, sword drawn. Immediately to his right a sweep of worn stone stairs curved up and out of sight.

"It's up there," he said over his shoulder. "I can almost see it now, like it's a ball a' purple flame, and the keep is all made out a' glass. Ten feet above us and thirty feet in, or thereabouts."

There was no need for a lantern or light-coin; the holes in the outer walls let enough sunlight spill through to illuminate the dusty, cracked stairs. After a full revolution the spiral staircase emptied out onto a second floor hallway. The floor was littered with moldering mounds and thickly coated with dust. A mostly disintegrated suit of armor leaned casually in a corner.

The hall was wide, with spears of sunlight stabbing down through gaps in the ceiling. One of these fell upon a wide doorless opening; beyond that was the Eye of Moirel, twinkling directly through the stone.

"In there," he whispered. Tor nodded, gave the others a hurry-up gesture, and dashed through the opening. Kibi half-expected they'd discover Sagiro, the Eye already in his pocket, and he drew his mining pick from his belt just in case. He and the rest quickly followed Tor.

They were now standing in a small throne room, and while their mustachioed rival was not in evidence, they beheld something equally alarming. At the far end of the chamber was a stone throne, modestly ornate, its back and arms carved with a braided cord design like intertwining snakes. Along the top of its backing was a row of scooped ovals, empty, out of which gemstones must long ago have been prised and carried off by looters.

The Eye of Moirel was highly conspicuous, at home in the eye socket of a skeleton seated comfortably on the throne. And while at first Kibi thought the skeleton had simply been arranged in a lifelike pose, hand on chin, left ankle on right knee, it surprised him by uncrossing its legs and standing up a moment after he observed it. Once on its feet, violet light surged from the gemstone in its left eye. A quick rime of purple crystal boiled from the apertures of its skull like ants stirred from a nest, coating the head before racing down its spine and out along its ribs and limbs.

Once the whole of it was encrusted with living amethyst, the skeleton stepped down from its throne. Kibi gripped his pick; was this skeleton going to attack them, the Eye defending itself with its possessed body? It took several unsteady steps towards him, swaying and clattering. He felt the others fan out around him, heard the hiss of Ernie drawing Pyknite, but his eyes were fixed on the Eye, blazing purple in the living skull of its host.

It advanced, tottering, until it stood less than ten feet away. From the corner of his eye Kibi saw Tor shifting his weight, preparing to strike.

The skull swiveled on its crystalline neck until it was looking directly at Ernie, who gulped audibly. A voice issued from the skull, a voice as dry and cracked as old sandpaper.

ERNEST. YOU ARE LOOKING WELL. I HAVE SEEN YOU AGAIN SOON.

Then it turned its baleful sockets to Kibi, and the purple gemstone flared a little brighter.

KIBILHATHUR. MY REGARDS TO YOUR GRANDFATHER. NOW BRING ME TO MY BROTHER. TIME RUNS SHORT.

The skull lolled once more, snapped off at the neck, and shattered upon the flagstones. The rest of the skeleton dropped like a puppet with its strings cut, collapsing into a jumbled heap of bones. The purple crystal all hissed away to nothingness, and a small round diamond with a heart of jet rolled from the skull and bumped gently against Kibi's boot. He picked it up.

"You know my grandfather?" he asked it. "You mean my ma's pa?"

It said nothing.

"Talk to me, you damn crazy rock!" he shouted.

Again, nothing. With a heavy sigh he dropped the Eye of Moirel into his pocket.

"'I have seen you again soon?'" said Ernie. "That doesn't make any sense."

"Aravia," said Morningstar. "Now that we have what we came for, can you get us back home? We shouldn't stay here any longer than is necessary."

"Agreed," said Aravia, and right there in the throne room the wizardess began the half-minute process of casting *teleport*. They all waited patiently, and Kibi steeled himself for the personal discomfort he was fated to endure. Aravia spoke the final syllable and twitched her left pinky just so, and there was the blackness, the sloshing contortions of his innards, and...

...he was still standing in the throne room. So was everyone else.

"Kibi, it's you," said Aravia.

"I was jus' standin' here!"

Aravia stared at him a moment, and he would have sworn he could see gears and wheels turning behind her eyes.

"No, it's the Eye of Moirel. Whatever physical or magical property makes my *teleport* spells have difficulty with you, it's much stronger on the Eye. I don't think I can teleport it."

Kibi's heart sank. He'd happily have tolerated the irksome displacement of a single *teleport* over another half dozen airborne stints on Vyasa Vya. But they could hardly leave the Eye behind.

"Let's get goin' then," he said. The others didn't hold it against him, and Ernie even patted his shoulder. He followed, last in line, as the group filed out of the room and down the spiral staircase, to emerge into the afternoon sun casting its rays into the courtyard.

Sagiro was there, standing ten feet inside the gatehouse, his mustache cast in up-curled silhouette. He was flanked by four Sharshun. Two of the bald blue-skinned Sharshun—one man, one woman—held long curved blades. The other two, both men, had such weapons at their belts but pointed cocked and loaded crossbows at the company.

"That answers that question," Dranko muttered.

"Stand still and my friends will not shoot!" called Sagiro, his voice cheerful yet hard-edged.

"You're too late!" shouted Tor. "We've already found the Eye of Moirel, so turn around and go back where you came from."

Kibi was no strategic genius, but he was pretty sure that was something they should have kept to themselves.

"I am pleased to hear you have been successful," said Sagiro, "but the Eye does not belong to you, and I would ask you to return it now." He sounded for all the world like a patient but remonstrative parent.

Kibi had his hands in his pockets, the Eye of Moirel clutched in a fist. He tried thinking to it. *I don't suppose you can blast them fellahs, like Sagiro did with his?*

No response.

Dranko pointed an accusatory finger at Sagiro. "And what if instead of handing over our lawful property, we tell you to stick your rapier up your arse? We have you outnumbered."

Sagiro frowned. "Your vulgarity is not appreciated. And what I would do is instruct my friends here to kill you, and take the Eye once you were dead. As before, my strong preference is not to cause you injury, but the Eye is not your property, despite that you possess it. It belongs to us, and always has."

"And who's 'us,' exactly?" asked Kibi. "You and your bald buddies there? We've heard some things about 'em, and they don't sound like fit company for a gentleman like yourself."

"There is nothing to be gained by further conversation," said Sagiro. "I will give you to the count of—"

Tor, it seemed, was not interested in math. He charged the closest Sharshun, drawing his sword as he did so, and this uncorked the chaos of battle. Both crossbows twanged, and while one bolt soared high, only grazing Tor's shoulder, the other sprouted from his thigh. It barely slowed the boy. Ernie and Morningstar leapt forward a second later, leaving Kibi to agonize over whether he should grab his pick and join the melee.

With Grey Wolf missing, Tor had insisted on continuing their nightly sparring sessions, but Kibi had usually stayed out of them. Despite his strength, he was ponderous, incapable of the quick footwork and side-to-side agility that hand-to-hand combat demanded. And so, while he went as far as to pull the mining pick from his belt and even took two hesitant steps toward Sagiro and the Sharshun, he moved no further. He'd be throwing his life away.

Much of his pessimism came from the obvious skill of the Sharshun in battle. The one who had shot Tor dropped his crossbow and unsheathed his blade in one unnaturally fluid motion, in time to deflect Tor's overhand swing. Now those two faced off against one another more warily, but the Sharshun's body language projected a contemptuous confidence. Blood flowed freely from Tor's leg.

While the second crossbowman hastily reloaded, the remaining two Sharshun engaged Ernie and Morningstar, and even to Kibi's untrained eye his friends were badly outmatched. Ernie stumbled hastily backward, giving up all pretense of attack and trying only to ward off the Sharshun's rapid strikes. Morningstar was knocked to her knees and rolled quickly out of the way to avoid her opponent's follow-up slash.

At his side Aravia flicked out her hand and spoke quick syllables. The Sharshun reloading his bow flew backward as if punched hard in the stomach; the crossbow twanged and sent its bolt soaring out over the walls. But Aravia herself fell backward from the effort; had her failed *teleport* still drained most of her casting energy? That was hardly fair.

"Kibi, they need you!" Dranko's voice barked from behind him.

Kibi again thrust his hand into his pocket and gripped the Eye of Moirel.

Damn you, you Hells-spawned rock, I know you can blast our enemies. I seen your brother do it.

IT IS NOT WHAT WE WERE MADE FOR.

An answer! That was progress.

I don't care what you were made for! Your green brother told us we had to collect you to keep the world from being unmade. Also we're gonna be dead in another minute, so come on!

Kibi took the Eye from his pocket and held it before him like a talisman. *Blast 'em!*

Sagiro, still standing in the back, looked wide-eyed at Kibi and barked an order. The Sharshun fighting Ernie spun and kicked the baker in the neck. Ernie dropped Pyknite as he fell onto his side, but instead of finishing him off the Sharshun strode rapidly toward Kibi. Her dark eyes flashed with cruelty and the pleasure of battle.

Knock the buggers out! Please!

I WILL BECOME DAMAGED. YOU MUST FIND ANOTHER WAY.

There is no other way! I'm about five seconds from being gutted like a fish!

It was closer to two seconds, but Kibi was saved from a filleting by Dranko, who leapt from the side and tackled the Sharshun. The two went down and rolled over several times, but the Sharshun ended up on top. Dranko's hands gripped her sword-arm, but the blue-skinned woman brought down her blade, inch by relentless inch, toward the channeler's neck.

"You know," Dranko gasped. "I like a...woman who knows what she...wants, but not if what she wants is to...cut my throat."

I don't care if you become damaged! Better that than Sagiro get his hands on you.

YOU DO NOT UNDERSTAND.

Kibi couldn't deny that! While he stood frozen, arguing with a talking rock, the battle was rapidly coming to an end. Ernie and Morningstar were each bleeding from numerous shallow cuts and had not inflicted any telling blows of their own. Both were fighting desperate retreating actions. Dranko had only seconds before the Sharshun's weapon would cut into his neck. Sagiro himself had drawn his rapier and was advancing straight towards Kibi.

Tor charged in from the flank, limping but with fury, and bowled over the Sharshun atop Dranko. The boy had incapacitated the Sharshun who had shot him, but not without terrible cost. Blood gushed from his off-hand and also down the side of his face from a cut to his scalp. The Sharshun popped to her feet while Tor struggled to rise. Her curved sword came sweeping down, and Tor barely deflected it.

Eye of Moirel, I command you to blast those damn bald bastards. Sagiro too.

THERE WILL BE CONSEQUENCES.

Dranko had gotten to his feet, and Kibi bellowed at him. "Dranko, get into the keep, *now.*"

"But Tor needs..."

"*Now!* Dranko, find cover *right now* or we're *all* as good as dead!"

Dranko dashed off toward the keep. Kibi couldn't follow his progress because Sagiro was nearly upon him.

"If you hand over the Eye, I will tell my friends to stand down." Sagiro sounded so conciliatory, even over the battlefield sounds of steel on steel. Unlike the indigo faces of the Sharshun, lit with battle-lust and malice, Sagiro looked regretful, almost apologetic. But he also wasn't stopping his advance. He pulled back his rapier and turned his wrist, clearly intending to skewer Kibi through the heart.

Now! Damn the consequences!

The tip of the rapier was nudging the fabric of Kibi's shirt when the blast went off. A purple sphere of force expanded outward from the Eye of Moirel, lifting everyone but Kibi off their feet. The shockwave was many times stronger than the one Sagiro's Eye had effected in the cave; it sent the combatants sailing upward and backward like windblown leaves. Two of the Sharshun, along with Ernie and Tor, were slammed bodily into the rough walls of the keep, where they fell into senseless heaps. Morningstar and the remaining Sharshun were merely flung a dozen feet across the courtyard, landing with rolling thuds. None of them stood up.

Behind him Aravia had been spared the worst of it by dint of already lying prone on the ground. The concussive force of the Eye rolled her backward nearly to the keep entrance.

Sagiro gave Kibi a final look of something like betrayal as he was picked up and thrown directly backwards, through the gap of the gatehouse and over the lip of the ravine. Kibi imagined the rest: his body spinning gracefully, possibly ricocheting off the far side of the chasm, and plunging into the churn of rapids and rocks at the bottom.

"Good riddance, you mustached bastard!"

Dranko poked his head out of the keep. "Hells' breakfast! Kibi, what happened? Are they all dead?"

Kibi looked at his friends, every bit as unconscious as the Sharshun, and prayed they were not. "Should just be knocked out and bruised. But Tor's badly cut up, and the others might be too. If you feel up to channelin', figure out who's worst off. Otherwise just patch 'em up best as you can."

Dranko nodded. "Right. But where's Sagiro? Did he get away?"

"Nope. The Eye knocked 'im into the river."

"Serves him right," said Dranko, before hurrying from body to body, inspecting their injuries. "Kibi, while I tend to our friends, I think our Sharshun buddies here should go play follow the leader."

It took Kibi a moment to figure that out. "You mean dump 'em over the edge?"

"No, I mean dance a jig and kiss 'em on the lips. Yes, of course dump them over! Those Sharshun are tougher than we are and will probably wake up sooner from your magic blast. It would be safer to drive your pick through their skulls; just choose whatever you can live with. Oh, and if you choose the toss-plummet option, loot the bodies first."

"But that might wake 'em up!" Kibi could hardly think of a less appealing activity than searching unconscious Sharshun for valuables.

"Then do it gently."

Kibi walked to the closest Sharshun, knocked senseless at the base of the wall. Even with an idea of the stakes involved, and knowing the Sharshun would not spare his life were their situations reversed, he knew he couldn't just skewer them while they were helpless. But would dumping them into a hundred foot ravine be any better?

"Yeah, it would," he muttered. "Still don't like it." He cursorily checked the Sharshun's pockets, found them empty, then picked up the body and slung it over his shoulder. Before his conscience could bring up any objections, he strode through the gatehouse and unburdened himself of the Sharshun at the ravine's edge. He didn't stay to watch the body fall, but went back for a second.

Dranko was applying salves and bandages to Morningstar and Ernie, even though Tor was clearly the most injured. But soon enough Kibi understood Dranko's methods. Once Dranko channeled, he might not have the wherewithal to help anyone else. Only when he had done his triage on the others did he kneel before Tor and pray.

By the time Kibi had tossed all four Sharshun (and thank the Gods none of them had stirred to consciousness while he carried them), Dranko had channeled for Tor and was sitting dazedly with his back against the front wall of the keep, next to where Aravia still lay sprawled following the Eye's wave of force.

"If you were wondering whether my healing could regrow lost body parts," he said, "I'm afraid the answer is 'no.' Incidentally, Tor has only nine fingers now."

Dranko closed his eyes. "Should be okay, though. It's only the last finger on his off hand. He'll get used to it." Soon thereafter, he was asleep.

Kibi took the Eye of Moirel from his pocket and held it up to his face. It didn't *look* damaged. It was still a perfect spherical diamond, just under two inches across, with that impossible dot of blackness in its center. There were no cracks, no scratches, not the slightest indication of wear or imperfection.

"You still there?" he asked it.

The Eye of Moirel was silent.

* * *

Tor was the first to wake, and he took the loss of his pinky with an optimistic equanimity. Dranko's healing had left only a faint pink scar over the knuckle.

Tor flipped his hand back and forth, admiring his wound from both sides. "What a story it'll make! Someday people will ask me how I lost it, and I'll tell them I was fighting as part of Horn's Company, saving the world from being unmade by a guy with a fantastic mustache. Don't worry, Kibi, you'll be famous too. We all will!"

Kibi wanted nothing to do with fame, but there was no point in trying to make Tor understand that.

It was another hour before the whole group was awake again. Aravia made a big deal over Tor's wounded hand, and the boy brightened noticeably at the attention. Kibi was no expert in such matters, but *something* was going on between those two. None of his business, though.

Since the wizardess couldn't teleport the Eye, Kibi feared there would be many hours on Vyasa Vya in his future, but Aravia gave him another option.

"Kibi, would you trust Tor to carry the Eye of Moirel for a day?"

Tor might be impetuous and unable to focus, but the boy understood the nature of responsibility. "I suppose so," he answered. "What're you thinkin' about?"

"I'm thinking that we're only ten hours from Tal Hae by carpet, if one were to fly more or less due north of here, across the strait between Nahalm and Harkran. I have to wait until morning before I can teleport us home, but if Tor were to start now…"

"Absolutely!" said Tor. "I have a good sense of direction. It won't be any problem."

"But what if the lad falls asleep?" Kibi asked. "He's bound to, before he gets all the way home."

"The carpet has magical safeguards while flying to prevent riders from falling off. And while it's in the air, if Tor tells it ahead of time, it will keep going at a constant direction and speed if the driver releases the tassels. Tor, find an altitude from which you can see the ground, but high enough to clear any trees and hills if you're still asleep on the other side of the channel. Set your direction due north, tell the carpet to keep flying even if you let go, and try getting a good night's rest. In the morning you should see Tal Hae when you reach the coast. If you're off by a few degrees, remember Tal Hae is at the northeast corner of the Bay of Brechen."

Morningstar argued, successfully, that they should find somewhere else to camp for the night. Sagiro and his allies might be out of the picture, but more Sharshun could be on their way. Kibi had to endure a final carpet ride after all, as Tor shuttled everyone to a sheltered valley some five miles to the southeast. There he handed the boy the Eye of Moirel.

"Don't drop it in the ocean, lad," he admonished.

"I promise I won't. See you back at the Greenhouse!"

And with that, Tor took off, vanishing into the dusky sky. The rest of them spent a quiet night camped beneath a stand of firs, talking about Sagiro and his Sharshun allies and how they planned to use the Eyes to "unmake the world." Morningstar's sister Previa had thought that the Eyes and the Seven Mirrors "combined to effect a form of magical transport." But if so, where would they take you? Maybe different Eyes sent you to different places. Aravia speculated that the Mirrors could be another way to reach the continent of Kivia and that Sagiro might even have known about the Crosser's Maze and had been hoping to get to it ahead of Horn's Company.

"Don't matter now," said Kibi. "Sagiro's dead. I checked to make sure he weren't clingin' to the side walls of the chasm, and there weren't no sign of him."

"Maybe you knocked him clean to the other side!" Ernie offered.

"Nah. I saw Sagiro go over the edge. Could be he survived a hundred foot drop onto the rocks, but I doubt it."

"Why did it take you so long to use the Eye?" asked Ernie.

"Damn thing took some convincin'. Kept complainin' that it would get damaged if I used it as a weapon, but I didn't see nothin' wrong with it afterward. I guess we'll see, but I'd do the same thing over again if I had the choice."

* * *

Aravia teleported them to the Greenhouse the next morning, and Kibi almost relished the wrenching of his innards since it meant no more carpet flying. Eddings greeted them warmly and offered them breakfast.

"Is Tor here?" asked Aravia.

"No, Miss Telmir. Did he not travel with the rest of you?"

"We sent him on ahead by carpet. He'll arrive any time."

Kibi gratefully accepted a plate of scrambled eggs. "Eddings, I don't suppose the Eye of Moirel in the basement busted out again and possessed Ernie's bear while we was gone?"

"I am happy to report that it has not," answered the butler. "Things have been calm in your absence. Abernathy is still asleep, though I have been tending to his survival and comfort. He does not seem to be suffering any effects of malnutrition, which I ascribe to some manner of wizardly preparation on his part. There have been no messengers or visitors. Was your venture more successful than the previous?"

"Yup. Got ourselves a second Eye of Moirel to keep the first one company. Tor should be showin' up with it any time, and then they can fight over who gets to make Bumbly talk."

Almost on cue, Tor appeared in the doorway, his hair disheveled and a huge grin across his face.

"That was fantastic! Cold, but fantastic."

He walked straight to Kibi. "Here's your Eye. I managed not to toss it overboard."

Kibi laughed with the boy, who immediately became distracted by the prospect of breakfast.

After the meal Kibi tromped down to the basement and unlocked the iron trunk containing the green Eye of Moirel. It took a bit of feeling around inside the opaque soupy sludge with which he had filled the iron pot, but his fingers found the Eye and he pulled it free.

"Here you are," he said, taking the purple Eye from his pocket. "We found your brother. Now what?"

The Eyes did not choose that moment to speak.

"I thought there was some terrible rush. You got somethin' to say, so say it!"

Nor the next moment.

"You're the one who told me time was short! Ah, a pox upon you. I suppose part a' the hurry was just to keep Sagiro from getting' his hands on you, but he's dead, so no more worry 'bout that."

He considered storing the Eyes in separate closets, but since his muddy cook-pot had finally done the trick of keeping the green Eye docile, he dropped the purple one in with it, resealed the pot, and locked the trunk.

"I'll check on you tomorrow," he promised. Kibi paused once on the stairs up from the basement, still holding out hope the Eyes would say or do something useful after all the trouble Horn's Company had taken to collect them.

Tor was practically bouncing around the living room. "What next?"

Aravia came in from the dining room and went directly to the bookshelf. "All we have left to go on is Hodge's prophecy about the Ventifact Colossus," she said absently. She pulled down one of Abernathy's tomes. "But until we find out where Ganit Tuvith is, there's not much we can do about it. In the meantime, if you need me, I'll be studying."

Morningstar came down the stairs. "Abernathy is still unconscious."

What would it mean if Abernathy never snapped out of whatever he was in? Maybe they'd have to find another archmage. And if the old wizard was comatose, what did that imply about Naradawk, the monster locked up in his prison world?

"Looks like we get a day off," said Dranko. "And a well-deserved one, too. I'm going to go out and buy us some celebratory bottles of wine."

"And I'll cook dinner tonight," said Ernie. "We can save the Icebox for lunch and dessert."

Morningstar called out to Dranko as the channeler was leaving. "Make a stop at the shrine of Werthis, will you? See if they know anything about a prophecy involving three of their number killing a giant turtle."

Kibi spent the afternoon relaxing, but his mind kept returning to the Eyes of Moircl. Twice he popped down to the basement to see if they had become communicative, but they remained silent in their closet.

When he closed his eyes and emptied his mind, he fancied he could sense them, two bright little sources of earthy magic, one green, one purple, twinkling in the darkness. They tugged at him, exerting an ineffable sort of gravity on his subconscious.

Dranko came back in the midafternoon, carrying a small straw-lined crate of bottles.

"Decided to splurge on the good stuff." He pulled out one of the bottles, uncorked it, and took a long swig. When he finally came up for air he gave the rest a defiant look. "Finder's fee."

"Did you talk to the Werthans?" asked Morningstar.

"Yeah. And let me tell you, they have no sense of humor. Make one joke about polishing their axe handles and they get all grumpy. Worshiping a god of war must do that to people."

Morningstar rolled her eyes. "And…?"

"And, huge surprise, they thought I was nuts when I mentioned a giant turtle. They had no idea what I was talking about, and the Stormknights I talked to had never heard of Ganit Tuvith."

"Then we'll just have to wait for Previa's report, assuming she finds anything."

"And what if she doesn't?" asked Ernie. "We seem to have come to a dead end. Abernathy hasn't given us anything more to do."

"Guess we just stay here in the Greenhouse," said Kibi. "Somethin' tells me we ain't gonna be waitin' too long before somethin' comes up. Just a feelin' I'm gettin'." He glanced nervously at the basement door. "Just a feelin'."

After dinner, when Horn's Company was finishing up a chocolate mousse from the Icebox and getting ready for bed, a messenger arrived from the Ellish temple with a letter for Morningstar. She grabbed it from Eddings and quickly read it.

"So is Ganit Tuvith actually Tal Hae?" asked Dranko. "'Cause that would be very convenient."

"No," said Morningstar. "Ganit Tuvith is what Sand's Edge used to be called, centuries ago."

Aravia looked up from her book, balanced on one knee while she ate her mousse. "I imagine many cities had different names back when Naloric was emperor of Charagan."

"So now we know everything!" said Tor. "A giant turtle is going to attack Sand's Edge, and three Stormknights will kill it, and then the Kivian archway will open up, and we'll be able to go get the Crosser's Maze."

"No, Tor, we don't know everything," said Aravia. "We're missing a critical piece of information, which is *when* that's going to happen."

"Or if we're supposed to do something to help *make* it happen," said Morningstar.

"Why would we?" asked Ernie. "We're not mentioned in any of the prophecies."

"Not by name," said Dranko. "But the madman wrote that someone would warn the Stormknights. Maybe Tor's right, and that's us."

"In my dream Eddings killed the turtle with a letter opener," said Morningstar. "Does that mean we should bring Eddings along when the time comes?"

"And where are we going to find a letter opener big enough?" asked Tor.

"Maybe the right thing to do is stop the turtle from being summoned in the first place," said Ernie. "If the Kivian Arch is going to open down on Seablade Point, I don't see how a giant turtle smashing half of Sand's Edge hundreds of miles away is going to bring it about. More likely, Hodge's prophecy just means the two events are going to happen one after the other. There's no reason a city needs to get destroyed and who knows how many people killed. Shouldn't that be what we care about most?"

"I agree with Ernie," said Kibi. The others regarded him curiously, probably surprised at him offering up a clear opinion. "I said many times before now, and I'm sure I'll say it again. I don't believe in no destiny. If a huge turtle is gonna stomp on folks, and we know a way to stop it, we should stop it. Everything else can work itself out after."

* * *

Kibi had trouble sleeping that night. Every time he closed his eyes, the Eyes of Moirel were staring back at him, glimmering, two crystalline foci of an indescribably powerful magic. Kibi tried to work out his vision's significance. Perhaps he was supposed to take them to the Seven Mirrors, and they would transport him somewhere important. Or could his stone-shaping skill work on diamond, and he needed to free the little dots of jet inside them? Or had they something of critical importance to say through Bumbly but couldn't because he had them trapped in sludge?

"Or maybe I have no Gods-damned idea," he grumbled in his bed. "If Aravia can't figure this out, how am I supposed to? All this magic business is far beyond me."

The bells had rung midnight before he finally drifted into an uneasy slumber. The Eyes of Moirel moved in and out of his dreams like colored phantoms. He dreamt of a grandfather he had never met and the earth whispering to him of its pain, of a splinter lodged in its heart. He dreamt that he held the purple Eye in one hand and the green Eye in the other.

"There will be consequences," said one.

"All the stones know your name," said the other.

And both Eyes glowed so brightly and with such heat that they melted his bones, and he poured through cracks into the ground until his being had merged with the molten fire at the center of the world.

He woke, sweaty, and heard a noise from downstairs, a sound of splintered wood. He knew immediately: the Eyes had found their vigor. Something momentous had happened, and it terrified him. Through his window the sun was just beginning to rise. Kibi swung out of bed and lurched into the hall, then hammered on the doors of the others.

"Wake up! All of you, wake up!"

Soon the six of them stood in the upstairs hall, dressed in their nightclothes.

"This had better be the best surprise breakfast in history," Dranko grumbled.

Kibi didn't bother to hide his fear. "It's the Eyes. I don't want to go down there alone."

The others must have seen how scared he was; they all followed him without question. Together they crept down the stairs, through the foyer, and into the living room.

Eddings stood by the fireplace, looking at them.

His right eye was a green ball of fire.

His mouth opened, and he spoke with a sharp, crystalline voice that was not his own.

THE VENTIFACT COLOSSUS WAKES FROM ITS SLEEP. THE WORLD IS AT A CROSSROADS.

His left eye burned with a purple radiance.

THE GREAT SAND TURTLE ARISES EVEN NOW FROM ITS SLUMBER, AND TODAY DESTINIES WILL SCATTER LIKE GRAINS OF SAND TUMBLING FROM ITS SHELL.

Living green crystal crept down the right side of Eddings' face as he spoke, covering it like a fast-spreading algae. A skin of amethyst did likewise on the left side. The green and purple Eyes spoke through the butler, alternating which had control.

HEED WELL MY WARNING. THE CHELONIAN HORN MUST BE SOUNDED ELSE THOUSANDS WILL PERISH IN WAR. IF IT IS SILENT, THE FUTURE WILL BE THROWN TO CHAOS TO SAVE AN EPHEMERAL PRESENT.

HEED WELL MY WARNING. THE CHELONIAN HORN MUST NOT BE SOUNDED ELSE THOUSANDS WILL PERISH IN WAR. SHOULD IT BE WINDED, THE PRESENT WILL BE SACRIFICED TO SAVE AN UNKNOWABLE FUTURE.

MY BROTHER IS CORRECT. THE COLOSSUS WILL RISE AND WREAK HAVOC. BUT ITS DEATH WILL OPEN THE GATEWAY TO SALVATION.

MY BROTHER IS CORRECT. THE COLOSSUS WILL SLUMBER AND THE WORLDS WILL BE JOINED. BUT IN WAKING IT YOU ONLY TRADE CONFLICT FOR CONFLICT, AND FOR THIS PAY WITH TERRIBLE DESTRUCTION.

YOU WILL STOP AKTALLIAN. THE FUTURE IS CARVED IN DIAMOND THAT NONE MAY ERASE OR CHANGE. YOU WILL INTERVENE.

NO. THE FUTURE IS WRITTEN ON WATER, AND YOU ARE ITS AUTHORS.

Eddings' two-colored harlequin mask was expressionless; it was impossible to tell if the butler was awake or even aware of what was happening. But if the Eyes of Moirel were indeed embedded in Eddings' sockets, his real eyes must have been burned away.

No one spoke. No one moved. Eddings stood stock still. But just when Kibi was sure they were done delivering their cryptic and contradictory messages, both Eyes flared and their light mixed. They had more to say, and now their voice became doubled, talking in an almost-unison.

YOU HAVE THE FOCUS, IN WHOSE VEINS RUNS THE BLOOD OF SANTO, AND YOU HAVE THE TALISMAN TO PRESERVE YOUR INTEGRITY. BUT THERE IS ONE MORE THING.

OUR CREATOR DID NOT FULLY UNDERSTAND US. WE ARE NOT ALL REQUIRED. TO TRAVEL NOWHERE, YOU WILL NEED ONLY THREE WHO ARE WILLING. TO TRAVEL NOWHERE, WE WILL NEED OUR LAST REMAINING BROTHER.

HE IS IN THE HOUSE OF HET BRANOI, BEYOND THE ARCH OF FIRE, AND HE CANNOT RETURN ON HIS OWN. THE CANARY HAS ENCIRCLED THE CAT. WHEN THE TIME IS RIGHT AND THE WORLD IS WRONG, RETURN HIM TO US, SO YOU MIGHT WALK IN THE FOOTPRINTS OF MOIREL.

CONTINUE TO KEEP US SAFE, KIBILHATHUR.

And with that final utterance, Eddings fell heavily to his knees. The two Eyes of Moirel popped gruesomely from his head and landed on the carpet, leaving the butler's eye sockets smooth but empty. The bi-colored crystal retreated from his face.

Eddings shook his head as if to clear it, and looked—no, rather, he pointed his face at them.

"Why am I on the floor?" he asked, his voice betraying embarrassment at the lack of decorum. "And why are all of you looking at me with such horrified expressions? What is going on?"

For a moment none of them could bring themselves to answer. Kibi had no idea what to say.

"Eddings, can you *see* us?" asked Ernie.

"Of course, Master Roundhill. Is there some reason that I shouldn't?"

"Because you have no eyeballs!" Tor blurted.

"Nonsense. If I had no eyeballs, I wouldn't be able to see you all standing there, looking as though I were a ghost. And I still await an explanation for what I'm doing here at all. Did I sleepwalk?"

"Not exactly," said Aravia in a small voice. "But…Eddings, we're delighted that you can still see, but…your eyes…"

Eddings' brows shot up as if he were rolling his eyes, which of course he wasn't, and he brought his hands to his face. He paled as his fingertips explored the unblemished depressions where his eyes had been.

"Oh, dear me. But if I have no eyes, then…"

Kibi stepped forward and picked up the Eyes of Moirel from the ground.

"I guess our friends here decided Bumbly weren't up to the job this time 'round."

"I see," said Eddings, immediately wincing at his turn of phrase. "Am I…am I likely to retain my sight? Aravia?"

"I don't know," said Aravia. "I think so. I hope so."

Eddings walked slowly to a mirror that hung on the wall.

"Oh, dear me," he repeated. "I am likely to cause a stir when I go into town, aren't I? No matter. If it all proves too much for people, I shall wear a translucent blindfold."

"I'm impressed how you're takin' it," said Kibi.

"Master Abernathy did warn me when he hired me that my life would become more…unusual. More unpredictable. Since this episode has had only cosmetic consequences, I shall simply count my blessings and move on. Now, shall I prepare breakfast?"

CHAPTER TWENTY-NINE

Dranko wolfed down his bacon. Today was shaping up to be a day for world-saving, and that wasn't going to happen on an empty stomach. "So the Ventifact Colossus might be walking through Sand's Edge right now, knocking over buildings?"

"The Eyes said 'must not be sounded,'" said Morningstar. "So fifteen minutes ago, it hadn't happened yet."

"I think you underestimate the damage the colossus could cause," said Aravia. Her expression was distant and troubled. "The purple Eye called it the Great Sand Turtle. Don't you realize what that means?"

"Sure," said Dranko. "It means the turtle lives in the Mouth of Nahalm. Maybe it's been riding around on one of the wandering islands all this time. Or the Black Circle could have been digging up a—"

"You're not thinking big enough."

Dranko stopped with a forkful of scrambled eggs halfway to his mouth.

"Oh Hells," he whispered. "The wandering islands…"

"Wait a minute," said Morningstar. "Are you saying each of those islands is just the shell of a giant…a Ventifact Colossus? I thought there was only one!"

"Not according to Romus the Mad," said Dranko. "Didn't he warn that if it wasn't killed, it would lead a turtle army to conquer the kingdom?"

"I doubt those islands are turtle shells," said Aravia.

"Oh, good," said Dranko, relieved. "For a minute there I thought you were implying that—"

"No, those are build-ups of sand that have mixed with secretions from the turtles' shells over time. The shells are at least as big around as the *bases* of the wandering islands. We're not talking about creatures the size of a house. No, something that big could flatten several houses with a single step."

Dranko tried to picture it. "Stormknights must be stronger than they look."

"We need to go now!" said Tor. "What's-his-name could be blowing the horn while we're finishing breakfast!"

"Aktallian," said Morningstar. "The red trespasser."

"The purple Eye seemed to think we were gonna stop him soundin' the horn in the first place," said Kibi. "But are we? The green Eye seemed to be sayin' we ought to let him blow the thing."

"We *have* to stop him," said Ernie. "If the turtle gets woken up, who knows how many people it will kill before the Stormknights even have a chance at killing it? We can worry about the consequences some other time."

"Consequences..." said Kibi, brows knitting. Dranko had learned to recognize Kibi's thinking face.

"Kibi, what are you—"

"We should let Aktallian blow the Horn," Kibi said. "It was the purple Eye telling us not to, but the purple Eye is damaged. It warned me. I'm guessin' that it wasn't talking about its physical self. It was talkin' about its judgment."

"Can we take that chance?" asked Ernie.

"Kibi's right," said Dranko. "The green Eye said letting the horn get blown will open the gateway to salvation. A gateway! The Kivian Arch! It all has to happen the way Hodge expected, so that we can go to Kivia and find the Crosser's Maze."

Ernie turned to Kibi. "Aren't you always telling us you don't believe in destiny? That's exactly what we're talking about now!"

Kibi shook his head. "But the purple Eye, that's the one tellin' us the future is carved in diamond. I don't hold no truck with that. The green Eye now, with the future in the water stuff, that tells me we control our own fates."

"Either way, we should go right now," said Morningstar. "Either we'll stop Aktallian from blowing the horn, or we'll have to figure out how three Stormknights are going to kill a turtle the size of a village. But both of those options involve getting ourselves to Sand's Edge as soon as we're ready."

Dranko had purchased a new bag of salves and ointments after buying the wine the previous day, and looking at his friends he knew he was going to need it. He had stitched up Ernie and Morningstar as best he could, but their cuts needed cleaning and fresh bandages. And if they wound up battling one of Naradawk's elite servants, they'd be at a significant disadvantage.

"Listen up," he told the others. "We may end up going sword to sword with Aktallian. I know I've channeled several times now, but that doesn't mean I can save you if you get injured. If two of you end up mortally wounded, at best I'll have the inner strength to save one. And if he hacks off your head with one blow…"

"We understand," said Ernie. "We'll be careful."

Dranko grimaced. There was something he hadn't told the others. His acts of channeling had cost him more than just temporary strength. Mortals were imperfect vessels of the Divine, and to serve as a conduit for Delioch's grace, Dranko had to relinquish some part of his own life. Priests trained as channelers could restore some of that lost vitality through weeks of dedicated meditation and prayer, but Dranko didn't foresee having that kind of luxury. Too much channeling and he'd die, his soul withered away. Would he do that for them?

I should have done it for Mrs. Horn.

That was why he had failed, why Mrs. Horn had died when he should have saved her. Only after he had healed the beggar had Dranko truly understood the price of channeling. When Mrs. Horn lay bleeding on the floor of the Shadow Chaser, a part of him, the cowardly part, the selfish part, had refused to make another sacrifice. Yes, channeling also required concentration, and Grey Wolf's haranguing hadn't helped, but he'd be lying if he said that was the whole of the problem.

He remembered Grey Wolf's tirade on the way back from Sand's Edge, when he wished it were Dranko who had died in place of Mrs. Horn. He understood the man's anger. And as he looked around at his friends, he knew that he would do whatever was needed should they come to harm.

A more cheering thought came to him: if a giant turtle menaced a large city, and he was instrumental in killing said turtle, a certain amount of fame would unavoidably attach to him. Not that saving hundreds or thousands of lives wasn't also a priority, but ever since Abernathy's summons so many weeks earlier, Dranko had been hoping for this kind of unique opportunity. It was one thing to tell tales of gopher-bugs in small-town inns, but this—*this* was a save-the-kingdom-from-obvious-destruction sort of affair. Hero stuff.

Now they just had to go do it.

He stood up and clapped. "No time like the present. Aravia?"

* * *

Aravia teleported them to their previous landing spot by the desert. Dranko spent only a second or two marveling at the awesome magical power that could whisk a half-dozen people hundreds of miles in an eye blink. After that, he fixed his attention on the wandering island that had made its way nearly to the edge of the Mouth of Nahalm's steep bowl.

Even at a few hundred yards' distance, it seemed to loom over them like a leaning mountain. Though he had scrambled about atop a similar island a month earlier, it was much more daunting now when he imagined it was merely a mound of hardened sand stuck to the back of a living creature. Dranko tried to picture something capable of carrying that sort of weight on its back. He failed.

It wasn't climbing up onto land, which was a relief, and a crowd had gathered at the lip of the Mouth not far away.

"We need to warn those people!" said Ernie. "They'll get stepped on!"

"We also need some information from them," said Dranko. "Come on."

The six of them jogged over to the crowd, several dozen denizens of Sand's Edge gazing upon the wandering island that had floated so close to shore. Dranko ran ahead and approached a young woman standing at the back of the gathering.

"Excuse me, miss. How long has that island been so close to the city?"

The woman turned and opened her mouth to answer, then drew back at the sight of his face.

"Look, miss, I'm…it's just a disguise. Forget the tusks for a minute and answer the question. How long—"

"Why would you disguise yourself as a goblin?"

"Gods damn it! Would you—no, forget it."

His friends were just catching up.

"Ernie, you're looking handsome today. Would you ask one of these fine folk how long the giant turtle has been sitting there?"

A scrawny teenaged boy nearby looked up. "Sir, did you say a giant turtle?"

"How long has it been there?" asked Ernie. "The island, I mean."

"Since yesterday afternoon. But why did you call it a turtle?"

"Yesterday," said Aravia. "So if we take what the Eyes said as the truth, the red trespasser hasn't blown the horn yet."

"You have to get out of here!" said Ernie to the boy. Then, louder, "Everyone! Please, listen to me! That island is actually a huge turtle, and any minute now it's going to climb out of the sand and step on your city. You have to flee!"

Most of the crowd didn't seem to hear him, and the few who did regarded Ernie with nothing more than curiosity.

A rotund and elderly woman emerged from the gathering and stood before Ernie. "Shame on you, boy. Are you trying to start a riot?"

"No, ma'am. I'm very serious." Ernie was painstakingly polite. "Underneath that island is an enormous turtle called a Ventifact Colossus, and if we don't stop it, today it's going to walk over your city and smash it to bits."

"And where did you come by such a fanciful notion, young fellow?"

"We, uh, read about it," said Ernie, obviously realizing how ridiculous he sounded. "In a prophecy. Two prophecies, actually. Plus my friend Morningstar is an Ellish Dream-seer, and she, uh, had a vision about a giant turtle." Ernie turned to Dranko with pleading eyes. "Help?"

"Excuse my friend here," said Dranko. "He has sunstroke."

"Already? The sun's hardly risen!"

"He's very sensitive. But you're obviously a knowledgeable woman. Would you happen to know what is the highest tower in Sand's Edge, and how best to reach it? We're from out of town and would love to take a look."

"Oh, of course," said the woman. "Arrowshot Tower is Sand's Edge's most famous building. It's popular with tourists; if you have a silver coin to pay the entry fee, the view is tremendous."

"I'm sure I can spare a silver for that," said Dranko. "Sounds glorious."

"Young man, what happened to your face?"

Dranko sighed. "Hunting accident. I ran face-first into a boar."

"We do have a small shrine to Delioch here in Sand's Edge. Perhaps—"

"We're in a bit of a hurry," said Dranko. "In which part of the city will I find Arrowshot Tower?"

"Old military quarter, to the north. Anyone on the street can direct you to it."

"Thank you, ma'am. You've been a great help."

"One more thing," said Aravia, stepping up. "Is there a Shrine of Werthis in Sand's Edge?"

"Of course," said the woman. "All of the Travelers' clergy maintain a presence in Travelers' Square, right in the center of the city. The shrine of

Delioch should be close at hand, in case your friend here wants to have his face attended to. They'll want a donation, of course."

"Ma'am, again, thank you," said Dranko. "But my face can wait. Also, one more thing. Ernie here wasn't kidding about the turtle. Don't say we didn't warn you."

* * *

They drew off from the crowd and formed a huddle.

"I have a plan," said Aravia.

"And I'm sure it's brilliant," said Dranko. "Let's hear it."

"Tor will fly three of us to Travelers' Square on the carpet. We'll fly high enough en route to see where Arrowshot Tower is, then do our best to convince the Werthans about their role in killing the colossus, assuming they don't already know. Once we've done that, we'll fly to the tower. The two on foot should just run straight there. If Aktallian is there, it would be best if we confronted him together."

"Are we going to stop him blowing the horn?" asked Ernie. "I still think we should."

"And I think we shouldn't," said Dranko. "Sorry, Ernie. But we don't have time to argue about it. Turtle clock's ticking, and Aravia's plan sounds good to me. Any volunteers for walking?"

"I'll walk," said Kibi. "I hate that damned flying rug."

"I'll go with you," said Ernie.

Tor unrolled the carpet and snapped it sharply to a hovering state. "All aboard!"

Dranko vaulted on behind Tor, and once Aravia and Morningstar were settled, Tor grabbed two of Vyasa Vya's tassels and the flying carpet launched upward into the brightening sky, trailing its tendrils of smoke. Below him Kibi and Ernie jogged toward the city, leaving the crowd to gape and gawk at the carpet.

Tor flew in a high arc, and from hundreds of feet up it was easy to spot Arrowshot Tower, built as a succession of tall rectangular sections piled one upon another. Its zenith was fifty feet higher than anything around it, a flat stone square trimmed with a shoulder-high wooden railing.

"Fly us closer," said Dranko, and Tor complied. The boy steered the carpet like he was born to its control, banking and swooping while the rug's magical protections kept them firmly anchored.

Dranko squinted down at the tower's rooftop, thinking he might see someone getting ready to, or even be in the process of, winding the Chelonian Horn, but the exposed tower-top was empty.

"Could we have missed it?" asked Tor.

"We're only here at the suggestion of two talking rocks and a page from a madman's diary," said Dranko. "I figure there's a good chance this whole thing is a big misunderstanding and the Ventifact Colossus is actually a fat bartender from Minok."

But he didn't believe that. Too many threads of fate were knotted together for this to be anything but what it seemed. The "wandering island" loomed at the edge of the desert, a living disaster waiting to wipe out Sand's Edge as surely as a hurricane.

Tor was already descending. "I remember where Travelers' Square is. It's where I got patched up after our fight with those Black Circle guys."

It was still early enough in the morning that the square was nearly empty. A flight of pigeons took wing as the carpet landed, and a nearby beggar stared wide-eyed for a moment before inching away. The Shrine of Werthis—a small two-story house with a miniature yard surrounded with an iron fence—was easily recognized by the insignia emblazoned above the door. Standing beneath the heraldic shield with its red gauntlet, Dranko considered what he knew about the Church of Werthis. Their priesthood doubled as a large battle-ready militia ostensibly under the command of King Crunard, but in practice they'd do whatever the Stormknight Lord Dalesandro ordered. The bulk of their fighting clergy was based in and around Hae Charagan, with lesser centers of power in Hae Kalkas and Hydra. In most other large cities they maintained a token presence; Dranko had seen their small chapter house in Tal Hae and wasn't terribly impressed. This one was even smaller.

Morningstar rattled the door handle. "Locked." She knocked, but after thirty seconds no one had come to let them in.

"It's barely past six in the morning," said Tor. "They could still be sleeping."

"I can get us inside," said Aravia. "Stand back."

Dranko put his arm on her shoulder. "No. Save your magic in case we need it later. I picked up a new set of tools the other day; allow me."

The lock on the door of the Werthan shrine was primitive, and Dranko had it open in less than half a minute. It creaked as it opened, but no one came to challenge them.

"Hello!" Dranko shouted. "Anyone here? Wake up, sleepyheads!"

There was a stirring from the second floor, some sounds of quiet voices, the creak of floorboards. Two people, a man and woman, came cautiously down the stairs, each holding a sword in front of them.

"Explain your presence here," demanded the woman. She was short and powerfully built, but hastily dressed, and her short brown hair spiked in amusing tufts from recent sleep.

"I'd have thought Stormknights would be up at dawn, practicing combat maneuvers or something," said Dranko. He held his hands to show they were free of weapons, and his friends did the same. "We're here because you have something important to do today."

"How did you get in?" asked the man. The fellow was tall, broad-shouldered and thin-waisted, with a salt-and-pepper goatee. Tor would look like that in another thirty years.

"I busted your lock," said Dranko. "But that's okay. You needed a better one anyway, and I'll pay you for it, assuming you're still alive tomorrow."

"Are you the only two Stormknights here?" asked Morningstar.

The Stormknight woman rubbed her eyes with her free hand and peered at them from the bottom step. "You wear Ellish robes. And you, half-breed, you bear the scars of a follower of Delioch. What is going on here? Why might I not be alive tomorrow? Do you threaten us?"

Dranko ignored the slur. "What I'm about to tell you is going to sound unlikely, but hear me out until the end. The four of us were hired by an important wizard to investigate some old prophecies. We found extremely clear indicators that right here in Sand's Edge, today, an enormous monster is going to attack the city, and the only people who will be able to kill it are three Stormknights. And that makes sense, right? Who's better trained to protect innocent lives and slay fearsome beasts than you?"

"This is a trick," said the man. "Some scheme to rob our house—"

Dranko sighed. "If my goal was to plunder your shrine, you'd still be asleep upstairs and I'd already be selling your silverware. In fact, I'm going to do the opposite of rob you."

He unslung his pack and produced a bag of silver talons he had hastily prepared for this moment. "Why don't we consider this a business proposition? I give you these hundred silver coins just for hearing me out. You go to the edge of the desert to see for yourself. If it turns out we're wrong about this, I'll come back and give you another hundred tomorrow morning."

He tossed the sack of coins to the floor.

"The monster is in the desert?" asked the woman.

"Yes. For now. But our sources tell us that today it's going to leave the desert and smash up Sand's Edge."

"You cannot possibly be giving credence to this goblin," said the man.

The woman shushed him with her hand. "What kind of monster is it?"

"You know those islands that float around the Mouth of Nahalm? They're actually giant turtles that live under the sand, and you Stormknights are fated to kill one."

Dranko was sure this was where his story would meet an unyielding wall of skepticism, but the looks on both the Stormknights' faces were so startled as to be downright comical.

"Giant turtles?" repeated the man.

"Technically it's called a Ventifact Colossus," said Aravia.

"It's too much of a coincidence," said the woman. "I'll go wake Corlea." She dashed up the stairs.

"You know what we're talking about?" asked Tor.

"Not exactly," said the man. "But…Corlea. Years ago she did her weapons training at the Swordyard of Hae Kalkas. Part of the regimen is to participate in free-for-alls, general melees with a last-one-standing objective. She was one of the final pair of combatants, but she slipped and fell, losing the melee in the process. Corlea is extremely sure-footed, and when she examined the ground afterward, she discovered she had tripped over a small turtle that had miraculously survived being trampled by fifty Stormknights for over twenty minutes. But Corlea was its downfall; she had crushed its shell and killed it. The other Stormknights gave her a nickname that we still use in jest. We call her Corlea Turtlebane."

Dranko blinked.

Beside him, Aravia said, "No, it's not a coincidence."

"Are there only three of you here?" asked Morningstar.

"Yes. My name is Sorent. You've already met Veloun."

Dranko glanced out a window at the sun rising over the square. "Right. Great. This is Aravia, Tor, and Morningstar, and my name's Dranko. Dranko

Blackhope. We're members of Horn's Company. And my deal still stands. Right now the giant turtle has moved right up to the edge of the desert. You three get dressed and head over there as soon as possible. If we're right, and the Ventifact Colossus climbs out, you three will have to think of a way to kill it. If not, I'll return tomorrow and pay you another hundred talons for the misunderstanding."

Sorent extended a hand. "I had heard that one of the islands had drifted close to the city but hadn't thought much of it. Dranko Blackhope, I accept your proposal." His eyes had lost their sleepy rheum, and he became excited, energized, his skepticism easily banished. Dranko supposed that when you've been trained as a warrior during peacetime, an opportunity to take some hacks at a city-threatening monster must be invigorating.

"Fantastic," he said to Sorent. Veloun was coming down now with a second woman, tall and limber, her long brown hair a tangled mess.

"What's this all about, then?" she said sleepily.

Dranko was done wasting time. "So that's the Turtlebane? Great. Corlea, you've got a new turtle to slay today. Sorent, I'm going to leave you to explain everything to your friend because we need to get moving. Good luck with the colossus!"

"Have you alerted the town guard?" asked Sorent. "We three are quite capable, but against a creature the size of a wandering island, we may need assistance."

That was likely to prove a fantastic understatement, but Dranko didn't say as much. He clapped a hand on Sorent's shoulder. "Something tells me that when the colossus makes its move, every man and woman in Sand's Edge with something to shoot, chop, or throw will be out there doing their best."

He gave his friends a grim smile. "Come on. We need to get to Arrowshot Tower before Kibi and Ernie."

* * *

The crowd gawping at the wandering island had swelled to a hundred people, maybe more.

"Why are they still there?" asked Tor, peering down.

Dranko snorted. "You mean, why didn't they believe a bunch of funny-looking strangers telling them the world's largest reptile was about to rise from an ocean of sand? Gosh, I can't imagine."

Tor had flown Vyasa Vya high above the city. The streets were filling with city folk getting the day's business underway. Arrowshot Tower rose up like a tall pine among saplings, and even from a distance Dranko saw that someone in red was now on the tower roof.

"There he is!" shouted Tor, swooping downward and banking smoothly left. "I'm going to land on the—"

"No, not yet," said Dranko. "Better if we confront him all together. Get closer and scan the streets for any sign of Kibi and Ernie."

The desert-side edge of the city was only a mile from Arrowshot Tower; assuming they'd met with no impediments, his friends should be arriving any time.

"There!" said Aravia. "In the tower. Look!"

Arrowshot Tower wasn't more than sixty or seventy feet tall, but it appeared taller due to its relatively slender footprint and the squat, even rooftops of its neighbors. Large rectangular windows were set into the red stone of its exterior, striped with close-set vertical metal bars.

Dranko at first saw nothing, but then caught a flash of movement behind one set of bars. Two figures were dashing up the interior stairwell.

"They'll be there in less than a minute. Tor, take us down to the roof."

"Keep approaching from the east," said Aravia. "If he's summoning something from the desert, he may be looking out that way. There's a chance he hasn't noticed us yet."

Given the streamers of smoke behind Vyasa Vya, Dranko was not optimistic about surprising the red trespasser, but it was worth a shot. Tor lowered the carpet down to the level of the roof and hovered just inside the railing along its eastern edge. By the railing on the far side, a lone figure in bulky red armor stood facing out toward the Mouth of Nahalm.

In the center of the stone roof was a wooden trapdoor, and this flew open even as Dranko and the others dismounted the flying carpet. Ernie emerged with Kibi on his heels, and the sound of the trapdoor banging against the roof caused the red-armored figure to turn his head.

"Aktallian," breathed Morningstar.

The red-armored man did not reply but turned fully to face them and gracefully drew his sword. His off hand held something distinctly horn-shaped. He stood some thirty feet away, but Dranko could tell he was smiling.

"Hey! Aktallian!" Dranko shouted. "Why aren't you off in dreamland terrorizing children?"

"You have me at a disadvantage," he called. "Who might you be?"

"I'm Dranko Blackhope."

"What a depressing-sounding name. Did you choose it yourself?"

"We have more important things to talk about," he called back. "Well, really only one thing. That's a nice horn you've got there."

"Oh," said Aktallian. "Are you here to stop me from blowing it?"

Ernie tensed. "Easy there," Dranko muttered.

"Why haven't you blown it already?" called Morningstar.

"Ah, Morningstar." Aktallian gave a little mock bow. "How surprising to see you alive! It seems you prefer to die with company. As to your question, I was admiring the view. There are no deserts this vast where I come from."

"And where is that?" asked Dranko.

"Nowhere you are ever likely to visit unless your luck is very, very poor."

"It might surprise you to hear this," Dranko called, "but we have no intention of stopping you. But I do have one question you could answer for me. If Emperor Naradawk wants to come back and rule Charagan, why would he want a bunch of giant turtles stomping all over it?"

It was a question intended to put Aktallian off his guard, but the red trespasser only laughed. "You are remarkably well informed," he said. "And yet also tragically naïve. But here's a question for you, Dranko Blackhope. If you believe I'm about to cause Ganit Tuvith to be overrun with Ventifact Giants, and you don't intend to stop me, why are you and your friends here at all?"

"To tell you the truth," said Dranko, "We haven't entirely agreed upon not stopping you. But I figured that either way, we're going to want to do something about you *after* you've either blown your horn or not."

Aktallian laughed. "'Do something about me?' Is that a euphemism for 'kill' on your world? If so, it's delightfully optimistic."

"We should kill him right now," said Tor.

"No," said Morningstar. "In my Seer-dream, Eddings killed the turtle, but the turtle was there to be killed. If we need to sacrifice this city to save the kingdom later on, so be it."

Ernie fumed but nodded his resignation.

"But we can kill him afterward, right?" whispered Tor.

"Oh, Hells yes," said Dranko.

Dranko wasn't *quite* as confident as he sounded. He was meddling in the proverbial things whose understanding was far beyond him, but the one thing that kept coming back to him was Abernathy's last pronouncement: that unless they found the Crosser's Maze, an ancient and unstoppable being was going to show up and lay waste to everything. There was also the possibility that Stormknight Turtlebane had some prophesied destiny—and by the Gods those things were lying thick on the ground these days—to kill the Ventifact Colossus before it got very far.

And of course, when the dust had settled and the colossus was slain, and the Stormknights were queried about what prompted their heroics, the name of Horn's Company was bound to come up.

"Aktallian, please, be our guest. Let the trumpet sound and the world's largest turtle have its tour of Sand's Edge."

Aktallian gave him and his friends a long, hard stare. Dranko belatedly worried that he had gone too far, that now Aktallian would suspect a trick and not blow the horn after all. The man adjusted both his stance and his grip on his black sword; was he going to rush them, figuring he could kill them all and summon the Colossus afterward? Dranko didn't doubt he was a formidable warrior even in the waking world, and unlike them he was heavily armored, but Dranko still liked the odds of six against one.

Without taking his eyes off of Dranko and the rest, Aktallian brought the Chelonian Horn to his lips. The bright green instrument was slightly bigger than a typical drinking horn; the sunlight brought multicolored reflections from its surface as though it were studded with a variety of gems. Despite the imminent enormity of consequence to Aktallian blowing it, Dranko couldn't stop himself from wondering: would he get more from selling the gems off individually or from presenting the intact whole as a collector's piece?

Its sound was low and piercing, a pure, even tone at the lowest register a person was likely to hear. A dull pain throbbed in Dranko's ears, his teeth vibrated, goose-flesh prickled his skin. Arrowshot Tower emitted an alarming percussion of crackling rock, like a whole block of stone houses settling at once.

Aktallian held the horn blast for ten full seconds before releasing it, after which a profound quiet rushed in. Dranko's eardrums popped from a sudden cessation of pressure. On the streets below, the pedestrians of Sand's Edge stopped, confused. The city held its breath.

The red trespasser himself stood on the westernmost side of the rooftop, closest to the desert. He must have been exerting superhuman self-control not to turn his back to them, to see if his summons had been successful.

"Ernie, go around to the left!" It was Morningstar barking orders. "I'll go to the right. Tor, straight ahead. Kibi, if you think you can fight well enough to make a difference, stay near Tor. Our best chance is to attack from different sides. Aravia and Dranko, support and healing."

Dranko was impressed; Morningstar must have been thinking this through since they first landed on the tower.

Aktallian tossed the horn aside and took a few relaxed steps forward, slashing the air with his shiny black sword and moving with fluid grace. For all it hindered him, the crimson armor he wore might have been made of woven grass. He made a feint forward, then sidestepped quickly right and turned to meet Ernie full on. Ernie grew wide-eyed and backpedaled, leaning backward as the tip of Aktallian's sword came close enough to trim his eyebrows. This spurred Tor into a run, and for just a second Dranko thought the kid might be able to take full advantage of Aktallian's divided attention, but the man in red armor spun and easily blocked Tor's overhand swing.

Dranko's experience in analyzing swordfights was not much cultivated, but he could tell that Tor was out of his league. The boy gamely took his hacks and dodged or parried Aktallian's counters, concentrating on defense until more help arrived. Ernie had regained his balance and took cautious steps in, looking for an opening while his enemy danced with Tor.

Behind him and off to one side Aravia shouted a pair of incomprehensible syllables, and Dranko waited for some magical effect that would sway the battle in their favor. When nothing obvious occurred in the following heartbeat, he guessed Aravia had done something subtler, like turn Aktallian's sword to wood or unbuckle his armor. But Aravia spit a most unladylike oath involving goats; had he taught her that? He must have. Either way, whatever Aravia had cast, it hadn't worked.

Morningstar moved up unnoticed and swung her mace down hard at Aktallian's head, but the red trespasser must have caught some glimmer of her movement; he ducked and leaned forward so that the head of Morningstar's weapon clanked against the back plate of his armor. Without even looking he spun and slashed Morningstar right across her stomach, opening a gaping wound, then finished his twirl in time to block a swing from Tor. He was a dervish, never still for a second, a fighting machine they had no business contesting.

"Kibi," said Dranko, "they need help. Our only hope is numbers." He dashed forward to where Morningstar had fallen, praying out loud as he ran. "Lord Delioch, whose might heals all hurts, time is very short right now."

He slid as he arrived and put his hands on Morningstar's gashed body. Aktallian flicked a look at him, then at Kibi. If nothing else, the stonecutter's arrival with a weapon drew Aktallian's attention away from him. Dranko's hand glowed golden, and energy was drawn from his body to heal Morningstar's wound. It came so easily now, a transferal of vitality made in full knowledge and acceptance of the price. His vision blurred, but with a mighty effort of will he retained his awareness.

"I'm becoming way too familiar with your insides," he said to Morningstar "And there's probably a good rude joke I could be making along those lines, but this isn't the time. Now get up and—"

Two things happened quickly then, much too quickly for Dranko to do anything but observe. As Morningstar rose to one knee, ready to return to the fight, Aktallian twisted away from Tor and executed a perfect backhand slash destined to take Morningstar's head off at the neck. At the same moment Aravia shouted a quick syllable and the Chelonian Horn sailed in from off stage, connecting hard with Aktallian's wrist. The black sword turned in his grip, and instead of the blade sweeping Morningstar's head from her shoulders, its flat struck the side of her head at a greatly reduced velocity. It was still enough to send Morningstar staggering back. She dropped to her knees, her mace falling from her fingers.

Dranko fumed. "Dammit, I just healed her!"

Aktallian spared him another brief glance, but Ernie and Tor diverted the red trespasser's attention. The three squared off, Tor and Ernie huffing a bit and bleeding from several shallow cuts each, while Aktallian spun and leapt like an armored dancer with not a scratch on him. Dranko had hoped that his allies' numerical advantage would translate into victory by attrition, but it wasn't working out that way. It didn't help that Kibi was still hanging back, looking for an opening that was never going to come.

The tower shook.

No, more than that, the *city* shook. Aktallian's nimble maneuvers had carried him back to the wooden railing on the west side of the roof, and over his shoulder a great gray hill was rising into view, heaving itself up out of the desert.

Faint but shrill, screams filled the air of Sand's Edge.

The swaying of Arrowshot Tower seemed to sharpen Aktallian's focus.

"I suppose we'll have to wrap this up," he said. Gods, he wasn't even breathing hard. Aktallian lunged and drove Ernie back, the baker barely lifting Pyknite in time to parry, and at the same time kicked high behind him, striking Tor in the sternum and sending him reeling backward. Aktallian was already cocking his arm back for a stroke that was likely to cut Ernie in half. Dranko doubted he had any channeling left in him.

Kibi finally found his opening. He lunged forward and swung his pick, driving its business end into Aktallian's breastplate. Knowing how unusually strong Kibi was, Dranko half expected to see the curve of the pick emerge from Aktallian's back. Aktallian himself was knocked three steps backward. Kibi looked up at him almost apologetically.

The point of the pick had made a deep dimpled dent in the breastplate, but had gone no further.

"Damn," said Kibi.

All hope left Dranko then. Aktallian scowled and hacked contemptuously at Kibi, cleaving through the wooden handle of the pick and chopping off the bottom two inches of the stonecutter's beard.

Another shockwave traveled through Sand's Edge as the Ventifact Colossus took another step. The tower swayed and shed flakes of stone.

Aktallian whipped around before Dranko and Ernie could get out of the way.

"You people are like gnats," he said. "But I—"

He turned again. Tor had regained his equilibrium and was charging forward. Aktallian's black sword flicked like a shadow and speared Tor's abdomen as the boy closed, splattering Dranko with blood. But Tor simply grunted, wrapped his arms around Aktallian, and continued his barreling run, bearing the man backward even as the black sword emerged from his own back.

The wooden railing had no chance. It splintered and gave way, and both Tor and Aktallian vanished over the lip of the roof, Morningstar's first Seer-dream coming to pass.

Aravia sprinted past Dranko in a blur, braced herself against an intact section of railing, and leaned out over it. She shouted a single word, then staggered back.

"Save Tor," she gasped before falling comatose onto the roof.

Dranko lurched to the railing and looked down. Tor was far below, on his back and looking up with wide, terrified eyes. Next to him was the sprawled body of Aktallian, but the armored man looked disproportionally small. Something was playing tricks with Dranko's perspective.

Red light shone out from Aktallian's body, and he disappeared, sword and armor and all.

Another temblor rocked Sand's Edge; clouds of dust rose from its streets and buildings. The Ventifact Colossus had its two front feet planted on the ground above the desert. Its turtle head was nearly level with the top of Arrowshot Tower and continuing to rise. Its immensity was of a sort that Dranko's mind could make no sense of.

Tor was another story. The boy was flailing around now, making swimming motions with one arm while the other was drawn in, hand tight against his side. The boy's body spun like something hanging on a string, and several pedestrians were reaching *up* to grab him.

He was levitating! Aravia had saved his life, at least for now. But Dranko had seen Aktallian's sword go right through the boy. He had little time left to live.

Dranko turned to Kibi. "Are you injured?"

"No, I..."

"Can you carry Morningstar and Aravia down the stairs? At the same time? I don't think this tower was built for what's coming."

Kibi nodded even as he gazed open-mouthed at the Ventifact Colossus dominating the horizon.

"Then do it."

Ernie was also looking dumbly at the world's largest turtle. Dranko grabbed his shoulder.

"Ernie, I need to go save Tor."

He pointed to the carpet, still hovering where they had dismounted. "You need to fly that thing. Find the three Stormknights. Two women and a man, probably wearing something with a shield and red fist. Make sure they're on the job and see if they need help."

"But I can't—"

"Yes, you can. And you will. Go."

Dranko bolted for the trap door.

Delioch, if Tor is still alive when I get down there, take whatever you need, even if it kills me.

CHAPTER THIRTY

Ernie's attention was uniquely divided.

On the one hand, there was the carpet, its orange fabric gently undulating two feet off the ground. As he had admitted back when they were taking turns flying the thing around the Greenhouse yard, he had no stomach for heights. More accurately it was *ledges* that sent some primordial cliff-fearing part of his brain into a blind panic. It didn't even have to be *himself* on the ledge. When his father climbed on the bakery roof to make repairs, Ernie literally couldn't look; his fear directed his head to turn away without consulting any rational part of his mind.

Vyasa Vya was not very large. It was all ledge.

On the other hand, there was the Ventifact Colossus. The great sand turtle had by now lifted its entire mountainous body out of the desert, its feet having pounded the cliff face and fifty yards of once-flat terrain into a compressed ramp of earth. Standing at the apex of a seventy-foot tower, Ernie was about even with its underbelly and the tops of its legs. Its enormous head was a hundred feet higher. Behind it the body stretched out like…like…

His mind balked. Other than mountains, there was nothing big enough for comparison, certainly nothing that could *move*. And it carried a mountain on its back already.

Its left foreleg was off the ground but descending in a kind of otherworldly slow motion, like a tree slowly toppling in a forest. It didn't seem to slam down with great force, but its impact set the tower to pitching to and fro even from a mile away. A cloud of debris the size of a city block plumed up from its foot.

Ernie was fascinated almost to the point of paralysis by the sight of the colossus, but the thought of standing on the roof when the tower collapsed spurred him to action. He ran to the carpet and stepped up gingerly, then spent a few seconds wiggling his backside in a vain attempt to feel comfortably stationary. Giving up on that, he grabbed two of the tassels along the front edge and willed the rug to rise a few feet. It responded to his wishes, sending fear creeping up his throat and thickening his tongue.

He imagined Old Bowlegs standing before him.

What are you waiting for, Ernie? Do you think all my training was about goblins? You will do great things in this life, Ernest Carabend Roundhill, if only you find a confidence to match your gifts.

And then, quite clearly, he saw Mrs. Horn smiling up at him, those wonderful wrinkles framing her face. *Stay positive, Ernest.*

"Fly forward," he said, and the carpet responded. It lurched a few times as Ernie's terrified subconscious fought to delay the inevitable, but then like a stone from a sling it shot out over the tower railing. Ernie's scream mingled with hundreds of others coming up from the streets.

It would have been easier had he not been obliged to look down, but he needed to find the three Stormknights. He willed the carpet to stop and hover, then leaned to the left and peered over the side. Thousands of people were running through the narrow, twisting streets, mostly away from the desert and the approaching colossus. A few souls, brave or foolhardy, were dashing closer, maybe to get a better look.

He couldn't imagine how he'd begin to find three people he had never met, from a hundred feet up, in a city teeming like a knocked-down anthill. If all had gone according to plan, the Stormknights would be attacking the Ventifact Colossus, though Ernie had no idea how they were planning to bring it down. His animal instincts yammered for him to turn around and fly to anywhere less imperiled than here, but Ernie collected his resolve and steered the carpet toward the gigantic turtle.

Another foot came down, and this one fell half on an outlying huddle of small buildings. These simply vanished beneath the turtle's brown-green claw, flattened and driven a dozen feet downward into the beast's footprint. A wooden shed that stood just outside the radius of the turtle's claw collapsed anyway from the shock, and several nearby gawkers were knocked over as the ground shifted.

Ernie flew higher, steering Vyasa Vya in fits and starts as he pummeled the terrified bits of his mind into submission. The ride grew smoother as he approached the impossible grandeur of the colossus, since it gave his fear a clearer object to embrace. Now he was of a height with its eyes, shimmering black walls showing only a slight curve. Its nostrils gaped like caves, and its mouth, slightly ajar, could have opened wide and swallowed the entire Greenhouse in a single gulp.

Though the turtle had been out of the Mouth of Nahalm for several minutes now, hundreds of gallons of sand were still streaming off its shell, creating shoulder-high mounds on roads and rooftops. Through these cascading sheets came volleys of arrows and bolts, as militiamen were firing bravely up at the giant beast lumbering through their city. It was impossible for them to miss, but none of the hissing projectiles were doing any good. The rough skin of the turtle's legs and belly repelled most of the missiles, and the few that stuck couldn't have bothered it any more than the tiniest splinter might trouble an elephant.

Its legs moved two at a time, foreleg with the opposite hind-leg, each rising and falling like a god's hammer. Aravia had been right; its next step landed in the city proper, and it crushed three buildings at once. Ernie prayed that its slow rate of progress had given everyone the chance to evacuate. Swooping around to its left he saw the crater left behind by its previous step. It was matted with pulverized debris, but without getting closer Ernie couldn't tell if any human remains were mashed into the wreckage.

An arrow whizzed by his head. The air had become thicker with projectiles as soldiers and armed citizens converged on the beast. He doubted they were aiming at him, but what might they think he was doing? A man on a flying carpet was probably just as strange a sight to a typical citizen as was a giant turtle. In the worst case they might decide that he was responsible for the colossus, or even controlling it! To his unspoken thought the carpet moved straight up like an elevator, until it was higher than the top of the wandering island perched on the turtle's shell, and well out of range of the bowmen. His fear of heights subsided a bit as the ground became more abstract, but if anything the colossus appeared even larger now that he could see it and the city at once. Slow as its footsteps were, another dozen of them would leave much of Sand's Edge in ruin, and that wasn't taking into account the prophecy of Romus the Mad, who foretold an entire regiment of turtles following the first one out of the Mouth of Nahalm.

Out in the desert two more of the wandering islands were much closer to the city than they had been this morning. A third wasn't too far behind.

Even as most of Sand's Edge's population was now streaming out of the city, spilling in a ragged column onto the north road, small crowds had gathered around the Ventifact Colossus's feet. Ernie took a wide spiraling course downward (so as to avoid the arrows that filled the air) to investigate.

The back right foot of the Colossus was large enough that over thirty people could stand in a ring around its circumference, and that's what they were doing. Each was armed either with a sword or else a pitchfork, hoe, or some other farmer's or tradesman's implement. They had scrambled and clawed their way through the local wreckage and were hacking at the foot with vigor, but obviously to no meaningful end. They might as well have been flogging a horse with handkerchiefs. A hundred men chopping at the leathery skin for an hour would maybe give the colossus the equivalent of a superficial cut.

Up went the leg, slowly, and the crowd scattered before reforming and running to continue their useless assault on the front right foot. Ernie admired their courage and despaired at the futility of it all.

A bystander who had been watching the circle of attackers from a safe distance noticed Ernie and pointed, shouting, but his words were drowned out by the thunderous roar of a massive foot coming down full upon the city, mashing another dozen buildings into fragments and knocking over, in part or in full, fifty more around it. Already the devastation was terrible, and nothing was likely to stop it before all of Sand's Edge was erased.

He still hadn't found the trio of Stormknights, but the foot-hacking squads were a likely place to look. Ernie steered Vyasa Vya clockwise around the back of the turtle, tilting his flight-path upward to avoid the creature's tail (which was stubby relative to the size of the body, but still a hundred feet long and wider than a toolshed). His control over the carpet was improving, though he was still nowhere as skilled as Tor. On the far side were forty more people bunched in an offensive cluster, attacking the turtle's back left foot while it was still planted in its crater, but none of them looked like a Werthan Stormknight.

As Ernie hovered, the foot rose from its indented footprint, and directly behind it were three people apart from the crowds. The Stormknights! They were beneath the center of the Colossus, two women and a man, standing alone and wearing tabards emblazoned with the shield-and-fist of the god of War. All carried long swords, and two had small shields strapped to their arms. They were looking up and talking as the majestic roof of the turtle's underbelly passed overhead. Had they found a weak spot?

He raced toward them, the carpet jerking at the excitement of his discovery. The taller of the two women noticed his approach, wheeled into a crouch behind her shield, and pointed her blade at him.

"Were you visited by four people including a half-goblin?" Ernie asked hurriedly. "Those were my friends."

The woman nodded. She was taller than Tor and had a warrior's bearing. Her long brown hair was tied behind her in a ponytail.

"They spoke truly," she said. "I am Corlea Turtlebane, but how I am to spell the death of this monstrosity is a riddle we cannot solve. Did your prophecies not include some hint as to how we might slay such a tremendous creature?"

"No," said Ernie. "One just said that that 'three children of Werthis would lay it low.' The other one said that 'three of your number would smite the beast.' Neither of them said how. We were hoping you had some kind of trick up your sleeves."

The ground shuddered as the Ventifact Colossus planted another foot; the three Stormknights swayed and clutched one another's shoulders to stay upright.

"It is impervious," said the man. "And even could we drive our blades into its flesh up to the hilts, it would feel nothing, not even a flea bite. Who could have dreamt there were such monsters on Spira?"

Ernie blinked. Who indeed?

The answer came to him like a thunderbolt.

"Eddings," he whispered. Then out loud he said, "I think I know how you can kill it. Hop on the carpet."

The man regarded him with skepticism. "Are you certain?"

"Yes! And every minute you stand there, the turtle is going to crush another piece of your city. Hurry!"

"I don't think that—"

"Sorent!" shouted Corlea. "Have faith. Can you not see the Gods' will at work?"

Ernie lowered the flying rug to the ground and the three Stormknights stepped onto it.

"Best if you sit." Ernie steered the carpet out from under the colossus and sent it rocketing straight up. "My name's Ernest, by the way. It's nice to meet you."

"I am Veloun." The shorter woman had to shout to be heard over the din. "Ernest, what is your plan?"

Ernie flew Vyasa Vya high over the turtle and towards its front. Enormous round pits marked its progress, and each footprint was carpeted with crushed debris. And as if that weren't destruction aplenty, its slowly sweeping tail had left its own zigzagging swath of devastation, houses and shops and wells knocked into rubble, statues toppled and trees felled.

"My friend Morningstar is an Ellish Dreamseer," Ernie shouted to the Stormknights over his shoulder. "She saw the colossus in a dream, and in that dream, our butler killed it by stabbing it with a letter opener."

"I hardly see how that helps!" Veloun shouted back at him.

Ernie swung the flying carpet in a wide and descending arc, returning to a hovering state a couple hundred yards in front of the monster. He held them at the same height as the giant turtle's head—at least a hundred feet from the ground—and facing it.

"He stabbed it in its nose! Don't you see? Its nostrils are plenty big for you to climb into. From there you just have to slice your way up into its head. It must have a brain in there somewhere, right?"

Sorent, Veloun, and Corlea all stared at him agog.

"Do you have a better idea?" he asked them.

They did not.

"Then take us closer," said Corlea.

Ernie directed the carpet straight at the head of the approaching colossus. The beast was still serving to distract the parts of his mind that would otherwise be succumbing to his acrophobia, so that was good. The colossus was on a course aimed directly for Arrowshot Tower; was it simply going to where the horn had been winded? Would it stop there? Or maybe that was where, according to Romus the Mad, it would call the other turtles from the desert and lead its slow but inexorable world-crushing march.

There was more missile fire in the vicinity of the head, as bowmen on the ground aimed for the turtle's eyes. Many of the arrows didn't climb high enough, and those that did had lost some of their force to the pull of gravity. Some missed their target and ricocheted from the monster's rough hide with a percussive plinking. A few stuck in its skin, but harmlessly. A scattering of arrows did strike the eyes, but none of them found purchase, as a thick translucent membrane covered the creature's banquet-table-sized eyeballs. The barrage of tiny sticks didn't appear to cause the turtle any discomfort, let alone discourage its advance.

Ernie edged the carpet closer. The Ventifact Colossus was moving towards him much more quickly than he had anticipated. Its head rocked slightly as it lumbered along, and what seemed like a smooth motion from far off was revealed as a brisk bobbing and swaying up close. The slightly upturned nostrils were enormous, but landing the carpet, or even hovering nearby so the Stormknights could leap into them, was going to involve some delicate and precise maneuvers. Behind him the Stormknights were uttering oaths of disbelief that anything could be so huge. The turtle's face was a wall of mottled brown-green skin, with features so large they hardly registered as parts of a living thing. Its lipless mouth was parted ever so slightly, which meant they could have flown into it with a dozen feet of clearance above and below.

"There won't be any light in there," said Veloun. "And there's no way a torch or lantern will stay lit."

She was right; the nostrils were gaping black pits. Ernie shuddered to think of what it would be like inside the head of a Ventifact Colossus—dark, hot, damp, with ropes of mucous and eventually veins and blood and Pikon only knew what else. Would there even be enough air to keep the Stormknights alive, once they had slashed their way in deep enough?

"I have a solution," called Ernie. "My friend—"

Another gargantuan foot smashed down onto the city, and the head lurched forward. Ernie frantically expressed a desire that the carpet move backward, and it obeyed instantly, though not before the bouldery nose of the Colossus had clipped the rug's front fringe.

"Pikon's flapjacks, that was close! I only have two of these, so you'll have to share."

This was a dangerous moment to test whether he could steer Vyasa Vya with only one hand gripping the tassels, but Ernie had no choice. He shrugged his pack from his shoulders and fished around with his right hand until he found his two illuminated coins.

"Take these. They don't need air, and they won't burn your hand."

Veloun and Corlea each took one and stuffed them into pockets.

"Are you ready?" Ernie asked.

"How could we be?" asked Sorent. "You are asking us to leap into the nose of the most monstrous being ever to walk upon Charagan! But our readiness does not matter. We are Stormknights, and guarding the kingdom is—"

"Yes, we're ready," said Corlea. "Move us closer, Ernest."

Now Ernie had to focus, to block out the distractions of occasional arrows hissing past, of his passengers shifting their bodies around as they prepared to disembark, and of the fact that he was less than fifty feet away from something that could breathe him in by accident. But once most of his concentration was dedicated to the finer points of piloting, the carpet reacted more strongly to every mental hiccup and second guess. Vyasa Vya tilted and bucked as he overcorrected, shifting sideways and then backward as Ernie tried to avoid crashing into the hillsides of the turtle's cheek ridges. And as his control of his cloth rectangle wavered, he panicked. This wasn't fair! His shoulders weren't broad enough for this responsibility. It should be Tor up here, ferrying these passengers of destiny…but then, Tor had likely given his life so that Ernie could have this opportunity. He shook his head. Focus!

Another leg came down with a noise like thunder, and once more the head shot forward. He was too close! Ernie yanked the tassels sideways in desperation, trying to nudge the carpet's position so it would wind up in the left nostril.

He almost made it. The end of the Colossus's septum crashed into the carpet, sending Ernie sprawling onto his back. With no one holding the tassels the rug defaulted to hovering and was simply pushed along by the inexorable bulk of the turtle's nose.

But the Stormknights had been ready. They leapt from the carpet even as it folded and spun. Ernie sat up in time to see Veloun jump cleanly into the nostril, vanishing into its darkness. Sorent landed against the nostril's lip, legs dangling, but his hands grabbed something inside the nose and he pulled himself up.

Corlea Turtlebane missed entirely, thumping against the cliff wall that was the skin between the turtle's nostrils. She scrabbled frantically for purchase even as she slid down. Ernie lunged for the tassels but knew there was no way he could swoop down in time to catch her. It was nearly two hundred feet to the city below, a fall that would be impossible to survive.

"Ernest!"

Ernie grabbed the tassels and went into hard reverse. Below him Corlea had grabbed onto an arrow that was lodged in a seam of turtle skin. She dangled by one hand, legs kicking. The arrow was bending.

You are destined for great things, Ernest Roundhill.

The voice of Old Bowlegs came to him again, even as he banked the carpet downward.

It is not ability you lack, or character, or intelligence. It is only confidence. But I cannot give you that. You will find it, probably in the most unlikely of places.

If the nose of a gigantic turtle was not the most unlikely place on Spira right now, Ernie couldn't imagine what might be. He forced his heart from his throat and back into his chest, executed a perfect plunge-and-spin maneuver, and brought the carpet directly beneath Corlea's waving feet. The Stormknight dropped down behind him, after which Ernie again backed up before there was another accident.

"It will be easier if you jump down from higher up," he said.

Corlea's face was pale, her lips trembling, but she nodded.

As Ernie brought the carpet up and around, a cone of radiance shone from inside the left nostril...a good sign. "I'll stay up here," he told Corlea. "After you three have killed this thing, get back down to the nose and I'll pick you up."

"You are a man worthy of Werthis," she answered. "Whatever happens this day, you are a hero, Ernest."

She jumped from the carpet and landed cleanly in the nostril. Ernie steered Vyasa Vya up and out, until he was a hundred feet or more above the top of the wandering island the colossus carried on its shell. Then he released the tassels and flopped down on his back, trying not to hyperventilate and praying that his heart wouldn't spontaneously combust from overwork.

For two minutes he lay there, panting, staring up at the sky. It was strange, looking at so much open space after the Ventifact Colossus had dominated his field of vision these past few minutes. (Gods, but it felt longer!) He closed his eyes and tried to pretend he was dreaming, but as he listened to the sounds of chaos from far below, worries crept into his mind.

What if there was no direct passage from the nose to the brain? Its skull must be three feet thick; the weapons of the Stormknights would never be able to crack a hole through it. Would they suffocate? Would the turtle simply sneeze them out, a titan's bellows launching them like grains of soot into the air? And how big was the brain of a Ventifact Colossus? Ernie had been assuming it filled up most of the head, but then animal brains were proportionally smaller, weren't they? What if the turtle's brain was only the size of a wine barrel? Would the Stormknights find it, or even recognize it if they did? And just as chickens could dash about in a panic without benefit of a head, might the turtle keep on stomping even if its brain was chopped to bits?

"Have faith in Eddings," he told himself.

Ernie rolled over until he could peek down over the edge of the carpet. Directly below was the thrashing tail, still leaving a wide swath of destruction. Many buildings had fallen merely from the tremors produced by the weight of the turtle's steps. And of course there were the footprints themselves, deep as wells, giant holes in the earth filled with the city's remains.

Another minute passed, and another, and the Ventifact Colossus trudged on, step by ruinous step. It was only a few hundred yards from Arrowshot Tower, and Ernie despaired. The Stormknights had failed, probably suffocated, or maybe they were still in the nose, chopping vainly through membranes and other interior bits that were not at all crucial to the beast's survival.

The thought came unbidden that the kingdom could be doomed by the world's largest booger. Ernie giggled as he imagined Sorent, Corlea, and Veloun carving through a barn-sized lump of hardened turtle snot, and the sound of his own snigger opened some sort of emotional floodgate that released a torrent of uncontrollable laughter mixed with sobs until tears blurred his eyes and ran down his cheeks.

By the time he mastered himself a minute later, the Ventifact Colossus was standing still. It slowly swung its great head back and forth, but for the first time since it emerged from the Mouth of Nahalm, all four of its legs were motionless.

Ernie sat bolt upright, gripped the tassels, and steered the carpet down and toward the head. As he flew, the colossus took a step *backward*, and its right eyelid drooped and closed. Though Ernie didn't have any good idea of how to interpret a turtle's facial expressions, he thought the thing was confused.

Its mouth opened, but no sound came out. Half a minute later its tail stopped swishing and dropped, flattening a row of shops that had miraculously avoided destruction before then. Just when Ernie dared to hope the Stormknights had finished their work, the colossus lifted its front left leg high off the ground, as though it was preparing for a final sprint. But instead of swinging forward, the leg splayed out at an awkward diagonal, and the whole of its body tilted leftward and collapsed.

When the underbelly of the colossus struck the ground, there was a shockwave of rolling thunder, a fast-moving ring of collapsing buildings and gouts of smoke and dust. From the folk who had not yet fled the city, a ragged cheer went up.

The turtle had fallen with its head only thirty yards from Arrowshot Tower.

The tower had stayed heroically upright throughout the city's ordeal, but now succumbed to the force of the beast's collapse. It buckled and cracked in several places, sending its multi-tiered red stone corpse spiraling downward, splashing the ground with a conspicuously odd pattern of debris.

Only one building had survived between the fallen colossus and the toppled tower, a low white dome made of limestone. A line of a dozen other buildings leading to it had fallen in the final shockwave, but the dome had survived. Did the people who lived or worked there appreciate how lucky they were? One more step and it would have been flattened like the hundreds of others. On the other hand, it was damaged badly enough that it would need to be knocked down and rebuilt anyway, and that was assuming the entire city wasn't simply evacuated as a total loss. Yes, there were even cracks in the dome's roof, and red light was slashing upward and out through those cracks like upside-down sunbeams. Was there a fire inside? Had the vibrations from the Colossus knocked over a brazier or—

The dome exploded in an inverted hailstorm of flame and rock, a blazing geyser that roared into the sky. The carpet responded to Ernie's instinctive flinch, zipping upward a hundred feet as if propelled by a giant spring. Ernie peered over the front of the carpet to see what had happened, and when the smoke had cleared, he just stared, wondering at the sight below.

The remains of the buildings that had fallen last were strewn in a very clear arrangement, like a man standing with his feet together, his arms raised and outstretched. The ravaged dome, its roof caved and leaking plumes of smoke, formed a nearly perfect head for the man. The fallen Arrowshot Tower resembled a crown of red rocks, and from hundreds of feet up looked like flames rising from the smoldering head.

Ernie had seen that figure before.

In Seablade Point. In Hodge's office. The statuette of the burning man was sculpted in the exact pose as the final pieces of wreckage from the Colossus's jaunt through Sand's Edge.

Ernie brought the carpet lower. As the smoke continued to dissipate, details inside the dome became visible. There were a dozen bodies lying amidst the chunks of limestone, each in an orange-red robe, and twinkling in the ashes were hundreds of little red-gold metal pyramids.

Even as his mind assembled the puzzle of what had just taken place, his eye was caught by unexpected movement from the giant turtle's face. The

Stormknights! He had nearly forgotten about them. Out of the black cave that was the reptile's left nostril, a human hand reached out, coated with yellow-green slime.

CHAPTER THIRTY-ONE

They made camp that night by the road, amidst a sea of refugees. Thousands of citizens of Sand's Edge were already making for the city of Hae Kalkas, following the same river the company had flown along en route to the Norlin Hills.

Morningstar gazed up at a sky ablaze with stars and prayed for undisturbed sleep. Her head ached terribly from the blow from Aktallian, and Dranko wouldn't be able to heal her until the next morning. Saving Tor's life had drained all the remaining energy out of him, and they had been obliged to carry his unconscious body out of the city following the death of the Ventifact Colossus.

She rolled to her side and looked across the ground at Dranko, snoring away like a logger's saw. In the ambient light of countless campfires his scarred and betusked face was almost noble. One could forgive his crudeness when he was so selfless in using his abilities to channel. He was an outcast, just as she was, and surely his lot had been harder. Where she had faced coldness and suspicion, he had endured the hatred of his grandfather and the cutting knives of Deliochan scarbearers—and probably something worse. She had worked to drive self-pity from her heart, but she ought to feel pity for him, however difficult he made it. It would take time.

Ernie was still awake, talking animatedly about his high-flying adventures with several refugees from the next campfire over. She was decidedly proud of the young man and hoped his achievement would burn off some of his excess humility.

Off by themselves sat the Stormknights Sorent and Veloun, faces etched with grief, journeying to Hae Kalkas to make their report to the Werthan church. The horrors they had described, climbing and hacking their way through a nightmare of blood, flesh, and slime, were difficult to imagine. And Corlea Turtlebane, who by their accounts had done the lion's share of critical damage to the Ventifact Colossus's brain, had either suffocated or drowned deep in the turtle's head.

The plan was for Aravia to teleport Horn's Company the next morning back to the Greenhouse, where they hoped Abernathy would have recovered. Now that the various prophecies had come true, was the Kivian Arch open? If not, what was there to be done? And if so, how would they get through it to find the Crosser's Maze?

In the meantime Morningstar needed to sleep, and though it felt blasphemous, she hoped her avatar would give her respite from their training sessions. She also hoped, fervently, that Aktallian would not visit her dreams. Though his fall should have been fatal, his body had apparently vanished. She couldn't be sure if he was dead, but she knew she was so very tired.

Morningstar hides in a forest thicket, watching the stone arch of Seablade Point pulse with a ruddy opaque luminance. A great noise comes from beyond that impenetrable glow, as if legions of warriors are clashing swords against shields and bellowing war cries in a foreign tongue.

The trees of the forest begin to uproot themselves, first singly and then in scores, shooting into the air like fireworks and exploding in balls of orange flame. In minutes the forest has become a clearing, excepting only the little cluster of elms that hides her.

The red glow vanishes from the arch, and now looking at it is like gazing through a picture window into another world. The land beyond is rocky and blanketed with snow. It is also covered with an army, a forest of tents and pennants. Smells of urine, horses, and cooking fires waft out.

A tall figure strides through the arch, passing seamlessly from the snowy realm to the cleared-away forest, a man with red hair and a warrior's bearing. He dusts some snow from his pauldrons, smiles with satisfaction, and scoops up a handful of soil from the ground, rubbing it between his fingers.

As soldiers begin to pour through from behind him, Morningstar's viewpoint shifts, zooming through the archway, then rising, a bird's-eye view of an eagle in flight, but faster, ever faster, streaking over and across an unfamiliar countryside. This new land is massive, many times larger than all of Charagan, and over a thousand varied miles pass beneath her, forests and mountain ranges, rocky plains and vast grasslands, and finally a dense jungle.

She looks up to the western horizon, and there is no sky. There is only an impossible iron wall, detailed with a complex pattern that resolves itself as she shoots towards it, and Morningstar realizes that her perspective is wrong; she is not flying toward something distant, but falling into it. She is plummeting, ever faster, into an infinite metal labyrinth.

She woke with a cry and sat up. Her friends stirred, roused from slumber by her shout, though it was still the dead of night. Kibi raised himself to his elbows.

"You okay there?" he asked. "Bad dream?"

"The Crosser's Maze," she whispered. "I know where it is."

EPILOGUE

G rey Wolf didn't puke, but Gods, he wanted to. The painful nausea had spiked, badly; he wouldn't have been surprised had he launched his stomach straight out of his throat. But on his hands and knees, he noticed that the ground had changed. It wasn't a planked ship's hold, which it should have been. Now it was beige marble, clean enough to show him his own blurry reflection.

It was warmer, too. He lifted his head—slowly, slowly, Gods, what a headache. Not more than twenty feet away, seated upon a massive stone chair, was a twelve foot tall purple-skinned being, human in shape, proportion, and features, bedecked in shining black armor. By his side, dwarfed by his immensity, stood a black-haired woman, human, also in armor, though hers was as red as blood.

There were others in the throne room as well, courtiers, guardsmen, and servants, all of them quiet, all of them staring at him. A dozen men bearing pikes lowered their points, making Grey Wolf the center of a wheel with sharp metal spokes.

"Let him be."

The voice of the purple-skinned sovereign was silk and steel. The guards raised their pikes and stepped back.

"My friends," said the sovereign, addressing his court, "do not be concerned with our visitor. His arrival was inevitable and a harbinger of our release."

He gestured to Grey Wolf. "Ivellios Forrester, come forward, as far as you are able. I wish to look upon you."

Grey Wolf shook his head, desperately wishing this was a fever-dream but knowing it was not.

"I can guess who you are," he said. "Emperor Naradawk."

The emperor nodded. "I said come forward. Do not worry. I will not harm you. I swear upon the Circle, that's the *last* thing I desire."

Grey Wolf took a step toward Naradawk. No one had disarmed him. If he moved close enough, he might be able to take this...thing...by surprise. Yes, Abernathy had told how even the mightiest wizards of the Spire couldn't kill this being's father, but who could say if the son was as impervious? Since he doubted Naradawk's words and figured he'd be dead either way in the next five minutes, he could at least go down fighting. But he would be cagey, deferential to this monster, until he was within striking distance. You didn't survive twenty years as a sell sword without a store of guile.

He took a second step, and that was harder. Something was radiating out from Naradawk, a hot, greasy force that pushed back on him like a headwind. There was nothing visible, but it was strong and sapped his will. Still a dozen feet from the throne, he could go no further. It felt as though his skin were burning, like Naradawk was a bonfire whose fuel was unalloyed malice.

The emperor turned to the woman at his side. "Meledien, this is Ivellios Forrester, the one the ritualists have told us about. As the time draws near, he will become unanchored more and more frequently, until the final moment when he is part of Spira and Volpos together. This won't be his last visit. Are you prepared, Ivellios?"

Volpos? That sounded familiar. Was it something Abernathy had mentioned?

He strained to move closer to Naradawk, but it was futile. Whether it was Naradawk's will or something inherent to the emperor's being, Grey Wolf thought he would burst into flames if he managed to struggle any farther forward.

That left only defiance. "I'm prepared to fight you," he spat.

A shocked murmur spread through the crowd of courtiers. Naradawk sat up straight in his throne, looking...surprised?

"Have you not been made ready for your sacrifice, Ivellios?"

Having no idea what the emperor was talking about, Grey Wolf just stared back.

"You haven't, have you?" Naradawk showed a smile full of dark gray teeth. "You're running loose on Spira with no idea of your importance."

"He knows who you are, my Lord," said the woman in red armor, the one the Emperor called Meledien. "He may even have been warned by the Spire."

"Let's find out."

Naradawk hardened his stare. Grey Wolf felt as though a fist had been jammed into his head, and this time he *did* puke, falling to his knees and splattering the marble tiles, drawing a titter of disgust from the courtiers. It was a horrible sensation, Naradawk rooting around in his memories, roughly, like a burglar turning out drawers and knocking over tables looking for valuables. His mind burned with anger and frustration. This purple monstrosity was reading his thoughts, and he was helpless to stop it.

After a torturous minute of this treatment Naradawk released him, leaving him coughing up droplets of bile.

"Interesting," said the monster. "The Spire has been disbanded. There's just the small cadre of wizards who are attending to the portal. They know I'm coming, but they don't know how. They don't know how to stop me. Ivellios here was hired by one of them to try figuring things out, but his team is a bunch of bumbling amateurs, one of whom has already been killed by our skellari. Their only plan is to use something called the Crosser's Maze, but Ivellios thinks that's an impossible long shot. They don't know what it is, or where it is."

"But Lord," said Meledien, "if their wizards don't know why Ivellios is important, why did they choose him from among all the people on Spira? That cannot be a coincidence."

"I don't know," said Naradawk, frowning. "He and his associates were summoned by Alander's apprentice, a wizard named Abernathy, but Abernathy himself claims not to know why his summoning spell chose them specifically. He could be lying to his slaves, but Ivellios here is convinced otherwise. Either way, Ivellios is entirely ignorant of his role in my plans."

Grey Wolf lifted his head from the floor to regard his captor. "And what are your plans?"

Naradawk smiled. "I and my armies are going to take back Spira, and you are the means by which it will happen. You'll serve your purpose as the place in common, scion of Moirel."

"Scion of Moirel? Place in common? What does that mean? Why aren't you just killing me?"

"Ah, Ivellios. I am not going to kill you because if you die here, I would have no way to return your body to Spira where it will be needed. No, like everyone else on your benighted world, you get to live a little while longer."

Naradawk leaned forward on his throne, and the invisible waves of pure repulsion caused Grey Wolf to slide backward a few inches on the marble tiles.

"But just a little."

Grey Wolf's stared into Naradawk's eyes.

Typical villain. Can't help but blab about your plans. So, if I die here, your master strategy is screwed? Easy enough to arrange, you arrogant purple monstrosity.

"You'll never see my world," he said. He struggled to his feet and drew his sword. "Not after I've lopped off that oversized eggplant head of yours."

Meledien made a move toward him, but Naradawk put out a hand to check her.

"You cannot even approach me," the emperor said, smiling. "Let alone lift a finger to harm me. I admire your fighting spirit, but you are fooling no one."

"I'm not?" Grey Wolf quickly flipped his wrist and extended his arm, so that the point of his sword touched his chest. He put his other hand on the hilt as well and drove the blade point-first into his own heart.

Or, rather, he meant to. He really did. He even thought he had, for just a second. But, no, the sword had not moved.

"No, you're not," said Naradawk. "How charming, that you imagined I would let you end your own life."

Grey Wolf didn't feel paralyzed. There was nothing wrong with his body, save that it was now responding to Naradawk's demands and not his own. This monster was dominating his mind, as surely as a puppeteer controlled his puppets.

"Ivellios, please. You're not going to remember any of this when you return because I am going to erase it from your mind. But be assured, I will leave the rest of your memories intact. It's just as well that Abernathy not discover your brain has been tampered with."

This was worse than when his memories had been looted. He knew for a surety that if Naradawk wanted him to commit murder, or slit his own throat, or debase himself in the worst ways imaginable, he wouldn't even hesitate.

He grew faint, and the throne room took on a strange amber glow.

"He's fading," said Meledien. "Returning to Spira."

"Then I'd best cleanse him," said Naradawk. A sickening agony gripped Grey Wolf as Naradawk shredded his memories of the past few minutes, like a clawed beast tearing strips of flesh from its prey. He tried to focus on the emperor, tried to at least remember what he looked like...and then there was something strange.

"What's the matter?" said Meledien.

"His memories," said Naradawk. All light was fading now, and in Grey Wolf's guts was that nauseating sensation of tugging. "He knew these things before! Someone has already erased—"

* * *

The throne room was gone. Grey Wolf was on his knees, bathed in moonlight. The night was cool and dry, the sawgrass whispering in the breeze and gently brushing his face. Above and around him towered the ring of great black obelisks, the Seven Mirrors.

ACKNOWLEDGEMENTS

First and foremost I wish to thank my wife, Kate Jenkins, for her unwavering support, insightful criticisms, and all the wonderful conversations we've shared about the story. As with all good things in my life, this book would not exist without her.

My children, Elanor and Kira, listened intently to the whole book and never tired of telling me how great it was. While their opinions may have held a *slight* bias in Dad's favor, they were still nice to hear. Thanks, kids!

Behind every author is an editor who knows better. Mine was the inestimable Abigail Mieko Vargus, whose encyclopedic knowledge and attention to detail are why there are about a thousand fewer problems with the book than there otherwise would have been. I cannot thank her enough though I'm surely going to try.

I employed a small army of beta readers, all of whom offered insights, suggestions, and support in varying degrees. At the top of the list is Edward Aubry, who bludgeoned me relentlessly with his merciless wisdom. I needed every kick he delivered to my authorial rear end. Just below Ed on the pyramid are Adi Rule, who overturned upon my head a necessary bucket of cold water after a very early draft; Alexander Hart, for whom no detail was too small to notice; and Michael Chaskes, who combined keen observations with exactly the amount of approval I needed to stay energized. Of course, the book would not be the same without the thoughtful input from *all* of my readers: Jim Blenko, Kit Yona, Benjamin Durbin, Jim Bologna, Christopher Cotton, Jeff Foley, Josh Bluestein, Karen Courtney, Aaron Size, Paul San Clemente, Phil Moriarty, Karen

Escovitz, and Andy Cancellieri.

At the end of the process, I employed a slightly smaller battalion of proofreaders, each of whom saved me from profound embarrassment in multiple places. Thank you to Fiona Heckscher, Bob Osborne, Corey Reid, Jeanine Magurshak, Darren Frechette, Christopher Wicke, Anise Strong-Morse, and (again) Alexander Hart.

As I ought to thank anyone without whom this book would not exist, I also extend my gratitude to Steven Cooper, Russell Morrissey, and all of my readers at EN World who told me over and over that I should do this thing.

And, finally, I want to thank my parents, Charlotte and Jacob, who have never stopped blowing wind into my sails.

ABOUT THE AUTHOR

Dorian Hart graduated from Wesleyan University with a degree in creative writing. This led circuitously to a 20-year career as a video game designer, where he contributed to many award-winning titles including *Thief, System Shock, System Shock 2*, and *BioShock*.

He is also the author of the interactive novella *Choice of the Star Captain*, published by Choice of Games.

Dorian now lives in the Boston area with his fantastic wife and two clever daughters.

THANK YOU
FOR READING

For information about the Heroes of Spira series, please visit
http://dorianhart.com/the-heroes-of-spira/

Made in the USA
Middletown, DE
19 January 2018